So Many Reasons to Die

Carole Sojka

ISBN: 0692358900
ISBN 13: 9780692358900
Library of Congress Control Number: 2014923022
Haven Press, Glendora, CA

ACKNOWLEDGMENTS

Thanks to my husband who has given me unstinting support in everything I've done, and to my friends and family who have helped me with writing and publishing my books. Thanks to Diane Wentworth, my first reader from the beginning, and special thanks to Candy Somoza who has edited my books thoughtfully and kindly.

ONE

The first thing Greg saw as he stood in the doorway of the motel room was the blood—— spilled on the rug, splashed on the headboard, spattered on the wall. Blood soaked the lacy blue nightgown and matted the long red hair of the woman lying on the bed. Her body was curled to one side, turned toward him. Her eyes were open, and she looked startled, as if she'd expected a better ending.

He caught his breath. When last he'd seen that face, it had been contorted with fury. Then later, in the dark, they had made love with savage intensity, and the next day she was gone. Now, looking at her body, Greg couldn't bring himself to touch her cold flesh.

The room was small and anonymous: a bed with a night table on either side, each holding a lamp; a console with the television set next to a small dresser with a mirror; a round table and two chairs by the window. A small duffle bag sat open on the luggage rack. How many times had he seen that bag when she'd come and gone without notice?

The Medical Examiner was bent over the body.

Greg spoke. "I'm Greg Lamont. I don't think we've met."

Ron Torres, the M.E., stood up from his work and said, "Greg. You're new in Burgess Beach, right?" He took off his glove and shook Greg's hand.

"You got here quick," Greg said.

"Yeah." Torres answered, "Quiet day." He put on a fresh pair of gloves and bent back over the body. Torres was in his forties, a short, compact man with neatly combed dark hair and a small moustache.

Greg checked the room and the bathroom before he beckoned to the patrolman who'd been first on the scene. He had only been in Burgess Beach a few months, and the young patrol officer was not someone he knew.

Greg reached out his hand. "Detective Greg Lamont. You are?"

"Pete Carlson, sir." Carlson was in his early twenties, tall and thin, still with some of the lankiness of a teenager.

"You touch anything?"

"No."

Greg noted that he sounded annoyed, as if Carlson knew enough to keep his hands off murder victims. Maybe uniforms were better trained here than in Miami. He'd see.

"Who reported this? What time did the call come in?"

"The manager, a guy named Ben Patel, reported finding the body around two, about an hour-and-a-half ago."

"Why'd he come in?" Greg made notes as he questioned the young cop.

"She didn't vacate the room by noon, and she didn't answer the door. Patel used his master key. When he saw the body, he could see she was dead. Nothing's been touched."

"Did you call anyone else?"

"The M.E."

"Just keep the nosy neighbors away." Greg turned away from Carlson and asked the Medical Examiner, "You figure time of death?"

"You can see rigor is fixed, so I'd say at least twelve hours ago, although it could be more. But don't quote me."

Greg asked the patrolman, "Patel say when she checked in?"

"Ten o'clock last evening," said Carlson.

"So time of death is between ten p.m. Friday evening and two or three a.m. Saturday morning."

"About that," said Torres.

"Okay. I'll call for a photographer and the crime scene techs. You ready?"

"I will be by the time they get here," Torres said.

"Let me know when you're done. I'll be downstairs."

Greg headed down to see Ben Patel. The day was hot: September in Florida, and the air clung to Greg's skin with moist tentacles. He paused at the foot of the stairs for a moment where no one could see his face. The dead woman had come and gone without warning in his life. She was trouble—he'd always known that—but he'd never thought she would be murdered, let alone that he'd catch the case. He knew he should tell Captain Bradley and have the case reassigned, but he couldn't. At least not yet. The decision wasn't one he had to think about. He owed Miranda that much, to find out who had killed her.

The office was in front of the U-shaped motel, and the parking lot was still nearly empty except for the police cruiser, the M.E.'s sedan, and his own. The office was small and dark, but there was a full pot of coffee that smelled fresh. Brightly colored posters and a vase of silk flowers decorated the room.

Ben Patel stood up when Greg entered. Patel was about fifty, Greg thought, dark skinned, his dark hair mixed with gray and cropped close to his head.

Greg showed his badge. "Detective Greg Lamont, Burgess Beach Police Department. I've been assigned to the murder in Room 204. I need to take a look at the guest register."

Patel produced the register and turned it around so that Greg could read it. The second to last entry for the night before had been Karen McCloskey with an address in Miami. That wasn't the name under which Greg had known her.

"Did she use a credit card?" he asked.

"No. She paid cash. She had quite a bit of money in her wallet." Patel spoke with a strong Indian accent.

"She have a car?"

"Yes. It's parked around at the back of the motel, next to the laundry room."

"How come?" Greg asked.

"She asked if she could park in a spot where it couldn't be seen from the street."

"Did she seem nervous?"

"Yes. She kept looking over her shoulder, and she wanted a second-floor room. When she wanted to park her car where it couldn't be seen from the street, I figured she was running away from a man who beat her or something."

"You get lots of runaways here?" Greg asked.

"Two or three times a month. Sometimes the same women."

"Anything else you can tell me?" Greg asked. "She just had the one piece of luggage—small duffle, right? I didn't see a purse."

"She took her wallet out of a purse. And she had another suitcase. It was heavy, and she had some trouble with it. I carried it upstairs for her."

Greg considered the room. He'd look again, but he knew he hadn't seen a purse or suitcase.

"Did you see her go out after she checked in?"

"No."

"Could she have moved the suitcase out of the room?"

"I didn't see her."

"Thanks," Greg said. "You'll be here the rest of the afternoon?"

"Until eleven o'clock."

Greg went back upstairs before he called for transport. The M.E. was packing up when he entered the room.

"When will the autopsy be done?" Greg asked as Torres turned to leave.

"I've got to call Fort Pierce to schedule."

"Oh. Right," Greg said. After years of working in Miami, he'd wasn't yet accustomed to the four-county sharing of morgue and coroner that was the case in Burgess Beach. "Let me know."

"Sure," said Torres. He left the room and headed down the stairs.

Greg looked again at the body of the woman who called herself Karen McCloskey. He tried to distance himself from the woman he had known, tried to see her only as a murder victim. Her wrists and legs showed no signs of having been bound. The murderer would have gotten blood on himself— or herself—as well as on the surroundings from the spurting carotid artery. There were no defensive wounds on her hands, which lay at her sides, and it seemed likely that she had been surprised in her sleep by her attacker. From a distance, he checked the floor around and under the bed. There were some smears in the blood on the rug which might have been footprints.

The photographer and the two crime scene techs arrived and greeted Greg. He didn't know any of them well, although he'd met them when he'd first arrived in Burgess Beach. They introduced themselves, donned their latex gloves and set to work, the photographer shooting the crime scene, the two techs measuring and cataloging each item of evidence.

Greg pointed out the bloody footprints on the floor and said, "I doubt there's much to be gotten from those."

Ginny, the female tech, said, "You'd be surprised."

"I guess I would," Greg said. "I'll call the morgue for transport," he said. "By the way, she had a car. It's in the back. The manager can show you. Check it for prints, then I'll have it towed."

Greg asked if they'd fingerprint and photo the duffle first so he could examine it. They did so and when they were done, he examined it carefully. It held a change of clothes and some cosmetics, but nothing else. The heavy suitcase and the purse containing her wallet were definitely gone.

TWO

Andi Battaglia stared at the stack of papers on her desk and sighed. What had made her want to be a detective? When she'd been a patrol cop in Tampa, she'd always been busy: answering calls, checking out neighborhoods, making arrests. There was paperwork, too, but the days flew by. Nights— well, not so much. Still, time had gone swiftly on patrol.

When she'd gotten the detective job in Burgess Beach, not only had she moved from the Gulf to the Atlantic coast, she'd moved from a city to a small town. It wasn't like Tampa.

But almost her first case in Burgess Beach had been a homicide. Of course she'd had to get her boss, Captain Bradley, to believe it was a homicide, but then, sorting through the six suspects and their motives and the final chase on the beach had been exciting. She knew that couldn't happen every day, but there were too many open-and-shut drug cases and car thefts in Burgess Beach and not enough challenge. And lots of paperwork. Too much paperwork.

Andi yawned, caught herself nodding, and sat up straight, glancing out the door of her tiny office to see if anyone had noticed. No one had. The detectives who had been there for years—McClain and Garcia—didn't seem to mind the paperwork. They didn't mind making phone calls on their cases and filling out forms. She wanted a little more action.

The new guy, Greg Lamont, had come from Miami, so maybe Burgess Beach would be dull for him, too. He was someone to talk to, and they'd had dinner a couple of times. He hadn't said he was bored, but from his stories, she gathered his life in Miami had been pretty exciting. Maybe he liked the change.

When he tried to pursue a relationship with her, though, she'd discouraged him. She knew better. She'd fled from a cop in Tampa. Cops were trouble. Not that Greg was married. Not like Jim. Still, he had his own baggage. She could tell. Maybe an ex-wife or a girlfriend.

She got up and walked over to the coffee pot, but the sludge at the bottom discouraged her from pouring a cup. Should she make a new pot? Hardly anyone there. McClain, who was retiring soon, had already left for the day. She'd noticed he was taking long lunches and working short days. Lamont was gone, too. He must be out on a call.

She returned to her office, finished reading an analysis of crimes committed by men under the age of twenty-five compared with crimes by men twenty-six to forty in the United States between 1960 and 2000. She decided that was enough torture for one day. She'd stop at the ladies' room and leave. It was almost five o'clock.

On the way home she thought about dinner. Nothing much in the refrigerator. Bread and eggs. Some on-their-last-legs mushrooms. She'd make an omelet.

The door to her apartment opened before she turned the key, and she nearly fell into the living room.

"What the hell!" she said. Then she saw Jim sitting in front of the television, remote in one hand and a drink in the other. "How did you get in?"

"Showed the manager my badge. He let me in." He grinned. His voice was slightly slurred.

She stood in front of him. "Well, you can just let yourself out," she said. "I told you I'm through. Go back to Tampa. Go back to your wife."

"And I told you I left. I told her about us, and I tried to tell you, but you wouldn't listen. You kept hanging up on me." He smiled again. "Sit down, sweetheart." The word sounded like schweetheart.

"I'm not your sweetheart. I told you I've had enough. You and I are through."

"But now we can be together. I've left my wife. I've moved to an apartment. I'm free." He smiled up at her.

That smile had always gotten to Andi, but now it had lost its magic. She wasn't even angry at him. She felt nothing. It was hard now to remember his pursuit of her and her reluctant, then enthusiastic, capitulation. She'd been such an idiot!

She perched on the edge of the chair across from him. "Look, Jim. The last time I saw you I told you I was tired of waiting. That was a year ago. It's too late. Go back to her, or not, I don't care. I'm here now. I have a new life." She watched his face. He'd been so sure of her. Now he looked as though he'd given her a present and she'd thrown in his face.

He shouted, "You can't do that! You ruined my marriage! She's suing me for divorce! My daughter hates me. Everybody I know looks at me like I'm scum. I did it for you! It's your fault!" Then he spoke in a lower tone. "You have to come back. I love you."

"Jim, that's enough. You're shouting. I'm not going back to Tampa. I'm not leaving the life I've built here to go back with you. If you'd left your wife two years ago—or even last year—I might have been waiting. But I've moved on. It's time for you to leave." She spoke quietly, hoping her tone would calm him down, but instead it seemed to inflame him more.

He stood up, towering over her. "Who is he? Who's the new guy? Somebody here, in Burgess Beach? Who is he? I'll kill him." His fists were clenched.

"Stop it, Jim. Don't be ridiculous. There's no one else. I have a new life here. I'm away from my family. I'm finally on my own. And I'm away from you. It's too late for us." Her reasoned tone wasn't calming him.

He stepped back and paced the floor behind her. She walked toward him, reaching out a hand to his arm. He pushed it away. "Leave me alone," he said. "Why didn't you tell me?"

"I did, Jim. I told you again and again I was through."

She stepped toward him, and he slapped her hard across the face. "Bitch!" he said.

Her head snapped back with the force of the blow, and her face stung. "Get out! Now!"

He turned. "We're not done." He flung open the door and stalked out, leaving it open behind him.

She didn't start to cry until she heard his car leave the parking lot. Half an hour later, she mopped her eyes and checked her face in the bathroom mirror. Her cheek was bright red and starting to swell. She made an ice pack and sat with it for a few minutes before she walked downstairs to the manager's office. She knocked, and a voice said, "It's open."

She opened the door, and Arnie got up to greet her. He was in his fifties, short and plump, and as he stood, he hitched up his trousers around his belly.

"Ms. Battaglia," he said. "What can I do for you?"

"You had no business letting that guy into my apartment."

"He said he was an old friend, and he showed me his badge. I thought you'd be glad."

"Well, you thought wrong. That was stupid. How did you know who he was? Would you let some murderer in, too?"

"No, no. Of course not. I thought you'd want him to have a place to wait for you."

"I'm going to be moving. You can take this as my notice that I'll be out by the first of next month. Do you need that in writing?"

"Why? Because of that guy?"

"Not your business, but I don't want to live in a place where the manager lets strangers in to my apartment."

"Look, he was a cop. He showed me his badge. We're supposed to let police in."

Andi's voice rose. "Just because he was a cop didn't mean he had a right to go into my apartment. He didn't have a warrant."

Arnie held out his hands in defense. "Hold on, Ms. Battaglia. I don't think I did anything wrong."

"Well, you did." Andi turned on her heel and slammed the door behind her. What an asshole!

Upstairs in her apartment, she poured herself a stiff scotch and drank it slowly, holding the ice pack on her cheek, until she could feel the tense muscles of her face and neck ease and she was able to relax. Jim was an asshole, too.

Her omelet tasted like cardboard, and she stared at the pages of the book she'd been reading, thinking only of Jim. She had a bad feeling he wasn't gone.

In bed, she finally dozed off at nearly one o'clock, only to be awakened by the phone.

"Hello," she muttered.

"Hello, sweetheart." Jim's words were slurred, and she could hear the sounds of people talking and glasses clinking.

"Don't call me again," she said. "I mean it."

"I love you," he said. "I'll always love…."

She hung up, cutting off his words. The phone rang again a moment later, and she picked it up, pressed "off," and put the phone on silent mode. She was going to have to get a new phone number, too.

THREE

After the attendants took away the body of Karen McCloskey, Greg and Pete Carlson canvassed the other rooms in the motel in case anyone had seen or heard anything during the night. Nothing .The techs had finished, and the photographer was gone. The car had been dusted for prints, but there was nothing of interest in the glove compartment or the trunk. No purse, no heavy suitcase.

Nothing more to be done here, but in case, Greg left the yellow tape in place and told Ben Patel not to have the room cleaned until he cleared it. Patel protested that would scare customers away, but Greg, while he was sympathetic, insisted.

It was after eight by the time he was ready to head home. He called Captain Bradley to update him. "I'll type up my notes in the morning and brief you, if you have the time."

"First thing," the captain barked.

"Yes, sir." Greg took a deep breath. He needed to be prepared for an interrogation.

Greg had lived in Burgess Beach for about four months, but home was still temporary. He wasn't sure if he wanted to stay. He'd wanted out of Miami, but Burgess Beach was pretty dull—or had been until today. Now that Miranda Duncan, the dead woman known as Karen McCloskey, had been murdered, he knew he wanted to stay and find out who had killed her. Miranda's death was linked to Miami, and he wanted to find Miranda's killer, no matter what it cost.

When he got to the apartment, he ordered a pizza. He thought about a drink, then decided against it. He wanted to be clear headed when he planned how he would deal with Miranda's death. He knew her real identity, but she had had no ID on her. Her purse was gone, and there was nothing in the duffle to show who she was. So for now, she'd be Karen McCloskey. She'd given an address in Miami, which might or might not be legitimate. He'd check for Karen McCloskey, then when her fingerprints showed her real name, he could go from there. He would stay on the case as long as he could.

He'd been with Miranda four years, off and on. A long time, he thought, but they'd parted a long time ago, too. When he'd known her, Miranda skirted the line between legal and illegal, sometimes slipping over, and Greg knew she had a police record—for writing bad checks on one of her forays away from him. She'd known some unsavory people, but who would kill her? What had she been involved in? Probably drugs, although she'd never been a user. Her body didn't show the traces of addiction. What had been in the suitcase? It was heavy, Patel had said. Heavy with drugs? Guns? Money?

Miranda's slashed throat haunted his dreams. On the way to work, he planned his morning. First, he'd write up his notes, then see Captain Bradley.

He knew Hank and Ed would be curious about the case, and of course, Andi Battaglia. He'd really thought he and Andi might get together at some point, but she'd made it clear she didn't like cops in her personal life. She'd obviously been bitten, probably in Tampa, but he didn't know what it was about.

Hank McClain was at his desk when Greg arrived. More than ready for retirement, he was reluctant to take on anything new, just marking time. Ed Garcia was out, and Andi was off today, so he didn't have to do more than tell Hank he'd picked up a murder at the Hibiscus Motel and was going to see the captain, then find out about the post-mortem. He wrote up his notes, then, report in hand, he headed for Bradley's office. He knocked.

"Enter."

Bradley's desk was, as usual, empty of anything except a telephone, in-and-out-boxes, both nearly empty, and a photo of his wife and children. The photo was an old one. Greg knew his kids were no longer teenagers, and Andi had told him Bradley's wife had died of breast cancer. Bradley's computer sat on the console behind him, the screen showing the Burgess Beach Police Department logo. In Greg's experience—and he'd confirmed this with Andi—Bradley's screen never had anything on it except the screen saver whenever anyone came into his office. No chance of finding him playing games or watching porn or even writing a memo to some hapless employee. They wondered if he ever used the computer.

Bradley indicated that Greg should sit, and said, "What do you have?"

When Greg finished his report, the captain barked, "Keep me posted," and turned to the computer behind him, dismissing Greg.

Greg headed back to his desk. So far, so good.

The address Miranda/Karen, had used to register at the Hibiscus Motel had a phone number in the Miami directory. He'd been sure the address was a phony, but when he called, he got an answering machine. A woman's voice, not Miranda's he was sure, asked him to leave a message. He hung up before the beep. He cross-referenced the phone number and got an address in Miami and a name–Kathryn Forbes.

He called the Medical Examiner's officer and learned the autopsy was scheduled for the following morning.

He decided to call a couple he and Miranda had known when they were together. Miranda had worked with Angela Ramirez at an insurance company in Miami, and she and her husband, Joe, had invited them to dinner a couple of times. He'd liked Joe, a contractor who built dry cleaning plants in the Miami's ever-expanding mini-malls. Greg wondered how business was since the recession of the last two years. When he called, he found the number was no longer in service.

The directory had seven listings for Joseph Ramirez, and he tried them all. Four rang to answering machines, and he left messages asking if he had reached the Joseph Ramirez he had known, and if so, would he call Greg Lamont. One call disturbed what sounded like a woman who didn't sound like Angela Ramirez and yelled at him in Spanish for bothering her. Two others simply rang and rang.

He tried to think of anyone else Miranda might have kept in touch with. She had held her private life pretty close, well hidden from him, but there was a woman she had stayed with once when she'd left Greg after a quarrel. The woman's first name was Cynthia or something similar, he thought, and at the time she sang in a band. Not enough to follow up on.

He checked on his other pending cases and made a few calls. Sunday wasn't a good day to reach people, so discouraged, he headed home at five o'clock. The only thing he'd learned was that the phone number Karen McCloskey had left wasn't a phony, although it might have nothing to do with Miranda.

FOUR

The autopsy was scheduled for Monday morning in Fort Pierce, a forty-minute drive. Greg cut it close and arrived just as George Parks, the Medical Examiner, was about to begin. Greg gowned up quickly and took his place by the body. Autopsies usually didn't bother him, not since the first few in Miami, but this was a woman he had loved. He had caressed this body that Dr. Parks was handling like a slab of meat, and he had to close his eyes before the doctor made the Y-shaped cut from shoulders to pelvis. He took a deep breath before he looked again.

Dr. Parks asked, "Do you want me to open the skull?"

Greg thought for a minute. If Miranda had been on drugs, they would show up in the organs. "No," he said. "Not if you don't need it." At least he wouldn't have to see the beautiful face destroyed.

When Parks was done, he said, "She died of blood loss from the severed carotid artery. Time of death sometime late Friday night or early Saturday morning."

"Can you tell if she was asleep or drugged?"

"She didn't fight. There are no defensive wounds, and don't expect anything from the fingernail scrapings. It seems likely she wasn't conscious. Drugs, we'll have to wait for the results from the lab. One other thing. She'd had a child born full-term." Greg left the autopsy room, glad to leave before seeing Miranda stitched up like a scarecrow stuffed with straw. All during the drive back to Burgess Beach, he thought about Miranda. She'd had a baby. Was it his? Where was this child? Whose child was it? When was it born?

At the station, he said hello to Ed Garcia, then he typed up his notes on the autopsy, and made phone calls on his other cases—a residential burglary and a hit-and-run with vehicle damage. This time he got some answers, but as he worked, he found his mind wandering to Miranda and Miranda's baby.

Then he decided to go to Miami and tell the woman on the phone that Miranda Duncan or Karen McCloskey was dead. He didn't want to do it over the phone. It was hard to tell friends and relatives about murder. Doing it in person was at least a courtesy.

As he drove, he thought back to his first sight of Miranda. It had been at least ten years ago. They'd met in a class on the new computer system the city had installed, and she'd been there from the D.A.'s office. He'd noticed her immediately and elbowed his way to a seat next to her, pushing a plump blond woman out of the way. He excused himself, but he hadn't meant it. Miranda had given him a cool gaze and gone back to reading the manual they'd been issued, although he knew she was checking him out.

When the instructor came in, Greg tried hard to concentrate, but he was aware of her next to him. He leaned close, his arm touching hers. "Just checking I'm on the same screen." The brief touch made his skin tingle, and she smiled as if she felt it, too.

He followed her to lunch, then later asked her to dinner. They ended up at his place, tearing at each other almost as soon as they'd gotten in the door. That night they set a pattern for their relationship: frantic sex; a fight; his anger; her depression; when she walked out, she'd be gone briefly; then she'd return to start the cycle over again. Then one day she walked out and didn't come back. Now she was dead.

.It took him two hours to get to Miami Beach and a little longer to find Kathryn Forbes' house. It was a good-sized ranch house in an area with well-kept lawns and palm trees. There was an SUV in the driveway, and someone was home.

He rang the bell, and a woman in her mid-forties opened the door. Her graying hair was cut short, she had gray eyes and an open, pleasant expression.

"I really am not interested in buying anything."

Greg showed his badge and said, "Your address was used by Karen McCloskey at a motel in Burgess Beach. Do you know Ms. McCloskey?"

"I don't know any Karen McCloskey," she said. "Why would this woman use my address? I don't even know where Burgess Beach is."

"Do you know a woman in her mid-thirties, red hair, blue eyes, about five-foot-eight inches tall, slender build?"

The woman caught her breath. "That sounds like Miranda. She lives here with me. Has something happened to her?"

"Is she available to speak with me?" Greg asked.

"No. She's been gone since Thursday. Sometimes she takes off, but usually I know she's leaving. She left sometime before I got home from work."

"May I come in, Ms ...?" Greg asked.

"Oh, yes. I'm Kathryn Forbes. Sorry."

She stood aside and allowed Greg to enter. The house was cool, the air conditioning on. The blinds were drawn, but she guided Greg to a small sunroom which looked onto a pool and a large area of trees and grass.

Greg pulled out the photo of Miranda and showed it to the woman.

She drew in her breath sharply when she saw it. The slash across Miranda's throat wasn't visible, but she didn't look alive. "That's Miranda Duncan. She's dead, isn't she?" she asked.

"Yes. I'm afraid so. What can you tell me about Ms. Duncan?"

Kathryn Forbes covered her face with her hands. "How did she die?"

"What can you tell me about Miranda Duncan's life in Miami Beach?"

Kathryn Forbes visibly pulled herself together. She clasped her hands tightly in her lap and tried to speak. Twice she opened her mouth, but the sound that came out was just a croak. She rose to her feet.

"I need a glass of water," she said hoarsely and walked out of the room. Greg could hear water running, then Kathryn returned with a glass of water from which she drank. "Tell me how she died," she demanded.

"She was murdered."

"Oh!" Kathryn didn't speak for a while. She was visibly stunned at the idea of murder. Then she asked, "Where?"

"In a motel in Burgess Beach. Tell me how you met Miranda."

"I met Miranda at the opening of my show. That was two...two-and-a-half years ago. She came home with me that night, and we've been together ever since."

"A show?" Greg asked. "What kind of show?"

"I'm an artist. I had a show at a South Beach gallery. I've had a couple of shows, actually, but that was the one where I met Miranda. She said she liked my work. Later she asked me to have a drink."

Greg wasn't surprised that Miranda had a female lover. There wasn't much left to surprise him about Miranda. "Where did she work?" he asked.

Kathryn Forbes thought for a moment. "When we met, she was working at a bank in Miami Beach. A few months later, she lost that job—I think she made someone mad, maybe her boss—and then she didn't work for a while." She paused.

"And then," Greg prompted.

"She didn't work, which was okay because I make a good living." She paused, and Greg could see her thinking back.

"You must be a good artist."

"I am, but I don't sell enough of my paintings to live on. I'm a graphic designer in my real life. That pays well. Miranda stayed home for a while. But she got depressed doing nothing. She needed to stay busy, so I pushed her to get a job."

That had been Miranda's pattern when she was with Greg. A job, then no job, depression, restlessness, and running away. "Did she find something else?"

"Yes. She was extremely bright, you know. She could do anything she tried." Kathryn looked a little defensive, as if Greg had criticized Miranda. "She got a job as a paralegal with a law firm."

"Do you know the name of the firm?" Greg asked.

"I think it was Pattis and Kearney. Or Kearney and Pattis. I'm sure you can find them."

"How long did she stay there?" Greg asked.

Kathryn thought for a little while. "More than a year."

"As far as you know, did she have any friends there?"

"She never talked about anybody in particular, although there was a man she said kept coming on to her. I can't remember his name, but it'll come to me."

Greg made a note to come back to that. "What happened at the law firm? Did she quit or was she let go?"

"She got mad about something. I don't remember for sure what it was, but she stormed out."

"Then what?"

"She stayed home again, but that didn't work. Same old thing. Then one day she picked a quarrel with me, accused me of 'mothering' her, and she left. She was gone for a few weeks, then she got arrested for passing bad checks."

"And so what happened? Did she call you?"

"Of course. She knew I would help her. I posted bond, and she came home. When she got six months' probation, I thought she'd feel better—and she did for a while—but then she got really depressed."

The story was so familiar to Greg that he could have written the script.

"How long ago did this happen," Greg asked.

"I don't know. Six or eight months. A month after her court date, she got really angry with me and left, but she came back on her own. She's been here ever since until Thursday. When I got home from work on Friday, she still wasn't back, and her clothes are still here."

"And this was unusual?" Greg asked.

"Yes. She usually made a production of leaving, packing, and storming out. To come home and find her gone was a surprise. It worried me."

"Did you call anyone?" Greg asked.

"Who would I call? She didn't have any friends that I knew, and she was still on probation, so I didn't want to call the police. I just assumed she'd be back." Kathryn's face crumpled. She sobbed quietly. "I'm sorry. I just can't believe it."

"Did she have any family that you know of?" Greg asked.

"I think she mentioned a sister," Kathryn said. "But I don't know where she lives or anything about her."

"Did she take all her personal records with her?"

"I didn't really check," Kathryn Forbes said. "You can see what's here."

She took Greg back to a room which obviously served as an office for the two women. There were two computers, each on its own desk. Miranda's desk was easy to identify. It was covered with a mass of unsorted papers, cancelled checks, three calendars, and half a dozen books, some open. Kathryn's desk, on the other hand, had two baskets on it with papers in each. A couple of books stood against the wall at the back of the desk. Greg shuffled through the papers on Miranda's desk, then asked Kathryn if she had any objection to Greg taking them back to Burgess Beach to look through more thoroughly. He asked if he could take the computer, too.

Since Kathryn had no objection, Greg piled the mess from the desk together as well as he could, added the sparse contents of the drawers, and put the papers into a sack that Forbes gave him. He wrote out a receipt for Kathryn for both the papers and the computer.

When he had done that, he asked, "May I look at her clothes? There may be something in one of the pockets that would help."

She looked startled at the idea of Greg going through Miranda's clothes, but after a pause, she said, "Her clothes? I guess not."

She motioned Greg to follow her to another bedroom that opened off the main hallway. She opened the closed door and walked in, Greg following behind her. "I haven't disturbed anything. She didn't like me to clean up in here," she said. "Her clothes are all in that closet."

Greg took in the room. The bed was unmade and looked as if it usually was rumpled. There were clothes on the floor and draped over a chair. Greg picked up a heavily spangled blue mini dress from the floor. No pockets in that. He gathered up a black bra and black thong from the floor and put them on the bed.

"She usually came home late and just went right to bed," Kathryn said, her explanation unnecessary.

Then she said in a shaky voice, "I'll go back to where we were before." She turned and left, and Greg picked up a dress from the chair, another short, low-cut number in emerald green with flounces over the hips. The dress smelled of Miranda's pachouli-scented perfume, and the odor brought her back to Greg in a way that nothing, not even the sight of her body, had managed to do. He caught his breath, feeling as if he'd taken a blow to his stomach, and almost collapsed onto the bed, but he remained standing, bracing himself against the chair that held Miranda's clothes. Finally he blew his nose and wiped his eyes and continued with his search through the clothing.

Most of the clothes in the closet were covered with plastic bags from the dry cleaners. Greg bypassed these and checked the jackets and coats with pockets to be sure they were empty. He found nothing, and closing the closet door, he returned to the sunroom where he found Kathryn Forbes. She was sitting staring out the window, the expression on her face bleak. He gave her his card and asked her to call if she remembered the name of the man at the bank who had come on to Miranda or if anything else came to mind. He picked up the bag of papers and the computer, let himself out and headed for his old station.

Greg hoped someone he knew would be around, and luck was with him. When he identified himself at the front desk, he found that his old partner, Caesar Fuentes, was in. A cadet buzzed Greg in, and he found Caesar on the phone, giving someone hell. Caesar was no more than five feet eight or nine, shorter than Greg by at least five inches, but he was broadly built with a massive chest and upper arms. He was a little older than Greg, and his full head of black hair was beginning to go gray around the temples. He smiled and motioned for Greg to sit.

"Stop giving me that shit," Caesar was saying. "You don't want the Miami P.D. to think you're not being helpful, do you? I just need to know who pawned the silver belt buckle.

Your records have to show that, but your 'assistant' couldn't tell us."

He listened for a while, then said, "Check your records and call me back. Pronto."

When Caesar clicked the phone, he turned to Greg and said, "Don't tell me you're tired of that burg already? Wanna come back?"

Greg said, "It's not Miami, that's for sure. How's Laura and the kids? How old's the little guy now?"

"He'll be two, and Laura's got another one in the oven."

"Congratulations, man. You trying to populate Miami entirely with Fuenteses?"

"If I can." Caesar laughed. "I gotta make up for you."

"Hey, I need some information if you've got a minute."

"Shoot."

"You remember Miranda Duncan? You called to let me know when Fraud picked up her up for passing bad paper. Do you know anything more about that case? Or do you know anyone in Fraud I can talk to?"

"Are you still seeing her? I thought she was out of your life." Caesar had never liked Miranda.

"She just got herself killed in a motel in Burgess Beach." He cleared his throat.

"Hey, man! I'm sorry about that. Murdered?"

"Yeah. Throat slashed." Greg swallowed, trying to rid his mind of the picture of Miranda's blood-soaked body in the motel room.

"Sorry, man." Caesar put out a hand and patted Greg's arm.

Greg took a deep breath and said, "I got the case, and I'm wondering if there's anything down here that could help me."

"You? Is that a good idea?" Caesar asked.

"I don't know, but I've got it. I'm doing what I can."

"I didn't follow up after her arrest," Caesar said, "but the Fraud guys might be able to help. I'll check that out." He looked at his watch. "They're probably gone now, but I'll call you in the morning."

"Great," Greg said. "Thanks." He looked at his watch and got to his feet.

"Hey, you want to come home with me for dinner. I'll be done here in an hour, and I know Laura'd love to see you."

"Thanks, but I got to get back. I'll be in touch."

"Okay." Caesar stood up. He shook Greg's hand and gave him a pat on the shoulder. "Don't stay away so long. We miss you, man."

"Thanks," Greg said, and turned toward the door.

FIVE

Andi Battaglia tried to sleep in on her day off without much success. She hadn't slept much after Jim's late night phone call, going over and over in her mind what she needed to do: rent an apartment, pack, hire movers, change her telephone. Last night Jim had been abusive, someone she didn't know at all. The Jim she'd loved had been tough, yes, but never abusive. He was a cop, and he'd worked his way up the ranks to captain. But she'd never thought he'd hit her nor had she ever seen him out of control like that. A couple of times in the past he'd called and sounded as though he'd been drinking, but she hadn't seen this side of him. She wanted out of her apartment before he came back. She wouldn't go through that again. This Jim was dangerous.

After coffee, she called her parents in Tampa. Mary Battaglia had a mastectomy six months before, and Andi had been driving to and from Tampa often, but she'd decided to give herself today off. Mary was doing well, expected to have reconstructive surgery later in the year, but of course was disappointed that Andi wouldn't be coming to see her.

"I'll come more often when the surgery gets closer," Andi said. "I need a little time here. I've got some shopping to do. I need some furniture and drapes."

"Well, I miss you," Mary said, "but I understand. You have your own life."

Andi said goodbye and hung up. Her mother didn't know what she really needed to do. Mary Battaglia didn't know about Jim. Some things were better kept from parents.

Andi checked the newspapers and found a couple of possible apartments, both close to work. She'd have to look at them, though. She'd rather not have a place with a lot of kids. Her hours were irregular, and she didn't want children to wake her—nor she them. She wanted to be some distance from her current place, and she wanted to find something with a closed garage so her car wouldn't be obvious from the street. The apartment she was in faced the front of the building, and while she'd liked that when she moved in, now she thought she'd prefer something with a rear outlook and even a back entrance.

She set up appointments for the two apartments, hurriedly ate a piece of toast and headed out. The first one was on the second floor, and she liked that, but it had an open garage, and her assigned spot would be visible from the street.

The second apartment was on the first floor with a front entrance from an interior hallway and a rear entrance to a narrow gated walkway backed by a high fence covered with bright bougainvillea. Covered parking spaces lay along both sides of the building, and although they weren't closed, the cars weren't visible from the street. She signed a one-year lease on the spot.

The manager said she could move in right away, so she hurried home, wrote a confirming note to her apartment manager about leaving, and called a moving company, leaving a message requesting a return call. She could be out of her current apartment by the end of the week, and with luck, Jim wouldn't know where she'd gone. First thing the next day she'd rent a post office box and leave the number with the manager with strict instructions to give the box number out to no one. She'd also cancel her land line and rely on her cell. She didn't think Jim had that number.

When she got back from her apartment search, she remembered the presentation on the dangers of teenage driving she was scheduled to put on at the local high school the next day. This would be her first community appearance, and she'd spent a lot of time on the power point presentation she'd prepared. She even had a couple of graphic accident scenes to bring the point home. She also planned, if time permitted, to let the kids ask questions about her work.

The next morning she woke up with a headache. Popping some aspirin with her coffee, she tried to talk herself out of the pain. She stopped at the post office and rented a mail box. When she got to the station, she checked in, reminded Lisa, the captain's secretary, about the scheduled presentation and got to the high school at nine o'clock.

The principal, John Lovis, took her to his office from the reception area. "I'm really sorry," he said, "but the computer system's down. I hope you didn't rely too much on visual prsentations."

Andi groaned. She'd have to talk for forty-five minutes. "That's okay. I'll manage," she said. It was going to be a bad day. "Is this part of driver education or social studies?"

"It's kind of both. It'll be juniors and seniors, and the prom is coming up. That's always a bad time, and two kids were arrested Friday night for drunk driving. They'll all know about it, so it should help bring your message home."

The students were chatting noisily and standing in the aisles when she and Lovis entered the assembly. A loud screech of the microphone helped to quiet them down, and Lovis told them to settle. When he introduced her, there were a couple of whistles. She had dressed carefully in a tailored gray suit and mid-height heels, pulling her hair up into a knot on top of her head, and she smiled and bowed to the whistles, saying, "Thanks," which brought a few laughs.

The kids mostly seemed to pay attention during her talk, although she ran out of material early without the power point presentation. She gave more time than she'd planned to the dangers of driving and texting or talking on the cell phone.

Finally John Lovis brought the questioning to an end and escorted her back to her car.

"You were a great success," he said. "When Detective Garcia was here, he was so boring the kids were bored, too."

She drove back to the station feeling pleased by Lovis' comments. She knew she'd done a good job. At the station, she called the movers and arranged to pick up boxes and have them move her to her new place on Thursday.

She asked Ed Garcia where Greg Lamont was, and Ed told her Greg had caught a murder at the Hibiscus Motel and had gone to Miami to notify next of kin.

Andi wanted a murder. She was tired of drugs and residential burglaries.

She settled in to make calls. No one would ID the drug dealer. She knew who he was, but without anyone coming forward, she couldn't do squat.

She turned to a burglary in a very upscale residence on Hutchinson Island, an area closed to the public. How had the burglars gotten into and out of the area with a shitload of expensive furniture and antiques while the road was supposedly closed to nonresidents? Andi decided to talk with the housekeeper again and headed out to her car. On the way out, she ran into Greg Lamont.

"Hey," she said. "Heard you caught a murder. Lucky."

"Yeah. I guess."

"Where have you been?" Andi asked.

"Today was the autopsy. Then I went down to Miami to notify the woman she lived with."

"Keep me posted," Andi said. "That's a lot more interesting than what I've got on my plate."

"Sure," Greg said.

SIX

Greg set up Miranda's computer on the desk in his office and turned it on. Perhaps she'd left something on her e-mails that would tell him why she'd been murdered. The screen lit up, then a message, "Enter password." Shit! He tried a couple of possibilities: her birthdate, which he always remembered: 070777.

"User name and password do not match."

7777. No. Her first and middle names. No. Kathryn. No. For the hell of it, he tried his birthdate. No. The computer beeped and the screen went blank. Too many tries. He was locked out. Damn!

The department had a computer guy who came in at one. Rob was good. Greg checked his watch. Ten o'clock. He'd work on the papers from Miranda's desk, then get some lunch and call Rob.

———

At Hutchinson Island, Andi buzzed for the housekeeper to open the gate. She was sure the woman knew more than she'd told Andi. Impatient, she buzzed again. She'd done some background checking on Leona Castro. Castro had been with the Palmers for five years, and when Andi had called them at their New York home, they had nothing but good to say about her. They refused to believe she had anything to do with the burglary.

The Palmers had come down to check what had been stolen—jewelry, paintings and some antiques—and they continued to defend the housekeeper. Castro lived at the Hutchinson Island house most of the time, but she had a home in Fort Pierce which she shared with her son and his girlfriend. The Fort Pierce P.D. had sent someone out to interview the son, and the report was in the file.

Andi buzzed a third time. Why didn't the woman answer? Finally she called the community security guard. He arrived a few minutes later and checked her ID.

"I called Ms. Castro," Andi told him, "and she said she'd be home, but I don't get a reply."

The guard buzzed her through and drove off before she could say anything. She drove past the gate and parked in the Palmers' driveway. When she rang the doorbell, there was no answer.

"Shit," she said, under her breath. She called the house again, but the phone rang to the answering message. Hoping she might be able to reach someone at the Fort Pierce address, she dialed that number. No answer there. Not even an answering machine.

There was also no response when she rang the doorbells at the houses on either side of the Palmers. Not that they'd be likely to have heard anything. The houses backed on the beach, and the noise of the surf and the distance of the properties from one another made them extremely private—and vulnerable. She buzzed the security guard again, and when he appeared, she asked him who had been on duty the night of the burglary, although she had already read the report.

"It was Frank," he said. "The cops took him to the station, but he didn't know nothing." The guard was a big guy in his forties, starting to go to fat.

"That would be Frank Alero?"

"Yeah."

"How about you? Do you know Ms. Castro?"

"Nah. She only hangs with Felicia." He hitched up his belt and turned, ready to get back in his car.

"Who's Felicia?" Andi asked.

"The housekeeper across the street." He gestured to a three-story villa set well back from the road.

There was no report in the file that Felicia had been questioned. "Thanks," she said and walked across to the house.

Andi heard quick footsteps after she rang the bell. The door swung open, and a thin dark-skinned woman wearing an apron asked, "May I help you?"

Andi identified herself and established that the woman was Felicia Gomez. Felicia said she was a friend of Leona Castro but that she didn't know where Leona was.

"She oughta be there. We had coffee this morning—her and me—like always. Then I come back here."

"You and Leona are pretty friendly, then? You have coffee every morning?" Andi asked.

"Yeah, most." Felicia said.

"I'm investigating the burglary at the Palmers." Andi was surprised Felicia wasn't more interested in why Andi was there.

"Oh, yeah. She said a bunch of stuff was stolen."

"Is that all she told you?"

"She said the insurance would pay for everything. She wasn't there or nothing, so the Palmers didn't blame her."

Andi had known everything was insured, but Leona Castro talking as though no one was worried about any monetary loss was interesting.

"Is the gate always locked?" Andi asked.

Felicia nodded. "Yeah."

"How do you get in and out if it's always locked?"

"I have a thing in my car that I press and it opens the gate. The gate opens by itself when I leave."

"And everyone who works or lives in Hutchinson Island has a remote?"

"I don't know. Mrs. Finch gave it to me when I started."

"Mrs. Finch is your employer?"

"Yeah." Felicia glanced around as if she needed to get to work.

Andi said, "So, no one would be able to get in past the gate if they didn't have one of those remotes?"

"I guess not. I always press the thing when I come in."

"Do you live in with Mr. and Mrs. Finch?"

"There ain't no Mr. Finch. No, I come every morning except Sunday and leave about six o'clock. I gotta house in Stuart." Felicia started to get to her feet.

"So you weren't here when the burglary happened at the Palmers. Where were you?"

"Home, I guess."

"Can anybody verify where you were?"

"My husband. He's usually there."

"Does the security guard patrol the area at night?"

"I don't know. I ain't here. But Frank does his job. Did Leona say he didn't?"

"Was there a reason why she would have said that?"

"No. He does his job." Felicia drew herself up and continued, "Frank's a nice guy. That's all I got to say."

"So you never heard anyone say that Frank might not patrol the way he should?"

"He does his job. Listen, I don't wanna say nothing more. I like Frank, and Leona's my friend."

"Right. I appreciate your help." Andi handed Felicia her card and walked toward the door. "If you think of anything else, please call me."

As Andi made her way back to her car, she thought about what she had just been told. The night guard might not be patrolling the way he should. She'd touched a nerve, but Felicia wasn't here at night, so it must have been something she'd heard. The Palmers didn't worry about what was missing because they were insured. Leona Castro hadn't been asked about how access to the gate was controlled. Was there a record of who had remotes for entering the gate? She needed to see Leona Castro again, do some checking on the Palmers' finances, and find out who issued the remotes and maintained the records.

Back at the station, she ate the lunch she'd brought in and made notes of her morning's activities. The high school was good, but the interview with Felicia Gomez had been even better.

———

Greg took the bag of papers Kathryn had given him and dumped them out on the table in an empty interview room. The papers were in no order, so he began sorting by type: check copies, bills, miscellaneous. The checks resolved themselves fairly easily. She didn't write many. She wrote a check to Kathryn once a month, usually for an odd amount. Maybe telephone bills.

A credit card bill had been paid in full every month until May when Miranda paid only the minimum amount. She continued to charge, paying only the minimum each month, but the amounts charged had been sharply reduced and she had taken cash advances: $1,000 in June and in July. By the end of July billing, the balance due had risen to $18,000. Greg wondered if Kathryn knew about these bills.

Then in August Miranda deposited $10,000 in the checking account. She also paid $8,000 on the credit card balance. Where had that money come from?

He looked at the charges Miranda had made on the card. Miranda had spent money at Miami Beach clubs, restaurants and shops. She'd been out of work, but she'd still been partying and eating out. He wondered why. Kathryn Forbes hadn't said anything about Miranda's clubbing.

Miranda's bank statements showed her checking account was overdrawn. Until May she had deposited $3,000 each month. In June and July the deposit had been only $2,000. When Greg found her savings account book, he knew that the June and July deposits had come from savings and the cash advance on her credit card..

He found more credit card bills from another card. That account had been opened four months ago. The May bill began, "Welcome to Credit Plus. We are pleased to have you as a customer." The bills were sent to a post office box in Burgess Beach, and all charges on the card came from that town. Miranda had also taken cash advances from that credit card until she'd reached the limit. She paid the minimum due each month.

At noon Greg went out and got some lunch. By 1:30 he had Rob working on Miranda's computer while he returned to the mess of paperwork.

Miranda had made six trips to Burgess Beach, but she hadn't stayed at the Hibiscus Motel before her murder. She had stayed at a small motel, the Flamingo, by the fishing pier. Greg knew it because there was a restaurant next door that served great pompano, and he'd seen the motel in passing.

She'd been up to her neck in debt, he thought. Until August. Was she being blackmailed? Did she have another lover besides Kathryn? Certainly she had needed money. Until a windfall in August. Where had that come from?

He checked on Rob and found him still struggling.

"I need a piece of software you don't have here. I was hoping I could get a clue without going that route, but I haven't had any luck. I've got to go to school and borrow the software, but I have two other jobs waiting before I can go."

"I need it today," Greg said.

"I'll do my best."

"I've got to have it. Put those other jobs on hold."

"Okay, but I'll tell 'em to see you."

"Fine. Just get it done."

Greg headed back to the interview room and picked up the paperwork. He wondered why there were no cell phone bills. Maybe Kathryn paid them.

There were no business letters, but Greg hadn't expected any. There were several photos, and Greg went through them, hoping to find some secret in Miranda's life. Several were of Miranda and Kathryn, arms around one another, two taken at Disney World and several on a beach, whether in Miami or elsewhere, Greg couldn't tell.

It seemed strange to him going through Miranda's life, like the life of someone he didn't know. Strange and sad. She seemed nothing like the Miranda he remembered. He didn't have any pictures of her. She had always hidden from the camera, not that he'd been much of a photographer. He did remember once at a local restaurant a photographer had taken their picture. He'd wanted to buy a print, but she'd insisted she looked awful in the shot and wouldn't let him. Now that he thought about it, she had been camera shy. Was there a reason? They hadn't gone many places together. He'd always been working, and she had come and gone with such suddenness that they never planned much of anything.

There were a couple of group photos of what looked like a company Christmas party. The people in the pictures were dressed up, and some held drinks in their hands. This could have been a party for the bank where Miranda had worked or the law firm. He needed to check further.

Miranda had had a life in Miami with Kathryn, maybe more of a life than she'd had with him. She'd had a job, gone places on weekends, gone to parties at work or with Kathryn. As he looked back, it seemed they'd spent most of their time in bed or fighting. Yet they had been drawn together time and again. He couldn't count the number of times she'd left and then come back after a few days, a couple of weeks or even several months, until one day she was gone for good.

He packaged everything together, put it on his desk, and left.

SEVEN

The Flamingo Motel was bright pink and dated from the 1950's. Burgess Beach hadn't been a tourist mecca then, and accommodations had been basic, designed mostly for fishermen. The "Vacancy" sign outside was lit, and the door to the small office was open. The woman behind the desk was about sixty, at least forty pounds overweight and wore a shapeless muumuu. She was watching a talk show on a small television at the end of the counter. She didn't hear Greg come in.

He knocked on the door. "Burgess Beach Police. I have a few questions."

The woman looked surprised at the intrusion but made no move to turn off Dr. Phil.

Greg pulled out his badge, gestured at the television and said, "Turn that off."

She pushed the mute button, then turned toward him.

This was going to be a long interview.

He showed her the badge and asked, "Are you the manager?"

"Yes."

"What's your name?" Greg asked.

"Alberta Smithson," she said, glancing over her shoulder toward the television.

Greg walked over behind the counter and snapped the TV off. He pulled out the picture of Miranda Duncan and showed it to her. "Do you know this woman?"

"Yes."

"Has she stayed at the motel?"

"Yes."

"So she's a regular?"

"Damned if I know."

"Why do you remember her?"

"I gotta good memory for faces." She smirked, pleased with her performance.

"What name did she use to sign in?"

"I have no idea."

"Don't you pay attention when guests sign in?" he asked.

"I look at faces, like I said."

"So you recognize her, but you have no idea what her name is."

"That's right."

"I need to look at your guest register, then." He was losing patience.

"That's private," she said.

"I can get a warrant, but that's going to cause you lots of problems. We'll go through the register with a fine tooth comb, examine all your rooms, check with your regulars to be sure you're not renting by the hour . . . ."

She interrupted him to stand and push the register toward him. "Here you go," she said.

She walked toward the television and pressed the "on" button.

"Leave it," he said.

She turned to glare at him, then pressed "off."

The register began in July. According to Miranda's credit card, she had stayed at the Flamingo on July 7th and July 15th. He turned to those days and checked the names. Two people had signed in on July 7th: James Baldwin and Amanda Parsons. They had been assigned Rooms 12 and 16. On July 15th, only one person had signed in: Amanda Parsons. She had been given Room 12. There was only a scribbled home address and license plate number next to Amanda Parsons' name on each sign in.

In August, Miranda had stayed only once, on August 12th. He checked that date and found Amanda Parsons' name and an illegible address and license plate number. The same was true for September 3rd, September 6th, and September 18th. It was now October 1st, and Miranda had been murdered at the Hibiscus Motel on September 27th, nine days after her last visit to the Flamingo.

"Did Amanda Parsons have any visitors when she stayed here?" he asked.

"Who's Amanda Parsons?"

"She's the woman in the picture. Did you notice anything about her?"

"I ain't paid to notice. I'm paid to check 'em in, get their credit card numbers, and give 'em a key."

"So you didn't notice anything unusual about this woman," he pointed to Miranda's picture, "when she stayed here? She had no visitors, left on time, didn't ask for anything special? Made no phone calls? Is that right?"

"I didn't notice."

"Do you have phone records for calls made from the rooms?" Greg asked.

"There's no phones in the rooms."

Greg thought. Miranda had a cell phone, but he hadn't found any cell phone bills among the mess on her desk. Where were they? He made a mental note to ask Kathryn Forbes about them. "So, what happens if someone wants to make a call and doesn't have a cell phone?" he asked the clerk, who was inching slowly along the counter toward the television set.

"We gotta pay phone," she gestured with her head toward a phone on the other side of the lobby.

Greg walked over to the phone. It wasn't very private, but it would do if Miranda's pay phone wasn't working. "Did you ever see Amanda Parsons use the pay phone?" he asked.

"I didn't notice."

He wrote down the number. He could get the records from the phone company with a subpoena. He'd narrow it down to the dates Miranda had stayed at the Flamingo.

"I'll be back if I need anything else."

Before he'd reached the door, the television was back on.

When he got back to the station, Miranda's computer was there but Rob was gone. He'd have to wait until tomorrow.

———

Andi's afternoon was not as satisfactory as her morning. Although she called the Hutchinson Island house and the one in Fort Pierce repeatedly, there was never any answer. She applied for warrants to look at the Palmers' bank records and their insurance coverage for the house and furnishings, and by the time they came back signed, it was four-thirty. In the meantime, she did some computer research on the Palmers and their social life. She found that Kenneth Palmer had recently traded his expensive Mercedes down to a less expensive Audi. Was he pinching pennies?

When the warrants finally arrived, she called three of the banks where the Palmers had accounts and arranged to meet with their vice presidents in the morning. She also called the insurance company and made an appointment to review the Palmers' homeowners' policy. Then she headed home.

As she pulled into her parking space, she noticed an unfamiliar car parked across the street. It wasn't Jim's car, or at least not the one she knew, but she didn't remember ever seeing it in her neighborhood. Her street was a busy one, and overnight parking was prohibited. She left her car quickly and headed upstairs to her apartment, but Jim was already there, slouched against the wall opposite her door.

"Hi, sweetheart," he said. He wasn't sober, she could tell, and she didn't like the tone of his voice.

"I have nothing to say to you," she said.

He moved across the hallway and leaned against her door. "Aren't you going to ask me in?"

"No. Move away from my door."

"We don't need to fight, baby. Just hear me out."

"You hit me," she said. "I want you to leave."

"Or what?" Jim's voice held a threat.

"I didn't say 'or' anything. Just leave. Go back to Tampa." She took her keys out of her purse and tried to push past him. He grabbed at them, and although she held them as tightly as she could, she couldn't manage to hold on against his strength. Her phone was in her pocket, where she kept it, and she pulled it out, held it away and hit speed dial.

Jim grabbed at the phone, but the operator was there, saying "911. What is your emergency?" Andi shouted her identity and said, "I have an intruder."

Jim managed to get the phone, but the operator had heard and said someone would be right out. He flung the phone and her keys down on the hallway floor.

"Bitch," he said bitterly. "Why can't we just talk?"

"Because you slapped me. Because we've said everything we have to say. Because you're drunk. Just go home."

He turned and walked toward the stairs. "I'll go now, but we're not done."

"Jim, don't be a fool."

He flung open the door to the stairway, and she could hear his heavy footsteps as he headed downstairs. A minute later she heard sirens.

Andi huddled in a chair, close to tears, until the police knocked on her door. When she opened it, she saw John Southby and Amelia Linch, Burgess Beach patrol officers. Shit, she thought. Of course she knew them. She hadn't considered that when she called.

She didn't want to tell them the truth: that he was a police chief in Tampa and that she knew him. If Jim didn't quit drinking and behaving like an idiot, he would lose his job, but she didn't want to be the one to make that happen. But she hadn't thought about what she would say.

She invited them in, and as she spoke, her voice shook. Jim had scared her badly. When Amelia put an arm around her and guided her back to her chair, she knew she looked as scared as she felt, and she nearly burst into tears. She was like any abused woman. Now she wasn't a cop. This was personal.

Amelia asked what had happened, and she told them that the intruder had been waiting in her hallway, that she hadn't seen him until he accosted her by the door, that she'd grabbed the phone and called 911, and that the intruder had fled down the stairs when he realized she had summoned help. No, she didn't know who he was. No, she'd never seen him before. But Amelia and John were experienced patrol officers. They knew there were things she wasn't saying.

Patrolman Linch asked if she had any idea why the intruder had waited by her door. Was Andi sure she'd never seen him before? Had he been hanging around her apartment? Then Southby asked if he might be associated with one of her cases. Had anyone threatened her? Andi knew she'd opened a can of worms. She couldn't call 911 again unless she was prepared to give Jim up, but what options would she have if he showed up again?

Linch and Southby finally left after Amelia got Andi a couple of fingers of scotch from Andi's supply. She knew they didn't really believe her, but they let it go for now. After they left, she drank the scotch, then poured herself another. It had been a stressful evening, she told herself. She thought about the move. She was scheduled to move on Thursday; maybe she could get it moved up to Wednesday.

EIGHT

The next day when Greg got to the station, he found Rob getting up from Miranda's computer.

"I was just leaving. I've disabled the password, and I got the e-mails. I retrieved the deleted one, too. I'll be working on Lisa's p.c. Let me know if you need anything else."

Greg sat down at his desk and looked at the current e-mails. There weren't many, and all of them had been received after September 27th, the day Miranda had been murdered. Then he looked at the deleted e-mails. Some were apparently from people she'd gone clubbing with, asking if she was going, wondering why she hadn't answered. There were also ads for clubs, for clothing stores, and the like. There were three, however, that drew his attention. They were from someone who called himself 'oldnick'. There was no salutation and no sign off, just a message on each one. The first e-mail asked, "Did you get them?" The second was only one word: "Ready?" The third was simply: "See you 27." All very cryptic, but since September 27th was the date Miranda had been murdered, Greg found them interesting.

He checked Miranda's e-mail address book and noted the names of some of her correspondents. He made a note to check the ISP's for the names of people who weren't on Miranda's address list. Miranda's documents contained a few poems she had written and a story she'd been playing with, but there were no other documents of interest.

He checked his other open cases, none of which had deadlines, although he needed to make a couple of calls. Then he asked Lisa for time with Captain Bradley, and when he went into the chief's office, he asked if his drug cases and a hit-and-run could be assigned to someone else while he was involved in the murder. Bradley asked for a report on his progress, and after Greg told him about the visit to Kathryn Forbes and his perusal of Miranda's paperwork, Bradley agreed to reassign his cases to Ed Garcia. He asked if Greg needed help with the murder and suggested that Andi Battaglai might be able to work with him.

Then Greg made a list of the people he needed to see in Miami including the e-mailers whose names he knew and found addresses and phone numbers for most of them in the Miami and Miami Beach phone directories. There were a lot of places to go and a lot of people to question. He sent Captain Bradley an e-mail to let him know he'd be in Miami all day Wednesday.

Out of the corner of his eye, he saw Andi Battaglia come into the squad room. He walked over and knocked on her door. He noticed that the walls of her office were bare, and there were few personal items on the desk. A couple of files were lined up neatly in a pile on the side of the desk.

"Haven't seen you all day." Greg said.

"I'm following up on that burglary on Hutchinson Island. How's your murder coming along?"

"Slow. I'm going to Miami tomorrow. I've got a lot of ground to cover. Think you could break free and come down with me? I could use some help."

"Sure. I can't do much until I get the information from the banks and the insurance company. They tried to tell me it would take six months—you know, the usual—but I doubt I'll see anything I can use for a week or two at best. I'm at a standstill until then."

"Okay. Great. I'll let the Captain know. He told me I could have help if I needed it, and I'd rather have you than McClain or Garcia."

"Gee, thanks for the compliment. Makes me the top of 'not much'."

"Sorry." Greg flushed. "I didn't mean it as an insult. I'd like to work with you."

"Okay. Give me some background and where you are with it."

Greg filled her in on Miranda's murder, her history with Kathryn Forbes and what he hoped to find out in Miami. He didn't tell her that he and Miranda had lived together, off and on, for four years until she'd left five years before.

"We'll each need a car so we can split up. If you leave about eight, we can meet for coffee when we get to Miami and divide up the interviews." He fished a map out of his desk and circled an exit. "There's a Starbucks here, just off I 95. I'll meet you there about 9:30."

"Okay."

—

That night Andi parked around the corner from her building. She walked cautiously to the front. There were no cars parked on the street, and no one seemed to be hanging around. She walked up the stairs to the second floor and opened the stairway door to check the entrance to her apartment. The hallway was empty. She went back and moved her car to a spot not easily visible from the street, one that belonged to a neighbor she knew was on vacation. When she entered her empty living room, she heaved a sigh of relief.

Andi had never settled into this apartment. She hadn't hung any pictures, and her books and ornaments were still in boxes in the second bedroom. When she'd first moved to Burgess Beach, she hadn't been sure she'd stay, and she'd spent no time fixing up the apartment or personalizing it in any way. She thought she'd try to do better in the new place.

She hadn't been able to change her moving date from Thursday to Wednesday, but Thursday was her regular day off, so that worked out okay. She intended to spend the evening packing up her remaining possessions, but first she sat down with a finger of scotch, just to relieve the stress of the day. The scotch was gone before she noticed she'd drunk it, so she poured another and finished that as well. Then she thought she'd better have dinner and had another as she prepared a salad with a grilled chicken breast. By the time she sat down to eat, she was unsteady on her feet. She picked at her food, then fell asleep in front of the television.

When the phone rang, she woke with a start. She'd been dreaming that someone was chasing her, and for a moment, the ringing of the phone became part of the dream. When the ringing persisted, she checked caller ID. Unknown caller. She hated unknown callers. It could be Jim, but it might be

Greg confirming something for tomorrow. She answered the call.

"Hi, sweetheart," said Jim's drunken voice.

She slammed down the receiver. When the phone rang again, she put it on silent mode and didn't answer. She double locked her door and, for good measure, stuck a chair under the doorknob. She wondered where Jim was. It was ten o'clock: time enough for him to have finished work in Tampa and gotten drunk on his own time. She considered the bottle of scotch, now more than half empty. She wouldn't have any more. She was getting to be as much of a drunk as Jim.

———

The next morning Andi set off at 8:00, a headache pounding her skull. Serves you right, she thought. She'd only started drinking the hard stuff since she'd been in Burgess Beach, first from the stress of breaking up with Jim, then the murder she'd gotten assigned to, later out of loneliness and worry about her mother's breast cancer. She knew these were all excuses, and she vowed to watch the drinking from now on.

Andi met Greg at Starbucks. She took a couple of aspirin and ordered black coffee and a pastry.

When Greg saw her take the aspirin, he asked, "Hard night?"

"Yeah, but these should take care of it."

"Never worked for me."

Greg produced a list of people he wanted to interview, and they talked about how they'd divide them up.

"We can both go to see Kathryn Forbes," he suggested. "You might be able to get her to talk more than I was.

Apparently Miranda was going out to clubs, but Kathryn never said anything about that to me. Maybe that's what their situation always was, but if so, how come she didn't say?"

"Okay. Then what?"

"Maybe we can split up on Miranda's past employment. I'll take the law firm, and you take the bank. By the way, Miranda told Kathryn that she was fired by the bank. See if you can find out why."

"Okay."

"We can meet for lunch and check our progress. Then I've got a list of the friends she went clubbing with and the places she went regularly. We can do those together.."

"Sounds good to me."

At Kathryn Forbes' house, the SUV was still in the driveway. Kathryn answered the bell.

"You're back," she said, not sounding pleased. She was dressed for work in a black skirt and long aquamarine jacket over a pale blue tee. Andi noted that she was an attractive woman, older than Miranda by perhaps ten years. She had some gray in her dark hair, but she was carefully made up, her hair well-groomed, and she wore a small silver and pearl necklace and earrings.

Greg introduced Andi. "We'd like to ask you a few more questions."

"I've got to get to work," Kathryn said. "Can't this wait?"

"No. We need to talk to you now."

Kathryn looked at her watch, sighed, then said, "Just let me make a phone call. Would you like some coffee?"

They both declined, and Kathryn led them to the living room and excused herself. Greg and Andi prowled the room, looking at the pictures and examining the bookshelves. There were several framed pictures of Kathryn and Miranda, similar to the ones Greg had found in Miranda's desk. There was one of what looked like a much younger Kathryn with an older man and woman. Maybe parents. There were no pictures of Miranda without Kathryn. Andi checked on her headache and found that the aspirin had helped, although there was still a dull ache over her eyes.

When Kathryn returned, Greg and Andi walked to the sofa and sat down. Kathryn asked, "Has there been any progress in finding out who murdered Miranda?"

"No. We're still gathering information." He paused for a moment, then asked, "Miranda seems to have spent a lot of time in the Miami club scene. Did you go with her?"

Kathryn looked uncomfortable and said nothing for a few seconds. "I didn't like that scene, okay? Miranda did, and she had a lot of friends she went with. I didn't have a problem with that."

"So you didn't care that Miranda went out every night with people you didn't know while you sat home and went to work and supported her?"

Now she looked angry. "It wasn't like that. Miranda needed excitement, stimulation. More than I did. We were happy together."

"Was there some question about whether or not you were happy?" Greg asked.

"No. No, of course not. We loved one another. We just had different needs."

Andi smiled. "Of course you did. We certainly understand that."

"Did you know any of Miranda's club friends?" Greg consulted his list and continued, "How about Eva Torres or Rashida Jackson?"

Kathryn didn't answer for a moment, than said, "I never met them."

"Did you remember the name of the man at the law firm who was pursuing Miranda? We'd like to talk to him."

"All I can remember was that Miranda called him Nick."

"I'm sure we'll be able to find out when we visit the firm," Greg said. "I didn't find any cell phone bills among the paperwork I took from Miranda's desk. Do you have them?"

"They're all on one bill. I paid the bills when they came in, and Miranda reimbursed me."

"We'd like to see the bills."

"Is that necessary?"

"I'm afraid so. I can take them and give you a receipt. Or I can copy them and return them today."

"Don't you need a warrant?"

"I can get one. You gave me the paperwork from Miranda's desk, so I assumed you'd do the same with the phone bills. Is there something special about them?"

"There are a lot of business phone calls on those bills. My business. I don't want you poking into those numbers and calling people I do business with."

"This is a murder investigation, Ms. Forbes. You don't have a choice. I'll get a warrant and come back later in the week."

He rose, and Andi followed. Outside, Greg said, "Interesting about the phone calls. She didn't feel any need to hide Miranda's e-mails."

"Some of the phone calls are hers. Maybe she has something to hide."

"Maybe. Kathryn said that the man who gave Miranda a hard time at the law firm was called Nick something. There were some e-mails from someone who called himself 'old-nick.' They seemed to be a signal of some kind. I'll check that out when I go there."

NINE

Greg and Andi split up outside of Kathryn's house. Andi headed for the Shenandoah branch of Florida First Bank where Miranda had worked. Her employment had terminated a little over two years ago, shortly after she and Kathryn had first met, and Andi wondered if there was anything to find out. The more interesting visit was the one Greg was going to make to the law firm.

Andi checked the address, then put it into her GPS. She loved that little gadget. It had prevented her from getting lost more than once in the three months she'd had it.

At the bank, Andi asked to see the person in charge.

The woman at the desk asked if she might tell Mr. Ramos what she wanted to see him about."

"Police business," Andi said. "About a former employee."

"What is the name of this employee?"

When Andi told her, the woman told her to have a seat. She waited for ten minutes, then fifiteen.

She went back to the woman at the desk and said, "Look, I'm a police officer. I want to talk to whoever's in charge. What's the delay?"

"Just a couple more minutes," said the young woman, lifting and tossing her long dark hair over her shoulder. "He'll be right out."

Andi sat down again, then rose and began to pace. After two more minutes by her watch, a man emerged from the offices at the back of the bank and identified himself as John Ramos, Vice President. He escorted Andi back to his office.

"Sorry to keep you waiting." He looked flustered. "I wanted to pull the file on Miranda Duncan before I asked you in." Andi thought he'd probably called his boss when he'd seen her ID.

He was young, no more than twenty-five, with blow-dried blond hair and a fashionable growth of beard. He looked like a kid to Andi. Not that she was that much older, but she'd seen more.

"So, what can you tell me about Ms. Duncan, Mr. Ramos? How long did she work at the bank?"

"Why are the Burgess Beach Police asking about Ms. Duncan? She left Florida First more than two years ago." He'd apparently been told to find out what he could before he answered any questions.

"Ms. Duncan was murdered in Burgess Beach last Friday evening. Is that reason enough for you?"

Ramos colored. "Oh," he said, then paused as if rethinking what he had to say. "Ms. Duncan was hired by the vice president then in charge of this branch, Joseph Adamski. He interviewed her in May of 2005, and hired her as a teller."

"How long was Miranda a teller?" Andi asked.

"Being a teller is a stepping stone to personal banker, and personal bankers get a commission on whatever accounts, loans, or credit cards their customers sign up for.

According to her file, Ms. Duncan was promoted to personal banker in August of 2005. She did well, earning substantial commissions."

"What happened to get her fired?"

Ramos' voice shook a little as he said, "She wasn't fired, Detective. She terminated her employment in November, 2006. According to her file."

"Really," Andi said. "She told her friends she'd been fired. Is there something different in the records?"

"The record doesn't say anything about being fired." He cleared his throat. "Her records say she left voluntarily in November, 2006."

"So, whatever she told her friends, Ms. Duncan left of her own volition? She was not fired. Is that correct?"

Ramos put a hand to his mouth and coughed. "The written record is somewhat ambiguous. I called Mr. Adamski before I asked you to come in. He said to tell you that Miranda Duncan left on her own."

"Is Mr. Adamski still an employee of Florida First?"

"Yes. He's the president now. If you want to know what happened to Miranda Duncan, you'll need to ask him."

Shit, Andi thought, barely keeping herself from saying it out loud. "Where can I find Mr. Adamski?"

"He's at our headquarters in South Beach." He scribbled on a piece of paper and passed it to Andi. "Here's the address."

Outside, Andi debated. Should she wait for Greg and a warrant? But Adamski knew she was in Miami. He was expecting her. She thought about calling Greg, then decided the hell with it. She got into her car, set up her GPS and headed to South Beach.

———

In the reception area of Pattis and Kearney, Attorneys At Law, the temperature must have been fifty degrees, and the blond receptionist seated behind a teak desk was wearing an expensive-looking sweater under a gray wool suit. Greg slogged his way across the blue-gray deep pile rug and showed her his badge. He asked to talk to either of the managing partners.

"Mr. Pattis is in court," she said. "and Mr. Kearney is in Washington this week. Did you have an appointment?"

"Is there someone in charge of personnel matters?" he asked.

"Mr. Epstein is the personnel manager."

"I'd like to see him," Greg said.

"I'll see if he's available." She picked up the phone and murmured into it, then said to Greg, "If you'll follow me, Mr. Epstein has a few minutes to see you."

Greg followed the receptionist down a long hall. He was watching the seductive sway of her hips so intently that he nearly ran into the woman when she paused to knock on an office door.

"Come in," said a voice, and the receptionist opened the door. "Mr. Lamont, Mr. Epstein," she said and stood aside to allow Greg to enter.

"Come in, Mr. Lamont. What can we do for you?" Epstein was tall and beefy, but his suit fit him impeccably.

"Detective Lamont." Although Greg hadn't been invited to sit, he took the chair in front of the large mahogany desk, noting that it was positioned so the guest faced one of the large windows and Epstein sat with his back to the light.

"Yes. Detective Lamont. Are you inquiring about one of our employees?"

"A former employee. Miranda Duncan. She left your employ in January, 2008."

Greg couldn't see the expression on Epstein's face clearly, but he didn't miss the way the attorney's body tensed when Greg said the name.

"Was she an attorney?" Epstein's tone suggested that anyone of lower status would hardly be worth asking about, but his well-manicured hands were clasped tightly in front of him as if to anchor them.

"A paralegal. I believe she was employed with your firm for a little over a year."

"Do you have a warrant?"

"I can get one, but I thought, since this is a murder inquiry, you'd want to help the police in any way you can." Greg fixed his eyes on the man and was rewarded by the sight of the involuntary flinching of his shoulders and a sharp intake of breath.

Epstein picked up a pen from his desk, clicking it open and closed. Finally he said, "I didn't know this was a murder inquiry." Then he cleared his throat and continued, "I'm afraid I didn't know Ms. Duncan personally. The hiring of paralegals and secretaries is handled by my assistant, Ms. Mendez. I'll have my secretary call her, and she can meet you in the reception area. Now, if you'll excuse me, I'm due at a partners' meeting." He rose.

Greg didn't move. "So you have no recollection of Ms. Duncan?"

"That's correct. Now . . . ." He gestured Greg toward the door. Greg sat. Epstein had not only known Miranda, he'd known her well.

"Ms. Duncan was a strikingly beautiful woman, Mr. Epstein. Long red hair, pale skin, very good figure. There aren't many men who didn't notice her."

"Well, I guess I'm the exception to the rule, Detective." He was still standing, but he picked up the phone from his desk. "Marge," he said, "will you take the Detective back to reception and call Paula. She'll need to talk to him." He turned back to Greg as a tall, almost painfully slender woman entered the room. "Detective . . . ."

Greg got slowly to his feet. "Thank you for your help," he said and followed the woman out into the hall and back to the freezing reception area where he stood waiting for Paula Mendez.

"Ms. Mendez will be right with you, Detective," Marge said.

Paula Mendez was a short, chunky Latina with the face of a severe fourth-grade teacher. "Mr. Lamont?" she asked.

"Detective Lamont. Burgess Beach Police Department."

"Police? All right. Follow me." She sounded more annoyed than curious.

It wasn't nearly as much fun to follow Ms. Mendez down another long hall as it had been the receptionist, but Greg did as he was told. Eventually they entered an office, the sole window of which overlooked an open area of women seated at desks, typing rapidly on computers.

In response to Greg's unspoken question, Ms. Mendez said, "Typing pool. Some of the attorneys haven't mastered computers and still use dictation equipment. Please sit down."

Ms. Mendez' chair faced the windowed wall, and Greg was able to see her face clearly. He said, "I understand you're in charge of the secretarial and paralegal staff. I'm interested in whatever you can tell me about a former employee, a paralegal."

"Yes. She, or he, would report to me. What is this person's name?"

"Miranda Duncan. I believe she left Pattis and Kearney in early 2008."

Ms. Mendez didn't look surprised at Miranda's name. She asked, "What has brought her to the attention of the police, Detective?"

"I'd like to know what you can tell me about the time she spent at Pattis and Kearney."

"Personnel records are confidential, of course. Do you have a warrant?"

"I can get one, but I hoped you would tell me something about Ms. Duncan now."

"I'm sorry. If you come back with a warrant, I'll be happy to tell you what I know. Without one, I can only confirm the dates of Ms. Duncan's employment and her job title when she left. I'll check that now." She turned to her computer and hit a few keys.

"Ms. Duncan began work in February 2007 and left the firm in January 2008. Her job title at that time was Senior Paralegal in the real estate division. That's all I can tell you." Paula Mendez pushed her chair back from her desk, getting to her feet. "I'll be able to give you additional information if you return with a warrant. Now, if you'll excuse me . . . ."

"Miranda Duncan was murdered in Burgess Beach last Friday night."

The woman sank back into her chair and took a deep breath. She said nothing for a long moment. Then she murmured almost to herself, "Murdered."

She was silent again while Greg waited. Finally she said, "I remember Miranda well. She was a beautiful woman, very intelligent, although apparently lacking much common sense. I'm sorry to hear she's come to such a bad end."

"What can you tell me about her time here?" Mendez' description of Miranda was right on.

"Look, Detective, I can't legally tell you anything more than I've already said without a warrant, but you're in luck today. I'm going to help you out." She paused.

"Today's my last day. I have another job, and I'm leaving here with no notice. I've been treated like shit, and I don't owe them a thing. So, ask away. I'll tell you everything I know about Miranda."

Greg was surprised at Paula's sudden about-face but happy to take advantage of the opportunity it provided. "Thank you. I'd appreciate information about her time with Pattis and Kearney, her work record, friends at work, that sort of thing."

"What did Mr. Epstein tell you about Miranda?"

"He said he didn't know who she was."

"He would say that, of course." She smiled, not in a friendly way. "Miranda was initially in a pool of paralegals who are assigned to some of the newer attorneys on an as-needed basis. She was very bright, and it only took a couple of months for her to come to the notice of some of the senior partners. Then she was assigned to work for Mr. Oldham, head of our real estate division. She also did some work for Mr. Epstein."

"Even though he said he didn't know her."

"I shouldn't tell you this, but I liked Miranda, although she behaved like a fool. When she was working for Mr. Epstein, she came to me one evening, complaining that he was pressuring her for sex. She was ready to file a complaint with the Miami Labor Relations Commission, but I asked her to wait until I had an opportunity to talk with him. I did, and of course he didn't want anyone else to find out about her allegations. He never admitted anything to me; in fact he denied he'd done anything, but then he would, wouldn't he? She didn't work for him after that, and the whole thing disappeared."

"That seemed like a sensible thing to do, both on your part and Ms. Duncan's. Why do you say she behaved like a fool?"

"Because she began an affair with a married senior partner and used that leverage to get a better office location, hours that suited her, and some significant pay increases. She referred questions to Mr. Oldham, but when these perks became too obvious, they cost her her job. She was allowed to resign, and the firm paid her severance pay in order to keep the matter quiet."

So like Miranda, Greg thought.

"What's Mr. Oldham's first name?"

"Nicolas."

"And he was the partner with whom she was having the affair?"

"Yes. Her behavior became so blatant that even he wasn't able to protect her. Everyone knew, except perhaps his wife."

"Do you know if Mr. Oldham and Ms. Duncan remained in touch after she left Pattis and Kearney?"

"No, I don't."

"I'd like to talk to Mr. Oldham. Can you arrange that?"

"I'll see what I can do. I'll take you back to reception while I check Mr. Oldham's schedule."

"Thank you for your help." Greg turned at the door and said, "And good luck!"

"Thanks," she said and walked him back to the reception area.

———

Andi parked in the lot reserved for customers of First Florida Bank and headed inside. She asked the greeter to direct her to Mr. Adamski's office.

"He's expecting me," she said.

She was directed to the bank of elevators. Mr. Adamski's office was on the third floor.

The receptionist asked her if she had an appointment, and she said again, "Mr. Adamski is expecting me."

The receptionist picked up the phone, but was told that Mr. Adamski was in conference and couldn't be disturbed.

"I'll wait." Andi sat in one of the comfortable chairs and picked up a magazine. She glanced at her watch. Eleven-fifteen. She'd give Adamski twenty minutes before she left to meet Greg.

The phone rang, and the receptionist said, "She's waiting."

At eleven-thirty, another woman came into the reception area and said, "Mr. Adamski will see you now."

She led Andi to Adamski's office. He was a plump man in his sixties, dressed in bankers' gray but sporting a bright red tie. Adamski rose from behind his desk and extended a hand to Andi.

After they were seated, he asked, "What can I do for you, Detective?"

"I'm inquiring about a former employee who worked at the branch where you were the manager when she was hired."

"Who is this employee? I left that branch nearly three years ago."

"Her name was Miranda Duncan. There seems to be some confusion as to whether she left the bank voluntarily in November of 2006, or whether she was fired. She told friends she was fired, but Mr. Ramos said that she left voluntarily."

"Why is that of interest to the police in . . . . where is it?" He checked a note on his desk, then continued. "Burgess Beach?"

"Just a matter of clearing up the record. A technicality, but something we need to know."

"And have you a warrant, Detective Battaglia?"

"No. I can certainly get one, but in view of the fact that Ms. Duncan was murdered, I thought you might be willing to talk with me about her work history."

Adamski got to his feet. "Come back when you have a warrant, Detective. Now I have another appointment." He waited for her to leave.

He was smooth, she had to give him that.

Andi got to her feet and extended her hand. "Thank you for your time, Mr. Adamski. I'll see you again."

"I'll look forward to it."

———

Nick Oldham was unavailable because he was in trial in Fort Lauderdale and not expected back for another day or so. However, when Paula Mendez provided this information, she pressed a piece of paper in Greg's hand. He thanked her for her help, and when he got outside, found she'd given him Oldham's home address and phone number.

He headed off to meet Andi for lunch. She was waiting at a table when he got to Deerfield's, and they compared notes.

"I'll get to work on the warrants as soon as we get back," Greg said. "Miranda sure raises red flags, doesn't she? What's your impression?"

Andi took a bite of her salad and thought for a minute. "I think she took advantage of her beauty and her smarts to get what she wanted. She used people, but she doesn't seem to have had any sense of how far she could go. People like Kathryn would put up with a lot for her, but others may not have been so willing."

"That sounds right. Maybe somebody got mad."

"Maybe. We don't know enough yet."

"No," Greg said. He thought about Miranda, how beautiful she'd been, how bright, and the way she'd used people.

Andi asked, "Earth to Greg. Did you hear me?"

"Sorry. I was thinking. Yes, the other people we need to see. I have a few work addresses for people she went clubbing with, so we can start there. The clubs don't open until eleven, but somebody would probably be there around ten. Let's go."

They found a lot where Andi could leave her car, then they met with Eva Torres who had a shop in Miami Beach that sold high-end beach wear. They found her alone in the shop unpacking a shipment of fancy flip-flops.

Greg identified himself and asked if they could talk with her for a few minutes about Miranda Duncan.

"Who?" Eva Torres was a tiny, dark-skinned woman with long, very curly black hair and a Cuban accent.

"We understand that you go to clubs with a woman named Miranda Duncan."

"I don't know her."

Greg pulled out the photo of Miranda. "This is Miranda Duncan."

"Oh, Red. Yeah, I know her, but not the name. What's wrong with her? She looks dead."

"She is."

"She's dead? Really? How'd she die?"

"She was murdered." Greg watched Eva's reaction, but there wasn't much, just a little shudder at the idea of murder.

"Murdered. I wouldn't have thought. . . . I really didn't know much about her. We e-mailed about getting together. I hadn't heard from her for a few days, so I wondered."

"What wouldn't you have thought?" Greg asked.

"I wouldn't have thought she'd get herself killed. I mean, she did play games, and she didn't much care if anybody got hurt. Maybe somebody really got pissed."

"Anybody in particular?"

Eva thought for a minute. "Well, there was a gay guy named Bobby. He said she stole his boyfriend, and they got into a shouting match one night. She slapped him, and he punched her, but somebody grabbed him and the bouncer threw him out."

"When was this?" Greg was interested now.

"Maybe last spring. May or June."

"What else do you know about Bobby?"

"Nothing. The bouncer may know. It happened at Victor's, I think."

"How about Bobby's boyfriend? Do you know him?"

"He was a real hunk. Blond hair and big muscles. French, I think." She thought a minute. "I can't remember his name."

"You said she played games. What do you mean?"

"Like she'd play up to some guy as if she was crazy about him, hugging and kissing him, telling him how great he was, then when he acted like he owned her, she'd get all mad and tell him to piss off. We all did some of that, but Miranda didn't care who the guy was."

"What do you mean?"

"There were some guys who you shouldn't piss off, but Miranda didn't care who they were."

"Who were the guys you shouldn't piss off?" Andi asked.

"You know. Gang guys, really connected guys. Dangerous."

"Did she do this at all the clubs?"

"Yeah. All the time. Different guys, different clubs."

"Do you remember anybody else in particular? Anybody who got mad, made threats?"

"I don't remember any names. Most of them got mad, but that didn't last long 'cause Miranda just laughed at them. Then they'd leave, like they knew they weren't good enough."

"Where did you meet Miranda?"

Eva tossed back her mane of hair and thought for a minute. "I don't know. One of the clubs. Cavelli's or Tux. Maybe one of the others. I can't remember."

"Was there anyone she was friendly with at these clubs, anyone she was in touch with outside the clubs?"

"I don't know."

"Do you think any of these guys she humiliated went after her?" Andi asked.

"I never saw any of them again at a club when she was there. Sort of like once she was done, they were too embarrassed to come back."

"Do you know where she lived?" Andi asked.

"No. Like I said, we e-mailed."

"So you and Miranda never went shopping together or to a show?" Andi was pushing a bit.

"No. We weren't like that friendly."

"Can you think of anything else?" Greg asked.

"No."

"Thanks." Greg gave her his card, asked her to call if she thought of anything else.

As they walked to Greg's car, Andi asked, "Think there's anything there?"

"Maybe, but it's gonna be hard to get anything that'll stick. Those guys aren't gonna talk."

"She certainly provoked a bunch of them. She really took chances."

"That was Miranda," Greg said, then stopped himself from saying anything more.

Greg and Andi visited the work addresses of four other clubbing friends of Miranda's, but none of them knew her any better than Eva Torres. Two confirmed the altercation with Bobby, but they didn't know anything more about him. They all said the same things about her.

When the detectives finished the last interview, they headed back to pick up Andi's car.

"There must be a bunch of pissed-off guys out there. Could one of them have been mad enough to kill her?" Andi asked.

"But why in Burgess Beach?"

"Good question. Maybe he stalked her there?"

"Maybe." Greg didn't sound convinced.

Andi looked at her watch. Seven-thirty. "What'll we do now?"

"I think we should eat. Then we can hit the clubs around ten. It's a little early, but someone might have time to talk."

Greg was feeling uncomfortable that he hadn't told Andi his history with Miranda. He had to watch what he said, and he'd almost slipped a couple of times. He missed Miranda, too. He wanted to talk to someone about her. They'd been so close, he'd never thought they would split up, but then she'd just left. And apparently hadn't looked back. Now he remembered, and remembering hurt like hell. He'd thought he was done with Miranda, but she was an open wound. He needed to talk, and he wanted to trust that Andi wouldn't tell the Captain.

TEN

Andi and Greg settled on La Locanda, an Italian restaurant in South Beach. Andi ordered a seafood pasta and Greg the veal scallopine. They skipped the wine.

They talked about the day and what they'd learned after the waiter had left with their orders. When the food arrived, Greg said, "I need to tell you something, but I don't want Captain Bradley to know, not until I can figure this case out."

"I'm not usually a confidant of the Captain's." Andi was annoyed.

"I know that. That's why I want to talk to you. I knew Miranda. We lived together in Miami for almost four years. She left me about five years ago."

"You what? You 'knew' her? You lived with her? And you're investigating her murder? What the hell are you thinking? You realize you could jeopardize the whole case."

"I know, I know, and I've thought about it, but I have to find out who killed her. I can't leave this to someone else."

"You know the Captain would have your head if he knew."

"Yeah, I know."

"And any defense lawyer with an ounce of brains would get the case thrown out of court. Even if you had eyewitnesses. Which you don't. It's crazy, Greg."

"I know, but I can't let it go."

Andi shook her head. She twirled pasta on her fork but didn't take a bite. Finally she put down her fork and folded her arms.

"Okay. I won't push it for now. But I don't see that you are anything but a dumb son-of-a-bitch. We'll come back to this later. Now, prove to me that you can be the detective on this one and not just an idiot. Tell me about her. What was she really like? What was her attraction for you, besides the obvious?" Andi smiled without humor.

Once Greg could talk about Miranda, he couldn't seem to stop. He talked about how smart she was, but how little patience she had with the details of daily life. She learned things: computer systems, gourmet cooking, the work of a paralegal, seemingly without effort, but she quickly became impatient with doing the same things day after day. She hated the daily grind of going to work, of doing what she was told, so sooner or later in her jobs she'd get into trouble with some higher-up who fired her, even though she was the best worker the company had ever had. Learning something new was challenging, but repeating it bored her.

"Then sometimes, she'd call in sick and spend all day in bed, crying. Of course bosses got impatient, demanded that she show up, and do her job. Sometimes she went to work; sometimes she told the boss to shove it. Let's just say, she had a checkered work history."

"That fits," Andi said. "Too smart for her own good. I wonder what kept her with Kathryn—or with you for four years, for that matter."

"I don't know," Greg said, but he did know and sure as hell didn't want to talk about it.

"You've told me this much," Andi said, "you'd better finish."

Greg didn't look at Andi, but stared down at his hands. "The sex. That was what kept her coming back to me. I'm sure it was the same with Kathryn. I don't think she was faithful to me—probably not to Kathryn either—but she always came back. At least until she didn't."

"Got it," Andi said. She wanted to change the subject. "Let's see where we are now." She took out her pen and notebook.

"The bank: was she fired or did she quit? Does it matter? What does Joseph Adamski have to do with that?

"The law firm: Epstein—what's his first name, by the way? Did he kill her because she wouldn't have sex with him? The other guy . . . ."

"Geoff. G-E-O-F-F. That's Epstein's first name," Greg said. "and she was having the affair with Nick Oldham. She was still getting e-mails from him, by the way, and very cryptic ones. They may have still been lovers. I wonder if his wife knew or cared? That'll have to wait until we see him. I have his home address and phone number. Courtesy of Paula Mendez and her war against Pattis and Kearney."

"Okay, now the clubs." Andi went back to her notes. "All the people we've talked to so far hardly knew Miranda at all, but they all mention this Bobby. Was he angry enough to kill her? Who is he?"

Greg said, "All those guys she pissed off. We don't even know their names. One of them could have been mad enough, I suppose."

"But not in Burgess Beach. They'd have followed her to Kathryn's, wouldn't they?"

"Unless they stalked her. What about Burgess Beach? What was she doing there? Was she meeting someone? What was she worried about?"

"Was she meeting you?" Andi asked, looking at Greg. She didn't understand this guy. He was clearly still hung up on Miranda. Had he been seeing her after their breakup?

"Good God, no. I haven't seen her in more than five years," Greg said. "You're right, though. Why Burgess Beach? Did she know I was there?"

"Okay. I'm not sure Captain Bradley will believe you."

"Probably not. And then there's the suitcase and Miranda's purse, both missing from the motel. The suitcase was heavy, Ben Patel said. What was in it? Drugs, guns, gold? What else is heavy?"

"Maybe the suitcase wasn't important and the important thing was in her purse." Andi liked this part of the case. It was better than talking about Greg's sex life with the dead woman.

Greg continued. "Why was she in Burgess Beach that night and the other nights? What was she doing? It looked like she was being blackmailed. She needed money, so maybe the suitcase was part of that. Why Burgess Beach? Why not Miami? I keep coming back to that."

"What makes you think she was being blackmailed?" Andi asked.

"Didn't I tell you? Oh, sorry. I thought I had." Then he filled her in on the bank accounts he'd traced with the paperwork he'd gotten from Kathryn Forbes.

Andi finished making notes and picked up her fork. The pasta was cold but still good., "We've got a lotta suspects, a lotta motives, and no evidence at all. What do we do now, boss?"

"What time is it?"

"Almost ten."

"Okay. Let's see what we can find out so we can add to our pool of suspects and motives. I've got a list of clubs."

Their first stop was Cavelli's. The line of hopeful entrants was already forming when Greg and Andi pushed past them to the door guard, a large African-American who definitely spent a lot of time working out.

"Get in line like everybody else," he said.

"We don't stand in line." Greg showed his ID. "I want to see your boss."

The guard took down the rope and motioned them in through the open door into the cool darkness of the club. The place was redolent of liquor and smoke. The lighted dance floor lay ahead of them, and they headed toward it. Two men sat at tables adjoining the lighted area, listening to a woman sing a version of "Poker Face," but she was, unfortunately, not Lady Gaga or even Madonna. She was young, no more than twenty, with the requisite big boobs and dyed blond hair, but those attributes didn't help her voice any.

One of the men, a thin, balding guy in his fifties with big bags under his eyes, said, "Okay, honey. That's enough. If we're interested, we'll let you know."

The woman behind the mic stopped singing in mid-phrase. "My agent was sure you'd like this one."

"Sure, hon. We'll let you know. Next."

The other man, younger, taller and in better shape, turned as Greg presented himself to them. Another singer hovered just out of the spotlight, waiting for her moment.

"Are you looking for somebody?" asked the younger man.

"Roberto Cavelli." Greg said.

"Who are you?" asked the man.

Greg showed his badge. "I have a few questions."

"I'm Roberto Cavelli," said the older man. "What's this about?"

"A woman named Miranda Duncan. Everyone called her 'Red.'"

"What about her?" asked Cavelli.

"What can you tell me?"

"Why are the cops chasing Red?"

"Because she's been murdered."

Greg watched Roberto Cavelli absorb this. He wasn't shocked, but he hadn't expected it, either, and he took a minute to process Greg's words. He wasn't a man who gave up information easily.

"Who murdered her?" Cavelli asked.

"We don't know. That's why we're here."

Cavelli studied him, then said, "Let's go in my office." He turned to the other man and said, "You can get rid of them. Listen if you want."

Greg and Andi followed him through a door next to the stage. In the office, Cavelli took a chair behind the large desk that crowded the room, and Andi and Greg sat in the two chairs in front.

"Now, what happened to Red?"

Greg introduced himself and Andi, saying they were from Burgess Beach.

"Why are you here from Burgess Beach?" Cavelli interrupted before Greg could finish.

"I'll ask the questions, Mr. Cavelli." Greg said.

Cavelli threw up his hands in a gesture of surrender, leaning back in his chair. "Okay," he said.

"Tell me about Red." Greg said.

Cavelli clasped his hands on the desk and thought for a minute. "She started clubbing here about two, maybe two-and-a-half years ago. She was a fucking knockout, and she attracted a crowd. She usually came with a coupla other broads—hot, too, but not like Red. Guys noticed them, and they bought drinks, and that was good for business."

"Did she have any particular friends? Anybody special?"

"Same crowd of gals—Eva Torres, Rashida something; some I only knew by sight. As to the guys, Red usually had a different guy every night, although sometimes they'd get a repeat. No more than two nights. I don't know any names. I talked to Red once though, about the way she treated some of the guys.

"She'd really piss 'em off when she was done with them. Just treat 'em like dirt, make out with another guy right in front of 'em. She caused a lotta fights, and my guys were getting tired of her. I warned her I might throw her out for good. There's just so much excitement a club can stand, and

I was getting tired of her trouble—and the damage. Some of those guys she pissed off were big, and they were mad."

"What did she say when you spoke to her?

"She laughed. Said she didn't care. Other clubs would have her if I wouldn't."

"How about a guy named Bobby, maybe with a French guy—big, tall blond?"

"Nah. Don't know 'em.

"Anything else can you tell us?" Greg asked.

"Why are you investigating the murder? Red lived in Miami."

"She was killed in Burgess Beach."

"Oh," Cavelli said. He looked as though he was about to say something else, but instead, he got to his feet. "If there's nothing else . . . ."

Andi asked, "Was there something else you were about to tell us about Miranda, Mr. Cavelli?"

Cavelli hesitated, then said, "I saw her once—I'm sure it was her—getting into a car with Joe Feragamo. I thought I was wrong then, but now I wonder."

Andi looked puzzled, but Greg got it. "Feragamo runs drugs and guns in and out of Mexico and further south."

Greg turned to Cavelli. "You're sure it was Miranda?"

"Yes. I'm sure."

Andi got the names and phone numbers for Cavelli and his assistant before she and Greg headed for Tux, next on the list.

The line at Tux wasn't as long as at Cavelli's, but the club was open now, and some of the hopefuls were already inside. Greg and Andi identified themselves and entered a huge room overlit with glare from the ceiling fixtures. Andi closed her eyes after the darkness outside and thought how the patrons must be taken off guard by the sudden brightness. There were a few couples gyrating on the dance floor.

Greg asked the doorman for the owner and was directed to a large table where several attractive young women sat with three men. The women glanced at them without interest and continued their conversation. Two of the men were big, bodyguard types, and the third was young, slim and bearded.

Greg asked to speak to the owner, and one of the bodyguards asked "Who wants to know?"

Greg produced his ID, and the man examined it intently. Then, at a barely perceptible nod Greg almost missed, the bearded man spoke. "I'm Tom Sarafian. This is my place."

Greg said, "I wanted to talk to you about Miranda Duncan. I think you knew her as Red.

"Sure. I know Red. Haven't seen her in a while." Sarafian invited them to sit, then continued, "Why are you here?"

"Miranda Duncan's been murdered. I want to know what you know about her."

This time the news that Miranda had been murdered produced a stunned silence. These people had known her, and her murder wasn't what they'd expected.

Finally Sarafian said, "I didn't know her well. She came here with a bunch of other broads, attracted a lot of guys, caused some trouble." He nodded at the other two men. "She got attention, though, and I liked that. Attracted customers."

Greg registered the disclaimer but didn't believe it. "Anybody in particular that she was in trouble with?"

"She had a knockdown with a guy named Bobby about his boyfriend. That time we threw Bobby out, but I told her to watch herself."

"Did she?" Andi asked.

"She was better. Maybe . . . . Right, guys?" He gestured to the two other men.

The darker-skinned tough said, "Yeah. We didn't have no more fights around her."

"D'ya know Bobby's last name?" Greg asked.

Sarafian looked inquiringly at the two men, and again, the dark-skinned man spoke. "Something Spanish. I don't remember."

Then the other man said, "Medina."

The first man said, "Right."

"Medina," Andi echoed, making a note.

"Do you know the boyfriend's name?" Greg asked.

Everybody shrugged, then one of the woman, a small blond with big brown eyes, said, "Etienne. He was French."

The other women looked at her in surprise. One said, "How'd you know that?"

"I thought he was hot, but I guess my gaydar wasn't working that day."

The other women laughed.

"Any idea where we can find Bobby Medina?"

Sarafian shrugged, "Haven't seen him."

"Was there anyone else in particular she hung around with?" Greg asked.

The group was silent. Then Sarafian asked, "How'd she die?"

"She was killed in Burgess Beach. The autopsy isn't in. Do any of you know why she might have been in Burgess Beach?"

Nobody spoke until Sarafian asked, "Where is it?"

"Up north of Palm Beach, on the coast. D'ya know anybody up there?"

There were a few head shakes. Nobody spoke.

"When was the last time any of you saw her?"

The question was greeted with silence. Finally, Sarafian said, "I don't think she'd been here for a while. I don't remember the last time."

The others at the table echoed that they hadn't seen Red for a while either.

"Did any of you see her outside of the club? Anybody ever take her home? Know where she lived?" Andi asked.

There were head shakes all around and murmurs of "no" in response to that question.

Greg asked again, "Anything else you can tell us about her?" Again, there were no responses, although Andi noticed two of the women glancing at Sarafian before shaking their heads.

Finally Greg said, "I'll leave you my card so if any of you think of anything, you can let me know. And we'll take your names and where you can be reached for our records."

Andi began with Tom Sarafian. Then the dark-skinned bodyguard balked. "Why d'ya need my name?"

"Just to complete the record of who we talked to." Andi waited, pen poised.

He finally muttered his name, added a phone number, and Andi moved on.

In the car, Andi said, "Somebody there knows more than they're willing to say. I'd be willing to bet the long-haired brunette in red had something—and the blond—but they didn't want to speak in front of Sarafian."

"I got some vibes, too. We need to follow up. What about the guys?"

"Nothing much there. They didn't like her; that you can tell."

"We need to talk to each of them alone."

Greg thought about Miranda. She had caused a lot of trouble in Miami, at least on the club scene, but she always went back to Kathryn. Was it because she loved her or because Kathryn's place was safe? Had she done the same thing when she was with him? The idea made him doubt his history with Miranda and gave him a queasy feeling. He pushed it away, not wanting to think about it.

ELEVEN

"What's the next club?" Greg asked as they left the parking lot.

"The Beach House," Andi gave him the address.

The Beach House was much less crowded than either Tux or Cavelli's, and the owner wasn't there. They got no new information, so they moved on to the Meta Lounge where strobe lights flashed and electronic music pounded. The room was crowded, and scantily clad women and sleek-looking men danced or watched four nearly nude women in cages gyrating to the incessant beat. The detectives were directed to a table by the dance floor where a gray-haired man sat with a woman who looked to be thirty years younger than he.

"I'm looking for the owner," Greg said, showing his badge.

"That'd be me," said the gray-haired man. He stood up and introduced himself as Jorge Acosta, extending a hand to Andi and then to Greg. "Sit down."

When Greg asked about Miranda Duncan, he was met with blank stares until he called her Red. Both Acosta and his companion indicated they knew her.

"What can you tell me about her?"

"Why are you asking?" Acosta countered.

This time when Greg said that she'd been murdered, the information didn't seem to come as a surprise.

After a silence, Greg asked again, "What can you tell me about her?"

The woman spoke, directing her remarks to Andi. "I'm Belle Acosta. He wouldn't think to introduce me." She jerked her head toward her husband, who looked embarrassed. "I knew Red. Better than he did." Again, a head movement toward her husband. "She was a smart woman, but she didn't know what she could get away with. She hung out here, and she and I used to lunch and shop when she wasn't working or when she had time off. I liked her. He thought she was a pain in the ass because she caused a lot of commotion wherever she went, but she was fun."

The woman was much older than Andi's first impression. She'd had some very good surgery and had maintained herself well, but she was probably closer to fifty than thirty, almost a contemporary of her husband. She wore a dress with a very short skirt and a scanty top, and her firm, tanned legs and well-maintained breasts didn't give away her age at first glance.

Andi asked, "You didn't look surprised that she'd been murdered. Why was that?""

Belle Acosta lit a cigarette with a tiny gold lighter. "Red pushed people around. She preferred women to men, so she was less ruthless with women, but she was pretty contemptuous of the men who were attracted to her."

"Were you and she lovers?"

"No. Just friends." Belle Acosta didn't seem affronted by Andi's question.

"So you think she might have pushed somebody around enough to get herself killed? Anybody in particular?" Andi asked.

Jorge interjected, "Don't listen to Belle. She didn't like Miranda."

Belle said sharply, "That's not true. We were friends."

"You didn't like the attention she got. You were jealous."

"Oh, be quiet, Jorge. I was <u>not</u> jealous. Red was my friend."

Andi said again, "Do you think she might have pushed somebody around enough to get herself killed?"

"I don't know that's what happened, but she didn't much care what happened to her or who got mad at her. And she had some sort of money problem."

"What do you know about that?"

This was the first time anyone had mentioned money.

"She asked me if she could borrow some money. Actually quite a lot of money. I was reluctant, but I lent her the money, and she repaid it within the month, so I knew she had some source of funds. She didn't ask me again."

"Did she tell you what the money was for?" Andi asked.

Jorge turned to Belle. "You didn't tell me about the money. Why didn't she come to me?"

Belle laughed. "Maybe she thought you'd ask for more than she was willing to pay.

Jorge bristled. "What do you mean by that?"

Belle smiled knowingly, then turned back to Andi who repeated her question. "Did she tell you what the money was for?"

"No. She said it was a short-term loan, and it was, so I forgot about it."

"When was this?"

She thought for a moment. "A coupla months ago? Maybe April or May?"

Greg indicated Jorge Acosta. "You didn't know her well?"

"No. I saw her when she came into the club. She always had an entourage—a bunch of different women. She teased the hell out of some of the guys. Whenever Red was around, business was good. That's all I knew."

Belle asked, "Where was she killed?" She directed her question at Greg.

"Burgess Beach," Greg answered.

"Not in Miami? What was she doing up there?"

"You tell me."

"Did you ever visit her home?" Andi asked Belle.

Belle took a deep drag on her cigarette, inhaled deeply and blew out a cloud of smoke. "No. She usually came here, or we'd meet somewhere. I don't know where she lived. She was pretty close-mouthed about her life outside the club."

"Did you ask about that?"

"Yeah. I asked a few questions, but I didn't get anywhere. She made it clear she didn't want to talk about it or about the past."

"What did you talk about?" Greg found it hard to picture them together, but it was also difficult to see her with Kathryn.

"Mostly books, movies, cultural stuff. She liked to read, and I'm a reader, so that kept us talking. And of course clothes, makeup, girlie stuff."

Andi and Greg took down their names and addresses, and Greg asked about Bobby and Etienne, but Jorge and Belle said they didn't know them.

It was one-thirty by the time they left the Meta Lounge.

The parking lot was blessedly quiet, although the temperature was still in the nineties. As they walked toward Greg's car, Andi said, "It's good to get away from that noise. Anything else we need to do tonight? I'm beat."

Greg said, "Let's pick up your car and head home."

In the car, Andi asked, "Still think you should be working on this case?"

"Yeah. I need answers. The more I find out, the less I think I knew Miranda."

"It's a mistake, Greg."

He didn't respond.

When they got to Andi's car, she said, "I'd like to come back to Miami with you when you talk to some of the people at Tux, and I'd like to have lunch with Belle Acosta. I think she knows more than she's saying in front of her husband."

"Sure," Greg said. "Good idea."

When Andi got home, it was close to four a.m. She'd had trouble keeping awake during the drive back and had stopped for a cup of coffee, which now jangled her nerves and kept her from falling asleep quickly. She knew she would feel lousy at work the next day.

But in the morning she felt invigorated when she remembered the day before and all the information they'd gathered in Miami. She'd been trapped by boring paperwork for more than a week before the burglary on Hutchinson Island, and the trip to Miami—as well as two days of questioning people involved in crimes and puzzling out what the answers meant—made her remember why she'd wanted to be a detective. Things were looking up.

Then she remembered Jim. She hadn't thought about Jim for a whole day. Maybe he was gone for good, but she didn't really believe that. She'd have to be careful. She couldn't call 911 again for help. They were too curious, and besides, sooner or later Jim would come to his senses. She didn't want to ruin his life, but if he didn't shape up, that meant that she'd have to deal with him on her own. She was no different from the threatened women she'd come to rescue or reassure when she'd been a patrol cop.

Enough of that, she thought. I need to take care of my job. At work, she typed up her notes of the interviews she'd gone on alone and then the information from their shared interviews. She forwarded them to Greg to add to his murder file, then she checked on her own cases. There hadn't been anything from the bank on the warrants for the Palmers' accounts nor anything from the insurance company. She looked over to see what Greg was doing, hoping he might have some more murder work she could do. He wasn't at his desk.

Andi made a fresh pot of coffee, then glanced through her inbox. As usual, it was filled with boring reports and statistical analyses. There were days when she could find those interesting, but not today. Sitting down with her notes, she made charts to organize all the information she had on the murder.

Miranda had lived with Kathryn for two-and-a-half years but had shared little of her life with her. Did Kathryn know anything about Miranda's financial problems? Miranda kept her finances separate and paid for her own telephone calls. She'd left her job at Kearney and Pattis more than a year ago, and it seemed, hadn't worked anywhere since. At least nowhere they knew. For a while, she'd had money in a savings account, but she'd gone through that quickly. Had she asked Kathryn for money as she had Belle Acosta? Kathryn hadn't said anything about that, but they hadn't asked. Andi made a note to herself.

Miranda had left Kathryn in early 2008, then had been arrested for passing bad checks. What had she spent money on? Andi looked at the reports of Miranda's expenditures. Clothes, makeup, a lot of pricey shoes, charges at several nightclubs including Tux, Cavelli's and the Meta Lounge, although she'd paid only the entrance charge and hadn't spent money on drinks. She'd been extravagant, at least in the first months after she left her job. Then she became more careful about her purchases, but there were still significant withdrawals of cash each month. Where was the money going?

She'd visited Burgess Beach six times between June and September and stayed at the Flamingo Motel. Then she'd checked into the Hibiscus with a very heavy suitcase, been murdered, and the suitcase and her purse were gone. Were her visits to Burgess Beach related to her need for money? What was in the suitcase? Was that why she'd been murdered?

Who was Miranda, anyway?

Greg described her as beautiful, sexy and smart. Roberto Cavelli and Tom Sarafian had said she was beautiful but a tease. She'd been good for business but often made trouble. She apparently didn't worry about what people thought. When Cavelli threatened to blackball her, she'd said she'd go elsewhere. No one would turn her away. Was she really that confident?

What was she like out of the spotlight? Her work history was spotty: a quick learner, but after she'd learned the job, there were patterns: a lot of absences; later, demands for raises or promotions, followed by angry outbursts when those didn't happen. She hadn't worked anywhere long. Her work history showed she'd had a number of jobs before the bank and the law firm: an insurance company, another bank, the office of a private school. She hadn't lasted long at any of them, at most two years at the private school. Where had she been working when she lived with Greg? Andi would have to ask him. She made another note.

Andi thought about whether she would have liked Miranda. No one except Belle Acosta and Kathryn spoke of her fondly—her clubbing companions, the owners of the clubs she frequented, the people she worked with. She seemed to use them and they her. Andi needed to talk with Belle again, without her husband. She'd said she liked Miranda, although her husband said Belle was jealous. She and Greg should also talk to Kathryn again.

What was there in Miranda's past that made her clam up with Belle? Women who became friends usually shared some of their history. Miranda didn't. Why? Did Greg know where she'd grown up, what her background was? Why hadn't she been willing to talk about her past?

She wondered what Miranda had been like with Greg? He had been sure to tell Andi the obvious: her intelligence, her beauty, her quick grasp of things, but what had kept her with him for four years? What was he really like? She hardly knew him, except for the little he'd shown her in the office. She'd been watching for the ways he was like Jim and therefore dangerous, but she'd forgotten to look at the ways in which he was different—and maybe equally a problem. She wished she could get a handle on that.

TWELVE

Andi looked up from her perusal of the files as Greg entered the room. He was scowling as he stomped to his office. Grabbing a box from those by the copy machine, he went to his office and began to shove things into it.

Andi watched for a moment, then walked over and asked, "What's up?"

Greg turned to her, clearly angry. "I've been suspended with pay and removed from the Duncan murder. I think the Captain will be calling you."

"So he found out about you and Miranda." Andi wondered how, but she wasn't unhappy it had happened.

"It didn't take you long to rat me out, did it?" Greg went back to his packing.

"What? I didn't tell him anything. I haven't even seen him."

"You were the only one who knew, and I told you because I thought you'd keep your mouth shut." Greg closed the box and moved toward the door.

Andi stepped back to let him pass. "I didn't say anything. I said I'd keep my mouth shut, and I did. What about your friends in Miami? Didn't they know?"

"They wouldn't say anything," Greg said with finality. "They're friends."

"And I'm not." Now Andi's voice was angry. "I didn't tell the Captain, but if you don't believe me, fuck you." She turned and strode back to her desk.

She watched Greg walk out of the room, carrying his box. The hell with him, she thought.

Her phone rang. "In my office," Captain Bradley said, "now." The phone went dead.

Andi grabbed her note pad and hurried along the hallway to the Captain's office. She knocked, and a gruff voice said, "Enter."

Captain Bradley looked up as she opened the door. He wasn't a tall man, but he held himself ramrod straight and projected an aura of barely contained energy. He had wiry black hair and a Dick Tracy profile.

"Sit," he commanded, so she did.

"You're aware of the mess Detective Lamont has gotten us into on the Miranda Duncan murder, Detective?"

"Detective Lamont told me yesterday that he had had a relationship with the deceased up until about five years ago."

"And did you tell him that he should step away from the murder investigation?"

"I did."

"And did he say he would tell his superiors the circumstances of his involvement with the deceased immediately?"

"No, he didn't."

"And did you tell your superiors of that involvement, Detective Battaglia?"

"No."

"Why not?"

"I didn't have an opportunity to do so. But I would not have reported Detective Lamont's involvement with the deceased even if I had."

"And why not, Detective?" This last question was delivered with some asperity.

"I didn't think it was my role to report on Detective Lamont. I told him he should tell you and resign from the case, but he said he wouldn't do that."

"Did he say why?"

"He wanted to find Miranda Duncan's murderer, mostly because of their involvement."

"What did he tell you about the deceased?"

Andi recapped for him what Greg had told her about Miranda, and then in response in Bradley's next question, recounted the gist of the interviews she and Greg had conducted in Miami the day before.

Then Bradley asked, "What would you do next in this investigation, Detective?"

Andi paused. Her response could determine whether or not the case went to her. "I'd go back to Kathryn Forbes and to Miranda's friend, Belle Acosta. I would check out the man she had a fight with at Tux, but I would also look at the parts of Miranda's past which she wouldn't talk about. I'd try to determine where she was spending money.

"There's a possibility she was being blackmailed, although I have no idea why, nor why she made six trips to Burgess Beach in the last four months. I want to know what was in the suitcase that was stolen from the Hibiscus Motel—if it was stolen. I'm not quite sure where to begin on that, but surely someone in Burgess Beach may have seen her on one of her visits and seen who she was with. I'd go out to the

Flamingo Motel again and talk with the manager, although she was less than helpful with Detective Lamont."

"Okay. You can have help from Detective Garcia if you need it, and if you require additional patrol staff, let me know."

"I may need to talk with Detective Lamont."

Bradley paused. Andi knew he wanted to sever Greg from any participation in the murder investigation. On the other hand, Greg knew the victim better than anyone else.

"Any information you obtain from him must be corroborated from other sources. And treat him as a possible suspect in Duncan's murder."

"Got it. I have the burglary on Hutchinson Island, and I'm waiting for the bank and the insurance to give me information about the Palmers' finances. I'm looking at an interesting angle on that. Do you want me to hang on to it for now?"

"Give me a report on where you are with Duncan when the bank and the insurance company respond."

"Okay." She was glad not to lose that case because she was pretty sure she was on to something, but she didn't want it to get in the way of Miranda Duncan's murder.

"That's all, Detective."

Andi left the room, suppressing the urge to salute.

Now that the Duncan murder belonged to Andi, she picked up Greg's murder file from his desk and read it thoroughly. She made new notes, then thought about how to determine what Miranda had been doing in Burgess Beach. She buzzed Captain Bradley and asked for four patrolmen to question businesses in Burgess Beach the following day. Then she inquired and found that Greg's warrant request for the phone records of the Flamingo's pay phone hadn't come in. Finally she headed out to the Flamingo Motel and another interview with the charming and helpful Alberta Smithson.

The motel was in an area of Burgess Beach Andi hadn't yet visited, and she drove around the neighborhood before she parked in front. It was an older part of the town, dating from the forties and fifties, before Burgess Beach had become fashionable. The houses were small bungalows painted pale yellows, greens and pinks when the paint hadn't faded beyond recognition and become dotted with mildew. The Flamingo fit right in.

Andi was pleased to see a man behind the motel counter. It must be Alberta Smithson's day off. She showed her badge and said she had a few questions.

The man was small and thin, his sparse hair a nondescript brown. He wore a loud Hawaiian print shirt.

Andi produced the photo of Miranda and asked if the man knew her. He stared at it for a while, then said, "She looks dead."

"She is," Andi said. "Did you know her when she was alive?"

"I think I checked her in once. Maybe during the summer."

"Are you here on a regular basis when Ms. Smithson is off?"

"Yeah. I come in one day a week."

"What's your name?"

"Frank Arenas."

"So you were only here once when this woman checked in? Is that correct?"

"Yeah."

"Is there a reason you remember when she checked in?"

"She was a good-looking redhead. My first girlfriend was a redhead, but mostly now you only see that funny purple color." Arenas paused, as if thinking of his first girlfriend.

"Any other reason you remember her?" Andi asked.

"She gave me forty bucks."

"Why?"

"Well, she asked could she have a room in the back, and then she said if anyone asked about her, I should tell them I hadn't seen her."

Arenas stopped talking when a man entered the office, dropped his room card on the counter and left.

Andi waited until the door closed behind the man, then said, "Did anyone come looking for her while you were here?"

"Yeah. Some dude asked whether a pretty redhead had checked in. Said she was his girlfriend, and they'd had a misunderstanding about where to meet."

"What did you say?"

"He slipped me a twenty, but I told him I hadn't seen anyone."

"Do you remember what he looked like?"

"A good suit. That's all I noticed."

"Anything else you remember? How tall he was, how old?"

"I don't remember nothing else. Just the expensive suit. And the ring."

"What ring?" Andi asked.

"He wore a gold ring with a big stone." Arenas said.

"Which hand was it on?" Andi asked.

"The one he gave me the twenty with."

"Was he left or right-handed?" She felt like she was pulling teeth, but at least she'd gotten more than Greg had.

"I don't know."

"What color was the stone in the ring?"

"Light blue. Big." Arenas said.

"You said this happened during the summer. Do you remember the date?"

"I only work Wednesdays."

Andi thanked Frank Arenas and left. This was new. Who was the guy with the ring?

She returned to the station, added the information Frank Arenas had given her to the file, and headed home. The next day, Thursday, was her day off, and she was moving.

She parked her car away from the front of the building in a spot assigned to an apartment she knew was vacant. There weren't any unfamiliar cars parked on the street. Walking quietly up the stairs, she looked along the hallway to her door. After tomorrow, thank God, she wouldn't have to do this again.

With a sigh of relief, she let herself in. This was her last night in this apartment, and tomorrow Jim wouldn't know where she'd gone. At least that's what she hoped.

There were ten messages on her answering machine, nine of them from Jim, one from her mother. All of Jim's messages asked her to call him back and apologized for his telephone calls. No apology for his confrontation with her on Monday, the day she'd called 911. Maybe he'd been drunk enough to forget he'd been there. Or maybe he didn't want to admit it.

Andi called her mother back and told her she was moving to a much nicer apartment. She gave her the address and the cell phone she planned to use. She finished packing, ate a can of soup and some crackers and watched television. Tomorrow she'd be busy with the movers, but tomorrow night she would talk to Greg about Miranda.

THIRTEEN

On Thursday the movers arrived early, and all the furniture and cartons were at Andi's new place by early afternoon. She spent some time unpacking kitchen items, then about four-thirty, hoping Greg would have calmed down, she called him.

He answered after a half dozen rings.

"Greg, it's Andi. Are you willing to talk to me?"

"About what?"

She said, "Duh. About the investigation. I need to get some more information. For the record, I'll say again: I didn't tell Captain Bradley about your involvement with Miranda."

The line was silent for a long time, but he didn't hang up. Finally, he said, "I was wrong. I know it wasn't you."

"Can I talk to you about Miranda Duncan? I could really use your help."

"I don't know."

"Look, you know more about her than anyone. I've got the case now, and I know you want to find out who killed her. I want that, too. And I <u>will</u> find the killer. I can do it with or without you. It'd be easier if you helped."

There was a pause, then he said, "What do you want to know?"

"Can we meet somewhere to talk about it?"

Again a pause, then he said, "Meet me at the Corner Diner, next to the theater in town. I'll be there around six."

"Okay," Andi said and smiled. The first step: Greg had agreed to see her.

Andi was half an hour early, and to her surprise, she found Greg already at a table.

"Hey," she said, sitting down opposite him in the booth. "You're early, too."

"Thought I'd get a head start," he said, picking up his wine glass.

The waitress appeared, and Andi asked for a glass of chardonnay. That out of the way, she looked down at the table, rearranged the water glass and the knives and forks before she finally took a deep breath and said, "Look, I have to treat you as a suspect because, like a lot of other people, you may have had reasons to kill Miranda."

"But I didn't . . . ," then he continued, "Of course. I'm a suspect because I hung on to the case when I should've backed off. I didn't kill her, though."

"Do you have an alibi?"

"Friday night I had dinner with an old friend in Miami. I left Miami about midnight and got back here about two. Saturday I started work at eight, and I was called out on Miranda's murder about three in the afternoon, after Ben Patel called the station to report the death."

"May I have the address and phone number of your Miami dinner partner?" Andi asked.

"Sure." He pulled out an address book, wrote the information on a piece of paper and passed it to Andi.

"Okay. I'll check it out, but this doesn't mean you couldn't have killed her. We'll see what the autopsy says about time of death. Now, tell me about Miranda. Where did you meet, where was she working when you met, who were her friends? Everything. You know what I need."

Greg went back over his meeting with Miranda and their instant mutual attraction. "She moved in with me about two weeks after we met."

"Where was she working then?"

"She was a paralegal in the Dade County D.A.'s office. I don't know how long she'd been there. She was smart, you know."

"And how long did that job last?"

"She said one of the ADA's made a pass at her and when she wouldn't come across, he put a note in her personnel file about her lack of cooperation. She got mad and quit."

"How long after you met her did she quit her job?"

Greg thought. "Five or six months."

"Did she work steadily at the D.A.'s office during your first months together?"

Greg scratched his chin. "She got weird maybe three months after she moved in. Wouldn't get out of bed, didn't go to work, cried a lot. That went on for a week, maybe two, but then she was okay."

"Did that make you mad?"

Greg didn't say anything for a while. "Yeah. Sure. I got mad. She wouldn't say what was wrong. All she did was cry."

Andi paused, pretended to make a note. Then she picked up her wine glass, took a sip and asked, "Did you guys fight about anything specific before she got depressed?"

Greg hesitated and looked about to say something, then shrugged his shoulders and said, "Not that I remember."

"So after she felt better, she went back to the D.A.'s office. And then she had problems with the ADA?"

"I guess so."

"Did she get another job?"

"Not for a while. She went back to bed. I finally told her she had to look for a job."

"And did she do that?"

"Yeah. Sure. I just had to push her."

"And what was her next job?" Andi was sure there was something Greg wasn't telling her.

"She worked in the office of a fancy private school. She was happy there."

Andi made a note. "What was the name of the school?"

"Brook something. Brook Haven, I think."

"It would've helped if you'd put all this in the file, Greg."

"Yeah. I guess."

"How long did she stay at the private school?"

"About two years. She liked it there, and she didn't have any problems. Then they had budget problems, and I think her position was eliminated. After that, she stayed home for a while, but it was different. She seemed okay."

"Did she get depressed while she was working for the private school?"

"A couple of times."

"Was she on any medication?"

"No. I said she should see a therapist, but she wouldn't, said it was just part of who she was."

"What do you think she meant by that?"

Greg gave Andi a look of annoyance. "I don't know."

Andi asked, "And as far as you remember, nothing started any of these episodes of depression. No other problems at work? No problems with you or with anyone? You guys weren't quarreling, were you?"

Greg answered quickly, "No. Nothing."

Andi looked at her notes, then asked, "Did she leave you more than once?"

Greg sipped his wine, then said, "She left a couple of times after we had a fight."

"What did you fight about?"

Greg didn't say anything for a while. "A lot of things. They didn't have anything to do with her murder."

"A lot of things like . . . ?"

"What do you think? Money, sex, our jobs."

"Did you start any of these fights?"

His answer came quickly. "No."

"Look, Greg. I have to ask you these questions. You know that. You're a suspect. Just because you're a cop doesn't mean you're exempt."

"I know."

Andi picked up the questioning again. "Did you expect her to come back when she left the last time?"

"At first I was mad and didn't care, but then I wanted her back. I expected her to come back. After a while, I looked for her, but she'd always come back before. We'd fight, she'd leave, then she'd come back. That was the pattern."

Andi checked her notes. "You said she did that 'a couple of times,' but it sounds like more than a couple. Did she leave often? It sounds like pretty often. And when she left for good?" Greg started to speak, but she went on. "Was that a surprise?"

Greg didn't speak for a while, his chin resting on his hand, his eyes turned inward in thought. "She left a lot, maybe three or four times a year, maybe more. I kind of lost count. The last time, I can't even remember what started it. We had a fight, then we made love, and I thought everything was okay. Then she was gone the following night when I came home from work, and she didn't come back."

"That was different from her usual pattern?"

"Yes. She usually stormed out when I was there to see the show, then stay away for a few hours or a day, but she'd always come back."

"Did you look for her other times?"

"I looked, but I never found her. I never knew where she went."

"And the last time?"

"I searched, but as usual, I didn't find her. I didn't know any of her friends, so I checked at work, but she hadn't been in."

"Where was she working then?"

"The bank, but they said she wasn't in."

"You didn't know any of the women she went clubbing with, the ones in her e-mails?

"No. All those names were new to me. The only friend I knew about was a woman named Angela Ramirez. They'd worked together somewhere, and she and her husband invited us to dinner a couple of times. His name was Joe. He built dry cleaning plants. I tried their old number after she was killed, but it wasn't in service. You might look for her."

"Is there anything else about her you think I should know?"

"That's it," Greg said. "I can't think of anything else."

They sat quietly while Andi pondered what Greg had said about Miranda. How could he have lived with her for four years and known so little about her?

When the waitress returned, they ordered dinner, then lapsed back into silence while they waited for their food to arrive. Andi looked around the restaurant at other tables, stared at her hands clasped together on the table. Finally, she said, "Look, you know I had to ask these questions. If our positions were reversed, you'd do the same thing. I'm sorry if I pushed you too hard, but you know it's what I had to do."

Greg said, "I know you did. It's just I've never been in this position before, and it sucks. Sorry."

Finally the food arrived, and then they were able to talk companionably about police work and cases they'd been involved with. Andi told Greg about her new apartment and gave him the address and her cell phone number.

"Let me know if you think of anything I should know," Andi said. "I need to go back to Miami to see a couple of people, and I think I'd like you to go along. Are you willing? Once you're cleared, of course."

"Sure," Greg said.

Greg headed home after dinner with Andi. He thought he'd done pretty well. He'd even drunk a glass of wine without feeling the craving. But he wondered if there was anyone who would tell Andi what he hadn't. He'd quit drinking— well, pretty much quit—about five years ago. Right after

Miranda left. His lieutenant had warned him he was pushing it.

Usually the fights had started after he'd had a few drinks.

"Who'd you go out with? Some girl from work? Damn you," she'd say.

"I had a drink with Caesar. He's my partner, for chrissakes."

"Yeah. Sure. Your partner."

He accused her of being jealous; she accused him of screwing around. They fought. He remembered her red hair flying about her face, her fists beating his chest. In the beginning, they'd fought like that, then collapsed into one another and fucked ferociously. Later, the quarrels, the jealousy, his drinking became more important, and the sex couldn't smooth things over.

FOURTEEN

Andi got to her new apartment, glad that she didn't have to worry about Jim.

She thought over her conversation with Greg. There was something he wasn't telling her, and it had to do with his culpability in their quarrels and in Miranda's disappearances. Probably he hadn't been as understanding as he'd led her to believe. But there was more to it. Something he didn't want her to know. If there was anything negative in his personnel record, the Captain wouldn't have hired him away from Miami. She didn't think Bradley would take that chance, so whatever it was, it wasn't in his file.

Now that she only had her cell, she didn't have a ton of messages from Jim. She felt free, as though a weight had been lifted. She blamed herself for her involvement with him, but in the beginning, he'd been so insistent. And so desirable. At least now she knew she didn't want to get involved with Greg or any cop. Cops were trouble.

The next day Andi woke early, pulled on a pair of shorts and a t-shirt and went for a run. She'd been lazy about exercise, not taking charge of her life. Now, in her new apartment, without Jim lurking in the background, she ran two miles to the beach, stopped to breathe for a minute, then did another mile along the sand before turning back. She was dripping wet when she got home, but as she stretched, she felt more in control than she'd felt since she found Jim in her apartment a week ago.

At work, she checked on the results of the warrants for the Hutchinson Island burglary. Nothing so far. She gave the Captain's four uniforms pictures of Miranda and instructions to look for anyone who had seen her in Burgess Beach during July and August. She had the results on the warrant for the pay phone at the motel, and checked those over. On July 15 there had been a call to Kathryn Forbes' number. That was undoubtedly Miranda. The next call from the phone was to another number in Miami. The call was short, but then within the next fifteen minutes four more calls had been made to the same number.

The number on her list was for Belle Acosta, the wife of the nightclub owner. Five calls. Another reason to see the woman again, this time without her husband.

Andi prepared warrants for Miranda Duncan's previous employers: the bank and the law firm, then one for Kathryn and Miranda's phone records at the house. When she went back to Miami, she'd serve the warrants and also check on Nick Oldham.

She spent some time looking for Angela Ramirez, but she didn't know where they'd worked together, and Greg said the number was no longer in service. She did some further searching and called four possibles. She left one a message; one was a woman who spoke only Spanish; one had no answering machine; and the fourth number reached a man named Joe Ramirez who used to build dry cleaning plants. His wife, Angela, knew Miranda Duncan. Andi arranged to meet the couple the following evening at eight o'clock.

The report of the autopsy was in. Miranda had died of blood loss from the severed artery in her neck. The results of drug testing weren't back yet. Miranda may have been drugged, or she may have taken something. In any case, it appeared that her throat was slashed while she slept. The time of death was estimated to be sometime between two a.m. on Friday morning and 3 p.m. on Saturday afternoon. This didn't eliminate Greg, which was something Andi didn't want to know. She wanted to work with him, but she couldn't before he was cleared. Damn!

The other interesting thing about the autopsy was that Miranda had had a child sometime in the past. Andi wondered if Greg knew about that.

She decided to go to Miami alone. She called Kathryn Forbes and arranged to meet her for lunch the following day. She told Kathryn she had a warrant for the phone records which Kathryn had refused to give Andi and Greg and asked her to bring them with her. Kathryn sounded annoyed but said she would. Then Andi called the number Belle Acosta had given her and left a message. She also called Greg's dinner partner, although he (it was a he) couldn't provide an alibi. Greg had left him about midnight on that Friday. Then she picked up the signed warrants and headed home. A good day's work, she thought.

The next day she checked in at the station before heading for Miami. Nothing on the Hutchinson Island case—again. The banks were really sitting on the information. If there was nothing by tomorrow, she'd have to push them for results.

She turned back to the Duncan murder file. The four uniforms hadn't uncovered any sighting of Miranda during the five times she'd been in Burgess Beach. What had she been doing? She wasn't working last summer, so she could have arrived at any time. The motel log didn't give arrival time. Where had she eaten? Had she shopped? Why hadn't she been seen? Why was she here at all?

As she sat in her tiny office gathering together the paperwork for her trip to Miami, she looked up in surprise to see Ed Garcia standing in her doorway. He had never come to her office before. He wasn't a sociable guy, even with people who had been in the office longer than she.

He was tall with a pronounced stoop, and his clothes, the routine suit and tie of the detective, were disheveled and messy-looking. His hair crept down over his collar and fell across his forehead. He definitely needed a haircut. He probably was only about forty, but he looked much older.

"Hi," he said.

"Hi," she repeated, waiting for him to speak. When he didn't, she asked, "What can I do for you?"

"What's happened to your pal?"

"My pal?" Andi asked.

"The guy from Miami. He hasn't been in for a couple of days."

"Greg? Did you ask Lisa?" Lisa was the Captain's secretary.

"She said he was on leave."

"Well, then, I guess that's the answer." Andi wondered what Garcia was fishing for.

"What are you working on?" Garcia asked. "Lamont had a big case, and I was wondering if it had been reassigned."

113

"It's mine now," she said.

"How'd you get it?" Garcia asked.

"I guess because I did some work with Greg on it."

"I'm the senior. It shoulda been mine." Garcia sounded angry, the first time she'd heard any kind of emotion from him.

Andi didn't say anything. Ed continued to hang in her doorway, then finally asked, "Do you know why he's on leave?"

"I'm not sure," she replied. The story wasn't hers to tell.

"It's a murder, right? I've had some experience on murders. You need any help on the case?"

On a cold day in hell, Andi thought, but said, "Yeah. It's a murder. I don't need anything at the moment, but I'll let you know. Aren't you busy now that Hank's gone?"

"Not so much. I'm here if you need me. Be glad to help." He turned and shuffled back to his office. She wondered how he had gotten to be a detective. He never seemed to leave the office, preferring to do everything on the telephone, and when he reported at their monthly staff briefings, his cases dragged on with very little forward movement.

Shit, she thought. He was the senior detective in the department. He was protecting his turf, and with Greg gone, they might be partnered. She hoped Captain Bradley wouldn't saddle her with him. But if Greg wasn't cleared, there might be no alternative. She shuddered. Don't borrow trouble, she thought.

At ten, she headed for Miami and her lunch meeting with Kathryn Ford. The woman wasn't there by noon, so Andi waited, wondering if Kathryn had decided to stand her up. Finally, at almost twelve-thirty, Kathryn hurried in. Her face was flushed, and her clothes wrinkled. Andi remembered her as businesslike and very much in charge when she and Greg had seen her two days ago. Now she looked disheveled—her makeup smeared and her clothes untidy—and she looked nervous.

She thrust a package at Andi. "Sorry," she said, "I forgot this and had to go back home." Andi opened the envelope and looked inside. Telephone bills. So those weren't the problem.

"Thanks," Andi said. "Do you have time to eat?"

"No," Kathryn said. "I'll be late back to work. I'll just have some iced tea." Andi thought she looked like she could use a glass of wine, but she didn't comment.

Kathryn ordered, and Andi asked her what she knew about Miranda's finances.

"We kept things pretty much separate. We shared food costs, and she paid me rent when she was working, but I really don't know anything about her money. I know she spent at the clubs, but that was her business. It wasn't my money."

"She spent several nights last summer in Burgess Beach where she was murdered. Did she tell you why she was going there?"

Kathryn avoided Andi's eyes. The mention of Miranda's time at Burgess Beach bothered Kathryn. Finally, she brought her eyes back to Andi's. "Yes. She said she had an old friend who had moved there and she went up to visit her." She took a sip of her drink and looked away from Andi again.

"Did she tell you the friend's name?"

"No." Kathryn played with her fork.

"Would it surprise you to learn she stayed at a motel when she went up there."

"She told me she was staying at the friend's house." She ran her hands through her short hair, making it stand upright in sharp spikes.

"Did you ever call her there?"

"Yeah. On her cell." Kathryn picked at her thumbnail.

"Did she tell you why she wanted to see this friend?"

"She was supposedly very sick, and Miranda was helping her with some legal issues." Kathryn didn't sound as though she had believed Miranda.

"I see."

So Kathryn had been jealous of this friend, but she didn't want Andi to know that because then she would have a motive. Andi paused for a moment, then changed the topic. "Do you know where Miranda grew up?" She watched Kathryn relax when she changed the line of questions.

"She never wanted to talk about her childhood, but I had the impression she grew up in Florida. Maybe up in the Panhandle. One time she said her parents lived in the sticks. When I asked her what she meant, she said they were real country people."

"She didn't elaborate?" Andi asked.

"No. That was all." She sipped her drink. Then she said, "Once she told me her education was the pits." Kathryn picked up her purse and pushed her chair back. "Listen, I've really got to go." She got up quickly.

"Is there anything else you can tell me about her?"

"No. I guess I didn't know a lot about her, but she was exciting, and I was willing to give her a lot of slack." There was a break in her voice.

Apparently, thought Andi. Kathryn hurried away without shaking hands. Andi paid the check and headed back to her car. The bank was next.

Andi went back to the branch of Florida First where Miranda had worked. She presented her warrant demanding copies of Miranda Duncan's personnel file, and after waiting half an hour, she was given an envelope containing what she wanted. The record reported that Miranda had been fired but didn't give a reason.

After she left the branch office, she headed for the headquarters of Florida First at Flagler and NW lst and asked to see Joseph Adamski.

"Have you an appointment?" the receptionist asked.

"No," Andi said, "but I believe he is expecting me."

A few minutes later Andi was ushered into Adamski's office. She sat down without an invitation.

"You wanted me to get a warrant to obtain Miranda Duncan's employment history," Andi said. "I did, and I have a copy of her personnel file. It says she was fired, but it doesn't say why."

Adamski cleared his throat and said, "Miranda Duncan was hired in May of 2005 and promoted to personal banker in August of that year. She was an excellent employee who brought in a lot of business to Florida First."

"I know all that. Mr. Ramos told me what a good employee she was. I want to know why she was fired."

"That can't possibly have anything to do with your murder investigation, Detective."

"I'd like to judge that for myself. She's dead, so it can't matter unless someone at Florida First killed her." Andi sat back and waited.

Adamski fiddled with a letter opener on his desk. Finally, he put the letter opener down and looked at her across the desk. "Ms. Duncan stepped on a few toes bringing in new business. I received a number of complaints from personal bankers at other Florida First branches about Ms. Duncan poaching their prospects. I spoke with Miranda three or four times about the complaints, but she refused to believe there was any merit to the accusations. I asked her if her prospects had been approached by other bank employees, and she answered that she hadn't asked them and didn't think she needed to. Finally, she stepped on the toes of an executive at the main branch, and she had to go."

"So you fired her?"

"Yes, although the bank provided a nice severance package. Miranda was just a bit too aggressive."

"What was your impression of Ms. Duncan?" Andi noticed he'd switched from calling her Ms. Duncan to referring to her as Miranda.

"I liked her. She was bright and quick to learn."

"And very beautiful, apparently."

"That, too. I was sorry to have to let her go, but she gave me no choice. For the greater good and all that, Detective."

"I assume that by 'the greater good,' you mean the pride of the executive whose prospect Miranda poached. Who was that, Mr. Adamski?"

Adamski paused again, looked away from Andi, then looked back at her and said, "Charles Worthington Abbott, then the president of the bank. You may have heard the name."

"I have. The Abbotts are very well known. I thought the family lived in Palm Beach."

"They do. Florida First is a statewide bank, so Mr. Abbott was still living in Palm Beach when he served as president. I live here, so I've moved the executive offices to Miami."

"You were protecting Mr. Abbott's name when you stonewalled me before?" Andi asked.

"Yes. But since it's obvious Mr. Abbott didn't kill her, I thought it best to help you find out who did." Adamski leaned back in his chair. "Does that answer all your questions?"

"For the moment. If I need anything else, I'll be back. Thank you for your time."

Andi rose, shook Adamski's hand, and left his office. As she headed back to her car, she thought about it. It would be hard to pin Miranda Duncan's murder on Charles Worthington Abbott. A waste of time, but she'd tied up a loose end.

She tried the cell number for Belle Acosta again. She'd left several messages, but Belle hadn't called back. This time, however, Belle answered, and Andi asked if they could meet.

"Do you want to talk to Jorge, too? He's pretty busy," Belle said.

Andi looked at her watch. It was three o'clock. She was not far from Pattis and Kearney, Nick Oldham's law firm. She could meet Belle about five-thirty.

"It seems to me you might have known Miranda better than he did. I'd really like to talk to you. I've got one more stop to make. Suppose we meet for a drink at five-thirty. Where do you suggest?"

"Come to the house," Belle said. She gave Andi the address. "It won't take you long from South Beach."

Andi headed off to the law offices where Miranda had worked. Thanks to Paula Mendez and her vendetta against the firm, Andi didn't need additional information about Miranda's work history there, but she wanted to talk to Nick Oldham, the partner with whom Miranda had allegedly been having an affair.

In Pattis and Kearney's freezing reception area, Andi learned that Nick Oldham was in court.

"Do you know when he'll be back?" she asked.

"When court is over for the day," the receptionist said helpfully.

Andi settled in with an old copy of *Vogue* and a cup of bad coffee from a machine by the elevator. She waited.

At four o'clock, a tall, thin man entered. He nodded to the receptionist and picked up a stack of messages from her desk. He turned to look at Andi, and she registered long gray hair that hung over his collar, a pair of piercing blue eyes and a gaunt, lined face. Then he headed back into the offices, clutching his messages, ignoring Andi.

Andi got to her feet and asked the receptionist, whose name was Denise, "I take it that's Mr. Oldham?"

"Yes," she said. "I'll call his secretary."

"Tell her I want to talk to him about Miranda Duncan."

Denise passed on the message. Time passed. Andi gave up on the coffee, but returned to the magazine. Finally, another young woman came out of the office area and said, "Mr. Oldham will see you now."

When Andi entered Oldham's office, he stood behind his desk and extended his hand. The office was large, larger than Epstein's, with a view of the bay and the ocean beyond it. The furnishing were dark mahogany and huge: a giant desk, a built-in credenza and an expensive sofa and chairs over on one side. Oldham was obviously important to the firm.

"Detective Battaglia. A pleasure to meet you," he said.

"Mr. Oldham," Andi said as she took his outstretched hand.

"Please have a seat. Now what can I do for the police department in," he paused while he looked at his messages, "Burgess Beach?"

"I'm inquiring about Miranda Duncan."

"Yes. Miranda," he said, gazing over Andi's head. "What about her?"

Andi was sure Epstein had told him that Miranda had been murdered. He was playing games with her, and she thought he was probably pretty good at that. "Well, as you know, Ms. Duncan was murdered in Burgess Beach. We're looking at her work history and the people she knew in Miami. What can you tell me about her?"

Nick Oldham sat back in his chair and steepled his fingers. "Miranda Duncan worked here as a paralegal for almost two years." Andi noticed he wore a gold ring with a large blue stone on his right index finger.

"Was she a good employee, good at her work?"

"Yes. She was very bright, very quick. She was a great help to me on a difficult case. That's why I remember her." He placed his hands flat on his desk, as if prepared to get to his feet and usher Andi out.

"And is that all she was to you—a great help in your work?" Andi didn't move.

"Yes."

"I've been informed that you and Ms. Duncan were having an affair."

He looked at Andi, his eyes cold. His face gave nothing away. "Miranda was an employee. She worked for the firm and did some work for me. That's it. We were not having an affair."

"I understand she was a very beautiful woman, Mr. Oldham."

"Beautiful women aren't scarce. Where are you getting this information about Miranda and me?" His voice was angry, but Andi sensed the anger wasn't genuine. It was part of his act.

"I was told about your affair, and I understood it was common knowledge in the firm. Did your wife know about it, Mr. Oldham?"

Nick Oldham smiled. It wasn't a pleasant smile. "I assume Paula Mendez is your informant, but she is not reliable. As a matter of fact, her employment was terminated a few days ago. She's a very . . . difficult woman. I'm surprised you believed her."

"So, you're saying there's no truth to the story of your affair with Miranda Duncan. Would you testify to that under oath, Mr. Oldham?"

"Of course. Now, if you have nothing further, I have some work to do before I go home." Again, he placed his hands flat on the desk and slid his chair back.

"Did you inquire about Miranda at the Flamingo Motel in Burgess Beach during the summer?"

"I've never been to Burgess Beach. I don't even know where it is."

"The motel clerk at the Flamingo Motel told me that a man in a suit wearing a gold ring with a large blue stone inquired about a red-haired woman. Was that you, Mr. Oldham?"

"No. Of course not. I told you I don't know anything about Burgess Beach."

"Aren't you interested in seeing that Miranda's murderer is brought to justice?" She held his gaze while his cold eyes seemed to bore into her. Just as she thought she could hold out no longer, Oldham looked away.

"I did not murder her, Detective. I'm sure you will find her killer."

"What did you think of Miranda Duncan?" Andi asked, trying to salvage something from this interview.

"She was an employee. She thought she was smarter than anyone else, and although she was very smart, I'm sure that assumption sometimes came back to bite her. Now, if you'll excuse me . . . ." This time he stood up, ready to escort her to the door.

Andi didn't move, although she had to look up to see his face. "Is there anything else you can tell me about her? She received a number of e-mails from someone who called himself 'oldnick' during the last several months. Was that you?"

"No. That's not my e-mail address, Detective. I haven't been in touch with Miranda in at least a year."

He was slick, she gave him that. She knew he was lying about their relationship. What about the e-mails? She didn't know, but she made a mental note to check with the e-mail provider.

"Thank you for your help, Mr. Oldham. I'll be back when I have additional questions." Andi got to her feet and extended her hand. Oldham took it reluctantly and opened the door of his office for her.

FIFTEEN

Back in her car, Andi made some quick notes about her interview with Nicolas Oldham before she plugged in her GPS and got directions to Belle and Jorge Acosta's residence in Coral Gables. It was a two-storied Spanish-style house in an area of expensive homes. The house was separated from the street by a wrought iron fence with a gate across the driveway.

Andi parked on the street and rang a bell at the entrance gate. A buzzer sounded and the gate opened. She walked to the massive oak door decorated with hammered copper strips and rang another bell. She waited, and as she was about to ring a second time, Belle Acosta opened the door.

"Detective, it's nice to see you again. Please come in."

"Thank you."

Belle Acosta guided Andi into a room to the left of the entryway. It was large enough to hold three conversation areas, each with a sofa, two or three chairs, and a rug, one focused toward a fireplace, the other two toward a large window with a garden view.

"Thank you for seeing me, Ms. Acosta," Andi said as she sat down on the sofa Belle had indicated.

"Please, call me Belle. I'm glad to have a chance to talk to you about Miranda. I was very fond of her, and I've been thinking about her a lot. I hope you've found out who killed her."

"Not yet, I'm afraid, but we're working on it. You knew Miranda outside of the club scene, isn't that right? You and she were friends?"

"Can I get you something to drink? Perhaps some tea?" Belle asked. Andi wasn't sure if Belle was just playing hostess or if she wanted to deflect Andi's attention from the question.

"Yes, tea would be nice."

"Hot or cold?"

"Hot, please. Were you and Miranda friends?"

"Yes. I liked her. Jorge says I was jealous of her, but that's not true. She was like a daughter or a younger sister to me. But she was someone who took risks, and that worried me."

A maid showed up, probably in response to an inaudible bell, and presented Belle with a glass of red wine. "Tea for my guest, Suzanne." She looked at Andi, "Unless you'd prefer a glass of wine?"

"No, thanks. Hot tea would be fine."

The maid nodded and left.

"What kind of risks do you mean?"

"She played men, one guy against another at the club. Some of those guys were powerful, and that worried me."

"Powerful how?"

Suzanne returned then with tea and scones, and there was a pause while Belle poured. It was English Breakfast, Andi's favorite, and she sipped approvingly.

"How powerful were these men Miranda played with?"

"They had money. Some of them were dangerous, but that never bothered Miranda. She was fearless."

"Did these men behave at the club?"

"Of course. We knew who they were, but the club was neutral territory. They still had their bodyguards of course."

"Do you know any particular guys? Any names you remember?" Andi asked.

"There was nobody in particular that I remember, and I don't know any names."

"Do you think one of the men she humiliated killed her?"

"Maybe. I don't know. I'm just thinking aloud. I miss her. She was smart, and she played a good game of bridge, and I miss that." Belle took a sip of wine, then sat back in her chair.

"Who did you play bridge with?" Andi asked.

"Some of my friends. Coral and Nonni, mostly. But others as well."

"Will you give me their names and addresses? I'd like to talk with them." Andi sipped her tea again, and Belle refilled her cup.

"I'll be glad to give you their names and addresses, but I don't think they ever saw Miranda except for bridge games with me."

"Is there anyone else you knew of who was involved with Miranda?"

Belle took a sip of wine, thinking. "No one I can think of. She didn't seem to have any close friends. Just the gals she hung with at the club."

"Have you ever met or did Miranda ever mention Kathryn Forbes?" Andi watched Belle process the name. It wasn't one she knew.

"Who?"

"Kathryn Forbes. The woman Miranda lived with."

"I never visited her home, and she never said anything about where she lived or with whom. Were they lovers?"

"I think so." She watched Belle absorb this information, but Belle's reaction made Andi pretty sure that she hadn't been interested in Miranda sexually. Still, she asked, "Were you and Miranda lovers?" .

"God, no! I'm totally hetero. You asked me that at the club. Why are you asking me that again." Belle's voice rose.

"What do you know about Miranda's financial situation? You said she had money problems."

"Money was definitely an issue for her. She didn't have any, and recently I know she wasn't working. I told you about the loan, but I don't know where she got the money for the repayment."

"Did she ever talk about a windfall or getting some money quickly?"

"When she repaid the money, she said she was sorry to have asked, but that money would be less of a problem from then on. I asked her what she meant, but she just mimed locking her lips with an invisible key, like a little girl, and I knew she didn't want to talk about it."

Andi took another sip of tea, ate another scone, vowing it would be the last, and said, "Do you have any idea why she was in Burgess Beach?"

"She knew someone there. One time I had scheduled a bridge game, but she said she couldn't come, that she had to be in Burgess Beach of all places. I asked if she couldn't postpone, and she said no, that she couldn't disappoint Toni."

Kathryn had mentioned someone in Burgess Beach, but both Andi and Kathryn had assumed Miranda was lying. Perhaps not. "What else did she say?"

"When I asked who Toni was, she just smiled, but I thought from her attitude that Toni was someone she was close to. It was the first personal reference Miranda ever made to me, and I was curious, but she changed the subject."

"Did she ever talk about family?"

"No, and whenever I mentioned my family or asked about hers, she never volunteered anything. But I had a feeling—nothing I could put my finger on—she had someone."

"How did Jorge feel about Miranda?"

"He complained about her constantly because even though she and her friends brought customers in, mostly men, she caused trouble. Still, I know he liked her."

"Do you think he was involved with her?"

"Absolutely not." Belle's voice was definite and a little angry. "Jorge's too busy to look for sex beyond what he gets with me. I trust him completely."

"May I have the information on your two bridge partners?"

"Of course." Belle wrote the names, addresses and phone numbers on a pad.

"Thanks. I appreciate your time," Andi said as she rose to her feet. "If you think of anything else, please give me a call." She left a card on the table.

Belle stood, and they shook hands. Back in her car, she thought about what she'd learned. Miranda did know someone in Burgess Beach. Toni. Family? Maybe. Or did it have to do with the suitcase? She wished Greg would get himself cleared so they could talk. She needed a partner, but not Ed Garcia.

She checked the addresses for Nonni and Coral. They lived close to Belle, so she thought she'd check them out before she left Miami.

Nonni Santiago lived about five blocks away in a Mediterranean-style house fringed with palm trees. When Andi rang the bell, she was greeted by a woman in her thirties wearing a smock and holding a paint brush in one hand. She looked at Andi inquiringly.

Andi introduced herself and showed the woman her badge. "Are you Ms. Santiago?"

"Which one? Do you want me or my mother?"

Andi said she wanted to talk to Nonni Santiago. "That's my mom," the woman said. "Come in, and I'll get her. I've gotta get back to my painting before I lose the light." She gestured to a seat in the large foyer and headed off toward the back of the house. Andi could hear her call, "Mom, somebody here to see you."

The house was large and imposing, but the furnishings that Andi could see looked old and rather shabby. The upholstery on the chair that she had been directed to was worn and soiled-looking. There had been money, Andi thought, but not now.

A woman came into the foyer from the back of the house, wiping her hands on her apron. She was about sixty, short and plump with a pleasant face. She smiled at Andi. "I'm sorry. Didn't my daughter even offer you any refreshment?"

"I'm fine, thanks. I just had tea at Belle Acosta's." Andi introduced herself and showed Nonni her badge. "I wanted to talk with you about Miranda Duncan. I think you played bridge with her at Belle's."

"Miranda?" Nonni thought a moment. "Oh, the red-headed woman who played bridge with us. Yes, I remember her."

"What can you tell me about her? Did you know her at all outside Belle's house?"

"I only knew her from bridge. Good player—cut-throat—but then so is Belle, and so are the rest of us. She fit in. I never talked to her away from the bridge table. Belle liked her, I know, but I, well, ... It's hard to say. I really didn't know her at all well. Why are you asking about her?"

"She's been murdered. In Burgess Beach. But since she was from here, I'm trying to learn what I can about her life here."

"Murdered? Really? Not an accident?"

"No accident. What were you going to tell me about her, what impression did you have about Miranda? You started to say something and stopped yourself."

"Just my impression. She was much tougher than she put on for Belle. I thought she was dangerous, but I can't tell you why I thought so. If Belle hadn't been so fond of her, I'd have tried to convince her not to get so close, but Belle wouldn't hear anything against Miranda."

"Are you surprised that Miranda was murdered?"

"She seemed to be one of those people who took risks and might get into serious trouble. I can't tell you anything more than that."

"What can you tell me about Coral Isaacson, your other bridge player?"

"Oh, Coral. Well, she's only interested in the game. She never notices who she plays with."

"So she wouldn't have any impressions of Miranda Duncan to share with me."

"I doubt it. She lives just around the block, and you can probably see her tonight. She never goes out except for bridge. If you want, I can call ahead for you. She has a gate guard, and sometimes it's hard to get in."

"Thank you, Ms. Santiago. That would be helpful. Is your daughter an artist?"

"'Struggling artist' is the description, I think. Can I help you with anything else, Detective?"

"No, this was helpful. Thank you for seeing me."

Andi got back in her car, wondering if a visit to Coral Isaacson was worth the time, then decided it was, even if only to close down a possibility.

Coral lived in a house on a large gated property about two blocks from Nonni. Andi pressed the buzzer when she pulled up, and a voice answered, "Yes?"

"This is Detective Battaglia. Ms. Santiago said she would call about me."

"Oh, yes."

The gate swung open, and Andi drove onto the property to a house surrounded by lush gardens of tropical plants. The property was bordered by water in the rear.

Andi parked her car in the roundabout in front of the Spanish-style hacienda and walked up to the front door. Before she could knock, the door opened, and a uniformed maid invited her in.

"Please," the maid said, "have a seat in the sitting room. Mrs. Isaacson will be right down."

Andi sat down in the room indicated, large and cool with tiled floors, expensive-looking area rugs, and huge pieces of dark wood furniture.

A woman entered just after Andi seated herself on a large Spanish-style sofa. She walked toward Andi, her hand extended. "You are the detective that Nonni called me about?" Coral spoke with a strong New York accent which years of living in Florida would probably never erase. She, too, was in her sixties, Andi thought, and almost painfully thin, her face etched with deep lines and the skin of her arms sagging with no flesh to support it. She wore a long, bright green caftan, its brightness draining even more color from her already pale face. She took a cigarette from the pack sitting on a small table, lit it with a gold lighter and inhaled deeply before sitting down.

"Yes. I wanted to talk with you about Miranda Duncan. You played bridge with her, I understand."

"Miranda. Yes, She was a friend of Belle's. A good bridge player, but I didn't like her at all. She was using Belle, I was sure, but I didn't want to say anything. My husband knew her. He said she was involved with a lot of suspicious people."

"How did your husband know Miranda?" Andi asked.

"He's in business with Jorge. They own a couple of clubs together. He told me to stay away from her, that she was dangerous. But Belle liked her."

"Did he say in what way she was dangerous?" Andi was getting tired of these vague accusations against Miranda. No one seemed to know anything that would give her a lead.

"She was seeing Philippe SanAngelo."

"The Miami drug dealer?" Andi asked. She hoped her surprise hadn't given her away.

"I hear he's the biggest dealer in the country." Coral looked pleased with her revelation. "He's also involved in smuggling guns. Or so my husband tells me."

Andi concealed her surprise. "Did Philippe SanAngelo go to the clubs with Miranda?"

"Oh, yes. He was always there with her, and my husband said he was selling drugs, but Jorge always said no."

"Do you have any idea where I can find Mr. SanAngelo?"

"No."

"What about your husband? Might he know?"

"I can ask him."

"May I talk to your husband?"

"I can ask him to call you."

"All right." Andi wrote her cell number on the back of her card and gave it to Coral. "Please tell him I'd like to talk with him as soon as possible."

Coral took Andi's card. "I'll give it to him, but I don't know if he'll call you."

"Ask him." Andi rose to her feet and extended her hand to Coral. "Thank you for your help."

Coral escorted Andi to the door which was opened by the maid, and she could feel Coral's eyes on her as she walked to her car. She slid into the driver's seat and drove slowly down the long driveway. Coral didn't seem that reliable, more inclined to want to shock Andi than to tell the truth. Andi needed to talk to someone at the Miami P.D. Greg would know who.

As she reached the highway, her phone rang. A woman's voice asked, "Detective Battaglia?"

"Yes."

"This is Angela Ramirez. I know we're supposed to see you tonight at eight o'clock, but something's come up. Can we do it another time—maybe tomorrow?"

Andi had nearly forgotten about the Ramirezes. She'd have to be in Miami again, probably in a day or two. Seeing them was really just dotting all the i's, covering all the bases. "That's not a problem. I'll be down here again in a couple of days. I'll call you, and we'll set another appointment."

Angela Ramirez sounded relieved. "Thank you, Detective. I'll wait for your call."

SIXTEEN

Now that she was on her way home, Andi decided to call Greg. She needed to talk things over with someone. She pulled off the highway and entered a coffee shop where she ordered iced coffee and dialed Greg's number. The phone rang four times before Greg picked up.

"Hello," he said.

"Hi. It's Andi, Greg. I'm in Miami—or some part of it—and I need to get some information on a Miami drug dealer named Philippe SanAngelo. Can you put me on to someone in narcotics at the Miami P.D. who might be able to help?"

Greg was silent for a long time. Andi wondered if he had hung up, but finally he said, "Probably Joe Patrone is the guy, but I don't think he'll give you much. He clams up with people he doesn't know."

"Even other cops?"

"Yeah."

"Would he talk to you?"

"Sure. We were uniforms together."

Andi thought for a minute about what she had learned today. She had Kathryn's phone records. They might yield a number in Burgess Beach that Miranda had called. She seemed to know someone there, this Toni, at least from what she'd told Kathryn and Belle. She was pretty sure Nick Oldham was lying about his affair with Miranda, but was he 'oldnick' in the e-mails? If he was, he knew something about Miranda's more recent activities.

She made a decision. "Are you still a suspect in Miranda's murder, or have you been cleared?"

"Nothing new. I'm still dangerous."

"Look," Andi said. "I need a partner. Ed Garcia came into my office last evening and tried to add himself to my murder investigation, but he's worse than no help. I need you."

"But I can't . . . ."

"Not if we ask the Captain. But if you come with me to Miami, talk with this Patrone, go over what I've found out, and provide muscle for me when I see these drug guys, you'd be a great help. Are you willing to do that?"

"We could both be fired, you know."

"I know. I'm willing to risk it. Are you?"

"Sure."

"I spent today in Miami, and I have a lot of questions. I need to talk to somebody. Can I come to your place? I'm just leaving Coral Gables. I'll bring dinner."

"That's an offer I can't refuse. Chinese, if you're picking it up."

"Good. See you."

Andi hung up and sighed with relief. She had a partner, even if Captain Bradley would fire her if he knew. She needed help and someone to talk to.

Andi picked up the dinner at her usual Chinese take-out place—all her favorites: moo shu pork, almond chicken and garlic shrimp—and headed for Greg's place. He lived in a gated development about fifteen minutes from the Burgess Beach Police Department. Andi found his number and called Greg to open the gate and give her directions. She found it in the rear of the development where his neighbors were the scrub pines and palm trees of rural Florida. At his apartment, Andi looked around with interest. She was surprised to find it fully furnished and decorated.

"Hey," she said as she entered with her food cartons. "You've really settled in. That's more than I can say."

"I got tired of living out of boxes. And, of course, I've been unemployed or on leave, you could say, for a couple of days. So, I've had some time."

"It looks good."

They sat down at the table and helped themselves from the cartons of food. Andi gobbled her first few mouthfuls, suddenly aware that it had been a long time since her lunch with Kathryn in Miami.

"Good," she said, putting down her fork and wiping her lips. "Sorry to be such a pig. I'm worn out and really hungry."

"So, tell me about your day."

Andi reported on her lunch with Kathryn Forbes, her visits to Florida First, Nick Oldham, Belle Acosta and her two bridge partners, which brought her to Philippe SanAngelo. She also told Greg about Miranda's friend in Burgess Beach and the name Toni.

"Does that name ring any bells with you?" she asked.

"Nothing. But Miranda never talked about her past or anyone she knew. Let's look at the phone records."

Andi pulled out the envelope that Kathryn had given her at lunch. She took a last bite of her dinner and a sip of jasmine tea, pushed the plate away, and laid out the phone records.

They worked companionably, each perusing a stack of the six months of records. The bills for each number were grouped together, and Kathryn had noted which were hers and which Miranda's. Andi started with Miranda's land line records while Greg took her cell.

Andi was nearly asleep, cruising through the numbers Miranda had called in September, just before she was murdered, when Greg said, "Here we go."

"What?"

"The numbers in Burgess Beach that Miranda called."

"How often did she call?" Andi asked.

"One number she called almost daily. But there are others."

"We'll call the phone company tomorrow and find out who the numbers belong to."

"I'm going to call tonight," Greg said. "I'll give them my police routine."

"Okay. I haven't found any Burgess Beach numbers in Miranda's land line records. Oops! Here's one." Andi read out the number to Greg, and he identified it as one she had called repeatedly from her cell phone.

"This was in August. Nothing in September," Andi said.

"She called other numbers in Burgess Beach," Greg said. "One is that motel she stayed at. I remember the number. I'll check them all."

Andi dozed on the sofa, at first listening to Greg on the phone, then falling soundly asleep.

Greg hung up and said, "Got 'em."

Andi jerked. "Who?" she asked.

"Two of the numbers are the motel where she stayed and the one where she was murdered. One, which she called often, is a pizza place that I know delivers. There are two other restaurants, and then there are a lot of calls to a residential address on Dixie Highway. I'll bet that's where she visited."

"Great. Maybe now we'll find out who Toni is and what Miranda was doing here."

"You'd better go there alone. I don't want the Captain to know I'm working. I'll call Patrone tomorrow morning. Maybe we can have lunch, somewhere in Stuart, away from here, and report our progress."

"Good idea." Andi's brief nap had refreshed her, and she was wide awake now. "Are we through with the phone info?"

"Yes. We've checked the land line and her cell." Greg paused, looking uncomfortable, then said, "There's something else you should know if you're going to be working this case."

"Shoot."

"It's about me." He stopped, reluctant to continue.

"What?" Andi asked impatiently. "What is it?"

"After Miranda left—and for a while before she left—I was drinking pretty heavily. That was part of the reason we fought. She would get angry about my drinking and I would get defensive, and then we'd get into it. Sometimes she'd leave, and sometimes I would."

"And? You're not drinking much now, are you? At least I haven't seen that."

"My lieutenant warned me. He was getting ready to put something in my file, but he gave me a last chance. I'd been cautioned before, but that time, I knew he meant it. So I quit completely for a while. Now I have a drink once in a while, but I'm okay."

"I knew there was something you were holding back. Thanks for telling me." Then she yawned, picked up the phone information and her purse, and headed out the door. "Goodnight. I'll call you in the morning."

Andi drove to her new home, pleased with the results of her day and the help she'd gotten from Greg. She was glad Greg had confided in her about his drinking. She'd been uneasy knowing there was something he was keeping back. She parked in her off-street parking space, grabbed her files and headed to her apartment. She was fumbling in her purse for her key when a voice said, "About time you got home. I've been waiting for you."

It was Jim.

SEVENTEEN

Andi's felt an adrenaline rush that made her want to get the hell out of there. She'd been so careful. Her options raced through her mind. Calling 911 hadn't worked nor had getting angry with him. She took a deep breath, thought what the hell, and turned to face him.

She put a smile on her face and said, "Jim, what a surprise. Don't you have anything to do in Tampa that you keep coming here?"

She could see he hadn't expected this. He was ready to react to anger or panic, but not to friendliness. "I drove over after work," he mumbled, as he took a wobbly step backwards.

"Long drive. Want some coffee?" she asked, at last fishing the keys from her purse and opening the apartment door. "I can make some."

She opened the door and motioned him to come in. She could smell the liquor on his breath. Maybe she could get him to fall asleep. He certainly shouldn't be driving.

"Where were you? I've been waiting for hours. Who's your new boyfriend?" His voice was slurred and angry, the way he'd been the last times she'd seen him.

"I'm not seeing anybody. I have a case involving Miami, so I was there interviewing witnesses. I'll make the coffee. Sit down. Make yourself comfortable."

"Yeah," he said. He really wanted to fight. "Hey, gimme a kiss, can't you?" He approached her, his arms outstretched, but she ducked around him and said, "I'll start the coffee. Have you had anything to eat?"

"Not hungry. Come on. Gimme a little kiss, damnit."

"Just a minute," she said. "I want some coffee, and I've got to take my shoes off. I'll be right back."

"Got anything to drink?" he asked. "Something to put in mine."

"Sure," she said. She stood behind the bar in her tiny kitchen, watching him wander around her bare living room. The furniture was in place, but almost everything else was still in boxes. She added water to the kettle on the stove and started the burner. Then she fished out a jar of instant decaf and got out two mugs.

"Just a sec. I've got some brandy in one of those boxes," she said. She brushed past him, ducking as he tried to grab her. Where had she put it? Then she remembered that the brandy was in a box in her bedroom, but she'd never find it while she was trying to elude Jim, and she didn't want him to follow her there.

"It's in the other room," she said, "but first I've gotta pee. I'll be right back." She fled to the bathroom and locked the door. Was there anything in the medicine cabinet that might knock him out? She looked over her meager supply of drugs, then saw half a bottle of cold medicine. Terrific. Twenty-five percent alcohol. Put some of that in his coffee. She hoped he wouldn't taste it. She flushed the toilet and returned to the kitchen.

Jim was still blundering around the living room, not settling anywhere. He'd taken off his jacket and thrown it on the arm of the sofa. "Where'd you go?" he asked, turning to face her.

"Just the bathroom," she said, passing as close to him as she dared. "Oops! There's the kettle." It was whistling, and she hurried to the kitchen to shut off the burner.

"Come on, baby," Jim said. "Forget the coffee. Just come here. I need you. I've been so lonely."

"I'll be right there," she said, pouring cold medicine into his cup along with hot water. This had better work.

"Here you go," she said. "Let's sit down." She moved toward one of the two chairs that flanked the front window and put a mug on the table between them.

He sat down on the sofa, loosening his tie. "Come on," he said. "Sit with me." He patted the cushion next to him.

"Just let me have my coffee," she said. "Then I'll come." When she put his cup down, he grabbed at her, but she stepped back quickly. She sat in the chair facing him and took a sip. The coffee was pretty bad, even without the cold medicine.

He picked up his mug and gulped. "What'd you put in here?"

"I told you. I found some brandy in the bedroom," she lied.

"It's pretty bad."

"I didn't say it was good brandy," she said.

"Awful," he said, but he emptied the cup.

"How'd you find my new apartment?" Andi asked.

"Just called your station. Told 'em I was an old cop friend from Tampa. Were you tryin' to get away from me?"

"No. Of course not. This place is much nicer than my old one, and it just became available." Stupid. She hadn't told anyone at work <u>not</u> to say where she'd moved.

"Yeah. I guess. Come here, baby. You've been running around too much. Come on and gimme that kiss." Again he patted the sofa.

Unless he fell asleep soon, he was going to be all over her, she thought, but she didn't have any alternative. She got up and sat down next to him. He immediately grabbed her, turning her toward him. He pressed his mouth on hers, forcing her lips open. She could feel his tongue probing. He tasted of coffee and liquor, cigarettes and that cold medicine. His hand grabbed her breast, kneading it. She was going to end up raped unless she did something. He was still a wide-awake drunk.

She pulled away from him and said, "So, how are things in Tampa? I miss everybody I worked with. How's Ellen?" She was babbling like an idiot, but she had to talk, keep him busy. "Are you smoking again?"

"You always bitched about it, but I started again when you left." He sat for a minute as if gathering himself together. "I don't want to talk. I've missed you so much." He pulled her close again, kissing her face and neck, his hands wandering over her breasts, trying to open the buttons on her blouse. She sat very still, letting him paw at her. "Oh, I love you so much, Andi. Why'd you leave me?"

She pulled away when his grip loosened and said, "Can I have a cigarette? Everybody here smokes, and I've started."

He pulled back and stared at her. "You? You're smoking?"

"Yeah, I've got a taste for it," she lied. "You got any?"

He pulled a crumpled pack from his shirt pocket and offered her one, taking one himself. He found a lighter, and, his hand shaking, lit first her cigarette, then his. She hoped she wouldn't choke as she took a puff and pulled herself out of his arms.

He dragged on his cigarette, turning to her. "I can't believe you're smoking. All the lectures you gave me."

"Yeah, well, sorry. I've succumbed to the demon." She leaned further away on the sofa and he, taking a drag, seemed not to notice. He swayed a little. She turned to watch him and saw his eyes close, then open quickly, then close again. Please, God, let him fall asleep.

She sat, watching the ash gather on the tip of his cigarette. Finally he slumped back against the sofa, and the ashes fell to the rug. His breathing steadied and deepened. She watched the cigarette as his hand relaxed, and she took it from between his fingers with the caution she would have used disarming a bomb. He didn't wake.

Andi sat watching him sleep for a long time. Then she brought out a blanket, went into her bedroom and wedged a chair under the doorknob.

She thought she hadn't slept at all, but she must have, for when she woke at seven and cautiously opened her bedroom door, Jim was gone.

She couldn't go on this way. He had to see she was through, that their love affair was over and she was starting a new life. But he was drinking so much it was hard to know how rational he was. She had wanted to run along the beach this morning, but in case Jim was still nearby, she settled for some stretching and floor exercises to a video before she showered and headed to work.

At the station, she quickly typed up her notes from the day in Miami before she checked messages and e-mails. The Palmers' two banks reported that they were both ready to release their records. The insurance company had e-mailed copies of the Palmers' homeowners' insurance policy: there were riders for some expensive jewelry, paintings and furniture. The current policy and the riders had been taken out in May. When Andi checked the items that had been stolen, most of them were listed as heavily insured under the riders.

She called the banks, and they e-mailed copies of the Palmers' bank records. They were interesting. Up until about four months ago, they had had plenty of money in the banks as well as substantial market investments which one of the banks handled in its investment program. But around the middle of May, money had been taken from their hefty savings accounts and stock had been sold. The proceeds had not been deposited in the bank. The balances in the bank accounts were low throughout the summer and often dipped into overdraft protection to cover checks. There seemed to be no regular source of income. What had happened to the Palmers' finances in May?

Andi now suspected they'd set up the burglary before they left for New York in late September and that Leona Castro and her son were in on it. She'd rather talk to the Palmers in person than on the phone. Although she'd be happy to have a case as interesting as this one, she longed to get back to Miranda Duncan's murder. She prepared her report on the information she'd obtained from the banks and the insurance company, then called the house on Hutchinson Island and Leona Castro's home in Fort Pierce. There was no answer on either phone. She could go up to Fort Pierce to Castro's home to see if she or her son were there, but she didn't want to do that before working on what she'd learned yesterday in Miami. The Palmer case would have to wait a while.

She checked out and headed for the address on Dixie Highway that Miranda had called repeatedly. Whatever was there could perhaps tell Andi the reason Miranda had been in Burgess Beach. The address was one of three small bungalows set close together on a weedy lawn. Three mail boxes were clustered together just off the road. Andi left her car in front and walked down the driveway to the cottage in the middle. A girl of about three sat on the front steps, combing a doll's hair and talking to her intensely. The child had very pale skin and red hair in two braids down her back. Andi thought about Miranda's nickname, "Red".

"Hi," Andi said.

The child jumped, surprised by Andi's voice. "Hi," she said. "Who're you?"

"My name's Andi. What's yours?"

"Toni," she said. "My real name's Antoinette."

"Pretty name. Is your mommy around?"

"She's not my mommy. My mommy doesn't live here."

"Is the person you live with at home?"

The door of the cottage opened then, and a woman standing at the top of the steps asked, "Can I help you?" She was no more than five feet tall and very slender, her dark hair beginning to gray in front. She was wearing jeans and a t-shirt too big for her, covered by an apron. Her voice was not welcoming.

Andi took out her badge. "I'm from the Burgess Beach Police Department," she explained. "I'm sorry to have startled you."

"I don't like strangers talking to Toni," the woman said. "What do you want?"

"A woman named Miranda Duncan frequently called this residence from Miami, and I wanted to know who she was calling."

"Why?"

The little girl had stopped talking to the doll and had turned to look at the woman in the doorway. "A police matter," Andi said. "May I come in?"

"Do you know my mommy?" Toni asked.

The woman shushed the child, and said, "Miranda Duncan isn't here."

"May I come in and talk to you?"

"Is Mommy coming to see me?" the little girl asked.

"Hush, Toni. This is for grownups." The woman took a step back and opened the door wider. "Yes. Of course." She turned to the child and said, "Please bring Annabelle in and play with her in your room."

The child sighed but did as she was told. As she walked down the hall, she turned and asked once more, "Is my mommy coming soon?" When no one answered her, she went into her room and closed the door.

"Please," the woman said. "Come in. I am Marta Perez, Toni's nanny."

"Andi Battaglia," Andi said. The living room was tiny but well-kept, and Andi could see a neat kitchen off to the left.

"Please sit down. May I get you anything? A glass of water?" Marta asked.

"Thank you, no. I'm fine." Andi sat down.

"I'm sorry to have to tell you," Andi paused, looking toward the little girl's room. She began again. "I'm sorry to say that Miranda Duncan is dead."

Marta drew back and put her hand to her throat. "My God! No!"

Andi waited as Marta absorbed the news.

"How did she die? She was not sick," the woman said.

"She was murdered."

"Murdered? She was murdered?" Marta's voice rose, and she flinched as if Andi had thrown something at her. When Andi nodded, Marta sat silent. She looked scared and turned to look down the hallway, as if to go to the child. Then she asked, "When? Who did it?"

"Her death is under investigation. She died in a motel in Burgess Beach last Friday night, September 27th."

After a couple of minutes, the frightened look drained from Marta's face, and she sagged against the back of the chair. Andi waited. After a moment, Marta straightened up and composed her face. She took out a handkerchief and blew her nose.

"What was your relationship with Miranda?" Andi asked.

"Well," Marta thought for a minute. "She was my employer. Toni is Miranda's daughter. How did you find us?"

Andi told her about Miranda's calls to this number. "I wanted to find out Miranda's connection to this address. When did you start to work for her?"

"Toni was about two months old, so almost three years ago."

"Did you live here all the time with Toni?"

"No. We moved here in May. Before that we lived in Miami."

"How did you meet Miranda?"

"I worked as a nanny for a friend of hers."

"You moved here in May? How often has Miranda come to see Toni since the move?"

"Miranda often came to see her in Miami, but since May," she gestured around at the living room, "mostly she talked with Toni on the phone."

"How many times has Miranda been here?" Andi persisted

Marta thought back. "Three, maybe four times."

"Do you know why you moved to Burgess Beach?"

Marta was quiet for a minute, thinking. Andi waited. "She didn't tell me, but she and her lover were fighting a lot. He loved Toni and was kind to her, but he and Miranda were not getting along. One night she just told me to pack up, that we were moving. I wanted to stay with Toni, so I did what she wanted."

"Who was this lover?" Andi asked.

"Miranda called him Pepe. He's a big man, Cuban, I think."

"Why Pepe?

"I don't know."

"What do you know about him?"

"People say he's a big drug dealer."

"Do you know his name?" Andi asked.

"No." Marta looked down at her hands in her lap. "I think he's a dangerous man." Andi thought she probably did know the lover's name but didn't want to say.

"Was he Toni's father?"

"I don't think so. Miranda never told me who Toni's father was, but I don't think she was involved with him when Toni was born."

Andi paused for a minute, then went on. "Do you know what they quarreled about?"

"Miranda never told me, but I overheard them fighting. Miranda wanted to quit going to the clubs. I heard her say she was tired of playing games with men, that she wanted to stay home with Toni at night, not be a whore."

"Was he violent?"

"Well, after that, I saw a big bruise on her arm. She covered it with makeup. A couple of times before her face was red, as though she'd been slapped, but I never saw him hit her. But I think she was afraid for Toni. The next time he was there, they fought again, and that was when she told me we had to move."

"And that was in May?"

"Around the beginning of May. She found this place and moved us here. It's nice, but we didn't see Miranda as much."

"Was he angry?"

"I don't know. I didn't see him again."

"Did Miranda support you?" Andi asked.

"She paid the rent and my salary and for the groceries. I love Toni, but I can't work for nothing."

So, Andi thought, that was the reason for Miranda's shortage of funds in the spring. She'd lost her sugar daddy's support. Had he killed Miranda? Or had Miranda been looking for a way to make some quick money and gotten herself killed?

"Did you know how to reach her when you needed to?" Andi asked.

"I could call Mrs. Acosta. She was a friend of the woman I worked for. I didn't this time, but I was beginning to be worried about Miranda. She'd always called us every two or three days. I know Toni was waiting for her call."

"But you hadn't yet tried to reach her through Belle Acosta, is that right? You didn't see anything on television about Miranda's death?"

Marta gestured to the small living room. "When we moved here, we only brought our clothes and Toni's toys. We don't have a television yet."

"Did Miranda still go to the clubs after she moved you and Toni to Burgess Beach?"

"I don't know."

"Tell me about last Friday night. Did Miranda come to see Toni that night?"

"She came Friday afternoon and played with Toni. We had dinner, and then when it was Toni's bedtime, she left."

"Did you know where she was going to stay on Friday night?" Andi asked.

"I thought she drove back to Miami."

"Where were you on Friday night after Miranda left?"

"I was here with Toni." Then her lips tightened. "You can't think I killed Miranda?"

"Sorry. Just covering all the bases. I'll alert Child Welfare Services about Miranda's death, but I'll ask them to leave Toni with you for the time being. Is that a problem?"

"Miranda set up an account that paid the rent here and sent me money for groceries and my salary. That's all okay until the end of October." She stopped, then continued, "What's going to happen to Toni?"

"Child Welfare will try to locate her father. If they can't find out who he is, she'll go into foster care."

"Oh," Marta said. She sounded shocked.

"May I have the address of the apartment you lived in with Toni in Miami?"

"It's in South Beach," Perez said, and recited the street address.

Andi thanked the woman for her help. Something else to check into in Miami, she thought as she headed to the station. She put together a timeline of Miranda's life in her head. Miranda had had a baby. Greg could be Toni's father. It seemed possible. Did he have any idea he had a child? Andi thought probably not.

Andi called Child Welfare Services when she got back to the station. She talked with a social worker named Paloma Marquez, who said she would go out to see Toni, check out the home and probably leave Toni there for the time being. Then Andi typed up her notes about the visit. She probably needed to tell the captain. Later, she thought.

She turned back to the burglary and once again tried the phone numbers on Hutchinson Island and in Fort Pierce, but there was no answer. At three-thirty, she went out again, heading for the Palmer's house on Hutchinson Island.

After she got the guard to open the gate, she asked about the Palmers and Leona Castro. The guard shrugged and said he didn't know whether there was anyone at the house. Castro, he said, could open the gate without calling him. When she asked about Felicia Gomez, Leona's friend who worked across the street, he said she'd left for the day.

Andi thanked him, drove to the Palmers' house and rang the bell. No answer. Where did that woman go? Wasn't she supposed to be taking care of the house, cleaning, watering plants, and generally keeping things in order? She was never there.

Andi left the island and headed to Fort Pierce. Traffic was heavy on I-95, and it was nearly four o'clock when she arrived at the Castro residence, a small, coral-colored stucco house on a street of similar houses, each with a small patch of yard in front, most planted with grass and a few decorative plants, some covered with small rocks and decorated with larger boulders and cactus.

She rang the bell at the Castro house, but there was no sound, so she knocked at the door. Then she knocked again. Nothing. She walked around to the back of the house and peered into the kitchen window. Nobody there.

Back at the front of the house, she tried to see through the blinds into the living room, but they were tightly closed. She sighed, then headed to the house next door. There was no answer to the bell there, nor was there one at the house on the other side. Across the street a small elderly woman opened her door but left the chain on.

"Not buyin' nothin'", she said and prepared to slam the door, but Andi, her foot wedged firmly in the gap, displayed her badge and asked about the Castros.

"Don't know. Ain't seen 'em," the woman said. "They come and go."

Andi gave the woman her card and asked if she'd let her know if she saw the Castros.

No one answered at any of the other houses that Andi tried, so she headed back to Burgess Beach.

EIGHTEEN

It was after five o'clock when she got back to station. She wrote up her notes quickly and headed to the captain's office. She knocked and heard his "Enter."

His chair faced the window, its back to the door, and she cleared her throat.

"Yes, Detective Battaglia. What do you need?" he asked, turning to face her across his desk.

"You told me to come to you when the Hutchinson Island burglary began to take me away from Miranda Duncan's murder. It's doing that. I need someone to check the Castro house in Fort Pierce again. There was no answer there today, and I couldn't get any information from any of the neighbors.

"I have to go back to Miami tomorrow on the Duncan murder. I'm going to ask for help from the Miami P.D. on Philippe SanAngelo, the drug dealer Miranda was involved with."

"Do you need a contact in Miami? I know people there."

"I've got the name of someone to see there. I'd like to find out about SanAngelo, and I don't want to do it on the phone."

"So, you want me to send Ed Garcia up to Fort Pierce to check on the Castros?"

"Yes, sir. I'd like to have him take over the whole burglary."

"Including any visit to New York to talk to the Palmers?"

How did he know about that? She must have been day-dreaming in her notes. Better read them over more carefully. "Maybe I'd do that. Or I could go with him." She knew she was getting pushy, but she also knew that in spite of himself, Bradley liked and respected her.

"You don't have much faith in Detective Garcia's skills, do you, Battaglia?"

Andi didn't want to bad-mouth Garcia, but surely the Captain knew his limitations. He'd probably get lost in New York. Certainly he wouldn't be capable of trapping the Palmers into an admission of guilt. "I didn't say that," she said. "He's just inexperienced as an interrogator."

"He's been a detective longer than you have, Battaglia. Inexperienced?"

"I've never seen him question a suspect, sir, and all I've ever heard him report on is telephone calls he's made and information he's gotten off the computer. Do you think he's a good interrogator?"

"Watch yourself, Battaglia. He's got years on you."

"I know that, sir." She stood, waiting for the eyes to release her.

Finally, Bradley sighed. "You're right, of course. If some-one needs to go to New York, it should be you. But I'll send him to Fort Pierce to see if he can get a line on Castro and her son."

"Thank you, sir."

Bradley picked up his phone, told his secretary to get Garcia.

"That's all, Detective."

Andi turned and walked out, meeting Garcia in the hallway. He looked at her questioningly, wondering, she supposed, if his summons meant good news or bad. She avoided his eyes.

She called Angela Ramirez and rescheduled their appointment for six the following evenng. What about Greg? She needed him to accompany her to Miami to talk to the Miami cops about SanAngelo, but even though he had known the Ramirezes, she didn't think he should go to the interview with her.

Everything about Miranda's visits to Burgess Beach had turned out to be dead ends except for the child. She'd stayed at the Flamingo Motel but left no trace. No one had seen her eating in a restaurant, walking, shopping, doing anything at all during her six visits. But she'd been murdered here, not in Miami, and she'd had a heavy suitcase and a purse with her, both of which had been taken from her motel room. Maybe Miranda had found some way to get money to make up for the loss of support from Philippe. Actually, until she talked with him, she really didn't know if he had been supporting Miranda and the child, but it seemed likely somebody had.

But the suitcase and her purse were gone, vanished, and no one seemed to know anything about them. The suitcase was big and heavy. That was all she knew about it. Maybe now the motel manager, Ben Patel, might remember something more about it. She decided to go and ask him.

Her phone rang. Greg said, "Did you forget you were going to call me this morning?" He sounded annoyed.

"I did. I'm sorry. Lots of material came in on a burglary I had since before I got Miranda's murder. I've been busy with that." She didn't want to tell him about Toni yet. She wanted to see his reaction when he heard.

"Did you get in touch with Patrone?" she asked.

"Yeah. He'll see us tomorrow at ten. He wants to know what you know about SanAngelo."

"You'll come with me to Miami, won't you?"

Greg was quiet, then said, "I guess. Did you at least see who Miranda was calling in Burgess Beach?"

"Yes. I'll tell you all about it tomorrow. Do you think Patrone can get us in to see SanAngelo?"

"I asked. He couldn't promise anything."

"Okay. I'll pick you up at eight tomorrow morning." She hung up quickly, cutting off any opportunity for more questions. Tomorrow would be soon enough.

At the Hibiscus Motel, Ben Patel was checking in a couple of middle-aged German tourists. They were blond and had gotten too much sun.

When Patel left to help them with their luggage, Andi sat down and waited. She'd never been in this motel before. It was definitely a step up from the Flamingo where Miranda had often stayed. It wasn't the Ritz, but it had a tiled entry way, and the pool had an attractive garden with tables and lounges around it. And it was closer to the shops and restaurants downtown.

Patel returned and asked how he could help her. She badged him and said she was working on the case of the woman who had been murdered at the hotel. Patel looked around nervously when she said "murdered," but there was no one around to overhear them. He motioned her to follow him into the tiny office behind the registration desk. She sat on the extra chair, her knees and Patel's nearly touching.

"I told the detective everything I know," Patel said. "I only saw her for a few minutes."

"I know. It's just that I'm new on the case, and I thought maybe you might have remembered something you forgot to tell the other detective. Did you notice anything about the suitcase other its weight? What color was it?"

Patel closed his eyes as if trying to remember the suitcase. "It was blue. Leather, no, it was that hard plastic kind of suitcase, one of those that don't break. No wheels. It had a strap around it."

Andi visualized the suitcase. Old, if it didn't have wheels. "Did it have any tags or labels on it?"

"It had a tag on the handle."

"What did it look like?" Andi asked.

Patel was still. He closed his eyes. Andi could see him reliving the moment of carrying the suitcase upstairs to Miranda's room. Now he had it in his hand again. Andi held her breath, not wanting to distract him from the memory.

"It was paper but heavier. It's what the airlines put on your luggage that you can write your name on." Patel said.

"Did you see the name of the airline?" Andi asked.

"The tag had blue and red on it. American Airlines? It was fairly new."

"The nearest airport is West Palm, isn't it?"

"Yes," Patel said.

Andi thanked him for his help. She'd find out about American Airlines at West Palm. If the suitcase had arrived by air, where had it come from? Had it arrived with Miranda or by itself? Maybe this would lead somewhere. Or maybe not.

She looked at her watch. Time to go home. Nothing more to do today. She drove home cautiously, on the lookout for Jim. She managed to get into her apartment without any problem, and she breathed a sigh of relief, shadowed by the knowledge that it was only a matter of time before she'd have to deal with him again. She should talk with him during the day when he was more likely to be sober. If he didn't leave her alone, she would talk to his superiors, and she knew, as well as he, that would mean his career. She didn't want to do that, but she might have to. She should take a day, drive over to Tampa, see her parents and then see Jim at work, when he was sober. But she couldn't do that until she'd solved Miranda Duncan's murder.

The following morning she felt brave enough to run three miles along the beach. She showered, dressed and picked Greg up at eight. She had brought coffee for them both, and they sipped in companionable silence for the first half hour of the trip. Then he asked, "So what did you find at the place Miranda called so often?"

"The house was rented by Miranda in May for her daughter and the daughter's nanny." She glanced sideways at him as she spoke, but his face told her nothing. "Did you know she had a child?"

"No. Yes. Autopsy report showed she'd given birth." He paused. "How old is this child?"

"She's three. Her name is Antoinette, but they call her Toni."

"Antoinette," he said. "She would have picked a name like that." He tried to control his voice, but Andi could hear his sorrow.

"Who's the father?" he asked abruptly. "That drug dealer?"

"The nanny doesn't know. Her name's Marta Perez, by the way. She doesn't think Miranda was seeing Philippe SanAngelo when Toni was born. Marta said he was good to them, but then he and Miranda quarreled, and she moved them up to Burgess Beach."

Greg was quiet. Andi glanced at him from time to time to see if his expression could tell her anything, but his face was impassive. Later she saw that his eyes were closed and his head rested against the seat back.

Just when Andi thought he was asleep, Greg spoke. "She could be mine. Miranda left me about five years ago. We'd been fighting, but there was no blowup that happened before she left. Just—one day she was gone."

He was quiet again for a while. "I didn't know where she'd gone. She could have been pregnant when she left. I don't know. Oh, my God. That's my daughter." His voice cracked, and he swallowed hard. Then he continued, "I know she's mine. Why didn't she tell me?"

Andi didn't know what to say. Greg and Miranda had made bad decisions throughout their relationship. It was too late to change anything now. If Toni was his child, maybe what Greg should do now was accept the past and bring her into his life, let her have at least one living parent. But they were both making assumptions. He didn't know whether the child was his. Neither did she.

They were both quiet for a long time. Then halfway to Miami, Andi broke the silence. "I didn't tell you what else I learned yesterday."

Greg didn't respond, and when she looked at him, she could tell he hadn't heard her. He was deep in his own thoughts. She let it slide.

At the Police Department, Andi found a parking spot, but Greg didn't move.

She looked at her watch. "Greg, let's go. We have an appointment."

Greg turned to look at her, his eyes filled with pain. "Why didn't she tell me?" he asked again.

"I don't know," Andi said. She was quiet for a moment more, then said, "We have an appointment with Lieutenant Patrone. We have to go."

He sat up straight in his seat and smoothed his face into an impassive mask. He was ready.

NINETEEN

Greg took the lead as they entered police department head-quarters. At the front desk, he was greeted by the woman on duty, a uniformed sergeant, with a warm handshake and an inquiring glance at Andi.

"Anita," he said, "this is my new partner, Detective Andi Battaglia. Andi, this is Anita Fonseca."

Andi held out a hand, and Anita shook it. "How you doing in the boonies, Greg?" she asked.

"Good," he said. "We have a Miami-related murder, and we're here to see Joe Patrone. Will you give him a ring?"

"Sure," Fonseca said. "Just a sec."

In a couple of minutes, Greg and Andi were buzzed into the offices. Greg led the way to the end of the hallway, and knocked on the door that read, "Lt. Joseph Patrone." A voice said, "Come in."

Patrone stood up as they entered. "Greg. How the hell you doin'? Good to see you." Patrone was nearly as tall as Greg's six-foot-two, with a full head of very dark wavy hair.

"I'm good, Joe." The men shook hands. "This is my Burgess Beach partner, Andi Battaglia."

Andi shook hands with Patrone before she and Greg sat down.

"So, what can I do for you, Greg?"

"Like I said on the phone, we have a murder in Burgess Beach. A woman from Miami was killed there. She was involved with Philippe SanAngelo. I know he operates mostly under the radar, but I hoped you could get us in to see him."

"I tried my contacts, Greg, but I couldn't get shit. We could stage a raid at one of the clubs where he hangs out, but that's probably not what you want. You think he killed her?"

"We don't know. Maybe he killed her, maybe not. Right now we're just trying to get some background."

"What do you know about him?" Patrone asked.

"Not much," Andi said. "He's Cuban, right? Big guy, tough. We think he was our victim's boyfriend."

"He is Cuban. And mean as a snake. He's legal, arrived in Miami from Havana asking for political asylum, which he got. He came with a lotta cash. He pays off the local cops to turn a blind eye, and he sells coke and heroin through little guys who won't talk because they're too scared of him. That's his real name—Philippe SanAngelo. His family's from Spain, been in Cuba for more than a century. They had money before Castro, but now they're poor like everybody else."

"You got a photo of him?" Greg asked. "That would help."

Patrone fished in the file on his desk and pulled out a black-and-white 8"x10". It was a mug shot. Andi asked, "When was he arrested?"

"This was taken about six months ago. He lawyered up right away and was released on bail. The charges didn't stick."

Andi looked at the picture. SanAngelo was a good-looking guy, well-built, his broad shoulders, thick neck and the
muscles of his upper arms visible through the long-sleeved
dark cotton shirt he wore. He had long dark hair combed
back from his forehead, a strong jaw, and dark intense eyes
that stared as if they were trying to intimidate the camera. He
radiated sensuality and power, and Andi could understand
Miranda's attraction to him. But his mouth was thin-lipped
and cruel. On the side of the picture were his particulars:
height – 6'4"; weight – 220 lbs; eyes - black; hair – dark
brown; scars – bullet wound, left chest.

"Can we get a copy of this?" she asked.

"Sure. So. Now that I've shared what I know, tell me
what you know."

Andi stepped in before Greg could answer. "Our victim is a woman who hung out at several clubs, mostly Tux,
Cavelli's, Victor's, and the Meta Lounge. She brought in a
lotta guys who followed her and her friends. Apparently she
caused a lot of trouble, a lot of jealousy, but she also turned
guys on to SanAngelo who supplied them with drugs."

Greg looked at Andi. "You didn't tell me that," he said.

"Sorry."

"How'd you find that out?" Patrone asked.

"She has a three-year-old daughter who lives in Burgess
Beach with a nanny. The nanny heard them quarreling about
the victim's role in SanAngelo's drug business. She didn't
want to do it any more."

"You think SanAngelo killed her?" Patrone asked.

"Maybe, but I think she also was looking for a way out of
her relationship with him, needed money and may have been
trying to get it by-passing SanAngelo."

Greg looked at Andi while she spoke, but after she finished, he said, almost to himself, "The suitcase."

"What suitcase?" Patrone asked.

Andi said, "When she checked into the motel in Burgess Beach where she was murdered, she had a very heavy suitcase. It was gone when her body was discovered. We don't know what was in it. Drugs, gold, guns, whatever. My guess it was something she planned to sell or had sold to get money to free herself from SanAngelo."

"So, you want to talk to SanAngelo?" Patrone asked.

"That's where I'm hoping you can help us."

"Who's the lead on this case?" Patrone asked.

Andi hesitated a moment, then said, "I am, but I've asked Detective Lamont to help on the Miami angle."

"Well," Patrone said, "I can reach someone who's close to him, one of his lieutenants, a guy named Juan Garcia. He's Cuban, too, but he's been here a long time and knows the city. He can put you in touch with SanAngelo. Tell him it's about your vic. What's her name, by the way?"

"Miranda Duncan," Andi said.

Patrone was still a moment. "Does your boss know about you and Miranda?"

Greg looked uncomfortable. "Yeah. I'm only here unofficially."

"Jesus Christ! What's that mean? Am I gonna get my ass in a sling 'cause I talked to you? You mighta told me."

"You're only talking to Detective Battaglia, Joe. I'm here unofficially."

"Okay, but you're sitting right there."

Andi asked, "Would you have told me as much as you did if Greg wasn't with me?"

Now it was Patrone's turn to look uncomfortable. "Maybe not."

"Okay, let's just see if you can set us up for a meeting with the big Cuban," Andi said. "Tell him it's about Miranda Duncan, and that she's been murdered. Today, if possible."

"Okay," Patrone said. He picked up his phone, dialed a number, then turned his back to them as he spoke into the phone. He talked quietly, then hung up. When his cell phone rang, he talked again, but Andi and Greg couldn't hear what he said. After he hung up, he said, "Three o'clock at Antonio's. You know where that is, Greg?"

"Sure."

"What got you the meeting was telling Garcia that you wanted to talk to SanAngelo about Miranda Duncan's murder."

"Thanks, Joe. Appreciate it." Greg said.

"Just so it doesn't come back to bite me," Patrone said, shaking hands with Greg and Andi.

"I hope not." Greg said.

Back in the car, Greg turned to Andi and put his hand on hers before she could start the engine. "Stop. Tell me what happened at your meeting with the kid and her nanny. Why the hell didn't you tell me about Miranda playing drug whore for SanAngelo?"

"Look, I know this is a lot to learn. When I told you about her child, you got quiet, like you didn't want to hear anything more. I started to tell you, but you weren't listening. I would've told you later, but I didn't realize Patrone knew about you and Miranda."

"Yeah, but still . . . ."

"Okay, I shoulda told you, but this whole case is fucked up because of your history with Miranda. I shouldn't have asked for your help, but I knew I wouldn't get to meet SanAngelo without a contact in Miami."

"What else didn't you tell me about her?"

"The nanny saw some evidence SanAngelo may have hit Miranda before she decided to move them out of Miami."

"He hit her? He probably killed her," Greg said. His mouth clenched tight.

"Maybe. We just don't know enough. How much good an alibi from him will be, I don't know, but we need to talk to him. This wasn't a killing in anger. This was planned. You saw the scene, and you were at the autopsy. She didn't even know her killer was in the room."

They sat for a while in silence, each thinking about Miranda, the puzzle of her murder and the enigma that had been her life. Finally Andi spoke. "I have a work address for Bobby Medina. He's the guy who hit Miranda when she took his boyfriend away. Let's go see him. He works at some ad agency in South Beach. If we have time after that, we'll get lunch before we meet SanAngelo."

Andi headed for South Beach and found a parking space not far from the lime green building that housed the ad agency. When they entered and asked for Bobby Medina, the very blond, very thin receptionist asked, "Have you an appointment?"

Andi flashed her badge and told her it was a police matter. The woman pressed a number on her phone, spoke into it briefly and said, "He'll be right out."

Bobby Medina was short and slim, dressed in tight black jeans. He held out his hand to Greg and said, "Bobby Medina. How can I help you?"

Greg shook his hand, then said, "You need to talk to Detective Battaglia."

Castro looked a little embarrassed, then held out his hand to Andi. They shook. "Andi Battaglia, Burgess Beach Police Department. Can we speak in private?"

"Of course." Medina led the way down a hall to a small conference room. "Please, sit down."

Andi and Greg took chairs opposite Medina. She waited until everyone was settled, then spoke. "We're here about Miranda Duncan."

Medina's face paled. "She didn't file criminal charges, did she? I didn't mean to hurt her. She just pissed me off."

"No, Mr. Medina. We're here because Miranda Duncan is dead. She was murdered in Burgess Beach. What can you tell us about your relationship with her?"

"Murdered? Oh, my God!" Medina looked stunned.

"You and Miranda had a confrontation at Tux, I think, about a man you were with. His name was Etienne."

"I don't know where it was. Probably Tux, maybe Victor's. Etienne's long gone."

"What happened?

"She was holding court as usual, and Etienne left me on the dance floor to take a look. By the time I found him, he was sitting next to Miranda, holding her hand and talking to her in French a mile a minute. Miranda was hardly paying attention, but that didn't seem to bother him."

"What happened then?" Andi asked.

"I knocked a few people out of the way and grabbed Etienne, but he shook me off, called that bitch a 'belle femme,' and told me to leave him alone. He said something about loving beautiful women, and that was the last I saw of him."

"So, your confrontation with Miranda wasn't that night?"

"No. About a week later, I saw her again. Etienne was gone, but I was still mad. Etienne is hot, and I got up in her face about losing him. Then she said . . . let me think. Something about if I couldn't hold on to a guy, how could I blame her? I think I slapped the bitch then, but she slugged me back. She gave me a black eye. She's a tough broad—was tough—certainly enough man for Etienne, but I haven't seen either one of them since."

"All right, Mr. Medina. Can you tell me where you were the night of September 27th? It was a Friday."

"I didn't kill her. I was just pissed off."

"I understand. Just for the record. Where were you that night?"

Medina turned to his Blackberry. "That was a week ago, right? I was in Key West. Big festival. I stayed over with someone I met." He thought for a minute, then said, "Jacob Something. Cooper. I'll give you his number. He lives down there."

They took down Cooper's phone number in Key West, thanked Medina for his help and headed back to the car.

They decided to stop for lunch at a Cuban restaurant Greg knew. He said it was close to Antonio's. "It'll get us in the mood to talk to SanAngelo. Cuban food, Cuban drug dealer."

"Yeah, yeah," Andi said.

They pulled up in front of a hole-in-the-wall in Miami's Cuban neighborhood.. "This is the best," Greg said. "You'll love it."

The place was cooled with a window air conditioner which wasn't doing much of a job, and it was crowded with customers. There were maybe eight tables, and each had six or seven people at it.

Andi turned to Greg. "We'll be all afternoon getting a table."

Greg said, "No worries." He called to a woman in a green off-the-shoulder dress with flounces at the hem who had just finished unloading a tray of food at one of the tables. "Hey, Carla. Got a table for us?"

"Ah, Señor Greg! Where you been?" the woman asked, walking over to Greg and giving him a big hug. "We miss you."

"Yeah. I moved to the boonies. But I miss the food. Can you find a spot for us?"

Carla turned and motioned to a busboy, gave him rapid directions in Spanish, and he brought out a small table and two chairs which he squeezed into a corner by the window. Carla brought them two menus, patted Greg's hand, then headed back to the kitchen.

"You're a good customer," Andi said.

"Not that. I got Carla's boyfriend off on some trumped up drug charges. I knew the guy who'd ID'd him was lying because I saw him somewhere else when he said he'd seen Carla's guy selling crack. The charges were dismissed, and Carla thinks I walk on water."

"Why'd you leave here?" Andi asked. "You've got friends, connections, as far as I can see your whole life was in Miami. What made you up and leave?"

Greg shrugged. "After Miranda left, I had a coupla really bloody drug killings to clean up. I got sick of it. After the last case, I swore I'd go anywhere. So when Burgess Beach came along, I took it."

Greg ordered for them both, his Spanish not fluent but adequate, and they chatted about Miami while they waited for the food to arrive.

After Andi had eaten enough to quell her hunger pangs, she inquired about what she was eating.

"Stuffed plantains—those big bananas," he said, pointing. "Then *tamal en hoja*—that's a Cuban tamale, and *papas rellanas*—potatoes stuffed with a spicy beef. Like it?"

"Terrific. It's different from the Cuban food in Tampa. That's more Americanized, at least at the restaurants I used to go to."

They left in plenty of time for their meeting with SanAngelo. Andi was nervous, and she wondered how Greg felt about meeting the man who might have killed Miranda.

TWENTY

When Andi and Greg got to the Cuban bar, the place was empty except for a bartender wiping glasses. He looked up at them, still wiping.

Greg guided Andi to a table near the bar where they could keep an eye on the door. Andi said she'd have a club soda, Greg ordered a coke, and they sat quietly sipping their drinks, waiting for Philippe SanAngelo.

At three o'clock exactly, a short, wiry man with a pony tail entered, nodded to the bartender, and headed toward them. He projected an air of strength and controlled menace. As he reached the table, two very large Hispanic men also entered the bar and stood on either side of the door.

"You are Detective Lamont?" he asked. He spoke with a Hispanic accent.

"Yes. This is my partner, Detective Battaglia."

"I am Juan Garcia. I understand you wish to speak to Philippe SanAngelo." He didn't shake hands or sit down.

Andi answered. "Yes. I'm the lead detective on a murder investigation. We're from the Burgess Beach Police Department."

"Did Señor SanAngelo know the person who was murdered?"

"We believe he knew Miranda Duncan. She was murdered at a motel in Burgess Beach on September 27th."

Garcia said nothing, and his face revealed less. Andi couldn't tell if Miranda's name meant anything to him or not. There was a long silence.

Andi finally asked, "Can you arrange for us to talk to Mr. SanAngelo?"

"Wait here." Garcia turned and strode out, followed by the two bodyguards.

In a few minutes, he came back to their table. "Señor SanAngelo will be here in ten minutes."

Garcia left again, followed by the two bodyguards.

Andi looked at Greg. "I guess we're going to meet the great drug dealer. I wonder if he knew Miranda was dead."

Greg shrugged.

They sipped their drinks in silence. They were still the only patrons. No coincidence, Andi thought.

At exactly 3:15, the door of Antonio's opened, and Philippe SanAngelo entered. The picture Joe Patrone had given them had been accurate, as far as it went, but it couldn't show the aura of power that SanAngelo projected. He wore a loose white linen jacket over a pale green t- shirt and white cotton trousers. In his left ear was a small gold earring, and a cross dangled from a fine gold chain around his neck. Garcia followed SanAngelo in and positioned himself half-way between the door and the table where Andi and Greg sat.

SanAngelo walked to Andi and Greg and pulled out a chair. Moving the chair at an angle, he extended a well-manicured hand to them. Then he sat so that he could see his two visitors as well as the door.

"I am Philippe SanAngelo. You wish to talk to me?"

Andi spoke. "I'm a detective with the Burgess Beach Police Department. I want to ask you about a woman who was murdered there last Friday night. I believe you knew Miranda Duncan. When was the last time you saw her?"

SanAngelo didn't look surprised but said nothing, looking first at Andi, then at Greg. When Andi said nothing further, he asked, "Who killed her?"

"We don't know that yet. That's what we're trying to find out. When was the last time you saw Miranda?"

"I don't remember."

"Were you and she living together?"

"I live in many places. Sometimes I was with Miranda."

"Señor SanAngelo, you're not being helpful. If you didn't kill Miranda, then perhaps you have an interest in finding out who did. Were you and Miranda lovers?"

"That is not your business."

Andi sighed. "It is my business. I'm a detective, Miranda was murdered, and it's my job to find out who killed her. Were you and Miranda lovers?"

"We were."

Andi thought she saw a grimace of pain cross SanAngelo's face when he answered her question, but then his face was as impassive as it had been before. Perhaps she had imagined it.

"Miranda had a child, a little girl named Antoinette. Did you know Antoinette?"

"Yes."

"Was Antoinette your child?"

"No."

"Do you know who Antoinette's father was?"

"No."

"Antoinette moved with her nanny from Miami in early May. Did you ask Ms. Duncan where Antoinette had gone?"

"She did not tell me."

"Did you try to find out why she had moved Antoinette?"

"No."

Andi sighed again. "What business are you in in Miami?"

SanAngelo turned to look at her, taking his eyes completely from the door. "Why do you want to know?"

"You're a suspect in the death of Miranda Duncan. We want to know as much as possible about you and to establish whether or not you may have killed her. What is your business?" Andi kept her voice firm and level. This man didn't get intimidated, but she was pretty sure she could get some answers, if only because he wanted to know who had killed Miranda.

"I am a coffee importer."

"Where do you import coffee from?"

Again SanAngelo turned to face her. "I did not kill Miranda."

"That may be true," Andi said, "but I still need to know where you import your coffee from."

"Mexico and Colombia." He settled back into his chair, glancing again at the door of the bar.

"Does your business have an office in Miami or South Beach?"

"Yes." His accent was that of someone who had learned English as a child, not without accent but with the intonation of an upper class Cuban.

"May I have the address?"

He snapped his fingers at Garcia who moved quickly and produced a business card which he gave to SanAngelo. Philippe passed it on to Andi. "My card, Detective."

Andi glanced at the card. It was printed on heavy stock, the company name embossed. There was a street address in Miami, a telephone number and a website address. Under the name "SanAngelo y Co." were the words, "Importers of Fine Coffees."

She wasn't getting much information, Andi thought. She considered. Maybe she could get an alibi at least, possibly eliminate him from consideration, although probably people would lie to protect any alibi he gave her. "Can you tell me where you were on the evening of Friday, September 27th?"

SanAngelo turned to Juan Garcia and held out his hand. Garcia handed him a Blackberry, and SanAngelo glanced down at it. "I was in Miami that night. Miranda was not here, but I was at the Meta Lounge all evening. I believe they will tell you I was there."

"They?"

"Jorge and Bella. They always know when I am there."

"Will they be able to tell me when you left?"

"I always stay until closing at two o'clock."

"Where was Miranda on September 27th?" Andi kept hoping for more information. He certainly gave nothing more than what was asked for.

"Not in Miami. She was gone."

"When did she leave?"

"I do not know." San Angelo rose to his feet, pushed the chair back under the table, and turned to Andi. "Find out who killed her, Detective. She did not deserve to die. And I did not kill her."

Andi stood up. "Just a minute, Senor SanAngelo." To her surprise, he paused as he turned to the door. "Where can I reach you if I need to ask you any further questions?"

SanAngelo said, "You have my card," and turned back toward the door. Juan Garcia and the two bodyguards followed him out of the bar.

Andi looked at Greg. He was staring after SanAngelo, and she thought he must be finding it difficult to picture Miranda in love with this cold amoral man. She could tell that the idea of Miranda that Greg had in his head was very different from what he saw when he pictured her with SanAngelo, but Andi understood how Miranda had been attracted to SanAngelo. He projected an aura of danger and daring that a woman like Miranda—reckless, smarter than almost anyone around her, wanting more out of life than ordinary living offered—might find captivating. Certainly more so than the cautious lawyers and bankers she'd previously been exposed to.

"Damn," she said. "He just walked out."

Greg looked at her. "He's a tough motherfucker."

"Doesn't give an inch. I think he does care who killed Miranda, but he's so busy protecting himself we probably won't learn anything from him. And his alibi isn't ironclad. He could have left Miami, driven to Burgess Beach and killed Miranda that night."

"You're right." He played with his drink, not really listening to her.

Andi wondered how she could tap into SanAngelo's caring enough to get him to let down his guard. He was protected physically by Garcia and his bodyguards, but he also kept his emotions totally under control. But she'd seen a small break in that protective wall. Could she use the feelings he still harbored for Miranda to get him to open up?

She turned to Greg and said, "I guess that's that. Let's go check out SanAngelo's business address. Then I have an appointment with Joe and Angela Ramirez at six. I'll leave you somewhere you can wait for me, and I'll pick you up when I'm through."

"I'd like to see them. Why don't you want me there?"

"You know why." Andi said. "Because you knew them from your time with Miranda. I don't want to fuck up whatever they can tell me about her with their memories of the two of you."

Greg said, "I won't interfere, but I'd like to see them."

Andi looked at him. What the hell was he thinking? If he was Toni's father, Angela might know that. She certainly wouldn't talk about any of Miranda's time with SanAngelo, if she knew about that, with Greg listening. He didn't get it. He didn't even get why Bradley had suspended him.

"No. Absolutely not."

Andi put some money on the table and got to her feet. She turned and strode to the door. Greg followed. They got into the car.

"I won't say anything," he said, "but I want to see them."

"No. You're a principal in this case." Andi started the car and turned to Greg. "You're trying to find out about the baby, about Antoinette, and whether they know who the baby's father is. You can't do that. Don't you get it?"

He didn't say anything, and she knew she'd hit a nerve. "Which way to SanAngelo's business?"

Greg glanced at the business card SanAngelo had given them, then gave her directions. It was after four o'clock, and traffic was heavy, but they didn't have far to go. Neither of them spoke again until they reached SanAngelo's office, which was housed in a small, tan storefront in Little Cuba. Behind the storefront was a warehouse.

Packets of coffee were artfully displayed among a tasteful array of rare orchids in the window of the storefront. Andi parked, and they entered. Inside, the walls held an array of oil paintings in a primitive style. On the left side of the room, an attractive young woman rose from behind a gleaming mahogany desk to greet them.

She was about twenty-five, small and slim and wore a close-fitting beige linen sheath that ended just at her knees. She had light skin, long dark hair held back by combs, and large green eyes. She wore small diamond earrings and a wide gold bracelet on her right wrist. Her left hand held a ring with a large diamond encircled by several smaller diamonds.

The woman extended a beautifully manicured hand to each of them.

"My name is Ana SanAngelo. How may I help you?" she asked, her words very slightly accented.

Andi showed her badge and said she had a few questions about SanAngelo's business, and the woman led them to a small table with four comfortable chairs at the right side of the front door.

"Please sit down. May I give you some coffee? We have just received a shipment from Mexico with a new coffee that has overtones of chocolate. I myself have not yet tried it. Or perhaps you would prefer our dark roast. I have fresh pots of both."

Andi asked, "Are you related to Philippe SanAngelo?"

"You know Philippe?" Ana asked.

"We've met. Are you his sister?"

"I am his wife," she said.

Andi sat back, stunned. Philippe had a wife! Where did Miranda fit into this scenario? She must have known he was married. Did this woman know about Miranda? Andi didn't know where to begin.

Finally she spoke. "We are here to ask about a woman named Miranda Duncan. Do you know Miranda?"

The answer floored Andi. "Of course. Her daughter Toni and my son Diego used to play together often. We have not seen much of them recently, however. Is something wrong?"

"Miranda has been murdered," Andi said.

Ana rose to her feet, her face turned away from them. Her composure seemed to be shaken. "I'm sorry. You did not tell me what kind of coffee you wished to try. Please . . . ." She gestured to the pots.

Andi wanted Ana to sit down and answer their questions, but the woman was already behind a counter at the rear of the room, placing cups on a tray. Greg chose the dark roast, and Andi elected to try the new coffee from Mexico. Ana filled the china cups and set cream and sugar on the small table. When at last they were settled, Ana spoke again.

"You said Miranda was murdered?"

"Yes. She was murdered on September 27th in Burgess Beach. That's where we're from. When did you last see her?"

Ana took a sip of her coffee and paused to think. "I saw her about two weeks ago. I had not seen her much during the summer, and she told me then that she had taken Toni up north somewhere to live. She was sorry Toni and Diego could no longer play together. Have you found out who killed her?"

"No, "Andi answered. "The case is still under investigation. Did she tell you why she moved Toni?"

"She said she wanted a better place for them to live. Miami can be a difficult place to raise children, and Miranda had no family here."

"How did you meet Miranda?" The answer surprised Andi.

"We met at a Mommy and Me class at the YWCA. Toni and Diego are the same age and seemed to get along, so we got them together to play whenever we could."

"Did Miranda tell you anything about the rest of her life?"

"Very little. I think she worked for a lawyer, but she didn't like it much."

"Did she ever talk about going to clubs?"

"No. What clubs?"

"Miranda had a busy night life. I assume you haven't been involved in that because of your son."

"When Philippe is here, I prefer to stay home with him."

"Is Philippe often gone?" Not gone, but out with other women and selling drugs, Andi thought. Was it possible this woman was so unaware of Philippe's life? Maybe this <u>was</u> his real life, and the Philippe who lived with Miranda and sold drugs just his business side.

"Oh, yes. He travels all over for the coffee business. I see him only a few days each month."

"Did your husband know Miranda as well?" Andi asked.

Ana thought for a moment, then said, "I think he met her one day when she brought Toni over to play."

Either Ana was very innocent or a good liar, Andi thought.

"Were you born in Havana like Philippe?"

"No. My parents came in the boat lift in 1980. I was born here."

"How did you meet Philippe? How long have you two been married?"

"Why do you want to know about my husband?"

Andi hesitated, then said, "We're looking at all the people who knew Miranda Duncan in case they can tell us anything that will help us find who killed her."

"Philippe hardly knew her. He could not tell you anything about her." Ana's tone had changed. Either she was protecting her husband from Andi's nosiness or she was covering for him. Andi pushed.

"Perhaps not, but we ask a lot of questions that don't seem relevant, but fit with other information we get. It may seem intrusive, but it is the way the police do their work. So, I'm going to ask again: how did you meet your husband?"

"My Tia Bella introduced us. She is not really my tia, but I have always called her that because she and her husband have been friends of my parents for many years."

"Tia Bella . . . . Is that Belle Acosta?"

"Yes. Have you met her?"

"We've met." And been lied to, Andi thought. Belle Acosta had certainly not been very forthcoming about what she knew. She had said she was Miranda's friend, but she hadn't told Andi and Greg that she knew Philippe or that he was Miranda's lover. Miranda must have known he had a wife and son, but Belle hadn't thought to mention the whole *ménage a trois* to them. And Ana? Was it possible she knew nothing about SanAngelo's drug business? She seemed totally innocent, but maybe she was just a good actress.

Or a murderer.

"Just for the record, would you mind telling me where you were the night of September 27th?" Andi asked.

When Ana found it was a Friday, she said she always left Diego with her parents on Friday night and spent the evening with a group of girlfriends. "We play bunko and gossip," she said with a little laugh. Andi got the names and phone numbers of the other women who had been with Ana SanAngelo that night.

She asked if they might be allowed to see the warehouse, but Ana said she wasn't allowed to let anyone in back because of the insurance. Andi made a note to come back with a warrant, thanked Ana for her time and the coffee, and she and Greg left. It was almost five o'clock.

TWENTY-ONE

"Well, that was a shocker." Andi said as they headed to the Ramirezes, "SanAngelo is a complicated man—drug dealer, coffee importer, Miranda's lover, Ana's husband, father of Diego, some relation to Toni. Who the hell is this guy?"

"And how do Belle and Jorge Acosta fit into SanAngelo's drug business?" Greg had his own questions.

"Maybe more intimately than we thought. This case is getting curiouser and curiouser."

As they got closer to where the Ramirezes lived, Andi asked, "Where can I drop you?"

"There's a coffee shop on the corner here," Greg said. "Sure I can't come along?"

Andi pulled into the parking lot and turned off the engine. "You're kidding, right?"

"Right," Greg said, as he stepped out of the car. "How long do you think you'll be?"

Andi glanced at her watch. "I'll figure to be back in about an hour. Don't think I've deserted you if I'm a little later."

"Okay," Greg said, and Andi headed off to the Ramirezes.

The house was small and well-kept, the lawn green and clipped, the flower beds filled with tropical plants. When Andi rang the bell, the door was opened by a tall man in his mid-forties with a pleasant, open face.

"You must be Detective Battaglia."

"That's right. Burgess Beach Police Department." Andi showed her badge and the man ushered her inside.

The living room was small but tidy and nicely furnished. Everything was in perfect condition, as if the room were used only on special occasions. Most of the living probably took place elsewhere in the house.

A petite woman rose from a chair and stepped forward. "I'm Angela Ramirez. I'm glad to meet you." Angela was older than Miranda, warm and vibrant-looking with no gray in her short dark hair but with a few lines around her eyes. Nice people, Andi thought.

Andi shook Angela's hand and then sat in the chair that Angela indicated.

"What did you want to see us about? Something about Miranda, you said on the phone," Joe Ramirez asked.

"Miranda Duncan was murdered on September 27th. I'm the detective assigned to find her killer."

There was silence for a long moment, then Angela asked, "Murdered? She was murdered?"

Ramirez said nothing. He looked stunned.

"Yes. I was hoping you could tell me something about Miranda and her life in Miami."

Neither of them spoke. They stared at Andi, disbelief and horror playing across their faces.

"That bastard! That bastard killed her!" Angela spoke. "I knew he was dangerous, but she said not to worry." Tears trickled down her cheeks, and she wiped her eyes, then took a tissue from a box next to her.

"Who are you talking about?" Andi asked.

"That drug dealer. Philippe SanAngelo. Son of a bitch." Joe Ramirez's voice was angry, his words almost a growl.

"Miranda told you about her involvement with Philippe SanAngelo?" Andi asked.

"Yes," Angela Ramirez answered, then turned to her husband. "There's no point in trying to hide anything now. Miranda is dead. We need to tell everything we know. We want to know who killed her."

"Miranda doesn't need our protection any more. But what about Toni?"

Andi said, "Toni's living in Burgess Beach now with her nanny. I have patrols checking on the house regularly. I don't think she's in any danger. It's Miranda we need to know about."

"Yes," Angela said, and her husband murmured agreement. She continued, "A little less than five years ago Miranda came to us. She had left that detective she was with, and she was pregnant. She didn't want him to know, and she asked if she could live with us during her pregnancy. She said she would get a job after the baby was born and pay us back. Miranda and I had not been close; but she knew I liked her, and I think she knew we would be willing to help. I told her I would talk to Joe," she indicated her husband, "and let her know. Of course Joe said she was welcome. We have no children, so it was like we were waiting for the birth of a grandchild."

"So she stayed here during her pregnancy? Then after the baby was born, what did she do?"

"She stayed home for a few weeks with Toni. Then she met a woman who knew a nanny, and Miranda hired her and went to work in a bank."

"Was she still staying with you when the nanny was taking care of Toni?"

"For a little while. Then she made enough money—I don't know how she did it—but she managed a place on her own. She did well at the bank. I believe they paid commissions on the accounts she brought in, but that's when she met Philippe, sometime during her first year at the bank when Toni was just a baby. I believe he paid for her apartment."

Andi considered what she knew of Miranda's history. She'd moved in with Kathryn Forbes not long after that, but from what Angela was saying, she'd also maintained another apartment where Toni lived with the nanny and where Philippe spent time. How did she keep everything straight?

Andi asked, "Do you know why she didn't want to stay with the detective—Greg Lamont?"

"She never said. I thought she loved him, and they were together a long time, but then she didn't want him to know about her pregnancy. I found it hard to understand."

"Was Toni his child?"

"I don't know. She never said, but at one point she told me she had been with someone else while she was with Greg or after she left Greg. I'm not sure about that, and she was hard to pin down, but I'm not sure the detective was the father. There was someone else, too."

"What did you think of Greg?"

"He seemed nice enough, although they fought a lot, even when we were around. But Miranda wasn't easy. She fought with a lot of people, including employers."

"Did she ever tell you what she was doing with SanAngelo?"

"What do you mean?" Angela asked.

"I mean, did she have a job with him or were they lovers? Did she tell you anything about their relationship?"

"No. After she met him, we saw her less and less. She had the place in South Beach by then, and she had the nanny. She was doing well at the bank, and . . . we lost touch."

"Do you know anything else about Philippe SanAngelo? Have you ever met him?"

"Miranda invited us to a club one night, and he was there. I thought he was frightening, but Miranda only laughed when I said that. Greg was tough, but he wasn't cruel. SanAngelo seemed cruel. I worried about him, and Miranda knew I didn't like her lifestyle with him, but she refused to listen."

"You and Miranda worked together a while ago, right? Where was that?"

"An insurance company—Mutual Life. We worked in agency: keeping the agents happy, checking commission statements, issuing commission checks. Not bad, but the pay wasn't much. Then she had a fight with a big agent and got fired. After that, she had another job."

"Do you know what the fight was about?"

"He thought he was entitled to more money on his commission check, and he threatened to go to the VP. She told him to go ahead, that the check was right. It was, but he was mad and said she was rude. He demanded she be let go. So she was."

"This was before she lived with Greg, right?"

"I think so."

"Have you seen him since Miranda came to you for help?"

"No." Angela looked inquiringly at Joe, who said, "We haven't seen him since Miranda left him."

"Why do you think someone would kill Miranda?" Andi asked.

"I think it was SanAngelo. He was scary, and Miranda loved danger, but I think she pushed him too far." Joe nodded agreement with what his wife said.

"Is there anything else you can tell me about Miranda?" Andi asked.

"I think we've told you everything we know." Angela looked inquiringly at her husband who nodded his head in agreement.

Andi gave them her card and asked them to call her if they thought of anything else. She thanked them for being so forthcoming about Miranda. Angela asked if she would let them know what progress was made on the investigation, and Andi said they could call her at the phone number on the card. Then she left to pick up Greg Lamont at the coffee shop.

She didn't want to tell him what the Ramirezes had told her, but she knew she had to tell him something about her visit with them. Damn! He had really screwed up this investigation by being in love with the murdered woman.

She thought about what she should tell him. Her first thought was to say nothing because it would only convince him further that Toni was his child, but she also considered how much she needed his help to solve Miranda's murder.

By the time she arrived at the coffee shop, she'd decided to tell him everything they had told her, including that the Ramirezes didn't know who Toni's father was.

Greg greeted her impatiently. "It's nearly seven-thirty. You said an hour."

"Stop," Andi said. "I said I didn't know how long. Let's sit for a minute. I could use some coffee, and we need to talk."

Andi ordered coffee and a sandwich, and Greg got more coffee and pie. He listened as she told him what the Ramirezes had told her.

When she finished, he was quiet for a long time, considering what she had said. Finally he said, "She must be my child. There wasn't anyone else."

Andi considered. "She told Angela there was someone else during or after she left you. So maybe Toni is, maybe not. You told me there were times when Miranda disappeared for days at a time. If she went to some other guy, he could be the father."

"I guess."

"Miranda's the only one who knew for sure, and we can't ask her. You can get a DNA test, I suppose, but what if she's not yours? Then what?"

"I've been thinking about it. A lot. She's gotta be mine."

"Greg," Andi said sharply. "Get over it. Maybe she is, maybe she isn't, but right now we've got to find out who killed her mother."

He didn't reply. After he took a sip of his coffee, he said, "Tell me the rest."

Andi told him about Angela and Joe's belief that SanAngelo had killed Miranda. "They don't even want to consider anyone else. I get it, but the suitcase bothers me."

"Me, too," Greg said. "I guess I'd like it to be SanAngelo. Get him off the streets."

Andi drank the last of her coffee. "We have one more stop to make before we head back to Burgess Beach. I have the address of the apartment Miranda rented in Miami where she lived with Toni. She may have given it up when she moved Toni and her nanny to Burgess Beach, but I'm inclined to think she might have kept it as a refuge."

"Let's go," said Greg.

The apartment was in a two-story building in South Beach but north of the restaurant and club scene. They roused the superintendent, who wasn't thrilled to be disturbed while he was watching what looked like porn on his TV. He let them in and told them to return the key when they were finished.

The place was tiny: living room, bedroom, bath and small kitchen.

The living room had a sofa and a couple of soft chairs facing a television set. Andi headed into the bedroom, which had pink flowered wallpaper and a single bed made up with sheets, pillows and a light blanket. The bed was pushed against one wall, and marks and dust patterns on the floor indicated that another bed and another piece of furniture, maybe a dresser, had been in the room. Andi checked under the bed and between the bed and mattress, but there was nothing. She stripped the bed but found only an oversized t-shirt under the pillow.

Andi considered, speculating. "I'll bet this was Toni's room. Maybe the nanny slept in the room with her. Two beds."

"I'll bet Miranda slept on the couch when she came home," Greg said. "She probably got in late after her clubbing, so she wouldn't want to disturb them."

Greg headed back into the living room. Andi checked the closet. There were a couple of dresses, spangled and very short, two pairs of shoes with very high heels, and a small chest which held underwear, two pairs of jeans and some t-shirts. She checked the bathroom. There was an array of toiletries, probably Miranda's.

Andi wondered if Miranda had a hiding place in the apartment where she might have kept cash or other valuables she might need in case she needed a quick getaway. When she came back into the living room, she found Greg in the kitchen. He had opened the refrigerator, revealing an outdated carton of milk, some containers of yoghurt, and a bedraggled head of lettuce in the cooler. The cupboards were similarly bare and contained only a can of soup and a box of cereal.

"Nothing in the freezer?" Andi asked.

"Nothing."

"There are some clothes in the bedroom closet and toiletries in the bathroom. She planned to come back. Think she had a hiding place here? In the floor, air ducts, I don't know. She must have had some place she stored cash and other valuables in case she needed to get away."

"Let's see."

There were few places in the tiny apartment for hiding anything. They moved the bed, tapped the floors in all the rooms, upended the mattress, checked the ventilation system. Nothing.

"She was a better hider than I am a finder," Andi said. "Let's check the bed again."

And they found it: a slash in the box spring that had been sewn together. It was closed so carefully they nearly missed it.

Greg cut the stitches with his knife, put his hand into the opening and pulled out a small box. He pried it open with the knife. Inside was a roll of cash and a passport in the name of Margaret Agnes Whitlock, born March 15, 1976, in Sebastian, Florida. The passport was issued on July 15, 1999. The woman in the passport picture was Miranda.

Greg stared at the picture. It was Miranda, but not the Miranda in the morgue and not the one Greg remembered. Nor did she seem to be the Miranda that everyone in South Beach knew as Red. Her hair was red but short, not the luxuriant mane of her later picture. She wore no makeup, and the striking green eyes receded in the picture to pale blurs. Margaret had become Miranda sometime between July of 1999 and the time Greg had met her in 2000.

"I guess this is the original Miranda," Andi said. "She did a heck of a job transforming herself."

"I met her two years after this passport was issued. She looked like the Miranda in the morgue photo by then. She was working as a paralegal for the Miami D.A."

"Well, we found the hiding place. We'd better get going. I don't think we need to tell the super about our find."

"No. He won't care. Let's just put the bed back together."

It was after ten o'clock by the time they got back in the car. Andi thought about going to the Meta Lounge to see the

Acostas, but decided against it. She was tired, and she needed to be alert when she challenged their lies and omissions. Besides, at the club, the Acostas would be on their own turf.

"Do you think we can use an interview room at the South Miami station where we saw Joe Patrone?" Andi asked. "We're going to need to see Belle and Jorge Acosta again, and I'd like to interview them out of their element."

"I'll call Joe in the morning."

Andi had a lot to think about. Miranda was still a mystery. Every time they uncovered one aspect of her life, another part showed up. Had she known about Philippe's wife? The Acostas knew about Philippe's wife. Did they also know about Miranda's drug whoring? Were they part of it? And what was in the suitcase and where was it? And for that matter, where had Margaret Agnes Whitlock come from?

Everyone they'd talked to today had lied about something. She needed to find out what they'd lied about and why.

TWENTY-TWO

Andi and Greg were quiet on the drive home to Burgess Beach. Andi was tired, and she was glad when she saw they were nearly home. A car behind them had its brights on, nearly blinding her. She turned the rear view mirror to deflect them, but they still reflected brightly in her side view mirror. The car was big and close. An SUV, she thought, dark. Andi felt a twinge of apprehension. Why was it so close?

"Greg," she said. "That car behind us. It's too close."

Greg had been dozing. He started awake and turned his head. "It's right on your bumper. It's tailing us. Can you lose it?"

Why would it be tailing us? Andi's heart was beating fast. She stepped hard on the gas—seventy, eighty, ninety—but the big car kept pace, always just behind her rear bumper, its bright lights nearly blinding her. She clutched the steering wheel, willing herself to stay calm, to drive carefully.

Greg pulled out his phone, then said, "Shit. We're in a dead area. There's an exit coming up. Get off. Maybe we can lose him."

"No. That road only goes toward the ocean. It's all dunes, no houses. There's nowhere to hide."

"Just keep going then, stay in the center. I'll try the phone again."

There was no other car on the road, and none passed them going the other way. The road was empty except for Andi and Greg and the big SUV.

"Still no service," Greg said.

'I'm going to slow down. See what he does.' Andi took her foot off the gas and let the vehicle slow to sixty. The car behind them slowed down as well, hugging her bumper. Then suddenly it sped up, bumped her rear bumper hard once, then again.

"Shit," she said. She pressed her foot to the gas pedal 'til they reached a hundred miles an hour. The car stayed behind her, close, but with a distance between them.

Then the lights behind them disappeared. She was relieved for a moment not to have those beams glaring in her eyes. Then she realized the SUV had pulled up next to them on her right. She clutched the steering wheel. At this speed she didn't dare take her eyes from the road. She heard a sharp crack.

"Jesus Christ, they're shooting at us!" Greg shouted. "Drop back. See if you can get behind them."

As she put on the brakes, she heard another crack. "Damn," Greg said.

"Are you hurt?" Andi asked as she slowed to seventy, then sixty. The SUV slowed as well, but she managed to pull her car in behind it.

"My arm," he said. "Not bad."

She didn't want to take her eyes off the road. She stared ahead. Dark SUV, she thought, blue or black. She could see the license plates. She repeated the numbers to herself: Florida plates, 234867.

The SUV was trapped in front of them. The driver tried to slow to get next to them, but Andi kept her car behind theirs. Then she saw an exit she knew, one that led to residential streets and then Highway 1A. She slowed even more, then veered to the right and exited. The SUV couldn't get off the interstate in time.

"The next exit is at least another two miles," she said. "How's your arm?"

"Hurts, but I think it's only a flesh wound," Greg said. "Good job. Where are we?"

"Cove Road. South end of Stuart. By the time he turns around and tries to find us, we'll be home."

"They—whoever they are—could be waiting at either of our homes," Greg said. "I don't think this was a random attack. It was meant for us."

"But who?" Andi asked.

Jim? Could it have been Jim? But he wouldn't try to kill her. Might he try to kill another man she was with? No. That wasn't a possibility.

"Take your pick. We have the drug lord, whoever took the suitcase, even the Acostas—any one of them might not want us messing around."

"We must have stirred something up."

"I guess. Maybe this was a warning."

"Can you shoot someone from a moving car and be sure you don't kill him?" Andi asked. "Seems like a real circus trick." They were traveling through a residential neighborhood that

Andi knew well. She made turns and more turns, keeping an eye on the road behind her, but there were no other cars. Her heart slowed to a more normal pace.

"I'm going to turn onto 1A and pull into the first gas station I see. We'll take a look at your arm, then decide what to do next."

Greg didn't answer. Andi found a gas station in the first block after she turned north. She pulled into a well-lighted area away from the pumps and said, "Okay. Let's see your arm."

Greg turned toward her and extended his right arm, wincing. He had managed to staunch the bleeding by stuffing a handkerchief into the wound. The bullet had hit above Greg's elbow, and although it had bled profusely, the bullet seemed to have passed through flesh and not damaged the bone or other tissue.

"I think I can bandage this up," Andi said. "It'd be better if we don't go to the emergency room. You're not supposed to be with me. Better to keep it quiet. Okay with you?"

"Sure."

"If they're following anyone, it's probably me." Andi paused for a moment, thinking about Jim. "I've got an ex-boyfriend hanging around."

"Let's go to my place." He directed her to his gated development, got out and pressed in the code that opened the gate. No one followed them to the complex, and the gate closed behind them.

Andi parked her car, grabbed her purse and when Greg didn't move, went around to help him out of the passenger seat.

"Sorry. Feeling a little woozy," he said.

"I'll get you inside," Andi said. "Which apartment's yours?"

"Right here. First floor. Number Five."

"Gimme the key."

Greg handed Andi the key, and she opened the door.

Andi asked, "You have bandages and peroxide or some other cleansing solution?"

"Whatever I've got's in the bathroom."

Andi found iodine and bandages and cleansed the wound, which was minor but bloody, then wrapped it in gauze.

"Okay. Got anything to drink?"

"In the cabinet under the TV."

She opened the cabinet door, pulled out a bottle of single malt Scotch whiskey and poured a shot into a glass. She gave this to Greg, then poured another for herself.

"Better," he said.

"Much better," she answered. She went back to the cabinet and poured each of them another shot.

Andi sat and sipped her drink. She could already feel the effects of the first one and thought to herself, "Be careful," but she kept sipping anyway.

"How's the arm?" she asked Greg.

"Numb," he answered. "I guess it's okay."

"Who do you think was in the SUV?" she asked,

"It could be any of those people we saw today. It seemed designed to scare us off, but the shots were serious."

"I'll say," she answered. "That wasn't just a scare."

"What next?" Greg asked. "Should we—or you—go to Sebastian to find out where Miranda came from or back to Miami to figure out who was lying?"

"They were all lying, except maybe the Ramirizes. They didn't seem to have anything to gain. But Philippe, his wife and the Acostas all told us stories that don't check out.

But first, I'd like to know about Sebastian. It's a whole new angle on Miranda and where she came from."

"I agree," Greg said.

"Will you come with me?"

"Couldn't keep me away. I don't know the Miranda in the photo."

"Okay. I have to bring the Captain up to date and tell him where I'm going. I just hope he won't suggest I take Garcia with me."

Greg moved cautiously and winced. "I'm getting sleepy." Greg said. "Are you ready for bed? I'll get you some sheets and pillows for the couch."

"I'm tired, and I can feel those drinks," Andi answered. "Just tell me where everything is, and I'll get what I need. Do you have a spare toothbrush?"

"Hall closet for sheets, blankets and towels. Toothbrush . . . in the medicine cabinet.

Andi came back with bedding, towels and the toothbrush and shooed Greg off to bed. As she made up the couch, she thought about the day. She and Greg were together now on Miranda's story, but she still worried whether Greg was concealing anything.

She slept restlessly, tossing and turning on the couch and dreaming about cars and head-on collisions. When she woke at seven, she didn't feel as though she'd slept. She wanted to do her morning run, but she had no clean clothes and would have to wear the ones she'd worn to Miami. Fortunately no one at work had seen her yesterday morning.

She wandered into the kitchen, fished around in the cupboards and found coffee and filters for the coffee pot. She opened the refrigerator and eyed its meager contents: a stale loaf of bread, a jar of jam, butter in a dish, a jar of peanut butter, and a quart of milk. She made a peanut butter and jam sandwich. The coffee tasted good, and by the time Greg arose at eight, she was ready for a shower.

Greg entered the kitchen and sniffed the coffee. "You found everything?"

"Yep. Now I need a shower."

"More towels, if you need 'em, in the hall closet. Not much food in the house."

"It's okay. I had peanut butter and jelly."

After she had showered and dressed in yesterday's clothes, she returned to the kitchen. Greg was still dawdling over a cup of coffee.

"I'll check out a car from the pool and come by to pick you up around ten."

Greg grunted assent, and she headed out to police headquarters. She dictated her notes from the interviews of the day before, aware as she did so how many pieces of contradictory information the notes contained. It was clear people were lying to her. Then she headed to the Captain's office, knocked and at his "Enter," opened the door.

"Well, we thought you'd left us," Captain Bradley said.

"No, sir. I've been dictating my notes, but I thought you should know somebody attacked my car on the way back from Miami last night. A big SUV. Bumped into me, then, I'm pretty sure, fired a couple of bullets. I lost them at the edge of Stuart and got home okay."

"You should have come to the station after you were attacked. Why didn't you?"

"I was pretty scared. I just went home, but I thought you should know."

"Damn straight I should know. Do you know who it was?"

"I stirred up a bunch of people in Miami yesterday. People have been lying to me, as you'll be able to see from my notes. It could have been anybody. I got a license plate: Florida plate 234867."

"I'll have it checked out, but you need a bodyguard, Battaglia."

"No, sir. I'll be fine on my own." She winced at the thought of Garcia accompanying her everywhere. "I have a lead on the murder victim in Sebastian. I want to go there today."

"Alone?"

"Yes, sir. I'll be okay." She couldn't say she already had a partner.

"You need any help from Garcia?"

"He's helping me by handling the burglary on Hutchinson Island."

"Where's the file on that?"

"He's got it."

"Okay. Let me know if you need help. Be careful, detective."

"Thanks. I will." Andi left the office.

She called the three women who had been playing bunko with Ana SanAngelo, but two calls went to answering machines and one didn't answer. The forensic report was in on the Hibiscus Motel. No fingerprints, but there were footprints that could be identified in the blood on the floor next to Miranda's body. Two footprints, both small, each from a different shoe. Two people? Maybe.

Then she spent a few minutes on the computer checking for Whitlocks in the Sebastian area. There were four, all of them north and west of the city. There was no listing for Margaret Agnes Whitlock, but there was one for Agnes Whitlock in Little Hollywood, and another for James Whitlock in Roseland. Two other Whitlocks had post office boxes in Brevard County. She printed out names, addresses and phone numbers and headed back to Greg's place. She pressed the button at the gate for his apartment number, and he buzzed her in. Maybe this was what she needed. A gated complex might keep Jim out.

Andi brought Greg up to date about her meeting with the Captain, and then they were quiet on the drive north and west to Sebastian. Brevard and Indian River counties were more rural than the area around Burgess Beach, but even the formerly unbroken stretches of green along the highway were now giving way to one development and strip mall after another.

Most of the houses were crowded onto scraps of land stripped of their native foliage and dotted with tiny lawns. Sebastian called itself "The Crown Jewel of the Treasure Coast," and real estate sale signs shouted slogans about "Celebrating the Good Life," and "Finding Your Haven in the Sunshine."

When they reached Sebastian, Andi plugged the address for Agnes Whitlock into the GPS. The house was in an older area of Hollywood, north and west of Sebastian. It was in a neighborhood of homes that probably dated from the fifties when the first waves of northern retirees had begun to move to Florida. The houses were built on large, irregular-sized lots set back from the two-lane road and without close neighbors. Agnes Whitlock's house was invisible from the road, and a narrow driveway led them to a small house almost overwhelmed by the trees and shrubs that surrounded it. Andi parked the car next to an old station wagon, and they headed toward what appeared to be the front door.

There was no bell, so she knocked loudly. There was no answer.

"Out?" Greg asked.

"Probably."

They peered through the window next to the door into a large kitchen. The sink was piled high with dirty dishes. Two cats slept on the table to the right of the door amid a tangle of mail, catalogs and newspapers.

Andi knocked again, more loudly. A cat raised its head, yawned and went back to sleep. Finally Greg circled to the left of the front door and Andi walked to the right along a narrow pathway that kept the shrubbery at bay. They met in the back, next to a screened swimming pool black with algae.

Greg spoke first. "There are two bedrooms on the left side, both empty, as far as I can see. Looks like a bathroom in between."

"Living room, and another bedroom, probably a bathroom, on this side. I didn't see any signs of life."

"Try the neighbors?" Greg asked.

"I guess."

As they turned to leave, they heard the sound of a car. They listened to the engine shut off, a car door slam, and then watched a woman plod along the path toward the house. She was tall, and probably two hundred pounds overweight. Her sandy hair was thin. She wore a flowered house dress and carried a plastic shopping bag.

"Who the hell're you?" she barked from ten feet away. The jowls of her many chins wobbled as she walked. Her accent sounded like pure Appalachia to Andi.

"We're with the Burgess Beach Police Department." Andi displayed her badge and waited until the woman got close enough to see it.

The woman peered at the badge. "Whadda ya want?"

"Are you Agnes Whitlock?"

"Yep. Whadda ya want?"

"Do you know a woman named Margaret Agnes Whitlock?"

"Why?" The woman set down her shopping bag and fished around in the pocket of her house dress for a set of keys.

"We're looking for Ms. Whitlock's family. We believe she may have been from the Sebastian area. Do you know her?"

"The bitch was my daughter, and I don't know nothin' 'bout her." She shuffled past Andi and put one of the keys in the lock. She pushed the door open and picked up her shopping bag with a grunt.

"Your daughter is dead, Ms. Whitlock. We're here to find out what we can about her."

"She been dead to me a long time, Officer." She stepped into the kitchen, but before she could close the door, Andi put her foot in the doorway.

"Your daughter was murdered. We're trying to find out who killed her."

"Find somebody else." The woman stepped into the kitchen, dropped the shopping bag, and when she realized she couldn't close the door, lumbered into the living room without looking back.

"Now what?" asked Andi

Greg shrugged. "You're the boss."

Andi followed Agnes Whitlock out of the kitchen into a living room that smelled of cat.

Every surface was covered with clothing, newspapers, magazines and unopened mail, all liberally sprinkled with cat hair. The woman threw a pile of newspapers and, judging from the sounds of indignation, a cat off the sofa and sat down, her arms folded across her chest, her several chins quivering.

"I told 'ya I don't know nothin' 'bout that bitch. Ain't seen her in years. Don't wanna see her neither."

"Is there anyone else who might be able to tell us more about your daughter?"

Agnes sat for what seemed a long time. She stared over Andi's head toward a window that faced onto a wall of greenery. Then, to Andi's discomfort, the huge woman began to cry, tears running down her cheeks and dripping onto her gigantic bosom. "Who kilt her?"

"We don't know that yet. We only found out her real identity yesterday."

"Who she bein'?" Agnes asked as she pawed into the pocket of her dress, apparently looking for a handkerchief. Her hand emerged empty.

Andi took a packet of tissues from her purse and handed them to her. "In Miami, she was known as Miranda Duncan. She took that name back in 2000."

Agnes Whitlock continued to cry, mopping tears with the tissues and blowing her nose. Finally she said, "I cain't talk 'bout her. Go see her daddy." She clasped her arms around herself and rocked forward and back, moaning. Finally she stopped and sat quiet, her head bent down. It looked as though her eyes were closed, but Andi couldn't see her face. She waited, hoping the woman would pull herself together. She thought about Antoinette, Miranda's daughter. She didn't think Agnes was up to hearing about her right now. Maybe later.

After several minutes, Andi asked, "Are you all right, Ms. Whitlock?"

The quiet continued, then Agnes drew a shuddering breath and raised her head. She stared out the window again, not meeting Andi's eyes.

"Her daddy kin talk to you. James Whitlock's his name. He seen her after me and kin maybe tell you somethin'."

"There's a James Whitlock who lives at 1534 Hibiscus in Roseland. Is that Margaret's father?"

Agnes Whitlock emitted a shuddering breath. "Yeah. He loved her."

"I think you loved her, too."

Agnes Whitlock was silent again, as if gathering her thoughts. "Maybe so. She went off with that colored man, though. I caint never forgive that."

"Thank you, Ms. Whitlock. We'll be in touch."

Andi rose and stood for a minute, looking down at the woman. Agnes' eyes gazed straight ahead.

Andi collected herself and returned to the kitchen, where Greg was waiting for her, petting one of the cats sleeping on the table.

"Cat lover?" Andi inquired, as she opened the outside door. Greg followed her back to the car, another cat following him down the path.

"Animal lover," he replied with a half smile. "My dog died just before I left Miami. I took that as a sign."

Andi beeped the car open. "A sign of what? That you should leave?"

"Yeah, I guess."

"Better get another dog so you can stay in Burgess Beach." She went around to the driver's side and entered.

Greg buckled his seat belt. "What'd the lovely Ms. Whitlock have to say?"

"She's really busted up about Miranda's death, but she doesn't want to talk. Said we should see the father, James Whitlock, in Roseland. So I guess that's where we're headed.

"I didn't tell her about Antoinette. I thought telling her about Margaret's death was probably all she could take right now."

Greg looked surprised but said nothing.

Following directions from the GPS, Andi drove south from Little Hollywood to Roseland, an area of homes abutting the Sebastian Municipal Airport. James Whitlock's house lay at the end of a cul-de-sac. Small planes were tethered on the other side of the chain link fence that separated his land from the airport property. The end of a runway lay just beyond those.

"Noisy, I'll bet," Greg said.

"Maybe. But I don't think it's a very busy airport."

The house was identical to the others on the block, although the Whitlock house was the best maintained. It looked freshly painted, tan with terra cotta trim; the lawn was green and well-groomed, and there were lush tropical plantings in beds close to the front door.

"James and Agnes seem to have a disagreement about living conditions," Andi observed.

"No wonder they don't live together."

Andi rang the bell and heard footsteps approaching the door. The door opened slightly, held by a chain, and a man in his sixties with a trim beard peered out.

"May I help you?" His speech was cultivated and sounded as if he came from well north of the Mason-Dixon line. He and Agnes were an odd pair indeed.

Andi displayed her badge and said they were there to talk to him about his daughter, Margaret.

"Margaret? Is she in trouble?"

"May we come in, Mr. Whitlock?" Andi asked.

"Sorry. Of course." The door closed, then reopened without the chain, and Whitlock motioned them to come in. He was probably half the size of his wife, his full head of hair graying over his ears. His posture was very straight, and his movements those of a man much younger than he.

"Please come in and sit down." He motioned for them to sit on the sofa, and he sat in a comfortable-looking chair that faced the television. "May I get you something? I can make coffee if you'd like."

Andi asked for water, and Greg said he didn't want anything. Whitlock brought Andi a glass of water and sat down.

"What's happened to Margaret? I haven't seen her in a long time. Is she in trouble?"

"I'm sorry to have to tell you your daughter was murdered. She was killed in Burgess Beach."

Andi always found this the hardest part—the flat statement of death she had to give to family who had no idea of what had happened. No one ever really thought they wouldn't see a family member again, even if they were estranged and hadn't been seen in ten or twenty years, even if their last contact was a vicious quarrel. Always, they were sure they would make up, see their child or husband or lover again, tell them how much they loved them. It was just a matter of time. But time passed and often, like now, death intervened.

"Margaret was murdered?" Whitlock leaned forward in his chair, his gaze focused on Andi. "Who would kill her?"

"We don't know that yet, Mr. Whitlock. We're here because Margaret was living in Miami under another name, and we've just found out her real identity. What can you tell us about her and about when you last saw her?"

"What was she doing in Miami? You said she was murdered in Burgess Beach." He shifted his gaze to Greg, then back to Andi.

Andi knew she needed to take control or Whitlock would be the only one getting answers. "I'll try to answer your questions later, Mr. Whitlock. First, can you tell us about your daughter and the last time you saw her."

His shoulders slumped, and he dropped his gaze to his hands clasped in his lap. "Yes, of course. I'll tell you what I know." He pulled a crisply ironed white handkerchief from his pocket and wiped his eyes. "Margaret was very smart, but she got in trouble a lot because she was bored." His voice dropped, and Andi had to strain to hear him. "Her mother and I . . . well, we had our differences and decided to live apart when Margaret was twelve and her sister was ten."

Andi jumped in. "Excuse me. Margaret had a sister?"

"Yes. She was two years younger than Margaret. Her name was Mary. She was born with a number of birth defects. We all loved her. She couldn't go to school and was at home with Agnes most of the time. She died when she was fourteen." Whitlock blew his nose and wiped his eyes, then returned his gaze to his clasped hands.

"Margaret was sixteen then?" Andi asked.

"Yes. Before Mary died, Margaret had her troubles at school, but after Mary's death, she cut school and began to hang out with a rough crowd in Fort Pierce. She had a driver's license by then and pretty much did what she wanted. She wouldn't listen to either her mother or me. She blamed us for Mary's death, although she knew we'd done everything we could." He wiped his eyes.

"Who did she live with after you and your wife split up?" Andi took a sip of water.

"She lived with me most of the time. Mary stayed with her mother, and Margaret spent time there as well." James Whitlock tucked the handkerchief back into his pocket and cleared his throat.

No one spoke for a moment, then Andi asked, "What happened after Mary died, Mr. Whitlock?

"Margaret was expelled. They said she could finish her G.E.D. at a continuation school, but she wouldn't go. She passed the exam when she was a little over sixteen." In spite of his sorrow, there was a hint of pride when Whitlock spoke of how smart Margaret was.

"Did she leave home then?"

"Yes. After she was expelled, her mother and I tried to talk to her, but she wouldn't listen. She left and went to live with some guy in Fort Pierce. She was using drugs then, I'm pretty sure." Whitlock took out his handkerchief again and mopped his eyes.

"Mrs. Whitlock said something about a black man she left with? Do you know who that was?"

"He was part of the crowd she'd been hanging out with. His name was . . . ." Whitlock paused for a moment, thinking. "I didn't think I'd ever forget his name. I hated him. So did Agnes. We blamed him for everything, but I know now she was just using him to get away from us. Gary Johns. That's his name."

"Do you know how long she stayed with him?" Greg asked, stepping in for the first time.

"I think she left him pretty quick. She got a job—waiting tables, I think—then enrolled in the two-year college in Fort Pierce. She came here to see me a couple of times. That was when she told me she'd left that guy. She said she was living with another woman in Fort Pierce, but I never met any of her friends. I don't know if she was telling the truth or not."

"Did you ever meet Gary Johns?"

"No. I saw him once in the car. That's how I knew he was black."

"When was the last time you saw Margaret?" Andi asked.

"About ten years ago. She came to say good-bye. She wouldn't tell me where she was going, just said she was leaving."

"Do you have any idea where we might find Gary Johns?"

"Sorry. No. Tell me what happened to her, Detective. I've told you everything I know."

Andi, with some help from Greg, told James Whitlock what they knew of Margaret's death and her life in Miami as Miranda Duncan.

Then Andi said, "There's something I didn't tell your wife because I thought she was too upset when I talked to her. Margaret has a daughter named Antoinette. She's about three years old and lives in Burgess Beach with a nanny." She wondered how James Whitlock would take this news.

"A daughter? I have a grandchild? That's wonderful." For the first time, Whitlock looked up and smiled.

Andi said, "We could go back to see your wife and tell her, if you think she would be ready for the news."

"You'd better let me tell her, Detective. Will we be able to see the child? Who's the father? Not that drug lord in Miami, is it?" He was bubbling over with questions, his face alight.

"We don't know who the father is." Andi could feel Greg stirring next to her and willed him to keep his mouth shut. "And I'm not sure when you can see her. I need to talk with my captain about that, but if you'll tell Mrs. Whitlock about the child, I'm sure she'll be glad to hear it from you."

Andi realized how complicated the story was getting. The Whitlocks were Antoinette's grandparents, and they had rights, but she wanted to find out who had killed their daughter before she involved them in the child's life.

Finally Andi and Greg told Whitlock how sorry they were for his loss, and Andi left a card for him to call her if he thought of anything else. Then they headed off to Fort Pierce.

Back in the car, Andi said, "I feel totally washed out. What an emotional rollercoaster this case is."

Greg said, "I lived with Miranda all those years, and I never knew her real name? It all fits, though. She was smart, that's for sure. And she could care less about anybody she thought wasn't as smart as she was. Everything fits except the depression. She had some black days when we were together, but Whitlock didn't mention that."

"Maybe that came on later." Andi said, then asked Greg to plug the Fort Pierce Police Station into the GPS.

"I don't even know where Fort Pierce is," Greg said.

"You've been there for autopsies, I know. That's where the Medical Examiner is."

"You're right, but I never went anywhere except to the M.E.'s office."

Andi was quiet for a minute, paying attention to getting back to a main thoroughfare and avoiding the many dead end streets that ended at the airport. "That's up by the college. I haven't been in much of the rest of Fort Pierce, either. I'm not sure where the police department is."

"They'll probably have something on this Gary Johns, if he was involved in drugs. Maybe even Miranda—Margaret. I can't think of her as Margaret Whitlock."

"She wasn't Margaret by the time you knew her. She'd become a whole different person."

At the Fort Pierce Police Station, Andi showed her badge and asked for the duty officer. A tall man in uniform came out and introduced himself as Sergeant Mattison. He led them back to an open area crowded with desks. Once they were seated, Andi told Mattison who they were looking for.

"Names aren't familiar, but that doesn't necessarily mean much. I'll check the computer." Mattison pulled up Gary Johns' name, and read through the material, then beckoned to Andi and Greg to come around behind him to see the screen.

"It looks like Johns is still around. Three arrests for possession of marijuana, one for pimping and two for possession with intent to sell. No convictions. Last arrest was about a year ago."

"Wonder why he was never convicted. Can you tell if he was charged?" Andi asked.

"I'd have to look at the court files to find that out."

"What about Margaret Whitlock?" Greg asked. Andi glanced at him as he peered over Mattison's shoulder at the computer screen. His face was impassive, and he held his body rigid as if he were afraid any movement might give something away.

"Margaret Whitlock is in the system, but there haven't been any entries since late 1998."

"For?" The word came out as a croak. Greg coughed and cleared his throat.

"Let's see. Possession of half an ounce of marijuana. Charged with possession but no intent to sell. She was given a suspended sentence."

"What about probation?" Greg asked. He cleared his throat again.

"Let's see." Mattison tapped away at the keyboard, clearing the screen and entering another set of files. "Ah, here we go. Margaret Whitlock reported once to her probation officer, then never came back. The probation officer apparently didn't follow up."

"What was the date of her first visit with him?" Greg again.

"Her. Gloria Gonzales. January 7, 1999. Nothing since then."

"Is Gloria Gonzales still around?" Andi asked. She probably wouldn't remember Margaret, but it was a loose end.

"I can check," Mattison said.

He put in a call to Human Resources while Andi and Greg went back to sit in the chairs opposite the desk. They could hear Mattison's voice but not what he was saying. He waited without speaking for several minutes, and when he came back to them, he said, "Gloria Gonzales retired in 2005 and moved to South Carolina. I have an address and phone number if you want to call her."

Andi got that information, then asked if he had a current address for Gary Johns. He gave that to them as well, they thanked him and left.

The area where Gary Johns lived was littered with small, dilapidated houses in yards where grass was a long-forgotten memory. Judging from the people on the street, the population of the area seemed to be mostly African-American. A few stopped to stare as they drove by, but mostly they were ignored.

The address they had been given for Johns looked deserted. It had been painted a bright yellow, but the paint was mostly chipped away. The front door opened directly onto the yard, but the steps that had led up to it were gone.

Andi and Greg parked in front, locked the car and headed up the broken concrete walkway. There was no bell, and the door was several steps above the level of the walkway. Andi considered how to knock. Even for Greg, who was several inches taller than she, it would be a stretch to reach the bottom third of the door.

"Let's try the back," Greg suggested.

They walked through the dusty yard, disturbing a dog tied next door that barked at them furiously. The back door was close enough to the ground for Andi to knock, but there was no answer.

Andi knocked again but got no response. A woman came out of the house next door and yelled at the dog to be quiet. Then she turned to Andi and Greg and asked, "What you want here?" Her tone wasn't friendly. She was in her fifties, Andi thought, her skin a light shade of cocoa, and she was wearing a faded house dress covered by an equally faded apron. A kerchief was tied around her hair.

"We're looking for Mr. Johns—Gary Johns." Greg stepped toward the woman as he answered.

"You the po-lice?" she asked.

"We're trying to find a woman who used to live here, maybe nine or ten years ago," Andi said. "Her name was Margaret. A white woman with red hair."

"Why you lookin' fer her?" She turned to the dog who had begun barking again and shushed him loudly.

"We're trying to find her for her parents," Andi lied.

"She long gone," the woman said. "Gary—he live now with Sophie."

"Does Sophie live in Fort Pierce?"

"Sure. She gotta fancy house. He live in her house."

"Do you know where Sophie lives or what her last name is?"

"She gotta big house by the beach."

"Do you know Sophie's last name?"

"Naw. Just Sophie. Gary know, I bet."

Andi took a twenty dollar bill out of her wallet, not offering it to the woman but being sure she could see it. "Do you know where the house is, Ma'am?"

The woman eyed the money, then said, "I don' know the address, but I kin show ya, you want."

"You'll come with us?" Andi asked. This was better than she'd hoped.

"Sure. You gotta bring me back, though. Bus don't run good."

"Of course," Andi said. "Will you meet us out front by our car?"

The woman yelled again at the dog, then went back inside her house.

"Let's hope we get something for our money," Andi said.

They waited for the woman by the car. When she arrived, she had taken off her apron but otherwise looked no different than she had before.

"What's your name?" Andi asked, as she opened the rear door for her.

"I'm Rashida."

"I'm Andi and this is Greg," extending a handshake to the woman over the seat back.

Rashida directed them to the road that ran along the beach, and about a mile up toward the center of Fort Pierce, she pointed out a large house on the side of the road that backed on the water. "That the place," Rashida said. "He livin' high."

"I guess so," Andi said. "Sophie's got a lot of money?"

Rashida shrugged. "Don' know. Gotta big house, and Gary say he living in paradise."

"That's what he said to you?" Andi asked.

"Uh, huh," Rashida said, her eyes focused on the mansion with its big front lawn and a wing on either side. The house was two stories, and Andi would bet the view of the ocean out the back would be spectacular. It was a far cry from Rashida's slum dwelling.

"Okay, Rashida. Thank you. Let's take you home." Andi handed Rashida the twenty, then pressed another into her hand.

They dropped Rashida off at her house, then went back to Sophie's. There was no answer to the doorbell. They walked down the driveway and saw two cars in the garage, but it was a four-car garage, so there was no telling where Gary Johns or Sophie might be.

Andi glanced at her watch. "It's after two. We could have lunch at Mangrove Mattie's, and try again after we eat. It's not far."

Greg agreed, and they headed down the coast. The day was beautiful, cool and bright, and the drive cleared Andi's head. There was so much to think about, so many tentacles to the story of Margaret/Miranda that she needed time to sort things out.

As they pulled into the parking lot, Andi said, "If there's no answer at Sophie's when we get back there, I vote we head back to Burgess Beach. I need to write up my notes, and I definitely need some time to think about what we've got."

"I'm with you."

Andi ordered the shrimp Caesar salad and Greg the crab cakes. They didn't talk about the case, just exchanged comments about the food and the view. The ocean was quiet and very blue with small whitecaps bubbling up on the white sand beach.

When they left the restaurant, it was three o'clock, and Andi drove back to Sophie's house. There was still no answer at the door, so they started back to Burgess Beach. Andi was glad not to have anything more to think about.

TWENTY-THREE

Andi dropped Greg at his apartment, then went to the station to dictate her notes. Then she pulled out a yellow legal pad, sat with the crime book and tried to outline the details of the murder. When she had the names of the players listed, she wrote her questions as they came up.

- What was in the suitcase and where was it now?
- Why was it so heavy? She made an assumption that the suitcase had, at some point, contained drugs or money. If the drug was marijuana, the suitcase wouldn't have been so heavy. If it was cocaine, it would, but if it was money from a drug sale, it would really be heavy. Guns didn't seem to make sense. One suitcase of guns wasn't a shipment and wouldn't yield that much money.
- So the next question had to be: Was the suitcase taken before or after a drug drop?
- Did Miranda know about Philippe's wife? If the Acostas knew, had they told Miranda? Did Philippe's

wife know about Miranda? She didn't seem to, but she could be lying.

- Did Coral Isaacson and her husband know more about Philippe SanAngelo? Andi didn't think so.
- What more could Gary Johns tell them about Margaret, her past identity and where she was now?
- How had Margaret so completely changed her identity that no one had ever questioned that she was Miranda? She'd worked for a law firm and even as an extra-help paralegal for the Miami D.A. That was where Greg had met her. How did she get the job? Had the D.A. even checked her references?
- How did Nick Oldham figure into all of this? Was he the money behind Miranda's drug sales?

Andi paused and dropped her head onto her desk. There were certainly more questions than answers in this case, and now she had a terrible headache. Better go home.

When she reached her apartment, she was so exhausted that she barely looked around as she headed upstairs and opened the door. Then, as she inserted the key, she was suddenly shoved against the door and into her living room, knocked so off balance that she nearly fell. She grabbed hold of a chair and managed to keep herself upright, but she was stunned and scared.

"What the hell?" she screamed.

"Where the hell you been?" Jim's voice was angry and his face bright red. He looked enormous standing in the doorway, silhouetted by the outside light.

"Oh, for God's sake," Andi said. "You?" She was scared, but she was so tired that her first response wasn't fear but anger.

"Whadda 'ya mean, you?" Jim asked. "Where the hell have you been? You never came home last night." He slammed the door closed behind him.

Andi switched on a table lamp. "Are you crazy? What the hell are you doing here?" she asked.

Jim hadn't moved from the doorway. He looked dumbfounded by her anger. "Where have you been?" he demanded, but his voice had lowered in volume and intensity.

"I've been working, goddamnit," Andi said loudly. "I've been working nonstop for two days, and then I come home to find you lurking around. Are you drunk?"

"I am not drunk," Jim said. "I've been waiting for you."

"You can't do that. You can't wait for me. You and I are through, and I don't work for you anymore. You need to get out of here. Go back to Tampa. If you don't, I'll call the Commissioner and say you've been stalking me, that you're drinking, that I left Tampa because you were harassing me, and that you need to be investigated by Internal Affairs. Do you understand what I'm saying, Jim?"

He looked shocked, as if her words had suddenly reached him.

"You wouldn't do that," he said. "You wouldn't make me lose my job."

"I'm not the one. I'm doing nothing. If you lose your job, Jim, it's because of what you're doing to me. If you think I'm gonna keep taking this harassment, well, just try me."

"But you love me," he whimpered. "You wouldn't do that to me. I left my wife for you. I love you."

"Jim, listen to me. Those are just words. You don't love me. I loved you once, but not any more. I stopped asking you to leave your wife a long time ago, long before I left Tampa and moved here. I've been in Burgess Beach for a year and a half. I moved because I wanted to get away from you. Please, for your sake and for mine, forget about me and get on with your life."

He walked to the sofa and sat, shoulders hunched, head bowed.

"Is that the truth, Andi? You don't love me?" His voice was so low she could scarcely hear him. Then he raised his head to stare at her.

"It's the truth, Jim. I fell out of love with you before I left Tampa. That's why I came here." She saw the longing in his face, but she felt nothing. "And you don't love me. Not the way you treat me. Go home. Don't come here again. And quit drinking or you'll be in real trouble."

When he stood up, he looked lost. Then he turned to the door, opened it, walked out and pulled it closed behind him.

He was gone.

Andi felt the tension leaving her body. She'd finally reached him. She collapsed on the sofa, tired as though she hadn't slept in days. She had finally reached him. Being afraid and trying to placate him hadn't worked. Avoiding the drunken behavior had simply made him go to sleep. But her anger, and most of all, her straightforward talk had reached him. She felt sure now that Jim had left for good.

Why hadn't she been that definite with him before? Would it have been so easy to get him to give up and go away months ago? No, she thought. Tonight he'd been sober and could hear what she'd said. If she'd said what she said tonight before, well . . . , she didn't want to think about what might have happened. Now he understood what she was saying and knew she was right.

Thank God, Andi thought, that this day had finally ended. In the last two days, she'd been chased, shot at, lied to, and stalked. She was exhausted. She headed straight for bed and slept soundly through the night.

To prove to herself that she was no longer afraid, Andi went for a run on the beach the next morning. It had been a couple of days and she felt out of shape, but after her good night's sleep, she finished four miles and felt new energy and renewal. It was a glorious day with bright sun and few clouds. The ocean would be chilly, but running the beach was paradise.

The euphoria carried her to work where she found the typed copy of the report she'd dictated yesterday on her desk. She made a few corrections and added to that the list of questions she had formulated yesterday afternoon. She gathered her material, then asked Captain Bradley's secretary if she could see him. Lisa called her ten minutes later.

She briefed the Captain on what she had discovered, careful to use "I", not "we" when she talked about what she and Lamont had done. Then she asked, "Is Detective Lamont still on administrative leave? I could sure use his help, especially in Miami."

Bradley eyed her suspiciously. "What do you want with him? He could be the murderer. There's no evidence he wasn't in Burgess Beach the night the victim was killed. He can't be involved in this case. You know that. He lived with the victim for years. A defense attorney would make hash of any case that involved Lamont as a detective."

"Of course you're right, Captain. It's just that he has so many contacts in Miami, people that could help with the case."

"What about Garcia? He can help."

"Has he got contacts in Miami? Can he help me there? He's got the burglary now. I don't want to take him away from that."

Bradley hesitated, rubbing his chin thoughtfully. "Perhaps I'd better consider replacing McClain. We could use another detective. Things around here warrant it."

She didn't say anything. Whoever he hired to replace McClain would need time to get up to speed on the murder. That wouldn't do her any good.

"Now, what's your next move going to be?" he asked.

"I talked once with Nicholas Oldham, the attorney with whom Miranda was having an affair. I didn't get much, but I know he was in touch with her by e-mail after she left the law firm. I'm sure it was he who sent those cryptic e-mails I copied in the file. He could be involved with whatever she had in the suitcase. I need to talk with him again, but first I need to check his e-mail ID. I also need to see the Acostas, preferably at a police station in Miami. Can I ask Greg who to get in touch with about that?"

"Let me call my contacts. I can see why you want to see the Acostas off their own turf. They've obviously lied about a lot of things. I'll let you know."

That was as much as she was going to get from Bradley.

Andi went down to Garcia's office to check his progress on the burglary. He'd tried to call the housekeeper at both addresses and gotten no reply. No additional financial records on the Palmers had come from the bank. She asked if he'd called the bank this morning to find out if there were any more records.

"Yes," Garcia said. "They told me they had nothing further."

"Who'd you talk to?"

"A guy named Larsen, VP in the investment section."

"Banks are never helpful. I talked with another VP. Carrillo. He didn't give me much either."

"Maybe I'll try him." He looked through the file on his desk.

She headed back to her office and checked the clock. Ten. She had to wait until Captain Bradley had a contact for her in Miami. She drafted a warrant to obtain the identity of "oldnick" from his ISP and asked one of the uniforms to take it to the courthouse for a judge's signature. Finally, she headed back over to Garcia and asked, "Have you tried the housekeeper again?"

"No answer. And nothing further from the bank, either Carrillo or Larsen."

"Okay. Let's you and me head up to Fort Pierce where the housekeeper lives. At least we can find out if they've skipped."

Garcia leaped to his feet with more alacrity than she'd ever seen him display. He grabbed the file from his desk and said, "I'll check out a car. Meet you out back."

Garcia drove, and Andi glanced through the file, refreshing her memory. "So, what's your take on this burglary, detective?"

"I'm pretty sure it was an inside job. Whoever did it must've had help from the housekeeper and her son along with having a gate clicker to enable them to get in."

"What d'ya think about the Palmers?"

"It looks to me like they were having money trouble. The burglary came just in time to bail them out. It was very convenient."

"Yes, it was."

Garcia went on. "I checked the insurance riders. They covered almost all the stuff that was stolen."

"You think the housekeeper and her son were in cahoots with the Palmers?" Andi asked.

"Yeah. I think so. They hired the housekeeper and her son to steal the stuff, then they put in the claim to collect the insurance money."

"I agree. I think the Palmers are far too fastidious to steal the stuff themselves. They must've had the housekeeper do it."

Garcia said, "The housekeeper probably had a clicker, anyway. She could've done it by herself with her son, or done it because the Palmers wanted her to."

"I intended to check who had clickers for the gate to the island, but I never got around to it."

"I checked. The security company issues the clickers and is supposed to get them back when an employee leaves or when a house is sold. But enforcement isn't very good."

"Have you talked with the Palmers?"

"Yeah. I asked if they thought the housekeeper had anything to do with the burglary."

"And they said . . .?"

Garcia imitated Mrs. Palmer's voice. "'Not Leona. We trust her a hundred percent. She couldn't have done it.'"

"Did you ever get to talk to Leona Castro?" Andi asked.

"No. Nobody was ever home at the Hutchinson Island house. Nobody ever answered the phone in Fort Pierce."

"Have you had a chance to go to the house on Hutchinson Island?"

"Yeah. I went twice. Nobody ever there."

"Did you ever get up to Fort Pierce to check on the Castros?"

"No. I called three or four times. No answer."

Andi said, "I went once, but nobody was home. Let's see if there's anybody home today."

They were quiet until they reached Fort Pierce. When Andi saw the coral-colored house, she told Garcia to drive past it. "We don't want to spook them."

He stopped the car about six houses past the Castro's home, and they waited, watching to see if there was any movement. Nothing.

"Let's go," Andi said.

They got out of the car, walked back to the Castro house and knocked. There was no answer.

"Either not home or not answering," Andi said. "Let's check the neighbors."

This time there were answers at the houses on either side, but no one had seen the mother and son for several days. No, they didn't know them very well. They weren't very friendly. Across the street, however, they talked to the elderly woman Andi had spoken with before. She was more friendly this time.

"You was here before?" she asked.

"Yes." Andi said and showed her badge again.

"They's gone. They gotta van and moved they stuff out. At night."

"When was this?" Andi asked.

"Maybe two days. Lemme think," the woman said, closing her eyes, remembering the last few days. "Today Thursday?"

Andi said, "Yes."

The woman continued, "Tuesday, I think. There wuz that movie on, and I watch it. Audrey Hepburn. See, she blind and some men try to kill 'er. Scares me. Always scares me. Couldn't sleep."

"What time did you see them?"

"Two-thirty, three o'clock. Quiet. They quiet, too."

"Did you see a name on the van?"

"Lemme think." She didn't speak for a moment, then said, "Seem like rent-a-something."

They thanked the woman and went back across the street.

"Damn," Andi said. "Let's take a look through the windows."

The front windows were covered with drapes, and they couldn't see in. Along the driveway, through the sheer curtains, Ed was tall enough to get a clear view.

"There's a bed on one wall, but the rest of the room is empty. No other furniture." He moved to the next room.

The kitchen held a standalone stove but no refrigerator or table. The room next to the kitchen was also empty, as was another bedroom on the side of the house.

"Shit!" Andi said under her breath.

"We can get a search warrant, but I don't think we'll find anything. Where would they go?" Andi wished she'd followed up on the Castros sooner, and she would have if she hadn't been so involved in Miranda's murder that the burglary had slipped from her mind.

Garcia called directory assistance for Rent-a-Truck and got the phone number for one in Fort Pierce. He called to find out if they were open and got the address.

The woman at the counter at Rent-a-Truck confirmed that the Castros had rented a truck there on Tuesday. She wasn't very enthusiastic about giving information, but finally she told them that the Castros planned to drop the truck off at the St. Augustine office in two days. She didn't have an address or a telephone number for the Castros, just a credit card number and a $500 deposit.

"Do you have GPS in those trucks that you rent?" Garcia asked.

"Yeah."

"That'll tell us where they went, right?"

"Yeah." The woman wasn't feeling helpful.

"So, you can tell us where they took the truck, right? Have they returned it to the Rent-A-Truck office yet?"

"You'll need a warrant," the woman said. "I can't give you that information without a warrant."

"I'll be back with your warrant," Garcia said. "Get the information ready."

They turned to leave, and Andi said, "Good, Ed. I didn't think about the GPS."

Ed looked pleased. "I won't have the warrant 'til tomorrow, and I'll have to show it to her. I hope the Castros haven't given me the slip by then."

As they left the Rent-a-Truck office, Andi said, "I have another stop. I may need your support. You can follow up on the Castros tomorrow."

"Sure."

TWENTY-FOUR

Andi and Ed got back into the car and headed to Sophie's house on the beach. On the way, Andi briefed Ed a bit about the murder case.

When they pulled up in front of the mansion, it was apparent someone was home. The front windows and drapes were open, and they heard the cerebral sounds of Miles Davis.

"Looks like my quarry is home," she said to Garcia. "Let's go."

They parked the car and headed to the front door of the mansion. Andi pressed the bell, but the sound of its ring was swallowed up by the music. After a moment she rang again, and she heard a voice shout, "Okay, okay. Be cool."

The door was opened by a man wearing khaki cargo pants and a t-shirt that read, "Wanna Fuck?" He wasn't tall, but his body was slim and athletic-looking. His head was shaved, and his skin the color of café latte. Beyond him, Andi saw the entry to a dimly lit hallway with doorways opening into the rest of the house.

"Yeah," he said. "Whadda ya want?"

Andi produced her ID. "Are you Gary Johns?"

Johns nodded yes, and Andi introduced Garcia. "May we come in?"

"What's this about?" Johns asked.

"We want to talk with you about Margaret Whitlock."

A relieved expression crossed Johns' face. Then he said, "Okay, sure," turned and led the way to the first room on the left. They stepped into a living area with two big sofas, several comfortable-looking chairs, a big-screen TV which took up a lot of one wall, and a stereo system that was now playing "Sketches of Spain." The man motioned to Andi and Ed to sit. He turned off the music and seated himself in a chair facing them across a coffee table littered with magazines.

"Okay," Johns said. "What about Margaret?"

"When was the last time you saw her?" Andi asked.

"I haven't seen Margaret in years, not since she left me and went off to live some place fancier than Fort Pierce." He was well-spoken despite his greeting at the doorway, and Andi thought the t-shirt and the rough speech were designed to establish a dominant position at the outset of any meeting.

"So you never saw her after 2000, when she left to go to Miami. You never knew she became Miranda Duncan."

He didn't speak for a moment. Andi could see him assessing her. He'd tried the Margaret game and lost.

"Well, you said 'Margaret'. I haven't seen Margaret, but I've seen Miranda Duncan a few times."

"When was the last time you saw Miranda?" She noted that Garcia had taken out a pad and pencil and was taking notes. Greg had always done that, but she hadn't asked Ed and was pleased he'd taken the initiative. He went up a couple of notches in her estimation.

"Oh, probably about six months ago," Johns said, his eyes meeting hers straight on in an effort to appear honest.

"Were you still living in your house in Fort Pierce when you last saw Miranda, or were you living here?"

Johns had to think about this, still trying to estimate how little he could get away with telling. "I think I was still at my old house," he said, "although maybe I'd moved here."

"Did Miranda know Sophie?" Andi asked.

He looked startled at Sophie's name, but he recovered quickly and said, "They're old friends. We all went to school together."

"In Fort Pierce?"

"Yes."

"Is Sophie around? Can we talk to her?" Andi wasn't surprised when he said, "She's not here right now. Went to see her mother."

"That's too bad. I guess we'll have to come back again to talk with her." Andi watched Johns move uncomfortably at the thought that Andi would be back to talk to his girlfriend. "When you last saw Miranda—you said about six months ago, right?—do you remember where she was working?"

"She didn't say. Why are you asking all these questions about Miranda? Is she is some kind of trouble?"

"Why would you think that, Mr. Johns?" Andi asked.

"Well, you're police, right? But you're not from Miami, so I wonder why you're asking about Miranda." He sat back in the chair, trying to look relaxed and unconcerned, but his left leg, crossed over the right, jiggled up and down.

"You knew that Miranda was living in Miami?" Andi asked, leaning toward Johns.

"Yeah. I knew she moved to Miami after she left here and changed her name. But what's the deal? Why are you asking about her?"

Andi watched Johns closely. "Miranda Duncan was murdered in Burgess Beach on September 27th."

"What did you say?" His body straightened quickly as if he'd been knocked back in his chair. His face seemed to draw into itself, grow longer and thinner, turn gray beneath the tan.

"I said Miranda Duncan was murdered in Burgess Beach."

Johns didn't speak. Andi continued, "We didn't know she was Margaret Whitlock until a couple of days ago. That's what led us to you."

She paused, and Johns stared at her. He seemed at a loss.

"Mr. Johns? Can you tell us why Miranda Duncan might have been murdered? Do you know why she was in Burgess Beach?"

Johns seemed to have lost the power of speech, even his power of movement. Andi and Ed sat waiting, watching him, and after a couple of minutes, he muttered, "She said it was safe. She said no one would know."

"What, Mr. Johns? What would be safe? What was it that you and Ms. Duncan were doing? Why was she in Burgess Beach?"

Andi watched as Johns hunched his shoulders and covered his face with his hands, breathing heavily. Finally he pulled himself upright, and looking at Andi, said, "She was so sure. No one would know, she said. It was perfectly safe. She wasn't hurting anyone."

"Tell us what you know, Mr. Johns. We're much less interested in the drug business than we are in who killed Miranda Duncan. I can't promise you immunity, but if you tell us what you know, I'm sure it will go less harshly with you in any prosecution for drug sales."

"I don't care about that," Johns said. "I want you to get whoever killed her. I loved her; I've always loved her. We were going to go away together when we got the money together. We were going to leave for Europe or South America. That was the plan."

Andi was stunned. Miranda certainly had an incredible power over men—and women. Greg, Nick Oldham, the Miami drug lord, Kathryn Forbes. Still she was surprised at Miranda's hold over this man she had known since she was Margaret Whitlock.

"What do you know about Ms. Duncan's visits to this area? Why do you think she was murdered?" Andi asked. She watched Gary Johns pull himself together as if sorting out in his own mind what had happened between him and Miranda Duncan.

Finally, he spoke. "Margaret had a connection in the cocaine trade in Miami. Her idea was to get a good supply of the drug from the people she knew, pay their price, and bring the stuff up here so we could sell it. It'd be worth at least twice the Miami price."

"Why was that?" Andi asked.

"Because the supply up here isn't reliable. Too many police raids on the suppliers. People'll pay a lot for a guaranteed supply. And it was quality stuff."

"Miranda wasn't stealing drugs from anyone in Miami. What she got, she paid for." Andi was thinking aloud. That let many people in Miami off the hook as far as Miranda's murder was concerned.

"That's what she told me. We got some cash together and started."

"That's why she said no one would get hurt. The drugs were bought and paid for. She didn't steal them."

"That's what she said."

"And you believed her."

"Why not?"

Andi could think of a lot of reasons why not, but if Johns was telling the truth, who had killed Miranda and why?

"Margaret's visit to Fort Pierce in late September, when she was murdered, was that her first trip with the drugs?" Andi asked.

"No," Johns answered. "She made a trip in July with a taste. That's all we had money for, and we wanted to see if it worked."

"And how did it work?"

Johns looked uncomfortable, as if he suddenly realized he was talking drug sales with a cop. But he continued, "No problems. The first lot went fast, and they were lined up wanting more. So Margaret brought up another batch in August and then again in early September."

"Who are you in all of this? Are you the dealer, the supplier, the wholesaler, what?" Andi asked.

"Let's just say I don't hang on street corners." Johns spoke carefully, not wanting to admit directly that he was selling drugs.

"Where did the money to buy the drugs come from?"

"Margaret got the money. She didn't tell me where it came from."

"Did you ask?"

"She said it was better I didn't know."

Andi watched Johns, not entirely sure this was the truth. She didn't push it, though. She had a good idea where the money came from.

"So, Margaret left on September 27th to go back to Miami. Do you know why she spent the night in Burgess Beach?" Andi wondered if Johns knew about Toni.

Johns looked puzzled. "I don't know. She always stayed there, but I thought when she left she was going straight back to Miami."

The nanny had said she'd seen Miranda on the day she was murdered. And Miranda had checked into the Hibiscus motel late on Friday night.

"What time did she leave on the 27th?"

"God, I don't know. In the morning. Late morning."

"Where did you and Margaret meet?" And asked, changing the time frame.

Johns looked surprised at the question and didn't answer for a few seconds. "I told you. We went to high school together."

"Why did Margaret go to high school in Fort Pierce? Wasn't there one in her area?"

Johns thought for a moment, as if casting his mind back. "I don't know. She rode the school bus until she could drive. I remember that."

"Did you have classes together? Was that how you got close?"

Johns smiled, as if remembering. "We didn't go to class much, but we hung out together. We hung out with the smokers, the drinkers, the potheads, the ones who didn't give a fuck. By the wall."

"The wall?"

"That's where we all hung out. At the edge of the campus. That's where the wall was."

"And did your friendship continue after she moved to Miami in 1999?"

"No. She lived with me for a while in that shack in Fort Pierce, but that was mostly to shock her parents. She blamed them for her sister's death. After a while, maybe before we graduated, maybe after, I don't remember, she left and moved in with some gal she'd met."

"So you weren't living together when she left for Miami?" Andi was getting a clearer picture of Miranda's relationship with Johns. Someone to shock her parents, someone to abandon when she had someplace else to go, someone to come back to when she had an illegal plan to make money.

"When did you and she reconnect?"

Johns seemed to be trying to recall, but Andi thought he knew perfectly well. "She got in touch with me early this year, February, maybe. Said she had an idea, wondered if we could talk."

"And?" Andi asked.

"She came up. The old attraction was still there, and then she told me about her plan."

"Did she ask you if you were still involved in the drug business when she came up?"

"Maybe. I don't remember."

Andi figured this was a face-saving lie. Miranda had come back to Fort Pierce to use the contact she had in the drug business, and if that involved rekindling an old romance, that was fine.

Andi switched topics again and asked, "When will Sophie be back?"

Johns looked startled as if he couldn't remember who Sophie was. Then he looked embarrassed. "Oh, hell. There isn't any Sophie. I made her up when I moved here. I didn't want my old neighbors wondering where the money came from. It was easier to say the house belonged to some rich bitch who'd fallen for me."

Johns was giving up his secrets at a great rate. Andi thought he must really want to catch Miranda's killer.

"So where did the money come from for this place? You haven't been here that long."

Andi was wondering if selling drugs in Fort Pierce could be that profitable.

"Margaret bought it. She said she had enough money saved to make a down payment, and she'd cover the mortgage payments. She hated where I used to live."

Not surprising, Andi thought. But this place was giant steps up, and Miranda hadn't had any money in July and August. Who did the house really belong to?

"Haven't you wondered why you haven't heard from Miranda since September 27th? That's nearly two weeks."

"She was always the one who called. She said not to call her. Margaret let me know when she was ready with another batch."

"Where did she call you?" Andi asked.

"Here. She used throwaway phones."

Andi thought about phone calls and remembered that no Fort Pierce number had shown up on her cell phone records.

Margaret's passport had been the first connection to Fort Pierce.

"Did she stay here at all? Leave any clothes?"

"Not many. You can look."

Andi followed Johns down the hall to a bedroom that still held the scent of Miranda Duncan. He pointed out the clothes hanging in the closet, the undergarments in the dresser drawers, the toiletries in the bathroom. "This is it."

Andi looked through the clothes, the bras and panties, the creams and powders. There was nothing to indicate that Miranda intended to leave nor that she intended to return. What she had left only showed it was a stop along the way.

Andi thanked Johns for his help, left her business card and said she would be in touch. They left Johns despondent, sitting on the comfortable couch in his mansion.

Andi leaned her head back against the passenger seat in the car and tried to clear her mind. There were so many things to follow up and so many things she'd believed that had turned out to be untrue. She had to begin at the beginning with Miranda. Who was she and what had she done?

Garcia turned to look at her. "I don't know anything about this case, but I gather from what that guy said that he told you a lot you didn't know."

"In spades."

They didn't talk for a time, then Andi said, "I had an entirely different picture of Johns and of Miranda. She's got at least four guys and a woman in love with her. Any one of them seems willing to do anything she asked. Any one of them might also have killed her. But I don't think any of them did. What am I missing?"

Garcia didn't answer, and Andi wasn't surprised. What could he say? The confusion was all hers to sort out.

They got back to Burgess Beach in mid-afternoon. Garcia gave her his notes from the interview with Johns, then went to prepare the paperwork for the warrants to search the Castro house and for information at the Rent-A-Truck office and take them to be signed.

Garcia's notes were both readable and complete, not like Greg's shorthand that required guesswork on her part. She always wrote or dictated her own first and then used Greg's as a supplement.

She was puzzling through the history of Margaret/ Miranda's life when her phone rang. It was Joe Patrone, the cop in Miami who had set up their meeting with SanAngelo.

"I thought you'd be interested to know about a murder in Miami, given your interest in Philippe SanAngelo."

Andi's heart beat faster as she heard SanAngelo's name. Another murder. "Who was it?"

"His name was Santiago Valencia. We think he was SanAngelo's importer. We knew about him, but he was hard to get hold of. Well-guarded and never where we thought. We didn't even know what he looked like until his body was found."

"How did you know who it was?"

"Somebody called, said he's been killed, told us where to find him. Our preliminary investigation says the body was Valencia. We'll be sure after the DNA results come back. He was pretty badly mutilated—tortured, then shot."

"Sheesh!" Andi said. "That bad?"

"Bad," Patrone said. "Wanna check it out?" His invitation sounded reluctant, but she accepted quickly, saying she would be down the next day about ten o'clock.

Now, she thought, should she take Greg or go on her own? She didn't need Greg, and Garcia would be busy with the search of the Castro's house in Fort Pierce. She decided to go alone. She wondered if the Captain had managed to get her a place to interview the Acostas.

She finished her reports, adding the information about the murdered Santiago Valencia and a question about the interview room. She took them to the Captain's secretary, adding that she would be going to Miami the next day to see the body and talk with Patrone.

Lisa buzzed her around four-thirty and said the Captain wanted to see her. Andi headed to his office and knocked.

"Enter."

Bradley was sitting at his desk, and he wasn't smiling. He held her request in his hand. "What's this, detective?"

"It's a mess and more confusing the more I learn."

"So, now you want to go to Miami and look at this body."

"Yes, sir." Actually, she didn't want to see the body. She didn't want any part of the drug wars. But she said yes.

"I've got you an interview room at the South Beach Station. Is that satisfactory?"

"Yes, sir. Who do I see?"

"Captain Al Johnson. He'll be expecting you."

She thanked the captain, then headed back to her desk. She set up an appointment with the Acostas at the South Beach Police Department at 2:00. Andi told them she had some news about Miranda's murder.

Next she called Pattis and Kearney and asked for an appointment with Nick Oldham. She didn't say who she was. The secretary on the other end of the phone tried to find out what this was about, but Andi would only say she needed to talk with an attorney and Oldham had been highly recommended. She had a feeling Nick Oldham would duck her unless she caught him unaware or got a subpoena, and she preferred the former. She hadn't gotten much out of him before, but this time she had more information about him and his connection with Miranda. The response to her warrant request about the online ID "oldnick" told her it belonged to Nicholas Oldham.

The secretary set up an appointment at 11:30.

In her apartment that evening, Andi decided against having a drink. She'd taken refuge in alcohol when Jim had been stalking her and she'd been afraid. He hadn't been around for a couple of days. She hoped he'd taken her threats seriously, and she hoped he'd gone into rehab. He needed that.

TWENTY-FIVE

The following morning, Andi was up early, her stomach roiling in anticipation of the day ahead of her. A four-mile run along the beach calmed her. The gray and white ocean forewarned a storm, but the tide was out, and she ran along the shore near the waves that thundered in. After she showered and dressed, she felt better equipped to handle the day ahead, although the thought of seeing Valencia's body still unnerved her.

Her first stop was the Indian County Records Office where she found that, as she had suspected, the house in Fort Pierce had been purchased by Nicholas Oldham and was in his name.

The drive to Miami gave her time to consider Miranda's life. Had she loved any of those men and women she'd used? Gary Johns had been useful in getting her away from her parents. Had there been anyone between Johns and Greg? She'd left Johns, gone to school, gotten her two-year degree and the paralegal certificate. Why had she gotten the passport? Maybe she'd wanted to disappear.

What about Nick Oldham? Andi was pretty sure he was the money behind the drug buys and sales, but now she knew he owned the house in Fort Pierce. Maybe he thought Miranda loved him. What about Kathryn Forbes? She just seemed to be a convenient place for Miranda to stay. Was there anything more to that? Who did Miranda love? Did she love anyone? Who loved her? Maybe they all did.

She reached Joe Patrone's officet a few minutes before ten. He came out to greet her. "Where's Greg?"

"He decided not to come."

Patrone looked annoyed when he realized Greg wasn't with her, but he led her into his office where he gave her the file on Santiago Valencia's killing.

Valencia's body had been dumped off the Tamiami Trail in the Everglades. He might never have been found had not the Miami Police gotten a phone call from a throwaway cell. It couldn't be determined whether the caller was a man or a woman, but the caller told them where to find the body and who it was.

The file indicated that Valencia had started as an importer of drugs for a number of local dealers but recently exclusively for Philippe SanAngelo. He brought in marijuana from Mexico and cocaine from Colombia. His routes and methods remained elusive: cocaine probably in the bellies of Colombians flying to Miami International Airport and marijuana carried by mules across the Texas border and then down to Miami. However the smuggling was done, the drugs arrived, and there was always a ready market.

The Medical Examiner's report said that Valencia had been tortured before dying from a gunshot wound to the head.

After Andi reviewed the file, Patrone asked if she wanted to see the body. She said she would, although her stomach protested at the thought.

It was freezing inside the morgue where the bodies were stored, and the smell of putrefaction lay like a miasma. Patrone pulled out a drawer. Andi registered that Valencia's eyes had been gouged out, then she glanced quickly at the body. Humidity, rain and heat as well as maggots and other insects had worked on the body after it had been burned with a branding iron and the nails pulled from the toes. The fingers had been chopped off as well. She couldn't look further and turned away in revulsion, though she managed to keep from vomiting.

"That's enough," she said to Patrone. "How could anyone . . .?"

He pushed the drawer in and led the way back to his office. "I don't know. Money and power, I guess." He lit a cigarette which, offensive as it usually was to Andi, dissipated the smell of death, and she welcomed the odor.

"Why the torture?" Andi asked.

"We think he worked directly for SanAngelo, so if he was cutting someone else in, this may have been a message to whoever it was. Even though his body was dumped in the Everglades, someone called to be sure we found him." Patrone stubbed out his cigarette on his shoe, then tossed the butt into the wastebasket. He explained, "No smoking in the building these days, but after a visit to the morgue, it does help to clear the senses."

"I'm with you." Andi glanced again at the file, then asked, "Do you think that Valencia might have been bringing in drugs for Miranda Duncan? She was buying them from someone in Miami, then reselling them in Fort Pierce for distribution up there. There was a good profit to be made from the resale."

"So that's what she was up to."

"That's what I think at the moment. But I still don't know who killed her."

"You may never know for sure." Patrone said. "Too many players, too much money involved."

"You may be right," Andi said, "but I think that Miranda's murder is simpler than a drug killing. I think she was killed for whatever was in the suitcase." She rose and extended her hand to Patrone. "Thanks for calling me."

At 11:30, Andi arrived at Pattis and Kearney and told the receptionist that she had an appointment with Nicholas Oldham. Then she sat in the freezing reception area. And waited. And waited.

At 12:30, a woman emerged from the offices behind the reception area and asked her to come in.

In his office, Oldham stood and extended a hand. "Miss Battaglia, I'm Nicolas Oldham. What can I do for you?" He obviously didn't remember her.

Oldham looked even more gaunt and his gray hair longer than on her previous visit, but his eyes had not lost their penetrating gaze. Andi shook his hand, then brought out her badge. "Mr. Oldham. You're a hard man to get to."

Oldham stared at the badge, then back at Andi's face. "What's this? I thought you had questions about a legal matter." His voice was annoyed.

"I do. I want to ask you a few more questions about the murder of Miranda Duncan in Burgess Beach."

He sat down heavily and motioned Andi to sit.

He sighed. "What is it this time?"

Andi decided to get right to it. "Your ISP tells us that 'old-nick,' is your e-mail identification. That's you, isn't it? You're the author of three e-mails to Miranda: 'Did you get it?' 'Ready,' and 'See you 27.' Can you tell me what those e-mails referred to?"

Oldham leaned back and closed his eyes for a moment, as if thinking, then opened them and said, "I haven't any idea. I don't remember sending them. It's possible my e-mail was hacked."

"Miranda was murdered on September 27th. Is that when you saw her? Did you kill her on September 27th?" Andi leaned forward in her chair. She'd be damned if she'd let him intimidate her this time.

"Of course not." Oldham's tone was indignant. "I didn't see her on September 27th. I haven't seen her in months. She was fired in January, and I only saw her once or twice after that, and not for several months."

Andi watched him, knowing he was thinking about getting to his feet and ushering her out. She hit him again. "Why did you finance Miranda's drug buys in Miami?"

Andi was sure she saw a flicker of surprise on Oldham's face, but it was gone quickly, and he asked, "Why would you think that?"

"And your e-mails were all sent in July and August. Why were you sending e-mails to her when you had severed your connection?"

"I didn't say I'd severed all connections, detective. If I did talk to her from time to time on the phone, that doesn't mean I sent any e-mails." His composure was just a bit rattled, Andi noted.

"Really. If you talked to her, what did you talk about?" Andi spoke quickly, trying not to give him a chance to gather his thoughts. She hoped he'd trip himself up in an attempt to keep his hands clean, but she knew she'd be very lucky if he did. Oldham was a seasoned litigator, accustomed to thinking on his feet in court.

"If she called me from time to time while she was job hunting, she may have asked for my help. I didn't have any problems with her performance here, and I certainly didn't want to keep her from getting a job, so I may have given her information about other law firms and I may have helped her get interviews. The usual things." Oldham sat back in his chair, looking calm, but Andi saw tension in his shoulders and neck. His hands were below the desk. She wondered if they were clenched.

"'The usual things,' Mr. Oldham? What 'usual things?'"

"Well, we'd been friends, so if she asked me to give her a good reference and put in a good word with some of the firms where she was applying, I would if I could."

"And did you?" Andi snapped.

"Did I what, detective?"

"If you could, did you give her a good reference? Did you put in a good word with the firms she was applying to?"

"If I could, certainly." He shrugged.

"You told me you hardly knew Miranda, that you only remembered her because she'd done some work for you on a difficult case. Now you say you were friends. Which was it? Or were you more than friends?"

"Are you accusing me of something?" The indignant tone seemed put on.

"Were you and Miranda more than friends?"

"Of course not. We were just work friends. I appreciated her brains. She helped me on a difficult case, and I would be willing to return the favor. I assume it works that way in the police department."

This was easy for him, Andi saw, and he wasn't tense any more. She needed to hit him again. "Actually, it's not. And what about the house in Fort Pierce?"

"House?" Oldham looked surprised although whether at her knowing about Fort Pierce or the house, Andi couldn't tell. "What house?"

"Your name is on the loan for 175 North Ocean Drive, the house in Fort Pierce where Miranda lived with Gary Johns."

Oldham didn't speak right away. He stared at the wall over Andi's head, then brought his hands from beneath the desk and clasped them together in front of him. "Well, I did lend Miranda some money. Are you saying she put me on the loan as co-owner? That's good. I can be repaid from her estate."

Oldham's expression seemed to say, "Gotcha." He was really quick, Andi thought.

"Your name wasn't just on the loan. You signed for the loan and put your house in Bermuda up as collateral."

He didn't say anything for a time, and a flash of anger crossed his face, an expression he didn't trouble to hide. Andi waited. Finally, he spoke. "Your questions are intrusive, detective. I've got nothing to hide, but I would advise any client of mine not to answer you."

"These are questions I have to ask," Andi said, "so, again, why did you purchase the house in Fort Pierce for Miranda?"

"She needed a place for her business. I loaned her the money. That was my choice."

Oldham looked ready to get to his feet, and Andi contin- ued quickly, "So you have seen Miranda more recently than 'several months ago'? Is that correct?

"Yes. We spoke in the spring." His tone was sharp.

"When you say 'business,' what 'business' are you talking about? Did you know that Gary Johns was involved with that 'business?'"

"Miranda told me she had a business in Fort Pierce and needed to put up a good front to convince people to buy from her and to attract other investors."

Andi was pretty sure Oldham was making things up as he went along.

"What kind of business was this?" Andi demanded.

Oldham didn't answer immediately. His face remained noncommittal, but she could almost hear him thinking. "To the best of my knowledge, it was some clothing she was importing," he said finally. "As I remember, she didn't want to set up a shop. She had fashion shows in the house, which was why she needed a good venue."

"Did you see any of the clothing she was importing? Where did it come from?"

"I didn't ask."

"So let me recap this. You mortgaged your house in Bermuda to finance a house for your ex-lover and her friend. You also provided money for her to import clothing and sell it out of this house. Is that right?"

Andi wanted Oldham to admit to something, but he always seemed to have an answer that got him off the hook.

"I invested in my friend's business," Oldham said. "That's true."

"How did you expect to be repaid for this investment? Did you have a contract with Miranda?"

"I was drafting a contract with her when she was killed. Initially, it was a handshake agreement, but I wasn't comfortable with that arrangement, so I was drafting a formal contract, the terms of which would allow me to share in the profits of her sales based on the percentage of my investment. It was a good investment, and the timing was right for her to get started, so we didn't wait until the contract was complete."

"Do you have a copy of the draft contract?" Andi asked. "I'd like to see it."

Oldham's face reddened, and he didn't speak for a minute. "I'm not sure where it is at the moment. I'll have my secretary send it to you."

"Please do that. Did you know Gary Johns, Miranda's lover?"

"I know about him, but I've never met him."

"Why was she setting up an imported clothing business in Fort Pierce? That doesn't seem to be a real fashion capital."

"Miranda had done a lot of impressive research about the market. She said there wasn't much competition up there, and there was money along the Treasure Coast.

"I'd like to see that research. Do you have it available?" Andi asked.

Oldham sighed and looked pointedly at his watch. "I'm sure my secretary can find it. I'll have her FAX it to you with the agreement. I have another appointment, detective. How much longer will you be?"

"Just a couple more questions," Andi said, then paused, as if she was thinking. "But Miranda was still living in Miami. Why didn't she move to Fort Pierce if that was such a great business opportunity?"

She had to admit that Oldham was fast on his feet. He'd spun a credible tale about importing clothing while she watched. She knew what he'd done, and she didn't think she could prove it was all a lie, at least not right now.

"I'm sure I don't know." He looked again at his watch.

"I'm surprised none of the friends she went clubbing with knew anything about her selling this imported clothing, Mr. Oldham. Why do you suppose that was?"

"You know more about it than I do."

Switching topics, Andi asked, "Do you know why Miranda spent time in Burgess Beach?"

"No. I know nothing about Burgess Beach."

Oldham didn't know about Toni. That wasn't a surprise.

"Mr. Oldham, can you tell me where you were the night Miranda was murdered? That would be September 27th."

Oldham turned to his computer and pressed some keys. "I was in Boston at a conference. My secretary will give you the information."

If that checked out, he couldn't have murdered Miranda. Andi didn't think he had, but he'd done a lot of other things. "Did Miranda tell you anything about Philippe SanAngelo?"

"Who?" Oldham looked genuinely puzzled.

She didn't think he was lying, but she couldn't really tell. Almost everything Oldham had said was a lie.

"Mr. Oldham, I don't believe a thing you've told me, except maybe about the conference. I think that Miranda Duncan was your mistress and that you are the money man behind her business in Fort Pierce, which is not in imported clothing but in selling drugs. I think that you financed her at least in her first drug buy from an importer in Miami, and that you shared in the profits. You also purchased the house in Fort Pierce, partly for Miranda, and mostly because she had convinced you that she would live in it with you when you'd cleaned up on the drug business. She never told you that she was living with Gary John in the mansion you bought and selling the drugs you purchased. You say you didn't know about her lover, Philippe SanAngelo, who was probably the supplier of those drugs. If those things are true, you've been a sucker, Mr. Oldham, but not the only sucker in Miranda Duncan's life."

Andi rose to her feet, nodded at Oldham and headed to the door.

When Oldham spoke, Andi turned toward him. "When you want to see me again, detective, don't try to sneak in as a client. Next time I won't see you without a subpoena and my lawyer present."

"I'll be sure to get a subpoena if I need to see you again," she said. Then she opened the office door and walked out.

After Andi got the details of the Boston conference from Oldham's secretary and told the woman about the documents Oldham had promised to FAX to her, she headed back to her car. It was one-fifteen. She had just enough time to get to her appointment with the Acostas at 2:00.

As she drove, she thought about her meeting with Oldham. Had she learned anything that she didn't already know? He hadn't admitted anything, not even that Miranda had been his mistress. And he'd spun a credible tale about imported clothing and the need for a fancy house in Fort Pierce. Probably nothing he'd told her was true, but it would take time and effort to expose his lies. It was possible that Oldham had killed Miranda, but Andi didn't think so. She'd put him on a back burner while she looked at other possibilities.

TWENTY-SIX

At the Miami Police Department she asked for Captain Al Johnson. Johnson was an African-American in his forties, a big guy who looked like he'd been a football player. He ushered her back to his office.

"Always glad to do a favor for Captain Bradley. He was my training officer when I was a new recruit." Johnson sat back in his chair and crossed his hands over his ample stomach. "Nice guy."

"Yes," Andi agreed, although 'nice' wasn't a word she thought of in connection with Bradley.

Johnson went on. "Not many African-Americans on the force in those days, but the Captain saw to it I was treated fairly. No, sir. A good guy."

Andi was afraid Johnson was going to sit all afternoon reminiscing, and the Acostas were due in less than fifteen minutes.

"Can I see the room you have for me to use?" she asked.

"Oh, sure, sure. Right this way." Johnson led the way to a small interview room. It was furnished with a battered table and four chairs. The window was obviously one-way glass. It was perfect.

"Thanks, Captain. I appreciate your help. I won't take any more of your time."

Andi began moving chairs around to seat the Acostas furthest from the door and herself facing them.

"I'll wait for my guests in reception."

"Nothing too good for a friend of Captain Bradley," Johnson said and left her alone.

Andi settled in the reception room to wait. By the time the Acostas arrived, it was after two-thirty, and Andi was beginning to wonder if they were going to show.

As they entered, Belle said, "I'm so sorry we're late. Jorge had an emergency at the club." In the light of the unforgiving fluorescents in the reception room, Belle Acosta looked her age, mid-to-late fifties, probably the same age as Jorge.

Andi shook hands and led them back to the interview room. She seated them in the chairs she'd staged and asked if they wanted coffee. They both declined, and she began the interview.

She opened the folder on the table in front of her and appeared to consult some papers in it. She looked up, holding a sheet in her hand. "I told you on the phone that I'd found out some interesting things about Miranda Duncan's murder. You knew that she was involved with Philippe SanAngelo, and that his main business was bringing in drugs from Mexico and Colombia." She watched them as she said this, and neither Jorge nor Belle indicated any interest in this information. "You never mentioned SanAngelo, although I believe you knew him from the club."

Belle looked at Jorge. Jorge looked down at his hands. Neither wanted to say why they hadn't mentioned the drug dealer. It was Belle who answered. "We only knew Philippe through his wife. She told us he was a coffee importer. I've known—we've known Ana SanAngelo for many years. I was her *tia,* her auntie, almost like her mother. She met Philippe—I don't know where or when— but she introduced us, and then about five years ago they got married. They are like family. We don't know anything about drugs."

"Ana SanAngelo told us that you introduced her to Philippe and you say she introduced you. Which is correct?"

Belle looked at Jorge, then said, "I guess we introduced her to Philippe. I'd forgotten that."

"So, why do you think that Philippe hung out at the Meta Lounge when he is married to a woman who is almost a daughter to you? What did you think he was doing there?"

Jorge spoke now, carrying on with Belle's story. "We didn't like that he was there, but it wasn't our business to tell Ana."

"What did he do at the club?"

"He danced some, drank and talked to people."

"You knew he was involved with Miranda Duncan? Is that correct?"

"Yes."

"But you didn't tell Ana."

"No. It wasn't our business." Belle answered.

"Belle said not to get involved," Jorge said.

"I wanted to tell Ana. <u>You</u> told me not to say anything." Belle's voice was sharp.

Jorge's look shut Belle up, and neither spoke again.

Andi broke the silence. "Why did Coral Isaacson tell me that Philippe was a drug dealer and that he was dealing at the Meta Lounge?"

Belle's look of surprise didn't look genuine. "Coral's a gossip. She doesn't know what she's talking about."

"You never saw Miranda send her boyfriends to Philippe to buy drugs?"

"Of course not. We wondered why he was there, but he was like family."

"So, your story is that you didn't know Philippe was a drug dealer or that he and Miranda were selling drugs at the Meta Lounge."

"It's not a story, Detective," Jorge said. "It's the truth."

Andi was quiet for a moment. She had thought the Acostas would have some story to tell, but she was surprised that they could keep straight faces at the tale they were spinning.

Jorge spoke again. "Do we need a lawyer, Detective?"

"That's up to you. If you want a lawyer, you are entitled to have one."

Belle looked to Jorge for a decision. He was silent, then said, "What else do you have to say, Detective?"

Andi continued, "Did Miranda know SanAngelo was married?"

Jorge answered. "She didn't know. She'd have been furious had she known. We were the only ones in that circle who knew he was married, and we were sworn to keep it secret."

"Did his wife know Miranda?" Andi asked.

"Yes, but she didn't know about Miranda and Philippe. Ana and Miranda met accidentally, and the kids played together. We tried to keep each of them unaware of the other's relationship to Philippe."

Andi remembered that Ana SanAngelo and Miranda had met at a Mommy and Me class. That had been the accident.

"How did you feel about Miranda's involvement with Philippe? After all, Ana was almost like a daughter to you."

After a minute, Belle spoke. "As I said before, I didn't like it, but there wasn't anything I could do about it."

Jorge said, "You tried to get Miranda away from Philippe, didn't you?"

"No. It wasn't my business."

"Miranda was trouble, Belle. You knew that."

"She was trouble for you."

"How was she trouble for Jorge?" Andi asked.

Belle didn't speak for a minute, then said, "You know, trouble at the club, fights and stuff."

Andi didn't think that was what she'd meant. She shuffled through some of the papers in the file. "So, let's see. From what you say, you two knew nothing about Philippe SanAngelo's drug business. He frequented the Meta Lounge, but all he did there was talk, dance and drink. Wasn't it your business to keep an eye on what people were doing in the club? You could lose you liquor license if there was drug dealing, and that would put you out of business."

"We didn't have any reason to think he was doing anything illegal. He was Ana's husband."

"Then why was he hanging out at the Meta Lounge with another woman? Didn't you wonder about that?"

"It wasn't our business," Belle said.

"But your business was the club, keeping the club open, keeping everything legal. Wasn't it?"

"Yes. And we did that."

"But SanAngelo was dealing drugs under your noses." Andi slammed her hand on the table. "How could you not have known?"

"We didn't know." Jorge said. "Perhaps we were blind, but we didn't know."

Andi paused. She wasn't going to get them to admit anything. She tried another subject. "What do you know about the drugs Miranda bought directly from Santiago Valencia? You know, the ones SanAngelo knew nothing about." This was a guess, although Andi thought they might have known about it. She hit the mark, though. The Acostas froze. Belle looked at Jorge.

After a long pause, Jorge said, "We don't know anything about any drugs. I will tell you again. We run a club, a place for people to drink and dance."

"I think you do know about the drug buys Miranda made. I think you either helped Miranda finance the drug buys, or you were in some way an intermediary. And now you're scared. As well you might be. Silvano Valencia is dead, and his death was not pleasant. It might be a good idea if you told me what you know, so the Miami police can provide you with protection. SanAngelo is not pleased with anyone who tries to cut him out of a drug operation."

Belle said, "We don't know anybody named Silvano Valencia. Who is he?"

"I think you know who he is."

No one said anything for a while. Then Jorge spoke. "We've done nothing, Detective. We kept some information about Miranda and Philippe from you, but we were not involved in Miranda's death nor the death of this Valencia and we know nothing about drugs. We will leave now, and if you wish to speak with us again, we will bring our lawyer."

"Okay," Andi said, closing the folder on her desk. "I wish you'd been more forthcoming with me. But be careful. SanAngelo is nobody to mess with."

The Acostas rose to their feet and headed to the door of the interview room. Belle held out a hand to Andi, but Jorge left without a backward glance.

It was after three-thirty when Andi finally left the Miami Beach Police Department. She'd poked her head into the Captain's office to thank him, but managed to avoid any further conversation.

She suddenly realized she was hungry. Her breakfast had been hours ago. She knew she'd never find Greg's café in Little Havana, and besides, that area had unpleasant memories of the bar in which they'd met Philippe SanAngelo and Juan Garcia. She decided to drive toward downtown Miami to find some place.

She found a coffee shop near the I 95 and ordered what the cops called "sissy food," a chef's salad, dressing on the side. Then she made notes about her interviews today and thoughts about what she would do when she got back to Burgess Beach. When she looked up from her notepad, she realized she'd been sitting a long time. Where was her food? It had been at least forty-five minutes since she'd ordered, and this was a coffee shop, for heavens' sake, and not even crowded. She called to her waitress and asked.

"The cook is out sick," the waitress told Andi. "The owner's filling in. Sorry it's taken so long."

Finally her food arrived, and she bolted it down, hungrily. It wasn't very good, although how anyone could screw up a chef's salad, she didn't know. By the time she'd finished and paid her bill, it was five o'clock. As she opened the door of the coffee shop, she saw that darkness had already fallen. And it was raining.

"Damn," she said. She had hoped to get home before it was dark.

She got on I 95 and made good time getting out of Miami. But the rain hit hard as she got to the Fort Lauderdale area, and she had to slow down, the windshield wipers working overtime but not keeping up with the rain. She saw other cars pulling off to the side of the road and considered doing that, but around West Palm, the rain slowed to just a downpour, and she finally reached her exit.

TWENTY-SEVEN

When Andi got to Burgess Beach, it was still raining hard, and she didn't bother with an umbrella because of the wind. She pulled up the hood on her coat and ran. When she reached her apartment, she noticed a small light in the window and wondered that she'd left it on. As she inserted her key in the lock, she found the door open. Jim, she thought instantly.

"Goddamn it, Jim! Don't you ever give up?"

But it wasn't Jim. A man she had never seen before was sitting in her living room.

She reached into her purse for her gun, but there was another man behind her. He pressed a gun to her ribs as he took her purse. He removed her Beretta and threw the purse aside.

The seated man said, "We want to talk to you, detective."

"Who the hell are you?" Andi asked. "How did you get into my apartment?"

"Your locks aren't very good," the seated man said. "If I were you, I'd get new ones."

The man with the gun pushed her further into the room and closed the door behind them. He didn't speak, just propelled her to the couch. Then, with gloved hands that were intimate but not in any way sexual, he patted her down. She squirmed away from his touch, but he continued, holding her tight while he checked her for weapons. Then he forced her to sit. After that, she could hear him take the bullets from her gun and place the empty Beretta on the table next to the couch.

Andi's first rush of anger was gone. Now she was scared. Her legs were shaking, and she tried to sit upright, clasping her knees tightly together to prevent the men from seeing her fear. She'd never seen either one of them before, but they looked as though they meant business, whatever their business was. The one seated in the chair opposite her was pale-skinned with slicked back dark hair and a compact build, and, like his partner, he wore leather gloves. The other man was taller, broader, and his brown face looked as though it had been carved, his nose chiseled, heavy brows overhanging his eyes and his mouth a broad slash above a jutting chin. He looked like an Easter Island statue.

The man in the chair said, "If you will give me your promise to keep quiet, we will not tie you up or gag you. It is more civilized to have a conversation if you are not tied up." His speech was formal and very slightly accented with the lilt of a native Spanish speaker. Its formality added to the menace of his words.

"I won't make noise unless you hurt me," Andi said. "Then I can't guarantee I won't scream."

"We do not plan to hurt you. Not now. This is a preliminary visit."

"Preliminary?" Andi asked.

"If you do what you are told, you will not see us again."

Andi didn't say anything, and he continued, "You have been looking into our business. Our boss does not like that, so we are here to suggest that you stop asking questions in Miami."

Andi listened, then after a minute she spoke. "Who's your boss?"

"That is not your business." He spoke with authority, as if the line between Andi's business and his boss was clear and distinct.

Andi tried to get up, but the big man pushed her back into her seat. "I'm a cop. It's my job to find out who killed Miranda Duncan. If those questions interfere with some business of your boss', I'm sorry. But it's my job."

"I do not think you understand, Detective," the compact man said. "If you continue to ask questions in Miami, you will not need a job. You will not need anything." He made a gesture with his hands, opening them toward her as if he was explaining something quite logical.

Andi stared at him, mesmerized. He looked like a cobra poised to strike. "You're threatening to kill me?" Andi asked.

"You understand, then," the compact man said. He folded his hands together in his lap, looking pleased.

She took a deep breath and paused for a moment, knowing she was pressing her luck. "Did your boss kill Miranda Duncan?"

"Our boss does not kill."

The man had reacted to her question as if he were saying his boss didn't play golf.

She hoped her next question wasn't the one that would make him angry.

"But he orders people to be killed? Is that right?"

As soon as she spoke, she shrank back against the couch.

"Sometimes such actions are necessary. I hope you understand the message we have been sent to give you. It would be regrettable if you did not understand." The voice had remained calm, but the level of menace had gone up a couple of notches.

"I understand," Andi said.

They weren't going to kill her now, but if she kept on doing what she was doing, her life was in jeopardy. Did she dare ask what she really wanted to know? Would they kill her now if she did? She breathed deeply and dug her nails into her palms.

"Can you tell me if your boss ordered Miranda Duncan to be killed?"

"I do not know the answer to that question," the compact man said. "I did not kill her, nor did my friend here." He turned his head to the statue who had not spoken. "We could have done so, but we did not. We were not told to do so."

"I'll keep your warning in mind," Andi said, relaxing her hands. She decided she could continue. "It may be necessary for me to go to Miami again and ask questions. If I do, I will be very, very careful."

"You cannot be too careful, Detective," the man said. He stood, smoothing the creases from his jacket.

"We will leave now. Be sure to lock the door behind us."

The two men walked to the door, opened it and closed it carefully behind them.

And change the lock and install a deadbolt, Andi thought.

Andi was shaking. Her heart pounded, and her muscles were clenched tight. A drink, she thought. She really needed a drink.

She stumbled to the liquor cupboard, poured brandy, neat, and downed it in one gulp. She felt the heat as it spread through her chest, her tense shoulders, her stomach, then down into her groin and her legs. She collapsed on the couch, all the strength gone from her body.

Forcing herself into action, she grabbed the pad next to the telephone and jotted down a description of the two men and her recollection of what they had said. Then she checked the other rooms in the apartment, looking for any signs of disturbance. There were none. She picked up her gun from the floor where it had landed and reloaded the clip.

Then, back on the couch, her notes clenched in her hands and her gun beside her, she considered. She should call the station, but she really needed to talk to someone, someone who knew her.

Greg answered on the first ring. "I hoped you'd call me. We haven't talked since we interviewed Miranda's family. Have you learned anything more?"

"Two men were just here," she said. "They scared the hell out of me." Her voice was a whisper.

"Hold on," Greg said. "I'll be right there. Don't move."

Andi didn't move until Greg arrived ten minutes later.

"Andi, it's Greg," he called through the door.

She hurried to the door. Then she stood motionless, staring at Greg, suddenly paralyzed, and he stepped inside and put his arms around her.

"Are you sure they're gone?"

She nodded. "They're gone," she said, barely able to speak as she fought to keep back tears.

Greg patted her back, muttered calming noises, and guided her into the living room. He sat her down next to him on the couch and put one arm around her. Andi tried to keep from crying, but his sympathy and the comfort of having him there was too much, and she let go. He drew her close to him while she sobbed.

Finally, she wiped her eyes and sat upright. "Damn," she said between sniffles. "I didn't mean to lose it like that. But they were so scary. They just talked, but I knew they would kill me if that was what they had been told to do."

"Are you okay for a minute? I want to search the apartment."

She whispered, "I did already," but he rose, and she could hear him checking her bedroom, the bathroom and kitchen.

He returned and sat down next to her on the couch. "It doesn't look as if anything was disturbed. How did they get in?"

"They said my locks were for shit. I had a deadbolt, but apparently it wasn't good enough to keep them out. I'll get a locksmith tomorrow."

"I'll look," Greg said. She could hear him prowling around, checking the front door, the windows and the patio door.

After a while, he dropped down next to her on the couch again. "I don't see anything. They're probably good at picking locks. They must have picked the front door lock and the deadbolt, but they didn't leave any scratches. There aren't any marks on the patio door either, and it was still locked. The windows were closed and locked as well."

She shivered at the thought of the men entering without leaving any sign. "They could get in wherever they want?" she asked.

"Guess so," Greg answered.

Andi thought about the menace in the man's words. He hadn't actually said they would kill her. But they had made it clear that if it had been their job, she would be dead. She huddled on the couch, but Greg reached over and gathered her in his arms, holding her close. His warmth was comforting.

After a while, he got up, found the brandy and poured each of them a stiff drink. Then he asked, "Have you eaten?"

She shook her head, "No," and as she sipped the drink, she could feel the warmth stilling the trembling in her legs and the fear in her gut.

"You'll feel better if you have something to eat. I'll order pizza. Any favorites?"

She didn't reply, just sat rocking herself back and forth. She heard Greg on the phone, ordering a large pizza with everything. Then he came back to sit beside her, pulling her back into his arms and rocking her like a baby. The brandy and the warmth of Greg's arms did their work, and she dozed, waking with a start when the pizza arrived.

Greg rummaged in her kitchen, finding plates, napkins, and glasses for water. "Do you want a glass of wine?" he asked, but she said no. He came over to the couch, pulled her to her feet, and guided her to the table.

Greg had been right. After she ate, she felt less frightened. The shaking stopped and her stomach settled.

She let Greg clear the table while she moved back to the couch. When he finished, he sat next to her. "Do you want to tell me what happened? You don't have to do this now if you'd rather not."

"I need to get this out. It'll make me feel better. I think."

"Okay. Whatever."

Andi told him the story, omitting her initial belief that it had been Jim who was in the apartment waiting for her. She referred several times to her notes. Her voice was so low that Greg had to ask her several times to repeat herself.

"They wouldn't say who their boss was?" Greg asked.

"No. Said it wasn't my business. I think it's SanAngelo, but that's only a guess." Then she also filled Greg in on what she'd learned in Fort Pierce and in Miami. As she spoke, her voice got stronger, and her mind returned to the puzzles she had uncovered. Only when she described the horror of Valencia's body did her voice sink back into a whisper.

"I can't give up, but I can't deny I'm frightened. They were a couple of scary dudes. They didn't do anything to me, and I'm not sure they were the ones who bumped the car when you and I drove back from Miami, but the threats . . . . I keep remembering what Silvano Valencia's body looked like. Not pretty."

Greg made a fist and hit his knee. "Damn. I wish I could help. Tomorrow tell Captain Bradley. He'll assign someone to be with you. Do you have to go back to Miami?"

She thought. "Not for a couple of days, anyway. I want to check on the nanny and the child. I haven't been there for a couple of days. I reported everything to Child Welfare, and I assume they're monitoring the situation, but I'd like to talk to Marta Perez, see what her plans are. She told me she'd been paid until the end of October, but after that, I don't know. She also may be able to tell me more about Miranda and SanAngelo.

"Are you thinking SanAngelo had Miranda killed?" Greg asked.

Andi frowned. "I don't know. Remember the suitcase? From what Gary Johns said, it must have been full of money. Or drugs. Heavy, Ben Patel said. Maybe SanAngelo had someone kill her, and the money was the payoff."

"Could be."

"Who else would have known about the drug sales and the suitcase of money? Who knew she was in Burgess Beach that night? She spent time with Toni and Marta before she checked in to the motel. I need to check my notes, but I think Patel said she got there late, after ten o'clock."

Greg said that the interview with Patel seemed a long time ago, but he was pretty sure that was right."

"And Gary Johns said she left Fort Pierce around ten in the morning. The nanny said she was there most of the day with Toni."

"I don't know. I wasn't there for those interviews."

Andi sighed. "I wish to hell you hadn't gotten yourself suspended. I need your help."

"And I want to help. I don't want you to have to face this alone."

"I can't do it alone. But there's nobody else. Garcia's okay, but he knows nothing about Miami."

They sat quietly for a while, his arm around her, her body leaning into his, each thinking about the case. Andi couldn't keep her thoughts from returning to the two men and their quiet menace. When she thought about being alone, her stomach roiled.

After a while, she said, "I don't want you to leave. I don't want to be alone."

"I agree. I don't think you should be by yourself tonight. I can sleep on the couch."

They sat again, not talking, Andi huddled in Greg's arms.

Finally, she got up and went to the hall closet and got out sheets, a blanket and pillow for the couch. They busied themselves making up the couch, not speaking.

When they were done, she said awkwardly, "Well, good night."

"Good night." He leaned over to kiss her on the cheek. As he came toward her, she moved her head, and he kissed her ear instead. They both laughed, then both turned to kiss lightly on the mouth. But as they kissed, neither pulled back, and the light kiss turned into something more urgent. He kissed her hard, and she kissed him back. They fell back onto the already made-up couch, and kissed again, this time with more passion. His tongue probed her mouth, and she responded.

He reached under her blouse and caressed her breast, and she tore at his shirt, craving the warmth of his skin, her hands sliding up and down his back. Then, as he unfastened her bra and touched her bare breast, she felt a surge of desire. "Bedroom," she gasped, and they stumbled from the couch and fell onto the bed. Their lovemaking was urgent, almost violent. Afterwards, they lay quiet, and she nearly fell asleep, but she responded immediately when he ran his hands down her body, and they made love again, more slowly and gently this time.

When they were done, she curled into Greg's arms and fell asleep.

She woke, startled, sunlight streaming into the bedroom. She was alone in her bed. She tried to remember the night before. She'd slept deeply, almost like she had as a child. Greg had been there. But where was he? Had he ducked out before she'd even awakened? She looked at the bedside clock. Seven. She was embarrassed. Perhaps it was good he was gone. What would she say to him in the daylight? It would be better not to have to see him.

Then she heard the sounds of movement in her tiny kitchen and smelled the odor of coffee brewing. He wasn't gone. Now she had to face him. She got out of bed and went into the bathroom. When she had showered, put on a robe and could think of no way to delay any longer, she headed out into the living room.

"Good morning, sleepyhead," Greg said. "Are you okay?"

"God, I really slept." She didn't look at him.

He turned away from the stove and smiled at her. "Coffee? I scrambled some eggs if you want, and I can make toast."

She returned his smile, relieved at his matter-of-fact attitude. "Lovely," she answered. "I haven't been waited on since my last trip home."

"Where's home?" he asked, not looking at her but busying himself with putting bread in the toaster and serving the eggs.

"Tampa's where I grew up. We moved there from Minneapolis when I was about two, so it's all I know. How about you?"

"I moved to Miami after college. Grew up in Michigan." He brought over a plate of scrambled eggs and toast. He'd even found butter and jam.

She took a bite and realized she was hungry. "Did you always want to be a cop?" she asked. "These eggs are delicious, by the way."

"Thanks. I went to Miami for a job with a hotel. I majored in hotel management, but I hated it. I had a friend who was Miami police, and he suggested I give that a try."

Her mouth full of toast, she muttered, "And you liked it better than hotel management?"

"Almost anything would be better than that. Hotel management is people yelling at you when you have to be nice to them. At least when you're a cop, you get to yell back."

She laughed. "I can see where that would be better." Then she glanced at the clock. "I'd better get going. Will you stay while I get dressed? I don't want to be here alone.""

"Sure. I'll stay."

She headed to her bedroom and took black slacks, a black-and-white blouse and a black jacket from her closet. When she pulled out the drawer that held her underwear, she saw that it had been slightly disturbed. She looked in the other drawers, and found the order had been altered slightly in each. She thought about the silent man rooting in her clothes and felt her stomach heave.

She ran to the bathroom, and hovered over the toilet, but after a couple of minutes, her stomach settled down. She sat on the edge of the tub for a long time, afraid to go back to the defiled bedroom. She'd have to have the locks changed, but she was also going to have to move. She couldn't stay here after those men had been through her clothing. What else had they touched?

Last night when she checked, nothing seemed disturbed, but her bedroom was no longer a refuge. It had been invaded, and she could feel the presence of those men.

Greg called from the living room. "You okay. I don't hear you moving around."

"I'm okay, I guess."

She showered and dressed quickly, then looked at herself in the mirror. She looked like a ghost, her skin the color of ashes. Make-up helped some, but she still looked as though she was recovering from a long illness.

When she came out to the living room, Greg asked, "What happened in there?"

"I'm gonna have to move. They went through everything. Some traces in the dresser of things moved. Scared the shit outta me."

"Bastards."

They left the apartment, and Greg walked her to her car. "What are you doing today?"

"I'm going to report to the captain first. I'm not sure what he's going to say. Probably want me to have an escort. I also need to get a locksmith to change the locks. You got anybody to recommend?"

"Yeah. Call me when you get to work. I'll give you his number."

"Thanks for coming over last night. I needed not to be alone."

"I'm glad you called." He took her key, opened the car door, and kissed her lightly on the cheek. "I'll talk to you later."

As Andi drove to work, she thought about the night before. She hadn't thought she'd been attracted to Greg, partly because he was a cop, and then especially after she'd learned about his relationship with Miranda, but he'd been comforting and caring last night. And then his lovemaking had been so passionate and her response so eager that she'd forgotten her misgivings. Now she wondered what she'd done. She was glad he hadn't wanted to talk about it this morning. They'd have to sometime, though.

She thought about the day ahead. She needed to have the locks changed—today, if possible. And when was she going to have time to find an apartment and move again? She'd thought this place was perfect—and look what it had brought her!

TWENTY-EIGHT

As soon as Andi got to work, she asked Lisa if she could see the Captain. She wanted to tell him as soon as possible about the threats. Lisa called her half an hour later and said the Captain was ready for her.

She knocked and heard the familiar "Enter."

"So, how'd you do with Johnson? He help you out?" the Captain asked.

"Yes. Thank you for that, sir. I wanted to tell you about some visitors I had last night," and she told him about the two men, omitting her terror and Greg's visit. As she spoke, the Captain's expression got more and more angry, his eyes darker and more piercing than usual. He listened without interrupting.

When she finished, he slammed his fist on his desk. "Goddamn it! Are you all right?"

"Yes. I'm fine."

"Why didn't you call the station? The duty officer would've called me. Who do you think you are—Wonder Woman?" His voice was angry. "What about prints?"

"Both men were wearing gloves, so there won't be any fingerprints."

"What did you do after they left?"

"I wrote down everything I could remember about them and checked the apartment to see if they'd disturbed anything. Then I called a friend to come over and stay with me. I didn't want to be alone."

"You should have called the station. What were you thinking? From now on, you'll have a bodyguard. A patrol officer will be with you at all times. I don't want you alone."

"Yes, sir."

"Do you think these were the same people who rammed your car a couple of nights ago?"

"I don't know. They didn't say anything about that."

"The plate number you gave me matched one belonging to a snowbird, down here for the winter. But his car was a red sedan, and you said this was a dark SUV."

"Oh. I got the number wrong, I guess."

"Or the plates had been altered." Bradley stroked his chin. "Do you have to go to Miami again?"

"I don't have to go for a few days. I have some details to follow up here and in Fort Pierce first."

"Let me know your plans. Every day. And don't you go anywhere without a bodyguard."

"Not even around Burgess Beach?" she asked.

"Nowhere."

She called Greg at home and after he gave her the name and phone number for the locksmith, he said, "Call me when you get home tonight. We need to talk."

Uh, oh! Andi thought. She hoped he wanted to talk about the case and not about last night. She didn't want to think about that now.

She called the locksmith, but he was booked for the day and couldn't come out until tomorrow. "Unless it's an emergency—broken window, door knocked down." Andi said she could wait, and Joe said he'd be out the next day at ten.

Then she dictated what she had found out the day before: Silvano Valencia's death, the interview with the Acostas, and the threats made by the two men when she returned home. She reread Greg's notes on his interview with Ben Patel. Miranda had checked into the Hibiscus Motel at ten minutes past ten on Friday night. Andi's interview with Marta Perez said that Miranda had been with her and Toni in the afternoon and stayed until Toni went to bed. Perez said she thought Miranda planned to drive back to Miami that night. Andi decided to see if the nanny could tell her anything more about Philippe and Miranda and the night Miranda was murdered.

Pat McCormack, a young patrol officer, was catching up on his paperwork at one of the desks when Andi called to him. "Can I get you to drive me on a call?"

"Sure," he said.

In his car, Andi directed him to Perez's house. Toni wasn't out front with her doll as she had been on Andi's last visit. Andi knocked and got no response. She knocked again. Nothing. She peered in the front window. No one home. Andi walked around to the side and then the back. There was no one there.

She called Paloma Marquez, the social worker, and got her answering machine. Identifying herself, she brought Marquez up to date on the empty house.

There were three small bungalows fairly close together on Bay Drive. The one Marta Perez and Toni had lived in was in the middle. Andi knocked on the door of the house to the left. No answer. She knocked again, and a voice said, "Hold yer horses."

An elderly man with a walker opened the door and asked, "Wha'cha want?"

"I'm looking for the people in the house next door—a woman and a little girl. They're not home. Do you know where they went or when they left?"

"Got better things to do than watch the neighbors," the man said, and slammed the door.

Andi went to the house on the other side of Marta Perez' rental and knocked. Again no one answered, and she knocked a second time.

"Just a minute," said a female voice. "I'm coming."

A tiny woman in her mid-seventies, Andi guessed, opened the door and asked, "What are you selling?"

"Nothing," Andi said and produced her ID. "Can you tell me when the people next door left, or when they might be back."

The woman took Andi's ID from her hand and studied it. She handed it back before she spoke. "They left in a taxi this morning. Had a couple of suitcases. She wasn't very friendly, the woman."

"No," said Andi. "She wasn't, I guess. What time did they leave?"

"About seven o'clock. I'm up by five-thirty most mornings."

"Did you talk to the woman or the child at all while they were here?" Andi asked.

"As I said, she wasn't very friendly." The woman stepped back, prepared to close the door on Andi.

"How long have they lived here?" Andi asked quickly.

"Don't know. Five, six months, I guess."

"Can you tell me anything about them or about the taxi that picked them up?"

"I never talked to them, but I saw the little girl once in a while. Cute little thing. The taxi was from town. Pierpont Taxis. You can call them."

Andi was left standing on the front porch, the closed door nearly hitting her in the face. Friendly enough, she thought. And nosy. Nosy is good.

She told McCormack where she wanted to go, and he drove to the headquarters of Pierpont Taxis. It was in a tiny storefront on a side street off the main avenue. Andi stepped into a long, narrow room which held two desks, one of which was occupied by a blond woman in her late forties. She had once been pretty but hadn't aged well. Too much sun had turned the skin of her face and neck leathery, and her bleached hair was lifeless. The woman stood up when she saw Andi.

"May I help you? I'm Betty Olson, the manager."

Andi produced her ID and asked about a pickup by the taxi service at Marta Perez' place on Bay Drive. The woman looked intimidated by the police ID and gestured to Andi to have a seat at her desk while she checked the records. It didn't take long for her to determine that the pickup, at seven o'clock that morning, had been done by their taxi number two. The destination was the West Palm Beach Airport, and they'd been dropped off at 8:30 a.m.

"The passengers," Andi asked. "Who were they?"

"The woman didn't give a name. She said her and her daughter."

"What airline did they request to be left at?"

"West Palm has a single drop off point, so we don't know."

"Anything else you can tell me?" asked Andi.

"No. If you want to talk to the driver, he'll be back about four when he checks out."

"I'd like to." She glanced at her watch. It was two-thirty. "I'll be back."

She asked Pat to take her back to the station, and he did so, returning to his paperwork until he left a few minutes later to take a call on a domestic dispute.

Andi called Paloma Marquez again and got her answering machine. She got a sandwich from the nearby deli and returned to her office to eat. At about a quarter to four, there were no other patrol officers in the building, and she decided to ignore the captain's instructions and drive to the taxi office herself.

A cab was parked on the street in front of the office. When Andi entered, she saw a man talking with Betty Olson. He was in his sixties, very bald with a combover and a big stomach. Andi wondered if he had trouble getting in and out of the cab. He and Ms. Olson both turned to look at her.

"Here she is now," the manager said. Then she said to Andi, "This is Ed Martinez, the driver I told you about."

Andi showed the driver her ID and asked him to tell her about the passengers he had picked up that morning.

"The little girl wasn't happy," he said. "She kept saying she wanted her mother and how would her mother know where they were. The woman tried to shush her, but she wouldn't stop. I felt almost as if the little girl was being kidnapped, but it wasn't none of my business, so I kept quiet. Finally, the woman said they'd see her mother pretty soon, and the little girl kind of quieted down."

"Tell me about their luggage," Andi said.

"They had a lot—four suitcases. One was big and heavy. Blue. It had a strap around it. The woman asked me to help, so I carried it to the cab and put it in the trunk."

"Anything else that you noticed about the woman and the child?"

"No. The little girl didn't want to get out of the cab at the airport, and the woman got a baggage handler and held the child tight by the hand. Almost dragged her out of the cab." Martinez looked embarrassed, as if he knew he should have done something but didn't know what. "I didn't want to interfere."

"No," Andi said. "I understand."

"She was being kidnapped—the little girl?" Martinez asked.

"Not exactly. Thank you for your help, Mr. Martinez." Andi extended her hand to him, then thanked Betty Olson and left.

Andi checked her phone. Why didn't the damn social worker call her back? The heavy blue suitcase with the strap around it. That was the one that Ben Patel had carried upstairs at the Hibiscus Motel.

She returned to the station and called West Palm Beach Airport Security. She explained what she needed, and Officer Manion said he would check and call her back.

While Andi waited, she dictated the day's events. That was when Lisa told her that the Captain wanted to see her immediately.

Andi stepped into the Captain's office after his "Enter."

"What the hell were Greg Lamont's prints doing all over your apartment?" he bellowed. His face was nearly purple, and she'd never heard him so angry.

"I called Greg last night after the two men left. He came over, and we talked for a while."

"You called Lamont and you didn't think to call the station? What kind of detective are you? Lamont is suspended. Why the hell are you even talking to him?"

"He's been giving me some help about Miranda, and he's been helping me with contacts in Miami."

"You've been discussing the murder of Lamont's ex-girlfriend with him, and he, a possible suspect, has been helping your investigation. Is that what you're telling me?" The Captain's face was, if it were possible, more purple with rage than when she had walked in.

"Yes, sir."

He turned away from her. He had not asked her to sit, and she remained standing like a schoolgirl in front of the principal. She knew she'd been a fool to get Greg involved and especially to have him come over the night before; but she'd known the men wouldn't leave prints and she really needed someone to talk to, not someone who would treat her apartment like a crime scene. She didn't know the captain would send out the crime scene techs.

She looked at the Captain's back. He couldn't take her off the case. There wasn't anyone else.

The Captain turned back to her. His face had returned to a more normal shade, and he no longer looked on the verge of a stroke.

"Detective, you are suspended with pay, pending further investigation. You are to turn over all your notes to me."

She stared at him. He couldn't do that. But of course he could. "Who's going to take over the case, sir?"

"That's not your concern, detective. You may not even have a job when this is over. Give me your badge and gun, your case file and murder book. Then pack up your things and go home."

She hesitated and almost spoke, but there wasn't anything she could say.

"Yes, sir."

"I'm going to have a car drive by your apartment complex every couple of hours. Just to be sure those men don't return."

"I don't want . . . ."

"You don't have a say."

"I do. I do have a say. You can suspend me, but I don't want anybody watching me. I'll sign anything you like to hold the department harmless, but no watchdog." She surprised herself by the force of her response.

Bradley put up his hands in front of his face as if to ward her off. "All right, Battaglia. I'll draft something for you to sign before you go. But I have to say that's not very smart. Be careful and watch your back."

She walked out of his office, fighting back tears. She hadn't thought he'd suspend her. Now neither she nor Greg had the authority to pursue the case.

Back at her desk, she saw that she'd had a return call from Officer Manion at the airport. The nanny and child had boarded a plane for Miami.

She took her badge from her pocket and her Beretta from her purse, and walked them to Bradley's office, knocking and leaving them on his desk.

"I need to finish my notes from today," she said quietly. "I'll leave everything with Lisa."

"Fine," the Captain said without looking at her.

As she gathered the case material together, she thought about what she knew. Miranda had been in Burgess Beach with Toni and Marta the day she was murdered. She'd left Fort Pierce, according to Gary Johns, at around ten in the morning and hadn't checked into the Hibiscus Motel until ten in the evening. Marta had said she thought Miranda had gone back to Miami, but Marta knew about the suitcase. Miranda had had it with her, and if it was full of money, she probably had brought it into the house. Had Marta left the child asleep and followed Miranda to the motel? Or had Miranda told her where she was staying? Perez had opportunity and motive. And now she appeared to have the suitcase.

Andi gathered her paperwork together, checked to see if Lisa was at her desk, and when the coast was clear, took her notes and case file to the copy machine where she duplicated as much of it as she could in ten minutes. When she returned to her desk, she found a hold harmless agreement that Bradley had drafted. She signed it, bundled the case file and murder book together and left everything on Lisa's desk with a note to give it to the captain. She didn't want to face him again.

Andi got a box from the copy room and gathered the few personal items from her office. She stuffed the copies of the case file material in the box and topped them with her calendar and a small owl figure that she considered a good luck charm. Hah! Some luck. She put her jacket on top to conceal the contents.

She could see Ed Garcia standing in the open office area watching her. She fought back tears as she worked, keeping her head down. Nobody was going to see her cry. Or lose her temper.

She picked up her things, took one quick look around and walked out without a backward glance. Out of the corner of her eye she saw Garcia walking toward her, but she kept her head down and headed for the door.

"What happened, Andi?"

She didn't turn her head as she spoke. "The captain and I had a 'disagreement.'"

"Will you be back?"

Andi didn't answer, just pushed the door open and walked out into the parking lot. Don't let him follow me, she thought. But of course he did.

"When will you be back?"

"Goddamnit, Ed, I've been suspended. Don't follow me."

Andi stuffed the box into the backseat, got in and started the car. She could see Ed standing in the lot, staring at her as she drove off. She held herself under control until the station was out of sight. Pulling into a supermarket parking lot, she found a space near a vacant store, turned off the engine and let her rage and frustration overtake her. She pounded the steering wheel and allowed her tears to flow.

Finally, when she had been reduced to a few last tears and her hands hurt, she started the car again and headed home. By the time she reached her apartment, her left hand was swollen and sore, but she was done with crying and ready to get to work. Andi made a pot of strong coffee, got an ice pack for her hand, and sat down to read the case material. She made notes as she read, noting any inconsistencies in that first talk she'd had with Marta Perez. When she was finished, it was eight o'clock. She called Greg.

"Hi," she said.

"I'm glad you called. I've done some thinking after last night."

In a sudden rush, she remembered. She'd been so involved with Captain Bradley and the case that she'd forgotten.

"Oh, yeah. But, listen, I have some really exciting news. I've been suspended."

"What?"

"The Captain found out I was using you as a consultant and hit the roof. I'm off the case until further notice. I'm on administrative leave. Sound familiar? "

"I'll be right over."

He hung up before she could say anything more, but she was glad he was coming.

Greg arrived twenty minutes later. "How did he find out?" he asked when she opened the door.

"Fingerprints. None from the bad guys, but lots from you."

"Oh. He sent the techs over?"

"Yeah. He didn't ask me. I guess it's a crime scene."

"I guess."

He looked at her hand, swaddled in an ice pack. "What happened to your hand?"

"Just a little bruise," Andi said. She didn't want to admit she'd done it to herself.

"Oh. Have you had anything to eat?" Greg asked.

She had to stop and think. "No. I guess I haven't." She realized then that not only hadn't she eaten, she hadn't combed her hair or washed her face since her tears on the way home. She must look like hell.

"Good. I've ordered Chinese."

Andi ran her day by Greg while they waited for dinner to arrive: the flight of the nanny and the child, Patel's description of the suitcase he had carried for Miranda, Bradley's fury at her working with Greg on the murder case and, despite her belief he wouldn't do it, her suspension.

"What do you think he'll do now?" asked Greg

Andi felt herself getting angry all over again. "I don't know. I don't care. I can't believe he'd suspend me. Who is there to take over the case? Garcia? Huh.

"Shit. That's cold. I can't believe it. There's nobody, is there? He'll have to get somebody from Fort Pierce or Lauderdale or take it himself. I suppose he was a good detective in his day."

"Who the hell's going to bring him up to speed? He's gonna have to spend days getting to know the case. He can't stop the investigation until whoever takes over learns the ropes. That's crazy. He's crazy. He can't find Miranda's murderer, but we can." By the time she finished, Andi realized she was almost shouting.

They were interrupted by a knock on the door, and Greg went to collect the dinner. Discussion of the case was put on hold while they got out plates, utensils and napkins and then sat down to their meal.

Andi realized how close to hysteria she'd sounded. Like she was the crazy one, not Bradley. She was embarrassed, and when she caught a glimpse of herself in the mirror by the front door, she looked like a crazy lady, too. Unwashed face, streaked makeup, uncombed hair. She wished she'd taken a little more time to pull herself together, mentally as well as physically, before Greg arrived.

"This is good," Andi said. "Where'd you get it?"

"Yung Chow, just past Dixie Highway in town."

"I've never tried them, although I've passed the place. They're only take-out, right?"

"They have a few tables, but they lack 'atmosphere.' Better to do take-out."

Finally, after she couldn't eat another bite, Andi said, "How'd you know I like Moo Shu Pork?"

"I figured you had good taste."

They cleared away the dishes and put the leftovers away. Although Andi wished Greg would leave, she knew he wouldn't, at least not yet, and she stalled, clearing up the kitchen for as long as she could before she headed back to the living room where Greg already sat on the sofa. She took a seat on a chair opposite him.

They talked about next steps, neither of them considering giving up the case. Each understood that they were committed to solving the mystery of Miranda's murder, no matter who told them to stop. They analyzed the suspects, particularly the nanny and where she might be now. "I hope she's not going to hold the child hostage," Andi said.

"That would be a problem."

"We're not giving up?"

"No. Absolutely not. Do you think Perez has gone to the Acosta's?"

"That's a good guess. Otherwise, I don't know where."

"You've got another gun?"

"Yeah. Another Beretta. But first, the locksmith is due tomorrow at ten. I can't go another day without doing that."

Greg agreed. "What you need is new locks—good ones—and a better deadbolt and something to keep the sliding glass doors from opening."

"First thing tomorrow," Andi said. "I'm sorry. I've run out of steam. I've got to get some rest."

Greg said, "I can't leave you alone tonight."

"I can't keep my eyes open. Let's talk tomorrow."

"I'll sleep on the sofa," Greg said. "The sheets and everything are already here. Then I'll be here when Joe arrives."

"Joe? Oh, okay." Andi got to her feet. "Thanks for coming over and for dinner."

"Yeah. Sure. I'll lock the door and the deadbolt."

Andi stood and headed into the bedroom. "Goodnight, Greg. Thanks."

"Goodnight, Andi," Greg said.

TWENTY-NINE

When she awoke the next morning, Andi thought about how her life had been upended. She'd never dreamed Captain Bradley would suspend her. She was needed. She was the one who could find the answers.

Bradley clearly put discipline before solving crimes, but that didn't make sense to Andi. Use what you've got, she thought. She'd used Greg because he knew Miranda and because he knew the Miami scene. She'd known it would be much harder to solve the crime as an outsider. She hadn't intended to get involved with Greg, just use what he knew to help her. But maybe she'd lost control of the relationship, like her relationship with Jim. No, this was different. She knew what she was doing.

There was no sound coming from the living room and no smell of fresh brewed coffee. Was Greg still asleep or had he left? She looked at the clock. Eight. As she got out of bed, she winced at the pain in her hand. It was still red and swollen. Served her right. She showered quickly, dressed, then headed into the kitchen. Greg was gone, the sheets and blanket neatly folded on the sofa.

She put on a pot of coffee, thinking about what she had to do. The locksmith at ten. As she poured a cup of coffee, there was a knock on the door. It was Greg carrying doughnuts.

"Good morning," said Greg. "Joe'll be here early if you're ready. What he doesn't know about locks isn't worth knowing."

"Sure." She took a bite of a doughnut. "Good."

Joe Anson, the locksmith, arrived a few moments later. He greeted Greg, was introduced to Andi, and they briefed him on the problem. "So, you've had some experts breaking in to your place."

"Experts—and scary ones. I need the best you can provide, although I think I'll be moving when I get a chance. What about an alarm system?"

"I don't do that, but I can put you in touch with the company I use."

Joe got busy while Andi and Greg sat drinking coffee.

"What are we going to do today?" Greg asked.

"Are we still together on this?" Andi asked.

"Of course. I've got to find Miranda's killer."

"Can you be objective about Toni? She could be your child."

"Look, I'm a cop. We need to find her."

"Right. So, what I was thinking is that we should go to the Acosta's first to find out if Marta Perez and Toni are there." Andi was leafing through her case notes, although she'd nearly memorized them the night before.

Greg nodded agreement. "If they're not at the Acosta's, we should probably check Miranda's apartment."

"Yeah. Even if the locks have been changed, we can probably get the manager to let us in."

"And if it's been rented, they won't be there." Greg said.

"It might be a good idea to check in with Kathryn Forbes." Andi was leafing through the case file and her notes. "We haven't seen her in a while. Does she know about Toni? She never said, but a lot of people never told us what they knew."

"Good idea. She'll probably be at work. Do you know where?"

Andi dug through her notes to their meeting with Forbes. "I just saw that last night. Ah, here it is. She works in Miami at a graphic design firm called Designs for the Future. I'll get a phone number and address."

Andi called information and got the phone number. She called and asked where they were located and whether a designer named Kathryn Forbes still worked there, explaining that Forbes had done some work for her firm and she wanted to talk to her again about a new project.

"Yes, Kathryn's still here. Do you wish to talk with her?"

"No. I'll just pop in when I get a chance. I won't take much of her time, but I'd like to reconnect."

Andi could hear another phone ringing as the receptionist asked, "May I tell her who called?"

Andi broke the connection before the receptionist had finished her sentence. She said to Greg, "The address is North East First Street and Second Avenue. You know it?"

"Yeah. It's one of those high rises downtown. What time is it now?"

"It's eleven now. Let's see how Joe is doing."

The locksmith came out of the bedroom just as she spoke. "I'll show you what I've done," he said.

Joe showed them the new locks and deadbolts, the locks for the sliding glass windows and the braces to keep them from being pushed open. Andi paid him, thanked him and she and Greg locked up and hurried out to his car.

It was two-thirty when they got to Miami. They parked under Kathryn's building and took the elevator up to the twelfth floor. At the reception desk, Andi showed her badge and asked to see Forbes. The receptionist called and told them Kathryn would be right with them.

When Forbes came out, she greeted them and led the way back to a small, glass-enclosed office with a spectacular view across Biscayne Bay to Miami Beach. Andi noticed that Kathryn was more assured than she had been when Andi saw her before, and she wondered if the finality of Miranda's death had allowed her to get on with her life. The last time they had talked, when Kathryn gave her the phone records, she'd been distraught and seemed jealous of whoever was taking Miranda to Burgess Beach and away from her.

Kathryn's desk was positioned with her back to the view, and she gestured to Andi and Greg to sit in the two chairs facing her. "It's not a big office, but the view is terrific. Still, I can't face out or I'd do nothing else all day." She smiled. "I only allow myself to look out when I'm taking a break.

"What can I do for you? I assume this is about Miranda. Have you found out who killed her?"

"Not yet, but we're working on it," Andi answered. "We wanted to ask if you knew anything about a woman named Marta Perez who lived in Burgess Beach."

Kathryn thought for a moment, then said, "I don't know the name. Was she Miranda's lover?"

"How about the name Toni or Antoinette?" Andi asked. "Does that ring any bells?"

Kathryn didn't even have to think about that. "No."

Andi stood and extended her hand to Forbes. "Thanks for seeing us so promptly. We're sorry to have bothered you."

Forbes, looking a bit puzzled, shook Andi's hand, then Greg's. She said, "Can you tell me anything about your investigation? Are you close to a solution? Miranda didn't deserve to die like that. Nobody does."

Andi paused. "We can't give you any details, but we believe we're close to a solution."

Kathryn seemed to hesitate, then asked, "Can you let me know when you have an answer? I think about Miranda a lot. I know I loved her more than she loved me, but we were close for a while."

"I'll try to let you know when the case is closed," Andi said, and followed Forbes back out to the reception area. Forbes pressed the elevator button for them and watched them leave.

"Well, I guess that was a waste of time," Andi said.

"And money. It's going to cost us a bundle for our few minutes of parking. Got any change?"

Andi fished twenty dollars out of her purse and gave it to Greg. "Here you go. We did need to know if she was involved. I wanted to see her expression, but she doesn't know about either Perez or Toni."

"You're right."

They headed to the Acosta's house in Coral Gables and pressed the button by the locked wrought iron gate. A voice asked, *"Si. Quien es?"*

Andi answered, *"Señora Acosta esta aqui?"*

"Si. Su nombre?"

"La policia."

There was silence, then a buzzer opened the gate. They headed up the path to the massive front door which was opened by a small, dark-haired woman wearing an apron over her dress. They could see a vacuum cleaner on the floor of the hall behind her.

A voice called from upstairs. *"Quien es, Elena?"*

"La policia."

After a moment, Belle Acosta started down the stairs.

She paused mid-way. "You again?" she asked.

"Yes," Andi responded. "We have a few more questions."

Belle continued down the staircase and stepped onto the marble floor of the entrance. "I've told you everything I know, detectives."

"Still," Andi said, "we need to talk with you again."

Belle noticed the cleaning woman watching the three of them with interest and said, "Elena, you can go on with your work. Start in the kitchen."

"Si, Senora," Elena said, picking up the vacuum and heading toward the back of the house.

"Oh, very well. Come in." Belle gestured to the living room where she and Andi had talked before. They sat in one of the conversation areas.

This time Belle didn't offer tea.

Andi began, "You remember Detective Greg Lamont. He was with me when we saw you and your husband at the Meta Lounge."

"Yes. I remember."

Andi glanced at Greg. Belle Acosta wasn't going to tell them much. "We believe you know a woman named Marta Perez. She works as a nanny."

Belle didn't react at the mention of Perez' name. "Yes. I've recommended her to several friends who have young children. What about her?"

"Did you recommend her to Miranda Duncan?"

"I may have. I don't remember."

"Did you know that Miranda had a little girl named Antoinette?"

"I think she told me she had a child. Was that her name? I don't recall." Belle's voice was calm and steady, but Andi noticed that her hands were clenched tightly in her lap.

"You told me when we talked before that Miranda never talked about her private life. Yet now you say you knew she had a child and that you recommended a nanny to her. Which story is correct?"

"Well, in thinking back, Miranda may have asked me for a recommendation for a nanny. I'd forgotten that when we talked before."

"Did you ever meet Toni?"

Belle's eyes shifted momentarily from her focus on Andi's face to the window above her. She had lied well so far, but her control was slipping. She didn't look at Andi when she said, "I never met her."

"Do you know where Marta Perez and Toni are now?" Greg asked, making Belle shift her focus to him. Andi thought she saw the shadow of a frown cross Belle's botoxed forehead, but then she resumed her innocent look as though she'd pulled down a mask.

"No. Should I?"

"It's not a question of whether you should, Ms. Acosta," Greg said. "Do you know where they are? They left Burgess Beach yesterday."

Belle didn't hesitate. "No. I don't."

Andi got to her feet. "Well, if you should hear from Ms. Perez, Belle, get in touch with us. Call me at my cell," scribbling the number on the back of her card. "Greg and I will be moving around. It's essential we find them. Marta Perez kidnapped the little girl, and I don't think you want to be a party to that."

"Certainly. I'll let you know." Belle stood and guided them to the front door, watching them walk down the path to be sure they did indeed leave.

"She knows," Andi said. "They may be there."

"Think the housecleaner knows?"

"Probably. She seemed curious about us." Andi looked back at the house as they got into Greg's car. "Let's wait for her to leave. We can use the threat of ICE to get her to tell us what she knows. How's your Spanish?"

"Better than yours," Greg said.

They got into Greg's car and drove off. Greg stopped when the street curved. He pulled to the side of the road, and they waited.

"This is a ritzy neighborhood. Hope some neighbor doesn't call the cops on us," Andi said.

"We'll have to chance it. Too bad I didn't bring the Rolls."

"And the chauffeur."

They waited for two hours, not talking much. Neither of them brought up their intimacy of the other night. They did need to talk, Andi knew, but not now, not while they had work to do.

After two-and-a-half hours, Andi had to go to the bathroom and hoped that Elena would show up before the need became urgent. A few minutes later an old Chevy truck passed them. Elena was driving.

Greg started the car and followed.

"Don't get too close," Andi cautioned.

"What? You think I've never followed a car before?"

Andi kept quiet.

In Little Havana, the truck pulled into the driveway of a small house painted bright orange. Greg drove past while Andi made a note of the address.

They parked further down the street and walked back toward the house. The front door was closed, the blinds drawn, and there was no sign that anyone was home. Greg knocked.

The door was opened by a burly Hispanic man who didn't look happy to see them.

"Yes," he said. "What do you want? We do not buy anything."

Andi showed her badge and said they would like to talk with Elena.

"She is not here. She is working." The man blocked the doorway so that neither Greg nor Andi could see inside the house.

"We just saw her go in. We know she's here." Andi said. "We are not with *la migra*. We just want to ask Elena a few questions."

The man stood quiet for a few seconds. Then he turned and called out, "*Ana, aqui hay unas gente quieran verte.*"

A voice called from the back of the house. "*Quien es?*"

Greg answered. "*La policia pero no es la migra. La niña? Esta en la casa?*"

There was silence for a few moments, then Elena emerged from the back of the house. Her face was tense with fear.

There was silence, then Andi went up to her and said, "*Elena, soy la policia pero no soy la migra. Digame. La niña y la mujer? Estan en la casa de Señora Acosta?*"

Elena didn't speak for a time, then went over to the burly man who put his arms around her. With her head buried in his chest, she emitted a torrent of Spanish which neither Greg nor Andi could understand. They looked at the man, and he said, "She says that a woman and a child are staying in the Acosta's house. They arrived yesterday afternoon by taxi. Señora Acosta tried to get them to go away, but the woman insisted, and la señora finally let them stay in the guest wing. They are still there, but the little girl cries for her mother."

Elena spoke again, and the man said, "She says Señora Acosta told the woman she had to leave tonight. The woman said she had nowhere to go, but Señora Acosta said she didn't care."

Andi looked at Greg. "We'd better get back there if we want to see where Perez goes with the child. Elena, can we see the guest wing from the street?"

Elena spoke again, and the man translated. "She says it is in the back. You cannot see it from the street."

The detectives thanked Elena for her help and headed back to the car. Andi said, "Before we go back, I need to make a pit stop."

Later, Andi said, "I'm trying to picture the Acosta's house. There's the wrought iron gate and the bell, but on the right, as you're facing the gate, isn't there a wall with a vine growing over it?"

Greg thought. "Yeah. It's only the gate that's wrought iron. The wall's not very high. Not dark enough yet, but in another hour, we could hop it."

"Better check the house across the street, too. Don't want nosy neighbors calling the cops on us. Embarrassing."

"More than embarrassing. Jail time."

They didn't speak again as Greg drove as fast as he dared the ten miles back to Coral Gables.

The neighborhood was quiet when they entered the Acosta's street, and they glided past the house. Greg said, "That's the wall. It'll work."

Andi looked carefully at the house across the street. "One light on downstairs and a fancy lantern outside. Security lights on a timer. Probably no one home."

Greg parked the car at the end of the block, which dead ended in a canal. There was a walkway alongside the canal and a bench overlooking it.

"Let's get out and sit. Looks innocent."

Andi checked her watch. It would be full dark in about forty-five minutes. They sat on the bench, gazing across the tiny canal.

"Pretty spot," Andi said. "Sorry we're not just sightseeing." Then she slapped her arm and swore. "Damn no-see-ums. We'll be eaten alive if we sit here. And I hurt that hand again."

"Not bothering me," Greg said. "What did you do to your hand?"

"Got mad at the steering wheel in my car," Andi said.

Andi couldn't see his face, but she was sure he was grinning. The street was very quiet. There seemed to be no one home at any of the houses adjacent to the canal. "Where is everyone?" Andi asked.

"A lot of university faculty live here. Maybe they're still in class. Don't know."

When Andi could no longer see her watch, she said, "Let's go."

Greg said, "I'll move the car up." He parked in front of the house next door, turned off the interior lights and left the car doors slightly open.

Andi walked along the sidewalk to the Acosta's house, and when she reached the side of the wall, she saw a narrow gate. She opened it. It led to a pathway at the side of the Acosta's house. They wouldn't have to jump the wall after all.

Andi grabbed Greg's arm as he left the car, and guided him to the gate she had found. He gave her a thumbs up, and they entered the front yard of the house. The grounds were planted with grass and a lot of small bushes that made walking treacherous in the dark. There were no lights coming from this side of the house.

"Now what?" Greg whispered.

"Back of the house. That's what Elena said."

They walked through the yard, trying to keep to the shadow. They rounded the side of the house and could see light spilling from a one-story ell-shaped extension to the main house. Andi grabbed Greg's arm, but he had stopped, too, still in deep shadow.

"The guest wing," Andi whispered, more to herself than to Greg.

At first there was no sound. Then they heard a voice.

"I said you can't stay." That was Belle Acosta. "Get your suitcases packed. I want you out of here tonight."

"Why won't you help us?"

"I don't know why you came here. You—and that child—they're nothing to us. I said you could stay last night, but now you have to go."

"I want to talk to Jorge. Jorge was good to us. Why won't you let me see him?"

Belle's voice came closer. "Why the hell is this window open? The air's on. Did you open it, little pest?"

A window slammed, and the voices became less distinct. Andi crept as close as she dared, but while she could still hear voices, she couldn't distinguish what was being said.

"Damn," she whispered. "Can you hear?"

"No," Greg said.

"I can't get any closer. The light's too bright."

They listened to raised voices, then a child's cry. Andi considered what they could do. If Marta left, they could follow, and when she reached where she was staying for the night, call Miami P.D. and have her picked up for kidnapping. They weren't going to learn anything now.

Then again, why had Marta asked to talk to Jorge? Had he been involved with Miranda? God knew almost every other male in Miami had been.

Then they heard another voice. Male. The voice was loud. "Belle, where are you?"

A door opened from the back of the main house. A figure walked onto the lawn, then turned toward the guest wing and knocked on the outside door.

"Belle. Are you in there?"

A door from the guest wing opened, and Belle emerged. Andi shrank back into the shadows, Greg behind her.

"What's going on?" Jorge said.

"Marta Perez is here with Miranda's brat. She wants us to help her. I told her she had to leave."

Jorge pushed Belle aside and walked through the open door into the guest wing. Belle followed, and Andi could hear her saying, "I told her we couldn't help."

Andi heard the child's voice. "*Tío* Jorge!"

"How's my little girl?" Jorge said.

Then Belle shut the door, and Andi couldn't hear anything except the murmur of voices.

"Damn," Andi muttered. "Just when it was getting interesting."

"Don't move," a man said. "Put your hands behind your heads."

THIRTY

"What the . . .?" Greg's voice was startled.

Andi did as she was told. A man in dark clothing walked around from behind them. He held a pistol in his hand, pointed at Andi's head.

"Who're you?" Andi asked.

"Put your hands behind your back." The man walked behind Andi and handcuffed her wrists. "Now you," he said to Greg and cuffed him as well.

"Who the hell are you?" asked Andi again.

"I am the security guard. Who are you?"

"We're police. From Burgess Beach." Andi knew she didn't sound very convincing.

The man pushed Greg toward the guest wing door. "Go. Open the door."

Andi pushed at the door with her shoulder, but it wouldn't open. The guard pushed the latch down, and they entered.

Andi took in the scene before the guard spoke. They were in a living room with comfortable chairs and a sofa, a large television on the wall, and an expensive-looking carpet. Jorge was sitting on the green and gold sofa with Toni on his lap.

Belle and Marta were face to face in the middle of the room, and Belle looked angry. They all turned as the trio entered.

Jorge carefully placed Toni on the floor and stood. "You!" he said when he saw Andi and Greg, then turned to the guard. "What's this, José?"

José said, "I found them outside, *Señor* Acosta. They were listening at the window and trying to see in."

"What are you doing here?" Jorge asked. "Have you not made enough trouble for us?"

Andi looked at Belle. She looked scared while Marta just stood quiet, her face giving nothing away.

Jorge took control of the situation. "Thank you, José. You may go on with your rounds. I will take care of them. Take off the handcuffs before you leave."

"*Si, Señor.*" José unfastened the cuffs from Andi and Greg's wrists, then turned and left.

"Why are you here?" Jorge asked.

"You have no right to be here. Do you have a warrant?" Belle seemed to have recovered her voice and her belligerence.

"We thought that Marta was here, even though you denied it," Andi said. She had to defend their actions. "We thought you were lying, so we came back to find out."

"Why are you looking for Marta?" Andi was startled when Jorge spoke.

"She kidnapped Toni, took her from Burgess Beach where she was under the supervision of Child Welfare Services and brought her to Miami."

"They were going to put her in foster care. I couldn't let them do that. Miranda told me to take care of Toni, no matter what happened." Marta's voice wavered.

"That's what Child Welfare is supposed to do. She doesn't have a mother or father, so she will go into foster care." Andi knew how she sounded, but she wanted to keep the attention on Marta.

"It is not true that she has no father," Jorge said. "I am her father."

Belle looked stricken. "Bastard! "she spat.

"I loved Miranda, and I love her child. You cannot take that from me."

"How could you? She was my friend."

Andi felt like the audience at a tennis match, turning from Belle to Jorge and back to Belle and still trying to keep an eye on what Marta was doing. Toni sat back on the couch, murmuring softly to a doll she held in her arms.

Andi took a quick glance at Greg. He looked as though someone had punched him. The news about Jorge and Miranda had come as a surprise to him, too.

Andi said, "We'd like to know what happened to the suit-case Miranda had with her in Burgess Beach."

No one spoke. Finally, Jorge said, "I do not think you are in a position to ask questions here."

He was quiet for several moments while everyone watched him. He seemed to be thinking. "I will not call the police." He held up his hand to quiet Belle as she protested. "But you will leave now. What you have done—trespass-ing—is not legal in America. Leave and do not come back."

Jorge motioned to the detectives to walk toward the door to the main house. Andi pushed the door open, and they walked down the hall to the foyer.

"Now you know my secret. I was in love with Miranda, but I did not kill her. I want you to find out who did." Jorge opened the front door and gently pushed Andi out. He pushed a button next to the door, and in a moment José appeared.

"They are leaving, José. See that they do."

José escorted Andi and Greg out the wrought iron gate and slammed it behind them. They walked silently back to the car. Greg started the engine, then sat, unmoving.

"Are you okay?" Andi asked.

"What makes him think he's the father?" Greg said. "That asshole. Who does he think he is?" He pounded the steering wheel. Andi had never seen him this angry.

"We don't know who Toni's father is." Andi kept her voice calm.

"Was she screwing him while she was still living with me? Was that where she disappeared to?" His voice rose.

Andi turned to look at Greg. The thought of Jim crossed her mind, and she remembered how his anger had turned to violence. She leaned against the passenger side door, pulling herself away from Greg.

Then she looked at him again. This was Greg, not Jim. As angry as he was, he wasn't going to take it out on her. Andi put a hand on his arm to quiet him. He was not someone to be afraid of.

Greg stopped talking, shoved the gear shift hard into drive and pulled quickly away from the curb, tires squealing in protest.

"Whoa," Andi said. "Slow down. Let's not have an accident."

"I don't want to talk about it any more."

"Okay." Andi took a breath and paused before she spoke. "I guess we just have to go back to Burgess Beach."

Greg didn't speak as he drove toward the highway that would take them to I 95, but Andi's mind was racing and before they left Coral Gables, she spoke again.

"Wait. Maybe we're being too quick. Belle wants Marta out tonight. Let's see if she leaves."

"Nothing's going to happen there tonight. Not with that asshole around."

"Maybe. But let's not leave right away. There's a pretty volatile mix of people in that house. Let's go back, see if anything happens."

"Your call." Greg shrugged, turned the car around and headed back toward the Acosta's.

When they were nearly back, Greg asked, "Where do you want me to park?"

Andi turned to face him, but he stared straight ahead, not looking at her. "Turn around and park next door. There's that big tree. Park under that. We'll just wait. It may be a waste of time, but let's see."

The Acosta's house was ablaze with light, but they couldn't hear anything. They sat quietly for a long time, then Greg asked, "Do you think Jorge is Toni's father?

"I don't know what I think. I've fucked this case up so royally that I don't know who did what. And I'm suspended. And you're suspended. We have no authority to do anything. We're lucky Jorge didn't call the police on us. The identity of Toni's father isn't a question I can answer."

"What now?"

"Just wait."

They sat quietly. Andi thought about what she knew, or what she thought she knew. She believed Marta had killed Miranda, but was that the truth? She had the suitcase, but she didn't act as if she were guilty of murder. So, if not Marta, who had killed Miranda? Did Belle know about Miranda and Jorge before tonight? Had she killed Miranda?

Andi thought about Greg. He'd loved Miranda, but she had betrayed him, not just with one, but with who knows how many others. She had had a child, who may have been his. Was it possible? Could he have killed Miranda? Her whole body turned icy. Why had she thought that?

She glanced at Greg, sitting next to her. Could he be Miranda's killer? She shivered violently. Suddenly she wanted to leap out of the car and run. If Greg had killed Miranda. . . , but no, he couldn't have. Could he? She looked over at him. His head was thrown back against the headrest, and he seemed nearly asleep. Could he be the killer?

She made herself gather the facts she was sure of. Greg had the opportunity. Captain Bradley hadn't cleared him of involvement in Miranda's death because he had no alibi. And exactly how had he felt about Miranda? When had he last seen her? Did he know about her life with Philippe, with Gary Johns, with Jorge, with Kathryn Forbes? Andi had dismissed him as a suspect without a thought, but now . . . . Maybe that was the problem—she hadn't thought. But she'd seen his anger tonight at Jorge. It was possible. Anything was possible now.

They heard no sounds from the house, but the lights stayed on. So they waited. At about half-past twelve, they heard loud voices. Andi got out of the car and walked toward the gate, hoping to hear better. Greg followed her.

"I want her gone. Tonight," a female voice said loudly. "I'll throw her out myself. I don't care what you say. She and that bastard have to go." It sounded as if Belle was outside.

Jorge's voice wasn't as clear. "Come on, Belle. Come back inside. Leave everything until tomorrow. Let's go to bed."

"No! I want her gone tonight."

Then Marta's voice could be heard, fainter. "You're afraid of what I saw, aren't you, Belle."

"You didn't see anything, bitch."

"Come in, Belle." Jorge's voice was soothing. "Don't tell everyone your business."

"I saw you." Marta said. Andi strained to hear, but whatever else Marta said was muffled.

"Shut up, bitch!"

There was the sound of a scuffle, then a scream. A child cried out, "Marta!" They could hear her sobbing.

"Come inside, Belle. You're scaring the girl."

"What the hell do I care? She's your bastard!" Her voice got fainter, and then a door slammed. They had gone back inside the house.

Greg and Andi moved back to the car.

"What did Marta mean? 'I saw you.' It sounded like something Belle didn't want Jorge to hear."

"I don't know," said Greg. "Could she have seen Belle in the motel where Miranda was murdered?"

"That's what I'm thinking. Could Belle have killed Miranda but not taken the suitcase? If Marta saw her, she could be in danger. Should we go in?"

"Cops can't enter without a warrant unless there's evidence of imminent danger, and we don't have enough for that. If we go in, Jorge'll just throw us out again."

"You're right. But we can't leave yet. In case."

They sat for a long time but heard nothing more. Gradually the lights went out, and by two o'clock, the house was dark.

"So, what now, chief?" asked Greg.

"Fuck off. I'm not the chief," Andi said. "We're in this together."

Andi was quiet for a long time. "I don't think we'll see anything more tonight, but I'm still worried. Marta might be in danger, and in any case, I'd like to catch her when she leaves tomorrow. She knows more than she's telling us."

"Then let's stay here tonight. We can sit in the car."

"I have to pee already."

"Go over in the bushes."

She sighed, got out to relieve herself in the shadow of the wall, then returned to the car.

Greg took his turn. When he returned, he said, "I hope we haven't killed all this expensive shrubbery."

"Fuck it," Andi said.

"Okay, chief."

Andi punched his arm at that. "Don't be a smart ass."

"Yes, Ma'am, Chief."

She hit him again, this time as if she meant it, then grabbed her sore hand and swore.

"Ow," Greg said. "Serves you right."

"Cut it out."

Greg said he wasn't sleepy, but by three o'clock he was snoring softly. Andi tried to stay awake, but found herself dozing as well. She woke with a start and checked her watch. 4:30. She was cold and wished she'd brought a jacket. Despite the chill, she dozed again.

Andi awoke to see a man walking a dog pause in front of their car. The dog, a German shepherd, sniffed at the tires while the man looked curiously at Greg sleeping in the driver's seat. He walked past the car, then turned and walked back. The dog stretched and placed his front paws on the driver's side window, and the man knocked.

Andi poked Greg. "Wake up. We have a visitor."

Greg came awake immediately. He opened the window and said, "Can I help you?"

"Yes," said the man. "Why are you sleeping here in your car? This is a nice neighborhood. We don't allow people to live in their cars here."

Greg brought out a badge and displayed it. "Police. Under cover."

"Oh," said the man. "I'm sorry. I thought you were homeless people." He hurried off, dragging the reluctant dog with him.

"Where'd you get the badge? Didn't you have to give it to Bradley?"

"On the internet. You can get a lot of genuine-looking stuff there."

"You're kidding."

"Scout's honor."

At seven o'clock, the driveway gate opened, and José drove out in a black SUV and headed toward the main road.

"Shift's over, I guess." Andi said.

Greg grunted.

They waited. At eight-thirty three children gathered in front of a house across the street, closer to the main road. A school bus picked them up a few minutes later, made a U-turn at the end of the block, then drove away. The street was quiet again. A car passed them from the end of the street by the canal. The driver didn't appear to notice them. By nine o'clock, they were desperately in need of coffee and a bathroom. They took turns entering by the side gate and relieving themselves in the bushes. The house remained quiet.

"How long do we wait?" Greg asked.

"'Til something happens."

"Forever, then."

At a quarter to ten a taxi pulled up in front of the Acosta's. The driver honked the horn, and Marta and Toni came out the wrought iron gate. Marta was carrying only one suitcase, not the heavy one with the strap. The driver loaded the suitcase in the trunk, and Marta opened the back door of the cab, ushering Toni inside. As Marta slid in, the gate clanged open, and Jorge, dressed in a robe and slippers, hurried out.

"Stop," he said, and banged on the window of the cab. "Marta, no. Don't leave. Where are you going to go? We need to settle this today."

"Belle said…," Marta said as she stepped back out of the taxi.

"I do not care what Belle said. Do not leave." He turned to the cab driver and said, "Wait a moment. Let me get some money." He turned and strode back to the house, returning a moment later with his wallet, from which he extracted some bills.

"I am sorry for the confusion," he said as he passed the bills to the driver. The driver counted them, then popped the trunk, stepped from the cab and lifted out the suitcase. He was smiling as he put the suitcase next to the gate where Marta and Toni stood. He got back into the cab and sped off.

Without a glance at the car where Greg and Andi had slid down in their seats, Jorge picked up the suitcase and ushered Marta and Toni back through the gate into the house. The front door slammed, and the neighborhood was quiet once again.

"Now what?" asked Greg.

"We have to get in the yard. That'll be closer to the action, whatever it's going to be."

"If we get caught this time, it's the police for sure."

"I know. Fuck it."

They opened the gate into the Acosta's yard. When they got close to the guest wing, they heard raised voices from inside the house although they couldn't hear what was being said.

Then, unmistakably, there was the sound of a shot, followed by a scream.

THIRTY-ONE

Andi tried to dial 911 as they ran, but her phone was dead.

"Damn," she muttered under her breath.

Greg pulled his weapon, pounded on the door and shouted, "Open up! Police!"

There was no response, but they could hear a child screaming and a man yelling. Greg kicked twice at the lock on the heavy door, but it didn't budge. He fired two shots into the door lock and pushed. The door opened.

There was no one in the living room or foyer. Greg and Andi ran toward the sounds. The guest wing door stood open, and Greg entered first. Belle stood pointing a gun at Jorge. Marta lay on the floor, bleeding from a wound to her shoulder, and Toni sprawled on the floor next to her, crying. Belle's gun was pointed at Jorge who stood in front of her.

"Drop the gun, Belle," Greg said.

Andi was startled at the change in Belle. Just yesterday, she had looked younger than her years, well-groomed, her clothing the height of fashion, her face carefully made up. Today, she looked thirty years older. Her hair was uncombed and matted around her head, she was wearing sweats, and her makeup was smeared with dark smudges of mascara around her puffy eyes.

When Belle heard Greg, she turned toward him slightly, and Jorge moved closer to her. She saw the movement and turned back to him.

"I'll shoot you," she said to Jorge. "You did this. You ruined our lives with that whore. We had everything, and you wrecked it. For what? For sex with a woman I thought was my friend? Don't think I won't shoot you, you piece of shit." Belle's voice was ragged, and tears streamed down her face.

"Don't be stupid, Belle," said Jorge. "Give me the gun."

"I don't want to kill you, Belle, but I can and I will shoot before you can shoot me." Greg's voice was firm and threatening. "Drop the gun."

"Don't try me, detective. I'll shoot you, too."

Standing behind Greg in the hallway, Andi took in the scene. She knew Belle hadn't seen her, so she turned and ran quietly back to the open front door to run around the house and take Belle by surprise from the yard.

She scarcely looked where she was going and smashed into a man coming in the front door. He grabbed her arm to hold her upright. It was Gary Johns, and he held a gun in his hand.

"Give me your gun," Johns said. "Turn around. Go on back."

"But . . .," Andi said.

"Shut up. Do what I say."

Andi did as she was told, turning and walking to the guest suite. She could see Greg, his pistol still focused on Bella.

Johns pushed Andi forward, the pistol at arm's length, then pointed it at Greg's head. "Give me the gun," he said.

Greg turned, ready to attack until he saw Johns' gun pointed at him. He dropped his.

"What the hell, Gary?" asked Andi.

He ignored her. Toni let out a terrified cry and flung herself at Jorge, nearly knocking him over.

"*Tío*," she whimpered. "Make him go away."

"Belle, get their handcuffs." Johns gestured to the detectives. He held the gun, and Belle did as she was told without emotion, handcuffing Greg and then Andi.

"Is there any rope and duct tape?" Johns asked.

"In the garage," she said.

Johns waved the gun at her. "Go. Get it."

Belle left the room by the back door. The two detectives, handcuffed, stood to the right of Johns, but well within his sight. Jorge turned slightly toward Johns.

Andi knew he wouldn't answer, but she couldn't stop herself. "What's this about? Belle killed Miranda. Did you know that? I thought you loved Miranda."

"You thought. You thought what? You didn't know fuck-all about what was going on."

He was right, Andi realized. She didn't know fuck-all.

Marta still lay on the floor, blood oozing steadily from the wound. Toni buried her face in Jorge's leg, sobbing, and he patted her shoulder, murmuring comforting sounds.

Andi said, "Marta's going to bleed to death if you don't do something for her.

"Shut up," Johns said.

Belle returned with a skein of rope and duct tape.

"Tie your husband to a chair," Johns said.

Jorge said, "Belle, don't do this," but she brought up a straight chair and pushed Jorge into it. Toni clung fiercely to him until Belle pushed her aside. She fell to the floor, her chest heaving.

"Bring that other chair for the detective," Johns said, and Belle tied Greg's feet and his cuffed hands to the chair.

"Okay, Belle," he waved the gun at Andi. "Hogtie her."

When Andi was trussed, he continued, "Now get something and try to stop the bleeding."

Belle brought towels out and pressed on Marta's wound, but the bleeding didn't slow.

Johns said, "Stop. That's not doing it. You hold the gun, and I'll do it." Then, with surprising skill, he applied a pressure bandage of towels to the wound, pressing it tightly until most of the bleeding had stopped.

Andi watched all of this in wonder. Who was this guy? She'd taken everybody in this case at face value until she was forced to see what the people really were like. Now another person had totally blindsided her. What a terrible detective she had turned out to be.

When the blood seemed to have slowed enough, Johns said to Belle, "Gag them."

"I don't know how," Belle said, protesting for the first time.

"Use duct tape. What's wrong with you?" Johns said.

"What about the kid" Belle asked.

"Tie her up," Johns said, but Jorge protested, "She's too little. *Mija,*" he said. "sit in the corner and be still like a good girl."

Toni looked scared but did as she was told. Then Belle started with Jorge, running duct tape around his head twice. Then she did the same to the others. When she got to Toni, she looked questioningly at Johns.

"Gag her."

After she had, Johns said, "Okay, Belle, let's go."

"We should shoot them," said Belle.

"You'd shoot Jorge?" asked Johns.

Belle didn't answer. She followed Johns out the door to the front of the house. The captives heard the front door slam.

The only sounds in the room were grunts as they each tried to loosen the ropes that held them. Time passed. How much time Andi didn't know. It seemed hours, but she couldn't judge. Then she heard a squeal from Toni

"I took the tape off, *tío*," the child said.

Jorge gestured with his head for her to come to him, and she moved to his side and loosened his gag.

"*Tío*, are you okay?" she asked.

"I am fine, *mija*," he said. "Good girl. Take the gags off the others. Does anyone have a cell phone?"

Toni did as Jorge told her, removing Andi's gag, and then cautiously approaching Greg, a little afraid of this man she didn't know. She pulled off his gag and then retreated to the protection of Jorge.

As soon as she could speak, Andi said, "My phone is in my pocket. Can you dial 911?"

Toni nodded, but when she retrieved the phone from the pocket of her jeans Andi remember that the battery was dead. "Shit," she said. "Greg, where's yours?"

"My shirt pocket." Again Toni approached Greg with caution, but she grabbed the phone and dialed 911.

"Can you give them the address and tell them we need help?" said Andi.

"What dress?" Toni asked, puzzled.

"I will help you," Jorge said. Toni had dialed 911, and Jorge gave the address while Toni held the phone close to his mouth. He said there had been a home invasion, that they were tied up, there was a woman with a bullet wound, and they needed help immediately.

The dispatcher asked, "Is there a need for the SWAT team?"

"No. The people who tied us up are gone," Jorge said.

"Police and an ambulance on their way," said the dispatcher.

The police arrived quickly, the sound of sirens piercing the air. Uniformed men and women swarmed into the room, followed quickly by EMT's and paramedics. Suddenly, the room was full of people, freeing the captives, asking questions, and yelling instructions across the room. The commotion made Toni start to cry again, and she held tightly to Jorge, still sitting in the chair to which he'd been bound. A detective from the Miami Police arrived to take charge of the chaos.

The EMT's put Marta on a stretcher and took her out to the ambulance. The loss of her nanny made Toni cry even more, and after he was freed, Jorge carried her over to the couch and held her on his lap.

Gradually, the noise subsided. Toni finally stopped crying and fell asleep in Jorge's lap. All but one man and one woman of the original responders left. The room was quiet but looked as if a tornado had hit: medical supplies of all kinds, some blood-stained, littered the floor; the furniture was pushed haphazardly against the walls; and every light in the room and outside was lit.

Lieutenant Arras of the Miami police settled down to question Andi, Greg and Jorge, "I'd like to get some preliminary information before we go back to the station to take your statements. What did this man and woman want? Was it a burglary? Do you know what they took?"

"Mr. Acosta hasn't had a chance to look, have you, Jorge?" Andi said.

Jorge didn't say anything.

"Can you give us a description of these people? If you talk with the police artist, maybe he can do a composite drawing. The woman who fired the shot? Had you ever seen her before? Or the man?"

There was a silence. Andi looked at Jorge, and he spoke for the first time. "She's my wife."

"Your wife?" Arras said. "So this wasn't a home invasion. This is her home."

He was quiet for a moment, then continued, "I need to talk with your supervisor," he gestured to Greg and Andi, "and get a handle on what you were doing here. You're way out of your jurisdiction."

Andi explained that the murder they were investigating had taken place in Burgess Beach but that the victim had been a Miami resident. She referred the lieutenant to Captain Johnson, Bradley's friend at the Miami P.D., hoping Johnson didn't know that she and Greg were suspended. "And," Andi said, "Detective Lamont worked for years on the Miami P.D. You can check him out."

"Okay. You're still out of your jurisdiction. Let's get back to the incident. The shooter was your wife," Arras gestured to Jorge. "Why'd she shoot the other woman?"

Andi said, "She was angry because the woman, Marta Perez, had brought the little girl here."

"So she shot her? Who's the kid?"

"My daughter," said Jorge.

"Our victim's daughter," said Andi.

"What the hell?" The lieutenant shook his head and looked over their heads for a minute. "Okay. No more preliminaries. Everybody down to the station. And" he motioned to the policewoman, "you. Take the kid back to the station and call Child Welfare to pick her up in the morning."

"Can we drive our car?" Andi asked. "I don't want to leave it here. It'll be towed."

"Okay. Detective Lamont, you know where the station is. Follow us, and don't get lost.

"Yes, sir."

They left the house, Jorge riding in a police car while Andi and Greg followed in Greg's car.

"Guess this is it for us," Greg said.

"I guess. Unless . . . ."

"What are you thinking?"

"Where would Belle and Johns go? What's a refuge for them? Who can help them?"

"Well, Philippe SanAngelo is the most powerful person in this scenario. Is there any connection between them? Johns was involved with Miranda and the drugs. Was Belle? Is there a connection between Belle and SanAngelo?"

"I don't think SanAngelo knew about the side drugs Miranda was selling through Johns. I think that was her way out of the relationship with him. Who else was involved?" She paused for a moment, thinking. "Nick Oldham. I'll best he was the original money for the drug purchase. Maybe they went to him for help."

"Good bet. SanAngelo didn't know about Miranda and Johns, but Oldham did. Where would he be?"

"At work, I suppose, but, wait a minute, what the hell time is it?" Andi looked at her watch. It was five o'clock. Close to dark. Oldham was probably still at work, unless Belle or Johns had called him, but she had his home address. "Let's go to Oldham's house. Just call it a little detour."

"Gotcha," said Greg.

Andi looked through her notes. God, her interview with Oldham seemed a long time ago. "Here it is." She read the scribbled note. "It's in Coral Gables. Can't be that far from here."

Greg plugged in his GPS and found that Nick Oldham lived about ten blocks west of the Acosta's. They had been following sedately behind the police car carrying Lieutenant Arras and Jorge. Greg slowed down, allowing other cars between them and the cop car. They missed a light and had to wait while the police car continued, assuming they would follow, but Greg made a quick right turn and headed back toward Coral Gables.

"Give me your phone. I'm going to try Oldham's office," Andi said.

The answering machine was on at the law firm. "If you know your party's extension, please press it at any time." Andi punched in the numbers, and the phone rang and rang. Finally, a female voice said, "Mr. Oldham's office."

"May I speak with Mr. Oldham?"

"I'm sorry. Mr. Oldham has left for the day. May I take a message?"

"I'll call again tomorrow," Andi hung up. "He's gone. Maybe he left to meet Belle and Johns."

"His house?"

"I guess. Let's go. We don't have any weapons, though."

"Look in the glove compartment," Greg said.

Andi pawed through the glove compartment and unearthed a small pistol. "This is it? It doesn't look big enough to even scare anybody."

"That's all we got."

When they reached Oldham's house, they drove by a big black SUV with tinted windows parked out front. Greg drove further along the street before he stopped.

Looking at the SUV, Andi said, "That's good enough for me. Let's go."

Greg parked, and they headed toward Oldham's house, a large two-story set far back from the road and surrounded by a wrought iron fence. "Damn these people and their fences," Greg said.

"I'll bet there's a passage between the houses, like at the Acosta's." Andi said. She walked past the house to the end of the fence. Sure enough, there was a small gate, padlocked.

"Can you pick it?" Andi asked.

Greg smiled at her. He took out a small kit from his pocket and squatted down beside the lock. "Not an easy one," he grunted, but after a couple of minutes, he opened it, and they entered a small alley between the houses. They opened another gate and entered Oldham's yard.

Inside, they stopped to reconnoiter, looking carefully around for security cameras or guards. There seemed to be nothing, but Andi didn't believe that Oldham would have left his house defenseless. She was right. Two large Belgian Malinois tore around from the back of the house, barking loudly. They stopped in front of Greg and Andi, growling.

Greg said, "Don't move. She won't hurt you if you stay still."

"I can feel his breath on my leg."

"It's a female. Just stay perfectly still."

"She's going to bite me." Andi's voice shook.

"Not if you stay perfectly still."

Greg made a sharp downward gesture with his right hand and said, "Sit," The dog guarding him dropped down on his haunches and stopped growling. "Good dog," Greg said.

He turned his attention to the dog guarding Andi. "Sit," he said, using the same downward gesture, but the dog continued to growl. "Back off," he said and gestured away from Andi. The dog didn't move.

"Make her stop. She's going to bite me."

"*Sitz!*"

The dog stopped growling and sat.

"*Braver hund,*" Greg said.

"What the hell was that?" Andi took a step back, but the dog didn't move.

"A lot of guard dogs are trained in Germany. These were trained to 'Stand and Growl,' but the female doesn't respond to English."

"I'm impressed. Where did you learn dog training?"

"I was a canine officer for a while. What'll we do with these two? They won't sit forever."

"Let 'em out the gate," Andi suggested.

Greg opened the gate and motioned to the dogs who walked obediently through into the area between Oldham's yard and the gate to the street.

No noise came from inside the house. Lights were on both upstairs and down, but they didn't hear anything. Greg and Andi moved quietly toward the front of the house.

"Well, here you are again, detectives. I don't know about you, but I'm getting tired of your visits." The voice was Gary Johns'.

THIRTY-TWO

Andi whirled around and saw the gun in Johns' hand.

"Drop your weapons."

Greg dropped the small pistol. "That's it."

"That's all you've got? What a pair of idiots!"

Johns gestured to them to walk ahead of him, and they headed to the front door. Nick Oldham was waiting for them with a gun in his hand.

"You could have come to my office, detective. Did you have to sneak around my property?" He turned to Greg. "Who are you?"

Gary Johns stepped forward. "He's the other detective, Nick. Name's Greg Lamont."

"Another fool." Oldham gestured to Andi and Greg to enter the house. He pushed them toward a large living room filled with overstuffed furniture upholstered in reds and blues. There was a gas fire burning in one of the two fireplaces.

Belle Acosta sat near the blazing fire. Her face was streaked with tears, her earlier defiance replaced by misery. She wore a man's coat over the sweatsuit.

Belle stood up when she saw Andi and Greg. "Where's Jorge?" she demanded.

Neither Andi nor Greg answered. Johns pushed them to a sofa near the fireplace and gestured to them to sit.

"Now," said Oldham. "What are we to do with you two? You've definitely become a nuisance."

"I said we should shoot them," Belle said, but her voice wasn't convincing.

"Where is Jorge?" Oldham asked.

"He's with the police. He knows everything we know," Andi said. "He knows Belle killed Miranda, he knows about you," she gestured to Oldham, "and he knows about Miranda and Johns' money-making operation and your help with it. He'll tell the police and they'll be here soon."

Oldham knew she was bluffing. If Jorge had known about Oldham, the police would be here already.

"Well," Oldham said, his voice smooth, "I guess we don't have a choice except to take you two for a boat ride. You'd like that, wouldn't you?" He looked at Andi as he spoke.

"They know we're not on our way to the police station. They'll be here soon," Greg said.

"Well, then, we should go," Oldham said.

He gestured to Johns. "Get some rope."

Johns handed his gun to Belle and left.

"Where's your car?" Oldham asked Greg.

"Down the street."

"Gimme the keys."

"Why?"

"I said, give me the keys."

"In my front pocket. I'll get them." Greg threw the keys at Oldham. They fell to the floor, and Oldham swore. He didn't pick them up.

A few minutes later Johns was back with rope and duct tape.

"Pick up the keys," Oldham said to him. "Smart guy threw them at me."

Johns picked up the keys and put them in his pocket, then grabbed the rope and Greg's hands.

"I shoulda tied you up myself," he said. After he tied Greg and Andi's hands, he hobbled them with the rope, so they could walk but not run. Then he gagged them both and pushed them toward the door. Andi thought about what options they had. Not many.

At Oldham's quiet command, Johns grabbed Belle's arms and tried to tie a rope around her wrists.

"What the hell?" she yelled, pushing Johns away and hitting at him. "Stop that! Leave me alone!"

Johns tried to hold her wrists behind her, but she fought him viciously, kicking and hitting. Still, he was stronger than she, and he finally got her hands tied behind her. She kicked at him with her unbound feet. "I'm in this with you!" she yelled. "Me and Jorge!"

Her kicking landed a telling blow on Johns' shin.

"Shit," he said.

Andi saw a smile on Oldham's lips.

Johns grabbed Belle and pulled her to him. She screamed, "Motherfucker!" turned her head, and bit the hand that pinned her arm to her shoulder.

"Goddamnit!" Johns said, and with his other hand, hit Belle hard in the stomach.

"Oof," she exclaimed, unable to breathe. They could hear the rasping of her breath, but her strength was gone.

Johns didn't stop there. Tilting her head back, he hit her in the jaw with his fist, and she slumped in his arms, unconscious.

"Well done," said Oldham.

Johns picked Belle up in his arms, fumbled to open the front gate and looked out at the street. Oldham walked behind Andi and Greg who were hampered by the rope that tied their ankles. Johns walked to Greg's car and threw Belle into the back seat. Then he brought the car up to the gate. Andi and Greg stumbled, but they got in.

"To the pier," Oldham said as he got in the car.

Johns put the car in gear and started off.

Andi looked at Greg. Would anyone miss them? Captain Bradley didn't even know where they were, although if Lieutenant Arras had gotten in touch with him, he now knew they were acting on their own, and they'd bolted instead of going to police headquarters. None of that would do them any good now. Arras didn't know about Oldham.

She nudged Greg with her shoulder and tried to telegraph a question. What could they do?

Greg shrugged. They were helpless right now.

Johns drove out of Oldham's street, turned right onto a wider avenue and made a left onto a highway. As the car moved along, she worked on the rope binding her hands behind her. The rope had some give to it, and she pulled and tugged, trying to get one wrist free. Then she had an idea.

The two men in the front seat were paying no attention to them, and Belle was unconscious. Andi nudged Greg with her shoulder and twisted her head and body away from him, hoping if he turned his back to hers, he could work on freeing up her hands. He turned very slightly so he could work on her bonds.

They drove for about half an hour, and when the car pulled off the highway, Andi turned her body to the front again and pushed Greg away. She continued to pull on her bonds. They were much looser and one hand was almost free. They rode another short distance and made a sharp right to the entrance of a parking lot. A number of cars were parked in the lot, and there were lights of a building to their right. This was good. Other cars meant other people around. Maybe someone would notice them.

Johns passed the lighted lot and moved forward to a darker area. He stopped the car but didn't turn off the engine. Andi saw Oldham pull a card out of his wallet and give it to Johns who pulled the car up close to a gate with an arm that barred access. Johns inserted the card into a slot, the arm lifted, and the car moved forward into a much darker area.

Johns parked the car near but not under an overhead light. "Where's the boat?" he asked Oldham.

"We have to take the dinghy."

"Where is it?"

"End of the pier. It's close."

"Okay," Johns said. "I'll carry Belle. You keep the other two under control."

"No problem."

Andi realized they hadn't planned this. There was a chance for a slipup. While Johns carried Belle, Oldham had to keep an eye on both of them. Could they make a move while they were walking out onto the pier or being loaded into the dinghy? She looked at Greg. He was listening intently to the conversation between Oldham and Johns. He winked at Andi. This was their chance. Andi kept her hands behind her as if the bonds were still fastened, but her hands were free. She stumbled getting out of the car.

The dinghy was tied at the far end of the pier. Johns walked in front, Belle slung over his shoulder like a sack of potatoes, while Andi and Greg followed slowly. Oldham and his gun brought up the rear. When they reached the dinghy, Johns put Belle down, pulled the boat within reach, and stepped into it. Then he picked Belle up and dropped her onto an aft seat.

Oldham nudged Andi with his gun, motioning her to step into the dinghy. She shook her head, gesturing with her head to the rope hobbling her movement.

"Oh, for Chrissake," Johns said. "I'll catch you if you fall."

Andi stared at the step facing her, lifted her ankle the width of the rope hobble, and shook her head.

"Do it," Johns ordered.

Andi shook her head again, hoping he'd take the rope off her feet.

Oldham said, "You're not that delicate." He pushed her forward off the pier. She fell into the dinghy, and Johns caught her in his arms and sat her in the stern. With effort, she managed to keep her hands behind her as if they were still tied.

"Go," Oldham said to Greg. He propelled him toward the edge of the pier and pushed. Greg crumpled as he landed, and his knee hit the seat next to Andi. He grunted through the gag.

Greg's face was screwed up in pain. Had he broken something? Had he only banged his knee? She couldn't tell, and Oldham and Johns didn't care.

"Okay," Oldham said, and Johns started the engine. The motor coughed once, then caught. Oldham untied the rope and threw it into the dinghy, then jumped aboard.

"Out to the left," Oldham told Johns. "Last boat on the right."

The harbor was calm, but as they headed further out, the waves tossed the light craft. Andi bumped Greg, and he grunted in pain.

She tried to see Greg's face to see how badly his leg was hurt, but the night was dark, the moon not yet up. If Greg was badly hurt, she couldn't count on his help against the two men.

Johns pulled the dinghy next to a 50-foot yacht. They were close to the harbor exit, near the open bay, and in the light from the yacht, Andi could see Greg wince with pain as the waves rocked the boat.

Tying up the dinghy and getting them aboard the yacht was going to take the attention of both men. Was this their chance? Once they boarded the yacht, their chances were dim.

Johns used the engine to hold the dinghy steady against the rubber buffering while Oldham waited, ready to climb the rope ladder that hung from the deck. Neither of them was paying attention to Andi or Greg.

Greg's eyes were closed, and he grimaced in pain each time the rocking of the dinghy threw him sideways. Andi nudged his foot and raised her eyes to the yacht and the ladder. She saw that he understood, but he dropped his eyes to his leg and shrugged his shoulders. Still they had to take advantage of this opportunity. Andi glanced at the still unconscious Belle. She looked again at Greg and motioned upward with her head.

By the time Oldham stepped onto the ladder, Andi had freed her hands. She stood, hobbled forward to fling herself at Oldham, and grabbed him around the legs.

Years of sitting behind a desk had weakened Oldham. He tried to hold on, but he fell backward into the boat. Andi jumped on him, pressing her knees on his chest and pummeling his face and head. Oldham yelled.

She didn't dare check to see if Greg had been able to attack Johns.

"What the hell!" That was Johns' voice.

Andi heard the sound of a punch.

"Goddamnit!"

Johns again.

Andi kept punching Oldham. He grunted, tried to push her off and landed a blow to the side of her face, but she was stronger than he. She hit him hard on the jaw, and he slumped into unconsciousness. She turned then to see what was happening between Johns and Greg. They were standing in the prow, Greg battering Johns with his head and kicking with his hobbled feet. The boat drifted toward the open bay.

Andi couldn't leave Oldham. He was only temporarily unconscious. She found his gun in the back of his trousers and tucked it into her waistband, then grabbed the rope that had held her hands and tied his together in front of him. Only then did she untie the hobbles on her legs and hurry to the prow to help Greg.

Johns was strong, and Greg was getting the worst of it. She grabbed an oar from the bottom of the boat, and swung at Johns' head, connecting with a *thunk*. Johns plunged overboard.

"Are you okay?" she asked Greg.

"Yeah. Shall we rescue him?"

"Why bother?" Andi untied Greg's hands, then flipped off her shoes, gave Oldham's gun to Greg and dove into the black water.

When she surfaced, she called out, "Got a light? I don't see him."

Greg grabbed a flashlight and shone it at the spot where Andi was treading water. She dove, but she couldn't see any trace of Johns. She dove again, trying to reach bottom, but the water was like ink. Johns seemed to have sunk without a trace.

Shots rang out, pinging on the water and hitting close to where she surfaced. The dinghy lay in the shadow of the yacht, and the shooter couldn't see it.

"Throw me a ring," she yelled.

Greg threw a life ring, and she grabbed it, holding on and catching her breath. More shots hit the water around her. Then she saw Johns a few yards from her, struggling to stay afloat. She swam toward him, holding the ring in front of her, but as he grabbed at it, another volley of shots came from the yacht, and he sank into the murky sea.

Andi swam quickly to the boat, bullets peppering the water all around her, and Greg pulled her aboard. She collapsed onto the aft seat next to Belle as more shots came from the yacht.

Greg had started the engine, but as he moved the boat away from the yacht, Belle jerked suddenly after another volley of shots. She fell to the bottom of the dinghy and wailed, thrashing around.

Greg gunned the engine and headed for the pier. Shots followed them as they fled, but they were soon out of range.

"I'll finish tying Oldham up," Andi said when she'd had a chance to catch her breath.

She made her way over to the lawyer who lay on his back as she had left him. His hands were tied together, his eyes closed. He seemed unconscious, but when she tried to tie his feet together, he slipped his arms over her head and grabbed her around the throat.

"Let me go," she yelled, hitting him in the face.

Oldham pulled her down onto the seat next to him, and she couldn't get a good angle to punch him. Greg turned from the wheel and jumped over the seats to reach them. The boat veered crazily, but they managed to subdue Oldham, finish tying him onto the seat, and Greg resumed the helm.

Belle moaned in the bottom of the dinghy.

Andi wanted to kick her, but contented herself with saying, "Shut up. You're gonna live."

"Who d'ya think was shooting?" Greg asked.

"Some caretaker on the yacht, I guess. Whoever it was must've been asleep, otherwise they would've shot at us sooner."

Then Oldham yelled, "Hey, I'm drowning."

She looked down and saw water seeping into the boat. Her feet were covered to the ankles. The shots had ripped holes in the aluminum dinghy, and it was leaking badly.

THIRTY-THREE

"We're leaking," Andi yelled to Greg. "I'll bail." She turned
Belle over face up in the bottom of the dinghy before grab-
bing a bucket and throwing water overboard. Not enough.
The dinghy was going under.

"Go faster," she yelled at Greg.

"This is it."

Oldham yelled, "Untie me, and I'll bail."

"Not even if we drown," she said.

Andi looked toward the pier. Still a hundred yards away.
She bailed as fast as she could, but she was losing. They were
going down.

"Can you tie up?" she called to Greg.

"Yeah. Maybe." He swung starboard toward a large boat,
grabbed the anchor rope to stabilize them and looked for a
ladder. The boat had only a small light, but it was enough to
steer to a ladder Greg could grab.

"We're sinking," Andi said.

Greg moved the dinghy around to the ladder and stepped
onto the ladder. "Shit," he said.

"What?" Andi asked.

"My knee. Went out from under me."

Andi watched as Greg stepped onto the ladder again. This time he managed to climb up to the boat deck.

Andi grabbed Belle, pulled her upright and waited for Greg to return.

Belle moaned and thrashed around until Andi said, "Shut the fuck up. We're rescuing you. Don't be such a pain in the ass."

It seemed like forever until Greg came down the ladder carrying a rope.

"How's your knee?"

"Not great." He tied the rope around Belle's waist and headed back up the ladder. When he reached the deck, he pulled her up, and she bumped along the side of the boat each time he pulled.

Greg brought the rope back down and attempted to tie it to Oldham's waist. As he worked, Oldham suddenly sat up and head butted Greg in the chest.

"Damn you," Greg said. He socked Oldham on the jaw, then on the side of his head, and Oldham subsided. By this time, the dinghy was nearly filled with water. Greg and Andi climbed the ladder to the deck.

When they both were on board, Andi asked, "You okay?"

"Yeah. Help me with Oldham."

It took two of them to haul Oldham's body aboard, and each time they pulled, his body bounced heavily off the side of the yacht.

"He's gonna be all bruised," Andi said.

"Fuck him. We shoulda left him."

Oldham lay on the deck, breathing but unconscious, and Belle whimpered and tossed from side to side.

"Guess I'd better look at Belle. She musta taken a bullet." Andi sighed.

She took the gag out of Belle's mouth, then when Belle whined and whimpered even more, quickly replaced it. "I don't want to hear any more from her," Andi said.

Andi found blood on Belle's chest but couldn't locate the source, so she turned her over on her stomach. Blood was coming from a wound in Belle's upper arm.

Andi found the exit. There was little bleeding.

"She needs bandaging, but she'll be okay. It's through and through."

"I'll look in the cabin," Greg said, and a few moments later he emerged with a first aid kit.

Andi applied disinfectant to the wound and then bandaged it. Belle moaned but didn't move. When Andi finished, she asked, "Whose boat are we on?"

"No idea. There's a radio in the cabin. I'll call the Miami Police."

When Greg reached Lieutenant Arras, the lieutenant was so angry he could hardly speak, but Greg took advantage of his sputtering to tell him their location and their need for assistance. Arras finally agreed to send help.

Hours later, Andi and Greg had told their story over and over to what seemed like hundreds of police officers. Captain Bradley arrived about five in the morning, ranting about their suspensions and their violation of the public trust. Andi and Greg sat silent. Until everyone stopped yelling, it seemed pointless to argue.

Belle went directly to the hospital from the boat where her condition was listed as stable. Jorge stayed at the hospital with her, but after Greg and Andi finally got to tell the Miami

Police what they knew, Jorge was arrested and charged with possession of illegal drugs with intent to sell. A search of the Acosta's house uncovered several kilos of marijuana and a slightly smaller stash of cocaine in the garage.

Toni would remain in the care of Child Welfare Services until it could be determined who her father was. Marta Perez was still in the hospital.

The caretaker on Oldham's yacht was brought in with an automatic rifle, and although he swore he thought they were pirates trying to hijack the yacht, he was booked on a weapons violation with a possible manslaughter charge, pending recovery of Gary Johns' body.

Divers were sent out at first light, but they had no success that day. They continued their search further out in the bay and along the shore.

After Lieutenant Arras had vented his anger about what Andi and Greg had done, he decided they should be present for Oldham's interrogation. Andi's face was bruised, her eye blackened and her clothes torn and filthy from her battle with Oldham. Greg wasn't in any better shape, his knees bruised from his fall into the boat and cuts and bruises on his face and body. But the interrogation was scheduled for that morning, so they cleaned up as well as they could and got ready.

Captain Bradley lost the fight to keep Andi and Greg from participating in Oldham's interrogation, so he settled for sitting in himself. Lieutenant Arras was in charge. They met with Oldham and his attorney in an interrogation room at Miami Police Headquarters.

When they entered the small, airless room, they found Oldham's attorney already there. He had spread paperwork out over the battered table and taken possession of several of the uncomfortable chairs. He introduced himself as Michael Flynn to the others. Then he gestured to them to sit down.

Flynn was not an attorney from Oldham's firm but a well-known Miami criminal lawyer. He was a tall, balding man in his fifties, with sagging jowls that made him look rather like a bulldog. He was dressed in an expensive gray suit, a white shirt and the requisite very expensive tie.

When Oldham was brought in wearing handcuffs, Andi was pleased to see that he was in worse shape than she, with a black eye, assorted bruises on the parts of his body that were visible, and a pronounced limp.

Arras reiterated that Oldham had been read his Miranda rights before he was arrested at the marina and asked if Oldham or his attorney had any objection to having the session recorded. After a discussion with Flynn, Oldham said they did not.

"How did you meet Gary Johns?"

Oldham turned to his attorney, and Flynn spoke to him quietly.

Then Oldham said, "I decline to answer on advice of my attorney."

Arras continued. "Did you buy a house for Gary Johns and Miranda Duncan at 175 Ocean Drive, Fort Pierce, Florida?"

Again, the sham consultation with Flynn, and again, "I decline to answer on advice of my attorney."

"Was that residence used for the sale of illegal substances?"

"I decline to answer on the advice of my attorney."

Of course this was how he was going to play it, Andi thought. No answers to the interrogation, and when he goes to trial, his attorney won't call him to testify. Then it will be up to a jury to decide his guilt or innocence based on the testimony of other people.

Exasperated, Andi interjected a question. Oldham looked at her warily.

"When Gary Johns showed up at your house late in the evening with people you knew to be police officers held at gun point, why did you take him in?"

Oldham looked at his attorney, then said, "I decline to answer on the advice of my attorney."

Captain Bradley spoke. "Did those individuals who came to your house identify themselves as police officers?"

"I decline to answer on the advice of my attorney."

Arras asked, "Will Mr. Oldham answer any questions about the activities, his and Mr. Johns', on the night of November 30?"

Flynn and Oldham consulted, then Flynn said, "My client refuses to answer on the grounds that he might incriminate himself."

Arras said, "That ends this meeting. I'm signing off the recording at 11:16 a.m. on December 1, 2009. Mr. Oldham, you will be arraigned tomorrow morning."

Flynn bowed to the group and said he would see Oldham the next day at his arraignment. Flynn left, and Oldham was taken back to his cell.

Captain Bradley said goodbye to the lieutenant and said to Greg and Andi, "I want to see you as soon as you get back to Burgess Beach, detectives. Call me for an appointment."

Later Andi, Greg and Arras sat in the lieutenant's office, talking about Oldham. Arras said, "Oldham's slick. We can still probably get a conviction based on your testimony. It'll be up to the D.A. to decide what he's charged with and some of that depends on whether we find Johns' body. That guy's a real weasel, and his attorney's no better."

Andi said, "I hardly got anywhere with him when I questioned him in his office—twice. He'll say anything to survive. What a bastard!

Arras asked, "Why did he get involved with Johns in the first place. He had plenty of money."

Apparently there's no such thing as enough," Andi said. "And, of course, he was in love with Miranda. She got him started on the path to selling drugs with her promise of lots of money and her love."

Then Arras said, "I'd like you to take a look at some photos to see if you can identify the men who went to your house."

"Sure," Andi said, "but not today. I'm exhausted, and I'm filthy. I need to go home. And at some point Greg and I need to talk with Marta Perez. I think she can point the finger at Belle as Miranda's murderer. That's what we came down here to find out, so we'll be back."

Arras nodded.

Andi and Greg headed home. They didn't say much until Andi said, "We need to talk about what went on between us the night those men terrorized me. That seems eons ago."

Greg yawned. "Yeah. Let's put that on the list of things to talk about, but right now I'd give everything I own for a good night's sleep."

"Bradley's still mad at us."

"Ya think?"

"Yeah, I think."

When Greg dropped Andi off at five o'clock that evening, they agreed to talk the next day. She examined her bruises and decided she could just do with a shower and some aspirin before she went to bed.

She was jolted from sleep several times by memories of the battle with Oldham and Johns and then by thoughts of what she needed to do. Each time she awoke, she groaned in pain, got up to take more aspirin, then started the cycle all over again.

The last time she woke up, it was dark outside. The clock said eight o'clock, and for a moment she thought she was late for work. Then she remembered. It must be eight o'clock in the evening. She'd slept almost twenty-four hours.

Sitting up hurt like hell, and standing was worse. She took some aspirin, made coffee and thought about what she had to do.

She called Greg. He sounded as groggy as she was.

"Just woke up," Andi said.

"Me, too. You hurt as much as I do?"

"At least. Let's wait 'til tomorrow to see Marta and for me to look at those pictures. More sleep wouldn't hurt me."

"How about I bring over some dinner? I'm starving, and there's nothing here to eat."

"Good idea. Chinese?"

"Sure. See you in half an hour."

THIRTY-FOUR

When Greg knocked on Andi's door, he carried a feast. "I'm so hungry I kept ordering," he explained as he limped to the table.

"Okay by me," Andi said. "I'm starving, too,"

After they had wolfed down the food, Andi wiped her mouth and said, "I guess that was good. I was so hungry I hardly tasted it."

Greg grunted assent.

"I've been thinking about Bradley and our suspensions. You belong to the PBA?"

"Of course. Don't you?"

"I never joined. My dad was against it."

"He was a cop?"

"Yeah. A captain."

"He wouldn't like unions."

"No. But you can get an attorney through the PBA. I'll have to get one for myself. Can we get them to work together?"

"I don't know. I talked with the local PBA chapter, but things have moved so fast we didn't ever get anything done."

"I guess I'll get an attorney. Maybe my dad can recommend one. I'm not sure I want to get my job back, but I don't want to leave under a cloud."

"Right. We need to clear our names."

She sipped some tea, and then said, "Look, I want to talk about the other night."

Greg looked at her, then picked up a fortune cookie and played with it. "Yeah. I guess we have to."

"I was scared that night. Terrified. What happened seemed okay. It was comforting, made me feel less scared. In fact, I slept well for the first time in a while. But . . . but now I don't know. When I look back, it makes me uncomfortable. I just don't think it was such a great idea. I don't mean you took advantage of me or anything like that. It's just that we changed our whole relationship."

"And so?" Greg said.

"Well, we work together. And we don't know one another that well. I don't think I'm ready to be involved."

Greg looked down at his hands as he spoke. "I hear what you're saying, but we've known one another for what? Maybe five months? We've dated, now we've worked together. I think we know one another pretty well.

"And, besides, you're saying what you want. What about me? What if that's not what I want? I'm not sure I can just put it behind me and go on as if nothing happened. I'm attracted to you. I have been . . . from the beginning." Greg played with the fortune cookie again, unwrapped it, then put it down. "The other night seemed right to me."

"I know there's something . . . an attraction between us." She stopped and rested her chin in her hands. Then she put her hands down and looked at Greg. "I had a bad experience with a cop back in Tampa, and I'm just getting over that. I'm scared. Scared of him and scared of getting back into the same situation. No, that's not fair. You're not like him, but being with him made me lose faith in my own judgment."

"All cops aren't bad, you know. Just because we're cops. Some of us are normal." He paused, then continued. "Well, sort of normal."

"The guy in Tampa was married, and he was my boss. It was a mistake all around, but I thought . . . I don't know what I thought. It turned really ugly.

"But also it's hard for me to think of you and Miranda. I know she was in your life a long time ago, but she was important. She may have had your child. You were together for several years. She's still a presence in your life. I can't just write her off. She was murdered, and she meant a lot to you."

"You're right, I guess. Maybe I want to put Miranda behind me too quickly. I did love her once." He opened the fortune cookie and read, "'Opportunities are quite plentiful when you say what you want.'" He smiled wryly. "Well, I said what I want, but I don't think opportunities are plentiful, are they?"

"I'm not sure you know what you want right now. Let's give it time."

Greg crumpled the cookie and its wrapping. "I guess we can try to put the genie back in the bottle, but I'm not sure how hard I want to work at it. It's not really what I want."

Greg picked up some of the leftovers and got to his feet.

Andi said, "Don't write me off entirely. Just give me more time to get my head straight. Can you do that?"

"That's the most encouraging thing you've said so far," he said as he headed into the kitchen. "I'll leave these leftovers with you. What time tomorrow?"

Andi still sat at the table, thinking of what he had just said. "What?"

"What time tomorrow?"

Andi pulled herself away from her thoughts, confused, and said, "Okay, okay. Let's start at eight-thirty. We'll see Marta first. I wonder if Lisa will give me my messages if I call in."

"She gave me mine long after my suspension."

"Good. I'll see what's going on there."

"Shall I pick you up at eight-thirty or do you want to drive?"

"I'll come and get you."

After Greg was gone, Andi sat at the table for a long time, drinking cold tea and thinking about what he had said. Jim had scared her, but how much was Greg like Jim? They were both cops, but was she only afraid of becoming involved with Greg because of that? When she thought about the night Jim had hit her and the night she'd called 911, she'd been scared, almost as scared as when SanAngelo's thugs had been in her apartment, but she'd never felt that way with Greg, even when she'd wondered if he might have killed Miranda. Still, what she'd said about Miranda was true. He may not yet be over her memory and their life together.

The cold tea and the memory of Jim chilled her, and she got up from the table, shivering. She needed to get to bed.

Andi slept restlessly, waking two or three times before finally getting up at seven to shower, do some stretching, and call Lisa at eight o'clock.

Lisa said, "Are you okay? We heard you were, but the boss hasn't told us anything. What's happening?"

"You know we're both suspended, but I think we're close to solving the case," Andi said. "I'm still working with Lamont, although the captain wouldn't approve if he knew. We're both okay. A bit bruised and battered, but okay." Then she asked, "Has Garcia made any progress with the burglary?"

"I think he's got it pretty well wrapped up. Yesterday he was smiling when he came out of the captain's office."

"That's good," Andi said, but she could feel a twinge of jealousy. "Can you give me my messages? I'm on my way back to Miami with Detective Lamont to finish things up today. At least we hope so."

"Sure. Hang on a minute." Lisa put the phone on hold, then returned and recited a number of messages, none of them pertaining to Miranda Duncan't murder.

"Thanks, and if you can, don't tell the captain I called."

"Oh, I won't. I hope you come back soon."

"Thanks. I hope so too."

THIRTY-FIVE

Andi dressed carefully in tailored black slacks, a long-sleeved blue silk blouse that flattered her eyes with a tailored blue-and-black-checked jacket. She examined her bruised face. There wasn't much she could do about the black-and-blue eye—nice she'd chosen a color-matching ensemble—but she tried to minimize the puffiness and carefully applied makeup and blusher, hoping to distract attention from her battle scars.

By the time she left, she felt ready to face whatever the day brought. She resolved to be all business with Greg this morning with no reference to last night's conversation.

Andi picked Greg up at eight-thirty, and their first stop was the hospital to see Marta Perez. She was still in the ICU after her blood loss, and when they saw her in the hospital bed, she seemed small and shrunken. Her face brightened when she saw them.

"Nobody's been to see me," she said. "It feels like I've been here forever. How's Toni?"

"She's with Child Protective Services. I'll try to check on her this afternoon if I have time."

"I understand," Perez said. "Do you think she's okay?"

Andi shrugged, then said, "We wanted to talk to you about the night Toni's mother was murdered. Did you go to the Hibiscus Motel where Miranda was staying that night?"

Perez was silent for a moment. Then she said, "Yes, I did. I should have told you when you came to see me before, but ...."

"Tell us from the beginning."

"Miranda was with Toni and me most of the day. She and Toni went to the park, and I made dinner for the three of us. Everything seemed fine, but Miranda was nervous, and she came in with this big suitcase, very heavy. She wouldn't let it out of her sight. I asked her what was in it, but she said I didn't need to know, it was security for her and Toni."

"What did you think was in it?"

"Drugs or money. Miranda was selling drugs up in Fort Pierce. The guy she was living with in Miami—SanAngelo—he was a drug dealer, so I knew she was involved."

"Did Miranda tell you where she was going?"

"She said she was staying at the Hibiscus Motel, and she left around nine-thirty. I knew where that was, and I wanted to see for myself what she was up to."

"Did she tell you her room number?"

"Yes. She said in case I needed her for Toni."

"What happened when you got to the motel?"

"I passed by the office. The guy—the manager—wasn't in the office. I went up to the second floor where her room was. I passed her door at first, but then I saw that it was open. I knocked and went in. She was lying on the bed, blood all over. She was dead."

"What time was that?"

"I took Toni with me. She was asleep, and the clock in our room said it was ten-thirty."

"You left Toni alone in the car?"

"She was asleep," Marta's voice was defensive, "and it was just for a moment. I came right back."

"Did you see anyone else?"

"No. Not then."

"What about the suitcase?"

"It was there. Whoever had killed her hadn't taken it. So I grabbed it and her purse, in case there was a key for the suitcase, and went back down the stairs. Then I saw a woman getting into a car out on the street. I thought it was Belle Acosta."

"What made you think it was Belle Acosta?"

"It was a woman with dark hair, and she got in a fancy black car like Belle has."

"Are you sure it was Belle?"

"Well, no. It's just that the car looked like hers. I couldn't really see the woman clearly because she had her back to me and she was pretty far away. But I know Belle didn't like Miranda because of Jorge."

"What about Jorge?"

"I heard Belle and Miranda fighting. Miranda said, 'You're too old. All the surgery in the world can't help you keep your husband. He wants someone younger—someone who can give him a baby.'"

"Did you hear what Belle answered?"

"She called Miranda a bitch and said Miranda wouldn't be anything without Belle's help."

"Did you hear anything more?"

"No. Toni ran in then to see Miranda, and Belle and Miranda stopped talking."

"Why were you there?"

"I was picking Toni up to take her back to Burgess Beach after she'd spent some time with Miranda. We met at Belle's because Miranda didn't want Philippe to know where Toni was."

Andi looked at Greg. "Do you have any more questions?"

"No. I guess that covers it. I wish you'd told us about seeing Miranda's killer before."

"I was too scared. And I wanted the suitcase, but I don't even know where it is now."

"The police have it. It was full of money," Andi said.

"That's what I thought. I thought it was my ticket out." Marta Perez sighed and gazed out the window. "I guess I'm not that lucky."

Andi called Lieutenant Arras who said he'd be ready to see them in half an hour. When they arrived, Arras greeted them, then turned them over to a detective who took them to an interview room with five books of photos of known drug dealers, most in the pay of the two major Miami kingpins: Philippe SanAngelo and his rival Joe Ferragamo. When the detective, mentioned Joe Ferragamo, something clicked in Andi's head, and she browsed through her notes. Sure enough. There it was. Roberto Cavelli, the owner of Tux, the first club she and Greg had gone to, had told them he thought he'd seen Miranda get into a car with Joe Ferragamo, but then he thought he must be mistaken. Maybe he hadn't been.

Andi and Greg looked over the five books of photographs, and in the fourth book, Andi found the man that she thought looked like an Easter Island statue, the one who hadn't spoken. Andi couldn't find any photos of the other man, but finding Manuel Cubano, the silent man who had visited her, brought back memories of that awful evening. For a moment, she thought she might throw up and took several deep breaths, clasping her hands tightly together.

"Are you okay?" Greg asked.

"Yeah. Just a little dizzy."

"Bad memories?"

"Yeah."

THIRTY-SIX

After they brought Lieutenant Arras up to date on what they'd found and left the station, Andi suggested lunch. They ate at Casa Juancho in Little Havana, not as good as the Cuban restaurant Greg had taken her to, but the atmosphere was pleasant, the food good enough, and they were quickly seated in a quiet booth. While they waited for their food to arrive, Andi read through her notes on Belle and Jorge Acosta and on Ana SanAngelo. Belle could have been in Burgess Beach the night Miranda was murdered. She could have killed Miranda out of jealousy. Marta thought she had seen Belle. Dark hair, fancy car. Could be.

Then Andi thought about what Marta had seen. Ana SanAngelo had dark hair, and Andi would bet she drove a fancy dark car. Andi checked her notes and saw that she'd never gotten any response to the phone calls she'd made about Ana's alibi. Her notes said that Ana was playing bunko with friends and had left Diego with her in-laws, and they'd gotten the names of the other women in the bunko group. She'd called and left messages, her notes said, but no one had ever called her back. One person hadn't had an answering machine.

"This is very interesting," Andi said.

Greg was reading the menu, although he'd already ordered. "What?"

"We need to find out what kind of car Ana SanAngelo drives?"

"Sure. I'll check. Do you think it's registered to her or to Philippe?"

"Don't know. Try them both."

While Greg called about the car, Andi called one of the women with whom Ana had been playing bunko. The phone rang several times and finally went to voice mail. Andi left her name and number and asked Anita Marengo to call her when she got the message.

The call to Stephanie Mardarosian had the same result, but Rosa Rodriguez, the third bunko player, the one without an answering machine, picked up on the third ring.

"Hello," she said.

Andi identified herself and told Ms. Rodriguez why she was calling. "Can you verify that Ms. SanAngelo was playing bunko with you on the night of September 27th?"

Rosa said, "I'll have to check my calendar. Can you hold on a moment?"

When she came back, she said, "We played that night. I remember that, but Ana had asked someone to substitute for her. I can't remember the woman's name—Alicia, I think. I don't remember her last name, if I even knew it. She was nice, but it was so odd because Ana hardly ever misses bunko."

"Do you think anyone else would remember Alicia's last name or know how to get in touch with her?"

"Maybe Belle Acosta. She's a friend of Belle's, I think."

Andi thanked Ms. Rodriguez for her help and hung up. "It would probably be better if we had all our ducks in a row, but I still think we can scare the shit out of Ana SanAngelo."

"I think you're right," Greg said. "You'll be interested to know that Ana SanAngelo drives a black Lexis SUV."

Andi dialed Ana SanAngelo's number. A woman's voice answered on the first ring.

"*SanAngelo y Compánia.*"

"May I speak with *Señora* SanAngelo?"

"This is she." Andi recognized the voice of the elegant woman she and Greg had met at Philippe's coffee importers.

Andi identified herself, then said, "My colleague and I would like to talk with you about the Acostas and about your husband. We'll be there in fifteen minutes."

"I don't need to talk with the police. What do you want to talk about?" Her voice was no longer smooth. She sounded wary.

"We'll be there in fifteen minutes." Andi clicked off the phone. "She sounds scared."

Their lunches arrived and as they ate, Greg said, "I want to be the lead on this one. I noticed when we talked to her before that she played up to me, and I think I can get more out of her. She's more likely to open up to a guy or maybe she'll think she can fool me."

Andi thought for a moment, then said, "I think you're right. She's probably used to playing up to men and not trusting women. Okay."

They finished their meal and headed out to SanAngelo's coffee importers. Ana SanAngelo was waiting for them.

She was as exquisitely dressed as she had been before, this time in a long red dress with a gold belt. She wore a gold necklace and the same gold bracelet she had worn before. Her feet were clad in high-heeled red and black beaded sandals. She greeted them and asked what kind of coffee they would like, talking nonstop about the coffee she was preparing, where it had been grown and how she brewed it.

Greg and Andi didn't interrupt, giving her anxiety the chance to build as she talked. She spoke faster and faster as she poured cups of coffee and got cream and sugar. Andi sat down while Ana moved around, but Greg stood, waiting for Ana.

"Ms. SanAngelo, we need to ask you some questions."

"Sit down, detective. I'll be right with you," she said, continuing to bustle about, getting napkins and some bite-sized cookies and placing them on the table.

Before Greg sat down, he asked, "Will you close the shop and lock the door, Ms. SanAngeleo, so that we won't be disturbed?"

"Is that necessary?" she asked.

"Yes, it is," Greg said. "Then, please, sit down."

Ana pulled the blinds on the front windows and locked the door, putting out the closed sign. She brought another chair up to the table where Andi was seated and sat, poised on the front edge.

She smiled at Greg, a bright, brittle smile. "Now what can I do for you, detectives?"

Greg looked at her and said, "When we talked to you the last time, you said you knew Miranda Duncan and that your son and her daughter used to play together. We told you at that time that Miranda had been murdered. When was the last time you saw Ms. Duncan?"

"I don't really know. She and Toni came to play . . ." her voice broke, as if she had run out of air, then she took a breath and continued, "about two weeks before you were here. I haven't seen her since." She kept her gaze on Greg as she spoke.

"So you didn't know until we told you that Miranda had been murdered?

"No. I was very surprised. Have you found her murderer yet?"

Greg went on, "Did you know that Miranda and your husband, Philippe, were lovers?"

"No, that's not true." Ana glared at Greg. "Philippe didn't even know Miranda. I met Miranda with the children at a Mommie and Me class. I told you that."

"I'm afraid it is true. Belle and Jorge Acosta knew about Miranda and Philippe, but they kept it from you."

"That's not possible. They're my friends, and besides Philippe would never . . . ."

Greg interrupted. "So now I'd like to ask you again where you were the night Miranda was murdered. That would be September 27th."

Ana clenched her hands in her lap, but she looked straight at Greg. "Didn't you already ask me that? I'm sure I told you where I was."

"Tell us again. Just for the record." Greg kept his voice even.

"What day was that? That was a Friday, wasn't it?" Ana tried to sound annoyed, but her voice trembled.

"Yes."

"Well, I'm sure I told you then that I always play bunko on Friday. I leave Diego with my mother-in-law. That's my night off." With an effort, Ana smiled and unclenched her hands.

"Let me check the names of the friends that you played bunko with," Greg said, referring to Andi's notebook. "That would be Stephanie Mardarosian, Rosa Rodrigues, Anita Marengo, and a woman named Alicia. I don't seem to have Alicia's last name."

"She's a friend of Belle's. I don't know her very well."

"You weren't there that night, were you, Ms. SanAngelo?" Greg asked. "Alicia made up the fourth at the bunko table because you didn't go that Friday night. You went to Burgess Beach and killed Miranda Duncan, your husband's lover."

Ana jumped to her feet, indignant. "That's not true! I was there!"

"Rosa Rodriguez says you weren't there that night," Greg said.

"She's wrong. I was," Ana said. "I was there." She sat back down, her eyes on Greg. Her face was pale, and she said, "I'm sorry. I don't feel very well."

"Let me get you some water, Ms. SanAngelo," Andi said. She rose and walked to the back of the shop. Greg crossed his legs and waited, looking over his notes. Ana turned to watch Andi behind the counter at the back of the shop, then turned back toward Greg when Andi returned holding a glass of water.

"Here you go, Ana."

Ana drank deeply, then put the glass down and sat quietly. She seemed to have regained her composure. "Why are you accusing me of killing Miranda? She was my friend. I wouldn't have killed her."

"You were seen leaving the Hibiscus Motel the night Miranda was murdered," Greg said. "A witness has identified you."

"That's not possible. I wasn't there. I was playing bunko with my friends."

"You might as well stop lying, Ms. SanAngelo. You have no alibi, you have a motive, and you were seen."

Ana got to her feet and picked up the glass. "I'm going to get more water," she said and walked to the back of the shop.

Andi rose to go after her, but Ana stepped quickly behind the counter, bent down, then rose with a gun in her hand.

"Don't come any closer," she said.

Greg jumped to his feet, and they started to walk toward her. "Don't be a fool, Ana."

"Stop," Ana said. "The gun is loaded, and I know how to use it. Don't move."

Greg said, "This is stupid, Ana. You can't kill two police and expect to get away with it. We know you killed Miranda, and you're the one who tried to run us off the road."

"I didn't, I didn't, but you're going to say I did anyway." She screamed the words.

Andi said, "If you killed Miranda, it was a crime of passion—killing your husband's lover. But you can't kill us and expect any kind of mercy."

"Think about your son? What will happen to Diego?" Greg sounded worried.

"Poor Diego. *Pobre hijo.*" Tears came to Ana's eyes as she thought about her son.

"And what about Philippe?

At the mention of her husband, Ana's face contorted with rage. "Philippe? That motherfucker went after anything in a skirt. He fucked that woman. Maybe Toni was his child. I hate him."

Andi and Greg each took a step toward the back of the store, Andi to the left and Greg to the right, easing slowly back toward Ana.

Ana tensed. "Stop right there," she said, swinging the gun from side to side.

They stopped.

"But you killed Miranda," Greg said. "She was your friend."

"My friend?" Ana spat out the words. "She pretended to be my friend and Belle's friend, but she slept with everybody: Philippe, Jorge, those men at the club. She didn't care about the wives, the children she hurt. She just took what she wanted and threw it away when she was done. And those stupid men—they all loved her."

Andi gestured to Greg to move forward, and she took over, trying to keep Ana's attention focused on her. Greg crept slowly forward while Andi spoke.

"You don't want to kill us, Ana. You were angry at Miranda. I can understand that. She took your husband and Belle's, too. She didn't care about anybody, did she?"

"I hated her." Ana's voice rose.

Then she turned toward Greg, firing a shot and hitting the floor in front of him. "Stop right there. No closer. I mean it. My next shot won't miss."

Greg stopped, and Andi kept talking, but now Ana was talking to herself. "I thought I'd feel better after I killed Miranda but I didn't. Philippe was so sad after she died. He didn't know who killed her. He thought it was that man who imported for him, and he had him killed. I couldn't tell him I did it. I was afraid. He'd have killed me if he'd known. He mourned for her. He loved her. Not me."

"Stop," she said again as Greg took a step forward. She swung the gun toward him. "I will shoot you."

Then she stared at the gun, turning the muzzle toward her. Andi screamed, "No. No, Ana."

"Why her?" Ana said. "Why not me? She was a whore. Why not me? I loved him."

Tentatively, Ana lifted her arm and held the gun to her chest, above her heart. She closed her eyes. Greg ran the few remaining feet and leaped across the bar. He grabbed Ana's arm, wrenching the gun from her grasp. Andi ran behind the bar, and they held Ana down. While Andi handcuffed her, Greg took the bullets from the gun.

Ana lay on the floor sobbing. "I love him. Why her? Why not me?"

Andi called 911, and the Miami Police arrived quickly. They took Ana SanAngelo into custody on charges of assault, murder and attempted murder. Andi and Greg drove back to police headquarters.

THIRTY-SEVEN

"Good job, you two," Lieutenant Arras said when they'd been shown into his office. "Although I don't think your captain's going to forgive you. But we're getting a lot of good stuff. Ana SanAngelo is spilling the beans about her husband and his drug operations. She's pissed. We have a team out to arrest him. I'm waiting for a call now."

As they talked, Arras' phone rang, and he took the call. "Good," he said.

He turned to Andi and Greg and said, "They've picked up SanAngelo and his lieutenant, Juan Garcia. He's lawyered up of course, but at the very least we should be able to deport him to Cuba. I'm sure he'll be welcome there." Arras smiled grimly.

Andi grinned at Greg. "Way to go."

"By the way," Arras said, "you were lucky Ana SanAngelo didn't shoot you. She's a crack shot, a member of the ISSF. Nearly an Olympic contender."

"What? You're kidding!"

"No. She's been shooting since she was a kid, has won medals and everything."

"Oh, my God!" Andi said. "She missed you deliberately, Greg. And probably the shot from the car wasn't meant to be serious."

Late in the day, Andi and Greg finally got into Andi's car and headed back to Burgess Beach, exhausted. They didn't talk much.

Andi said, "I'm gonna call my dad and get the name of an attorney. We have to go in tomorrow to see the captain."

"Not my favorite idea, but yes, we have to."

"We should each call separately for an appointment."

"Yes."

Andi dropped Greg off at his apartment, and tired as he was, he didn't even attempt to ask her in. He kissed her lightly on the forehead, and said goodnight.

Andi called her father in Tampa the next morning.

"Hi, Dad."

"Well, we haven't heard from you in a while, although I guess you've been busy. The paper says you put a bigtime drug dealer out of business."

"Yeah, it's been busy. Caught a murderer, too. How's Mom?

"She's good. She's playing bridge right now. Her usual group. Are you going to visit us next weekend?"

"I'm planning to. Listen, Dad, I need an attorney. Do you know anyone who specializes in police personnel stuff?

"Why do you need an attorney?

"It's a long story, but I've been suspended and so has Greg. We'll need to have the attorneys work together. If they will. Greg's in the PAB, and I'm not, but the job rules call for arbitration for suspensions of more than five days. Do you know anyone who'd take me on?"

"You're what? Suspended? What the hell? You caught the drug lord and the murderer. How can you be suspended?"

"I know. I know. It's weird. I'm sorry."

He was quiet for a moment. "Okay. I won't judge, and anyway, now you're a hero. Let me see. Joe Shapiro, He's done good work for the Tampa police. Usually not on management's side. Let me find his phone number."

Andi's father gave her Shapiro's office and cell numbers. After Andi thanked him, she said, "Give Mom a big hug and tell her I'll be there to visit next week."

She called Shapiro's office, but the call went to voice mail. She tried the cell phone number, and after two rings he answered, "Shapiro." His accent sounded like he'd just moved to Florida from New Jersey.

Andi introduced herself, told him her story. She explained that she needed an attorney in what would probably be an arbitration. There was another police involved.

"Do you have a schedule already?" Shapiro asked.

"Not yet. We just finished a big case, and I'm going to make an appointment today to see the captain."

"You okay on your own?"

"Yeah. The other cop has an attorney through the PAB, but I never joined."

"Your father's daughter, huh?"

"I guess."

"Okay. Call me when you know the schedule, and then you and I can meet. Later we'll want to meet with this other cop and his attorney."

"Okay," Andi said. Having an attorney made her feel a bit less nervous.

Andi made an appointment to see the captain at 2:00. That left a lot of time to fret while she waited. She wondered if Greg would be there before or after her. Should she call him? No. They should keep this separate.

She couldn't relax, first sitting down, then getting up to get a cup of coffee and put some dishes away. Next she tried to read a book she'd started weeks before, but she couldn't concentrate and found herself reading the same paragraph over and over.

She decided to burn off some of her nervous energy with a heroic cleaning effort on her apartment. She'd been home so little in the past couple of weeks that it was pretty messy, so she scrubbed the kitchen floor on her hands and knees, moved the furniture to vacuum behind it, scrubbed the bathroom until it gleamed, and even cleaned out kitchen drawers. The physical exercise felt good and almost made her forget her upcoming ordeal.

At 12:30 Andi took a shower and dressed carefully in a blue suit with a peach-colored blouse. She opened a shoe box and pulled out a pair of blue patent leather shoes with three-inch heels she'd bought when she'd first arrived in Burgess Beach. She tried them on with the suit and they really flattered her legs, but on second thought, she decided they made her look frivolous, and she settled for a comfortable pair of navy pumps with a one-inch heel. She wore the pearl earrings her parents had given her when she graduated from college, and the pearl necklace that commemorated her graduation from the police academy.

When she was dressed, she stood in front of the full length mirror on the back of her bedroom door and looked herself over. She looked professional and businesslike, she thought. Serious but not too severe. She tried on several facial expressions, trying for one that appeared concerned but not nervous.

Satisfied, she said aloud, "Okay. I'm ready."

THIRTY-EIGHT

When she walked into the police station, everyone turned to look. Ed Garcia gave a wave and a smile, and she smiled back at him. Lisa stood to welcome her. She looked at the office as though she'd been gone for weeks rather than just a few days. There was a new person where McClain had sat, and some of the cubicles were empty, including the one that had been hers.

Lisa said, "Go right on back."

Andi headed down the hall toward the captain's office, dreading the meeting. She knocked, heard Bradley's gruff, "Enter" and opened the door.

Bradley sat at his desk, unsmiling. "Detective," he said. "You're quite the celebrity. Picture all over the papers." He didn't sound pleased.

"I haven't seen them, sir."

"The chief wants to see you." Bradley came from behind his desk and guided her out the door, further down the long hallway to an office she been in only once. Chief Roger Stoneham had welcomed her on her first day on the job, but she hadn't seen him since and barely remembered what he looked like. The chief spent most of his time in Tallahassee, schmoozing with politicians and getting as much grant money for Burgess Beach as he could wrestle from the grips of Florida's other police chiefs.

Bradley knocked on the door and pushed it open, guiding Andi in before him. The chief, a tall man with graying blond hair and very blue eyes, stood as they entered and held out his hand.

"Congratulations on your work on the Miranda Duncan murder."

Andi stepped forward and took the proffered hand which gripped hers in a practiced but somehow intimate shake. "Thank you, sir."

"Sit down," Stoneham said. "I want to hear how you and Detective Lamont managed to solve the murder and catch that drug lord and his accomplices in the bargain."

Andi sat in the chair in front of his desk, and the chief sat down just after she did. Bradley remained standing next to her. "Well, sir, we just did our job." She knew Stoneham wasn't interested in the details of the case, just in the results.

Stoneham nodded, then said, "Now, the captain here has some problems with the way you and Lamont got the job done. Is that right, Captain?"

"Yes, sir."

"He thinks you should have kept Detective Lamont out of the case, once it was determined he knew the victim and had been suspended. Of course I believe he's right in a technical sense, but I can see your point in that you needed Lamont's help to solve the murder and bring the murderer and the others to justice. Which you did."

"Yes, sir."

Stoneham placed his hands together on his desk in a decisive gesture. "I know the captain won't agree with my ruling on this, but I appreciate the initiative you and Detective Lamont took in solving the case. I am therefore terminating your suspension and restoring any back pay which you are due. The matter of the suspensions will be deleted from the record, and a letter commending your work on the Duncan case placed in your file. There will be nothing on your record or that of Detective Lamont regarding any reprimand or suspension."

"Thank you, sir," Andi said, breathing easily for the first time since she had entered the office.

"Now, is there anything else you would like to talk about with me?" Stoneham had risen to his feet and was ready to usher them out.

"No, sir. Thank you, sir."

Bradley opened the door and gestured for her to walk in front of him. He closed the door behind him, then said, "I have a few things I'd like to say to you."

"Yes, sir."

They entered Bradley's office, and he took the seat behind his desk while Andi stood in front of him.

Bradley's eyes looked like glittering stones in his impassive face. "You understand that wiping the slate clean is due only to the fact that you and Lamont were successful?"

"Yes, sir." Andi could feel her legs quivering, and she worked at keeping her body from showing her weakness. She felt tears in the back of her throat as she thought about how unfair Bradley was.

Bradley went on, his voice rasping, "I want you to understand something that I'm not sure you appreciate. You violated the rules of this department with your behavior. This department is run by the rules. I won't forget what you did, and I sure as hell won't forgive it. In the future, you will <u>always</u> operate strictly by the book. Have I made myself clear, Detective?"

"Yes, sir."

"You will be at your desk at 8:00 tomorrow morning to close out the Hutchinson Island burglary case. Garcia's gotten the Palmers and Leona Castro and her son charged with the burglary. He's been waiting for you to come back to close out the case. See him first thing tomorrow morning. Now, you are dismissed." Bradley rose to his feet, his hands braced on the desk in front of him.

Andi felt her cheeks redden as she said, "I guess Garcia's done a great job."

Bradley grunted, and Andi turned and left his office, her legs shaking and her throat tight. Garcia had done a good job in her absence, and she'd be watched carefully from now on. She wondered when Greg was due to come in. Did he already know?

Andi stopped to tell Lisa that she'd be in in the morning. Lisa smiled and stood up to give her a hug. Andi congratulated Garcia on closing the Hutchinson Island burglary and made arrangements to get together with him to close the case the next day. Then she headed out to her car.

Back in her apartment, Andi changed to jeans and a blue and white t-shirt. There was a message on her machine. When she heard Jim's voice, she almost hung up, but something in the way he sounded made her keep listening.

"Hi," Jim said. "I guess you're not in, but I wanted to congratulate you on your success. It's all over the papers. You not only solved the murder but caught the big time drug lord as well. Good job."

There was a pause, then he continued, "I wanted you to know I'm in AA, not drinking at all. I'm back with Elaine and trying to pull my life together. Thank God I managed to save my job. You were right about what I needed to do, Andi.

"And I apologize to you for all the ways I fucked up. I want you to know I'll always love you."

Andi sat with the phone in her hand for a long time, playing over in her mind what Jim had said. The drunken man who had terrorized her had overwhelmed her memories of the man she had loved. Now she could get some of the good memories back.

After a while she called Greg. His phone rang several times before his answering machine picked up. She left a message. "Damn," she said after she hung up. She'd wanted to talk to him, but what she really wanted to do was run along the beach shouting "Yippee!" She contented herself with doing aerobic exercises to release some of her energy.

She called her parents, told them the good news, and reconfirmed that she'd be in Tampa next weekend for a visit.

She called the lawyer to tell him what had happened at her meeting with the chief. "Keep my number just in case the captain gives you any static in the future," Shapiro said.

She needed dinner, but when she looked in her refrigerator and considered its contents, she decided there was little that could be done with a jar of olives, a mostly empty tub of margarine, an aged hunk of cheese, and a six-pack of diet soda. She pulled on a jacket and headed to the market.

By the time she returned, Greg had left a phone message. He had said simply, "Great news! Call me when you get back." She did.

When Greg answered, Andi shouted, "We've been pardoned! Can you believe it?"

"Not really. I didn't think about Chief Stoneham. I've never even met the guy."

"I met him once, but I know what you mean. I've been used to Bradley being the boss. He was livid, by the way, but there's not much he can do. He answers to Stoneham who doesn't want to look bad for the media.

"What are you doing now? I just went shopping and have the makings of a celebratory meal. Want to join me?"

"Sure. Be right over. You're cooking?"

"Yeah. I'm pretty good, too. Give me a minute though to get organized. Come in about an hour."

"Okay." Greg hung up.

Andi browned boneless chicken thighs which she cooked with a sauce of lemon, butter and mushrooms. She made rice pilaf, green beans and a strawberry and spinach salad. That was the nice thing about Florida. Fresh strawberries in November! Her mother, who had grown up in Minneapolis, had often talked about the dismal choices of fruits and vegetables in the Midwest in the cold months.

When Greg arrived, he hugged her, then said, "Smells good. You want wine or champagne?"

"Champagne, of course," Andi said, and they sat in the living room, toasting their salvation with glasses of bubbly.

They talked about Stoneham and Bradley and laughed ruefully at Stoneham's political savvy.

Greg said, "He's really a non-elected politician. And a good one, at least for his department.

"I guess. Do you think he knows anything about the guts of police work?"

"Does it matter?"

"Probably not."

Then Greg said, "Life with Bradley isn't going to be a picnic from now on. Stoneham's not going to be around any more than he has been, and Bradley's going to see that we don't get any breaks. Maybe I'll give it a few months while I look around. I might try out west—California or maybe Washington. I don't think I want to go to a big city like L.A., but there're lots of small towns. I know a guy in Southern California I worked with in Miami. I'll get in touch with him. I've been thinking about it. I don't want to stay around with Bradley gunning for me."

"Wow! Sounds like you've been doing a lot of thinking." Andi was a little taken aback by his planning and a little hurt by the way he ignored her situation. She was quiet, though, while she finished her champagne, then said, "Come on. Dinner's ready."

They spoke little as they ate. When he was done, Greg pushed his plate away with a satisfied sigh, and said, "You are pretty good at this cooking stuff. How come I kept bringing take-out?"

"Take-out's a lot easier, but I really like cooking." Andi got up to make coffee and brought out some cookies she had bought.

As she sipped her coffee, she said, "How come you're talking about leaving Burgess Beach? What about Toni? You were so sure she was your daughter. You can't just leave without knowing."

"You're right, but then I found out when she was born. She couldn't be mine. Miranda was gone over a year before Toni was born. I could have a DNA test, but it's pretty clear Miranda went to someone else when she left me. Maybe

Jorge, maybe Philippe, maybe someone else. Toni couldn't be my kid." Greg bowed his head.

"Are you disappointed? You seemed like you really wanted her."

"I wanted something left from Miranda. I loved her once, and I clung to that, but I guess I didn't know her at all until I investigated her murder. She was no good, and there were a lot of reasons she was murdered." His voice broke as he spoke.

"I guess you're right. I wonder where Toni'll end up."

"I don't want to think about that. She has grandparents, though."

They each thought about the incompatible man and woman who had fathered Miranda. Maybe Toni would be better in foster care.

They sat in silence for a couple of minutes. Then Greg reached across the table and took Andi's hand. "I've been thinking about what you said. I'm not going to push you. Let's take it slow. But we have a common interest in protecting one another from the captain, and we are the best detectives in the Burgess Beach Police Department. Let's keep it on a friendly level, like you said. I'm still attracted to you, but I'm willing to wait and see how it goes."

"Thanks. Right now I need a friend. Don't cut me out of your life, though. And don't leave Burgess Beach without thinking about me."

"Sure. I'm not giving up on you. I want you to come with me wherever I go. I'm just willing to take it slow like you asked."

THE END